THE RED AXE

CONTENTS

CHAPTER		
I	DUKE CASIMIR RIDES LATE	9
II	THE LITTLE PLAYMATE COMES HOME	16
III	THE RED AXE OF THE WOLFMARK	22
IV	THE PRINCESS HELENE	28
V	THE BLOOD-HOUNDS ARE FED	34
VI	DUKE CASIMIR'S FAMILIAR	40
VII	I BECOME A TRAITOR	46
VIII	AT THE BAR OF THE WHITE WOLF	52
IX	A HERO CARRIES WATER IN THE SUN	59
X	THE LUBBER FIEND	66
XI	THE VISION IS THE CRYSTAL	72
XII	EYES OF EMERALD	80
XIII	CHRISTIAN'S ELSA	88
XIV	SIR AMOROUS IS PLEASED WITH HIMSELF	93
XV	THE LITTLE PLAYMATE SETTLES ACCOUNTS	99
XVI	TWO WOMEN—AND A MAN	106
XVII	THE RED AXE IS LEFT ALONE	111
XVIII	THE PRIME OF THE MORNING	116
XIX	WENDISH WIT	122
XX	THE EARTH-DWELLERS OF NO MAN'S LAND	127
XXI	I STAND SENTRY	132
XXII	HELENE HATES ME	138
XXIII	HUGO OF THE BROADAXE	144
XXIV	THE SORTIE	149
XXV	MINE HOST RUNS HIS LAST RACE	154

XXVI	PRINCE JEHU MILLER'S SON	159
XXVII	ANOTHER MAN'S COAT	165
XXVIII	THE PRINCE'S COMPACT	172
XXIX	LOVES ME—LOVES ME NOT	179
XXX	INSULT AND CHALLENGE	187
XXXI	I FIND A SECOND	192
XXXII	THE WOLVES OF THE MARK	199
XXXIII	THE FLIGHT OF THE LITTLE PLAYMATE	206
XXXIV	THE GOLDEN NECKLACE	211
XXXV	THE DECENT SERVITOR	216
XXXVI	YSOLINDE'S FAREWELL	221
XXXVII	CAPTAIN KARL MILLER'S SON	226
XXXVIII	THE BLACK RIDERS	232
XXXIX	THE FLAG ON THE BED TOWER	237
XL	THE TRIAL OF THE WITCH	244
XLI	THE GARRET OF THE RED TOWER	249
XLII	PRINCESS PLAYMATE	255
XLIII	THE TRIAL FOR WITCHCRAFT	265
XLIV	SENTENCE OF DEATH	271
XLV	THE MESSAGE FROM THE WHITE GATE	276
XLVI	A WOMAN SCORNED	281
XLVII	THE RED AXE DIES STANDING UP	289
XLVIII	HUGO GOTTFRIED, RED AXE OF THE WOLFMARK	295
XLIX	THE SERPENT'S STRIFE	301
L	THE DUNGEON OF THE WOLFSBERG	305
LI	THE NIGHT BEFORE THE MORN	314
LII	THE HEADSMAN'S RIGHT	319
LIII	THE LUBBER FIEND'S RETURN	326
LIV	THE CROWNING OF DUKE OTHO	331
LV	THE LADY YSOLINDE SAVES HER SOUL	337
LVI	HELENA, PRINCESS OF PLASSENBURG	342

CHAPTER I

DUKE CASIMIR RIDES LATE

Well do I, Hugo Gottfried, remember the night of snow and moonlight when first they brought the Little Playmate home. I had been sleeping—a sturdy, well-grown fellow I, ten years or so as to my age—in a stomacher of blanket and a bed-gown my mother had made me before she died at the beginning of the cold weather. Suddenly something awoke me out of my sleep. So, all in the sharp chill of the night, I got out of my bed, sitting on the edge with my legs dangling, and looked curiously at the bright streams of moonlight which crossed the wooden floor of my garret. I thought if only I could swim straight up one of them, as the motes did in the sunshine, I should be sure to come in time to the place where my mother was—the place where all the pretty white things came from—the sunshine, the moonshine, the starshine, and the snow.

And there would be children to play with up there—hundreds of children like myself, and all close at hand. I should not any longer have to sit up aloft in the Red Tower with none to speak to me—all alone on the top of a wall—just because I had a crimson patch sewn on my blue-corded blouse, on my little white shirt, embroidered in red wool on each of my warm winter wristlets, and staring out from the front of both my stockings. It was a pretty enough pattern, too. Yet whenever one of the children I so much longed to play with down on the paved roadway beneath our tower caught sight of it he rose instantly out of the dust and hurled oaths and ill-words at me—aye, and oftentimes other missiles that hurt even worse—at a little lonely boy who was breaking his heart with loving him up there on the tower.

"Come down and be killed, foul brood of the Red Axe!" the children cried. And with that they ran as near as they dared, and spat on the wall of our house, or at least on the little wooden panel which opened inward in the great trebly spiked iron door of the Duke's court-yard.

But this night of the first home-coming of the Little Playmate I awoke crying and fearful in the dead vast of the night, when all the other children who would not speak to me were asleep. Then pulling on my comfortable shoes of woollen list (for my father gave me all things to make me warm, thinking me delicate of body), and drawing the many-patched coverlet of the bed about me, I clambered up the stone stairway to the very top of the tower in which I slept. The moon was broad, like one of the shields in the great hall, whither I went often when the great Duke was not at home, and when old Hanne would be busy cleaning the pavement and scrubbing viciously at the armor of the iron knights who stood on pedestals round about.

"One day I shall be a man-at-arms, too," I said once to Hanne, "and ride a-foraying with Duke Ironteeth."

But old Hanne only shook her head and answered:

"Ill foraying shalt thou make, little shrimp. Such work as thine is not done on horseback—keep wide from me, *toadchen*, touch me not!"

For even old Hanne flouted me and would not let me approach her too closely, all because once I had asked her what my father did to witches, and if she were a witch that she crossed herself and trembled whenever she passed him in the court-yard.

Now, having little else to do, I loved to look down from the top of the tower at all times. But never more so than when there was snow on the ground, for then the City of Thorn lay apparent beneath me, all spread out like a painted picture, with its white and red roofs and white houses bright in the moonlight—so near that it seemed as though I could pat every child lying asleep in its little bed, and scrape away the snow with my fingers from every red tile off which the house-fires had not already melted it.

The town of Thorn was the chief place of arms, and high capital city of all the Wolfmark. It was a thriving place, too, humming with burghers and trades and guilds, when our great Duke Casimir would let them alone; perilous, often also, with pikes and discontents when he swooped from the tall over-frowning Castle of the Wolfsberg upon their booths and guilderies—"to scotch the pride of rascaldom," as he told them when they complained. In these days my father was little at home, his business keeping him abroad all the day about the castle-yard, at secret examinations in the Hall of Judgment, or in mysterious vaults in the deepest parts of the castle, where the walls are eighteen feet thick, and from which not a groan can penetrate to the outside while the Duke Casimir's judgment was being done upon the poor bodies and souls of men and women his prisoners.

In the court-yard, too, the dogs, fierce russet-tan blood-hounds, ravined for their fearsome food. And in these days there was plenty of it, too, so that they were yelling and clamoring all day, and most of the night, for that which it made me sweat to think of. And beneath the rebellious city cowered and muttered, while the burghers and their wives shivered in their beds as the howling of Duke Casimir's blood-hounds came fitfully down the wind, and Duke Casimir's guards clashed arms under their windows.

So this night I looked down contentedly enough from my perched eyrie on the top of the Red Tower. It had been snowing a little earlier in the evening, and the brief blast had swept the sky clean, so that even the brightest stars seemed sunken and waterlogged in the white floods of moonlight. Under my hand lay the city. Even the feet of the watch made no clatter on the pavements. The fresh-fallen snow masked the sound. The kennels of the blood-hounds were silent, for their dreadful tenants were abroad that night on the Duke's work.

Yet, sitting up there on the Wolfsberg, it seemed to me that I could distinguish a muttering as of voices full of hate, like men talking low on their beds the secret things of evil and treason. I discerned discontent and rebellion rumbling and brooding over the city that clear, keen night of early winter.

Then, when after a while I turned from the crowded roofs and looked down upon the gray, far-spreading plain of the Wolfmark, to the east I saw that which appeared like winking sparks of light moving among the black clumps of copse and woodland which fringed the river. These wimpled and scattered, and presently grew brighter. A long howl, like that of a lonely wolf on the waste when he calls to his kindred to tell him their where-abouts, came faintly up to my ears.

A hound gave tongue responsively among the heaped mews and doggeries beneath the ramparts. Lights shone in windows athwart the city. Red nightcaps were thrust out of hastily opened casements. The Duke's standing guard clamored with their spear-butts on the uneven pavements, crying up and down the streets: "To your kennels, devil's brats, Duke Casimir comes riding home!"

Then I tell you my small heart beat furiously. For I knew that if I only kept quiet I should see that which I had never yet seen—the home-coming of our famous foraying Duke. I had, indeed, seen Duke Casimir often enough in the castle, or striding across the court-yard to speak to my father, for whom he had ever a remarkable affection. He was a tall, swart, black-a-vised man, with a huge hairy mole on his cheek, and long dog-teeth which showed at the sides of his mouth when he smiled, almost as pleasantly as those of a she-wolf looking out of her den at the hunters.

But I had never seen the Duke of all the Wolfmark come riding home ere daybreak, laden with the plunder of captured castles and the rout of deforced cities. For at such times my father would carefully lock the door on me, and confine me to my little sleeping-chamber—from whence I could see nothing but the square of smooth pavement on which the children chalked their games, and from which they cried naughtily up at me, the poor hermit of the Red Tower. But this night my father would be with the Duke, and I should see all. For high or low there was none in the empty Red Tower to hinder or forbid.

As I waited, thrilling with expectation, I heard beneath me the quickening pulse-beat of the town. The watch hurried here and there, hectoring, threatening, and commanding. But, in spite of all, men gathered as soon as their backs were turned in the alleys and street openings. Clusters of heads showed black for a moment in some darksome entry, cried "U-g-g-hh!" with a hateful sound, and vanished ere the steel-clad veterans of the Duke's guard could come upon them. It was like the hide-and-seek which I used to play with Boldo, my blood-hound puppy, among the dusty waste of the lumber-room over the Hall of Judgment, before my father took him back to the kennels for biting Christian's Elsa, a child who lived in the lower Guard opposite to the Red Tower.

But this was a stranger hide-and-seek than mine and Boldo's had been. For I saw one of the men who cried hatefully to the guard stumble on the slippery ice; and lo! or ever he had time to cry out or gather himself up, the men-at-arms were upon him. I saw the glitter of stabbing steel and heard the sickening sound of blows stricken silently in anger. Then the soldiers took the man up by head and heels carelessly, jesting as they went. And I shuddered, for I knew that they were bringing him to the horrible long sheds by the Red Tower through which the wind whistled. But in the moonlight the patch which was left on the snow was black, not red.

After this the crooked alleys were kept clearer, and I could see down the long High Street of Thorn right to the Weiss Thor and the snow-whitened pinnacles of the Palace, out of which Duke Casimir had for the time being frightened Bishop Peter. Black stood the Gate Port against the moonlight and the snow when I first looked at it. A moment after it had opened, and a hundred lights came crowding through, like sheep through an entry on their way to the shambles—which doubtless is their

Hall of Judgment, where there waits for them the Red Axe of a lowlier degree.

The lights, I say, came thronging through the gate. For though it was moonlight, the Duke Casimir loved to come home amid the red flame of torches, the trail of bituminous reek, and with a dashing train of riders clattering up to the Wolfsberg behind him, through the streets of Thorn, lying black and cowed under the shadows of its thousand gables.

So the procession undulated towards me, turbid and tumultuous. First a reckless pour of riders urging wearied horses, their sides white-flecked above with blown foam, and dark beneath with rowelled blood. Many of the horsemen carried marks upon them which showed that all had not been plunder and pleasuring upon their foray. For there were white napkins, and napkins that had once been white, tied across many brows. Helmets swung clanking like iron pipkins from saddle-bows, and men rode wearily with their arms in slings, drooping haggard faces upon their chests. But all passed rapidly enough up the steep street, and tumbled with noise and shouting, helter-skelter into the great court-yard beneath me as I watched, secure as God in heaven, from my perch on the Red Tower.

Then came the captives, some riding horses bare-backed, or held in place before black-bearded riders—women mostly these last, with faces white-set and strange of eye, or all beblubbered with weeping. Then came a man or two also on horseback, old and reverend. After them a draggled rabble of lads and half-grown girls, bound together with ropes and kept at a dog's trot by the pricking spears of the men-at-arms behind, who thought it a jest to sink a spear point-deep in the flesh of a man's back—"drawing the claret wine" they called it. For these riders of Duke Casimir were every one jolly companions, and must have their merry jest.

After the captives had gone past—and sorry I was for them—the body-guard of Duke Casimir came riding steadily and gallantly, all gentlemen of the Mark, with their sons and squires, landed men, towered men, free Junkers, serving the Duke for loyalty and not servitude, though ever "living by the saddle"—as, indeed, most of the Ritterdom and gentry of the Mark had done for generations.

Then behind them came Duke Casimir himself. The Eastland blood he had acquired from his Polish mother showed as he rode gloomily apart, thoughtful, solitary, behind the squared shoulders of his knights. After him another squadron of riders in ghastly armor of black-and-white, with torches in their hand and grinning skulls upon their shields, closed in the array. The great gate of the Wolfsberg was open now, and, leaving behind him the hushed and darkened town, the master rode into his castle. The Wolf was in his lair. But in the streets many a burgher's wife trembled on her bed, while her goodman peered cautiously over the leads by the side of a gargoyle, and fancied that already he heard the clamor of the partisans thundering at his door with the Duke's invitation to meet him in the Hall of Judgment.

CHAPTER II

THE LITTLE PLAYMATE COMES HOME

But there was to be no Session in the Hall of Judgment that night. The great court-yard, roofed with the vault of stars and lit by the moon, was to see all done that remained to be done. The torches were planted in the iron hold-fasts round about. The plunder of the captured towns and castles was piled for distribution on the morrow, and no man dared keep back so much as a Brandenburg broad-piece or a handful of Bohemian gulden. For the fear of the Duke and the Duke's dog-kennels was upon every stout fighting-kerl. They minded the fate of Hans Pulitz, who had kept back a belt of gold, and had gotten himself flung by the heels with no more than the stolen belt upon him, into the kennels where the Duke's blood-hounds howled and clambered with their fore-feet on the black-spattered barriers. And they say that the belt of gold was all that was ever seen again of the poor rascal. Hans Pulitz—who had hoped for so many riotous evenings among the Fat Pigs of Thorn and so many draughts of the slippery wine of the Rheingan careering down the poor thirsty throat of him. But, alas for Hans Pulitz! the end of all imagining was no more than five minutes of snapping, snarling, horrible Pandemonium in the kennels of the Wolfsberg, and the scored gold chain on the ground was all that remained to tell his tale. Verily, there were few Achans in Duke Casimir's camp.

And it is small wonder after this, that scant and sparse were the jests played on the grim master of the Wolfsberg, or that the bay of a blood-hound tracking on the downs frightened the most stout-hearted rider in all that retinue of dare-devils.

Going to the side of the Red Tower, which looked towards the court-yard, I saw the whole array come in. I watched the prisoners unceremoniously dismounted and huddled together against the coming of the Duke. There was but one man among them who stood erect. The torch-light played on his face, which was sometimes bent down to a little child in his arms, so that I saw him well. He looked not at all upon the rude men-at-arms who pushed and bullied about him, but continued tenderly to hush his charge, as if he had been a nurse in a babe-chamber under the leads, with silence in all the house below.

It pleased me to see the man, for all my life I had loved children. And yet at ten years of age I had never so much as touched one—no, nor spoken even, only looked down on those that hated me and spat on the very tower wherein I dwelt. But nevertheless I loved them and yearned to tell them so, even when they mocked me. So I watched this little one in the man's arms.

Then came the Duke along the line, and behind him, like the Shadow of Death, paced my father Gottfried Gottfried, habited all in red from neck to heel, and carrying for his badge of office as Hereditary Justicer to the Dukes of the Wolfmark that famous red-handled, red-bladed axe, the gleaming white of whose deadly edge had never been wet save with the blood of men and women.

The guard pushed the captives rudely into line as the Duke Casimir strode along the front. The women he passed without a sign or so much as a look. They were kept for another day. But the men were judged sharp and sudden, as the Duke in his black armor passed along, and that scarlet Shadow of Death with the broad axe over his shoulder paced noiselessly behind him.

For as each man looked into the eyes of Casimir of the Wolfsberg he read his doom. The Duke turned his wrist sharply down, whereupon the attendant sprites of the Red Shadow seized the man and rent his garment down from his neck—or the hand pointed up, and then the man set his hand to his heart and threw his head back in a long sigh of relief.

It came the turn of the man who carried the babe.

Duke Casimir paused before him, scowling gloomily at him.

"Ha, Lord Prince of so great a province, you will not set yourself up any more haughtily. You will quibble no longer concerning tithes and tolls with Casimir of the Wolfmark."

And the Duke lifted his hand and smote the man on the cheek with his open hand.

Yet the captive only hushed the child that wailed aloud to see her guardian smitten.

He looked Duke Casimir steadfastly in the eyes and spoke no word.

"Great God, man, have you nothing to say to me ere you die?" cried Duke Casimir, choked with hot, sudden anger to be so crossed.

The elder man gazed steadily at his captor.

"God will judge betwixt me, a man about to die, and you, Casimir of the Wolfmark," he said at last, very slowly—"by the eyes of this little maid He will judge!"

"Like enough," cried Casimir, sneeringly. "Bishop Peter hath told me as much. But then God's payments are long deferred, and, so far as I can see, I can take Him into my own hand. And your little maid—pah! since one day you took from me the mother, I, in my turn, will take the daughter and make her a titbit for the teeth of my blood-hounds."

The man answered not again, but only hushed and fondled the little one.

Duke Casimir turned quickly to my father, showing his long teeth like a snarling dog:

"Take the child," he said, "and cast her into the kennels before the man's eyes, that he may learn before he dies to dread more than God's Judgment Seat the vengeance of Duke Casimir!"

Then all the men-at-arms turned away, heart-sick at the horror. But the man with the child never blanched.

High perched on the top tower, I also heard the words and loved the maid. And they tell me (though I do not remember it) that I cried down from the leads of the Red Tower: "My father, save the little maid and give her to me—or else I, Hugo Gottfried, will cast myself down on the stones at your feet!"

At which all the men looked up and saw me in white, a small, lonely figure, with my legs hanging over the top of the wall.

"Go back!" my father shouted. "Go back, Hugo! 'Tis my only son—my successor—the fifteenth of our line, my lord!" he said to the Duke in excuse.

But I cried all the more: "Save the maid's life, or I will fling myself headlong. By Jesu-Mary, I swear it!"

For I thought that was the name of one great saint.

Then my father, who ever doted on me, bent his knee before his master: "A boon!" he cried, "my first and last, Duke Casimir—this maid's life for my son!"

But the Duke hung on the request a long, doubtful moment.

"Gottfried Gottfried," he said, even reproachfully, "this is not well done of you, to make me go back on my word."

"Take the man's life," said my father—"take the man's life for the child's and the fulfilling of your word, and by the sword of St. Peter I will smite my best!"

"Aye," said the man with the babe, "even so do, as the Red Axe says. Save the young child, but bid him smite hard at this abased neck. Ye have taken all, Duke Casimir, take my life. But save the young child alive!"

So, without further word or question, they did so, and the man who had carried the child kissed her once and separated gently the baby hands that clung about his neck. Then he handed her to my father.

"Be gracious to Helene," he said; "she was ever a sweet babe."

Now by this time I was down hammering on the door of the Red Tower, which had been locked on the outside.

Presently some one turned the key, and so soon as I got among the men I darted between their legs.

"Give me the babe!" I cried; "the babe is mine; the Duke himself hath said it." And my father gave her to me, crying as if her heart would break.

Nevertheless she clung to me, perhaps because I was nearer her own age.

Then the dismal procession of the condemned passed us, followed by my father, who strode in front with his axe over his shoulder, and the laughing and jesting men-at-arms bringing up the rear.

As I stood a little aside for them to pass, the hand of the man fell on my head and rested there a moment.

"God's blessing on you, little lad!" he said. "Cherish the babe you have saved, and, as sure as that I am now about to die, one day you shall be repaid." And he stooped and kissed the little maid before he went on with the others to the place of slaughter.

Then I hurried within, so that I might not hear the dull thud of the Red Axe, on the block nor the inhuman howlings of the dogs in the kennels afterwards.

When my father came home an hour later, before even he took off his costume of red, he came up to our chamber and looked long at the little maid as she lay asleep. Then he gazed at me, who watched him from under my lids and from behind the shadows of the bedclothes.

But his quick eye caught the gleam of light in mine.

"You are awake, boy!" he said, somewhat sternly.

I nodded up to him without speaking.

"What would you with the little maid?" he said. "Do you know that you and she together came very near losing me my favor with the Duke, and it might be my life also, both at one time tonight?"

I put my hand on the maiden's head where it lay on the pillow by me.

"She is my little wife!" I said. "The Duke gave her to me out in the court-yard there!"

And this is the whole tale of how the Little Playmate came to dwell with us in the Red Tower.

CHAPTER III

THE RED AXE OF THE WOLFMARK

Just as clearly do I remember the next morning. The Little Playmate lay by me on my bed, wrapped in one of my childish night-gowns—which old Hanne had sought out for her the night before. It was a brisk, chill, nippy daybreak, and I had piled most of the bedclothes upon her. I lay at the nether side clipped tight in my single brown blanket. It was perishing cold. Out of the heaped coverings I saw presently a pair of eyes, great and dark, regarding me.

Then a little voice spoke, sweetly and clearly, but yet strangely sounding to me who had never before heard a babe speak.

"I want my father—tell him to send Grete, my maid, to attend on me, and then to come himself to sit by the bed and amuse me!"

Alas! her father—well I knew what had come to him—that which in the mercy of the Duke Casimir and in the crowning mercy of the Red Axe, I had seen come to so many. The dogs did not howl at all that morning. They, too, were tired with the hunting and sated with the quarry.

All the same, I tried to answer my companion.

"Little Maid!" said I, "let me be your maid and your father. I will gladly get you all you want. But your good father has gone on a weary journey, and it will be long ere he can hope to return."

"Well," she said, "send lazy Grete, then. I will scold her soundly for not bringing the sop of hot milk-and-bread, which, indeed, is not food for a lady of my age. But my father insists upon it. He is dreadfully obstinate."

Now there was no one but our old deaf Hanne in the kitchen of the Red Tower. She stayed only for cooking and keeping the house clean. My father never paid her wages, and she never asked any. She did her work and took that which she needed out of the household purse without check or question. It was long before I guessed that Hanne also owed her life to my father's care. I had noticed, indeed, when he had upon him the red headman's dress, which fitted him like a flame climbing up a tall back log on the winter's fire, that old Hanne trembled from head to foot and shrank away into her den under the stairs. Many a time have I seen her peeping round the corner of the kitchen-door and tottering back when she heard him come down the stair from the garret. And I guessed so well the reason of her fear that I used to cry to her:

"Come out, good Hanne; the Red Axe is gone."

Then would she run, pattering like a scared rabbit over the uneven floor, to the window, and watch my father stalking, grim and tall, across the open spaces of the yard towards the Judgment Hall of Duke Casimir, the men-at-arms avoiding him with deft reverence. For though they hated him almost as much as did the fat burghers, they feared him, too. And that because Gottfried Gottfried was deep in the confidence of the Duke; and, besides, was no man to stand in the ill-graces of when one lived within the walls of the Wolfsberg.

So this morning it was to the ancient Hanne that I ran down and told her how, as quickly as she might, she must bring milk and bread to the little one.

"But," said she, "there is none save that which is to be sodden for your father's breakfast and your own."

"Do as you are bid, bad Hanne!" cried I, being, like all solitary children, quickly made angry, "or I will tell my father to drive you before him when next he goes forth clad in red to the Hall of Justice."

At which the poor old woman gave vent to a sharp, screechy cry and caught at her skinny throat with twitching, bony fingers.

"Oh, but you know not what you say, cruel boy!" she gasped. "For the love of God, speak not such words in the house of the Red Axe!"

But, like an ill-governed child, I was cruel because I knew my power, and so made sure that Hanne would do what I asked.

"Well, then, bring the sop quickly," said I, "or by Peter-and-Paul I will speak to my father. He and I can well be doing with beaten cakes made crisp on the iron girdle. In these you have great skill."

This last I said to cheer her, for she loved compliments on her cooking. Though, strange to tell, I never saw her eat anything herself all the years she remained in our house.

When I was gone up-stairs again I looked about for the Little Playmate. She was not to be seen anywhere. There was only a tiny cosey-hole down among the blankets, which was yet warm when I thrust my hand within it. But it was empty and the top a little fallen in, as if the occupant had set her knee on it when she crawled out. A baby stocking lay outside it on the floor.

"Little maid!" I cried, "where are you?"

But I heard nothing except a hissing up on the roof, and then a great slithering rumble down below, which boomed like the distant cannons the Margraf sent to besiege us. I listened and shuddered; but it was only the snow from the tall roof of the Red Tower which had slipped off and fallen to the ground. Then I had a vision of a slender little figure clambering on the leads and the treacherous snow striking her out into the air, and then—the cruel stones of the pavement.

"Little maid, little maid!" I cried out again, beginning to weep myself for pity at my thought, "where are you? Speak to me. You are my playmate."

Then I ran to the roof, and, though the stones chilled me to the bone and the frost-bitten iron hasps of the fastenings burned me like fire, I opened the trap-door and looked out. There above me was the crow-stepped gable of the Red Tower, with the axe set on the pinnacle rustily bright in the coming light of the morning—all swept clean of snow. But no little maid.

I ran to the verge and peered down. I saw a great heap of frozen snow fallen on its edge and partly canted over, half covering a deep red stain which was turning black and horrid in the daylight. But no little maid.

Then I ran all over the house calling to her, but could not find her anywhere. I was just beginning to bethink me that she might be a fairy child, one that came at night and vanished like the dream gold which is forever turning to withered leaves in the morning. At last I bethought me of my father's room, where even I, his son, had never been at night, and indeed but seldom in the day. For it was the Hereditary Justicer's fancy to lodge himself in the high garret which ran right across the top of the Red Tower, and was entered only by a little ladder from the first turning of the same staircase by which I had run out upon the leads.

I went to the bottom of the garret turnpike. The little barred door stood open, and I heard—I was sure that I heard—light, irregularly pattering footsteps moving about above.

It gave me strange shakings of my heart only to listen. For, though I was noways afraid of my father myself, yet since I had never seen any man, woman, or child (save the Duke only) who did not quail at his approach, it was a curious feeling to think of the lonely little child skipping about up there, where abode the axe and the block—the axe which had done, I knew so well what, to her father only the night before.

So I mustered all my courage—not from any fear of Gottfried Gottfried, but rather from the uncertainty of what I should see, and quickly mounted the stair.

I shall never forget what I saw as I stood with my feet on the rickety hand-rail of the ladder. The long dim garret was already half-lighted by the coming day. Red cloaks swung and flapped like vast, deadly, winged bats from the rafters, and reached almost to the ground. There was no glass in any of the windows of the garret, for my father minded neither heat nor cold. He was a man of iron. Summer's heat nor winter's cold neither vexed nor pleasured him. So it was no marvel that at the chamber's upper end, and quite near to my father's bed, lay a wreath of snow, with a fine, clean-cut, untrampled edge, just as it had blown in at the gable window when the storm burst from the east.

My father lay stretched out on his bed, his head thrown back, his neck bare—almost as if he had done justice on himself, or at least as if he waited the stroke of another Red Axe through the eastern skylight which the morning was already crimsoning. His scarlet sheathings of garmentry lay upon a black oaken stool, trailing across the floor lank and hideous, one of the cuffs which had been but recently dyed a darker hue making a wet sop upon the boards.

All this I had seen many a time before. But that which made me tremble from head to foot with more and worse than cold, was the little white figure that danced about his bed—for all the world like a crisped leaf in late autumn which whirls and turns, skipping this way and spinning that in the wanton breezes. It was the Little Playmate. But I could not form a word wherewith to call her. My tongue seemed dried to the roots.

She had taken the red eye-mask which came across my father's face when he did his greater duties and tied it about her head. Her great, innocent, childish eyes looked elfishly through the black socket holes, sparkling with a fairy merriment, and her tangled floss of sunny hair escaped from the string at the back and fell tumultuously upon her shoulders.

And even as I looked, standing silent and trembling, with a little balancing step she danced up to the Red Axe itself where it stood angled against the block, and seizing it by the handle high up near the head she staggered towards the bed with it.

Then came my words back to my mouth with a rush.

"For the Holy Virgin's sake, little maid, put the Red Axe down!" I cried, whisperingly. "You know not what you do!"

Then even as I spoke I saw that my father had drawn himself up in bed, and that he too was staring at the strange, elfish figure. Gottfried Gottfried, as I remember him in these days, was a tall, dark, heavily browed man, with a shock of bushy blue-black hair, of late silvering at the temples—grave, sombre, quiet in all his actions.

But what was my surprise as the little maid came nearer to the bed with her pretty dancing movement, carrying the axe much as if it had been an over-heavy babe, to see the Duke's Justicer suddenly skip over the far side of the bedstead and stand with his red cloak about him, watching her.

CHAPTER IV

THE PRINCESS HELENE

"What devil's work is this?" he said, frowning at her severely.

And I confess that I trembled, but not so the little maid.

"Do not be afraid, mannie," she said, laying down the axe on the stock of the couch, against which its broad red blade and glass-clear cutting edge made an irregular patch of light. "Come and sit down beside me on your bed. I shall not hurt you indeed, mannie, and I want to talk to you. There is nothing but a little boy down-stairs. And I like best to talk with men."

"I declare it is the dead man's brat I saved last night for Hugo's sake!" I heard my father mutter, "the maid with the girdle of golden letters."

Presently a smile of amusement struggled about his mouth at her bairnly imperiousness, but he came obediently enough and sat down. Nevertheless he took away the heavy axe from her and said, "Put this down, then, or give it to me. It is not a pretty plaything for little girls!"

The small figure in white put up a tiny fat hand, and solemnly withdrew the red patch of mask from before the wide-open baby eyes.

"I am not a little *girl*, remember, mannie," she said, "I am a Princess and a great lady."

My father bowed without rising.

"I shall not forget," he said.

"You should stand up and bow when I tell you that," said she. "I declare you have no more manners than the little boy in the brown blanket down-stairs."

"Princess," said my father, gravely, "during my life I have met a great many distinguished people of your rank; and, do you know, not one of them has ever complained of my manners before."

"Ah," cried the little maid, "then you have never met my father, the Prince. He is terribly particular. You must go *so*" (she imitated the mincing walk of a court chamberlain), "you must hold your tails thus" (wagging her white nightrail and twisting about her head to watch the effect), "and you must retire—so!" With that she came bowing backward towards the well of the staircase, so far that I was almost afraid she would fall plump into my arms. But she checked herself in time, and without looking round or seeing me she tripped back to my father's bedside and sat down quite confidingly beside him.

"Now you see," cried she, "what you would have had to put up with if you had met my father. Be thankful then that it is only the little Princess Helene that is sitting here."

"I think I had the honor to meet your father," said Gottfried Gottfried, gravely, again removing the restless baby fingers from the Red Axe and laying it on the far side of the couch beyond him.

"Then, if you met him, did he not make you bow and bend and walk backward?" asked the Playmate, looking up very sharply.

"Well, you see, Princess," explained my father, "it was for such a very short time that I had the honor of converse with him."

"Ah, that does not matter," cried the maid; "often he would be most difficult when you came running in just for a moment. Why, he would straighten you up and make you do your bows if you were only racing after a kitten, or, what was worse, he would call the Court Chamberlain to show you how to do it. But when I am grown up—ah, then!—I mean to make the Chamberlain bow and walk backward; for you know he is only taking care of my princedom for me. Oh, and I shall have you well taught by that time, long man. It is cold—cold. Let me get into your bed and I will give you your first lesson now."

So with that she skipped into my father's place and drew the great red cloak about her.

"Now then, first position," she commanded, clapping her hands like a Sultana, "your feet together. Draw back your left—so. Very well! Bend the knee—stupid, not that one. Now your head. If I have to come to you, sir—there, that is better. Well done! Oh, I shall have a peck of trouble with you, I can see that. But you will do me credit before I have done with you."

In a little while she tired of the lesson.

"Come and sit down now"—she waved her hand graciously—"here on the bed by me. Though I am a Princess really, I am not proud, and, as I said, I may make something of you yet."

My father came forward gravely, wrapped himself in another of his red cloaks, and sat down. I shivered in my blanket on the stair-head, but I could not bear to move nor yet reveal myself. This was better than any play I had ever watched from the sparred gallery of the palace, to which Gottfried Gottfried took me sometimes when the mummers came from Brandenburg to divert Duke Casimir.

"My father, the great Prince, took me for a long ride last night. There was much noise and many bonfires behind us as we rode away, and some of the men spoke roughly, for which my father will rate them soundly today. Oh, they will be sick and sorry this morning when the Prince takes them to task. I hope you will never make him angry," she said, laying her hand warningly on my father's; "but if ever you do, come to me and I will speak to the Prince for you. You need not be bashful, for I do not mind a bit speaking to him, or indeed to any one. You will remember and not be bashful when you have something to ask?"

"I will assuredly not be bashful," said my father, very solemnly. "I will come and tell you at once, little lady, if I ever have the misfortune to offend the most noble Prince."

Then he bent his head and raised her hand to his lips. She bowed in return with exquisite reserve and hauteur; and, as it seemed to me, more with her long eyelashes than with anything else.

"Do you know, Black Man," she said—"for, you know, you are black, though you wear red clothes—I am glad you are not afraid of me. At home every one was afraid of me. Why, the little children stood with their mouths open and their eyes like this whenever they saw me."

And she illustrated the extremely vacant surprise into which her appearance paralyzed the infantry of her native city.

"I am glad my father left me here till he should come back. Do you know, I like your house. There are so many interesting things about it. That funny axe over there is nice. It looks as if it could cut things. Has it ever cut anything? It is so nicely polished. How do you keep it so, and can I help you?"

"I had just finished polishing and oiling it before I fell asleep," answered Gottfried Gottfried. "You see, little Princess, I had very many things to cut with it last night."

"What a pity the Prince had not time to wait and see you! He is so very fond of going out into the forest with the woodman. Once he took me to see the tallest tree in all our woods cut down with just such an axe as that—only it was not red. Have you ever seen a high tree cut down?"

"I have cut down some pretty tall ones myself!" said the Duke's Justicer, smiling quietly at her.

"Ah, but not as tall as my father! It is beautiful to see him strip his doublet and lay to. They say there is not a woodman like him in all our land."

Helene looked at my father, whose arms were folded in his great cloak.

"But you have fine strong arms too," she said. "You look as if you could cut things. Did my father ever see you cut down tall trees?"

"Yes," said Gottfried Gottfried, slowly, "once!"

"And did he say that you cut well?" the little maid went on, with a strange, wilful persistence in her idea.

"He neither said that I did well nor yet that I did ill," replied Gottfried Gottfried.

"Ah!" said Helene, "that was just like the Prince. He was afraid of flattering you and making you unfit for your work. But if he said nothing, depend upon it he was pleased."

"Thank you, Princess," said my father. "I think he was well enough pleased."

Just then there came a noise that I knew—a sound which chilled every bone in my body.

It was the clear ring of a steady footstep upon the pavement without. It came heavily and slowly across the yard. The outer hasp of our door clicked. The door opened, and the footstep began to ascend the stair.

There was but one man in the world who dared make so free with the Red Tower and its occupant. Our visitor was without doubt the Duke Casimir himself.

For the first time I saw my father manifestly disconcerted. The little maid's life might be worth no more than a torn ballad if Duke Casimir happened to be in evil humor or had repented him of his mercy of the past night. I saw the Red Axe look aimlessly about for a hiding-place. There was a niche round which certain cloaks and coverlets were hung.

"Come in here," he said, abruptly.

"Why should I hide, whoever comes?" asked the Little Playmate, indignantly.

"It is the Duke Casimir," whispered my father, hurriedly, stirred as I had never seen him. "Come hither quickly!"

But the little maid struck an attitude, and tapped the floor with her foot.

"I will not," she said. "What is the Duke Casimir to me that am a Princess? If he is good, I will give him my hand to kiss!"

But at this point I rushed from the ladder-head, and, taking her in my arms, I sped up the turret stairs with her out upon the leads, my hand over her mouth all the time.

And as I ran I could hear the Duke trampling upward not twenty steps in the rear. I opened the trap-door and went out into the clear morning sunshine. And only the turn of the stair prevented Casimir from seeing me go up the narrow turret corkscrew with my little white burden.

Then I heard voices beneath, and I knew, as if I had seen it, that my father stood up straight at the salute. Presently the voices lowered, and I knew also that the Duke Casimir was unbending as he did to none else in his realm save to the Hereditary Justicer of the Wolfmark.

But I had my hands full with the little Princess. I dared not go down the stairs. I dared not for a moment take my palm off her mouth. For as like as not she would call out for the Duke Casimir to come and deliver her from my cruelty. So I stuck to my post, even though I knew that I angered her.

The morning was warm for a winter's day in Thorn, and I pulled open my brown blanket and wrapped her coseyly within it, chilling myself to the bone as I did so.

It seemed ages before the Duke strode down the stair again, and took his way across the yard, with my father, in black, after him. For so he was used to dress when he went to the Hall of Judgment, to be present and assist at the discovery of crime by means of the Minor and Extreme Questions.

Then, so soon as they were fairly gone, I took my hand from the mouth of the Little Playmate, and carried her down-stairs; which as soon as I had done, she slapped my face soundly.

"I will never, never speak to you any more so long as I live, rude boy—common street brat!" she said, biting her under-lip in ineffectual, petulant anger. "Listen, never as long as I live! So do not think it! Upstart, so to treat a lady and a Princess!"

And with that she burst into tears.

CHAPTER V

THE BLOOD-HOUNDS ARE FED

But the Princess-Playmate spoke to me again. I was even permitted to call her Helene. Me she addressed uniformly as "Hugo Gottfried." But neither her name nor mine interfered with our plays, which were wholly happy and undisturbed by quarrelling—at least, so long as I did exactly what she wished me to do.

On these terms life was made easy for me from that day forth. No longer did I wistfully watch the children of the street from the lonely window of the Red Tower. They might spit all day on the harled masonry at the foot of the wall for aught I cared. I no longer desired their society. Had I not that of a real Princess, and if my companion was inclined to be a little wayward and domineering—why, was not that the very birthright of all Princesses?

Helene and I had great choice of plays within the walls of the solemn castle. So long as we kept to the outer yard and did not intrude upon the Duke's side of the enclosure, we were free to come and go at our pleasure. For even Casimir himself was soon well accustomed to see us run about like puppies, slapping and tumbling, and minded us no more than the sparrows that pecked in the litter of the stable-yard. Indeed, I think he had forgotten all about the strange home-coming of the Little Playmate.

The kennels of the blood-hounds especially were full of fascination for us. That fatal deep-mouthed clamoring at morn and even drew us like a magnet. Helene, in particular, never tired of gazing between the chinks of the fence of cloven pine-wood at the great russet-colored beasts with their flashing white teeth, over which the heavy dewlaps fell. And when my father, with his red livery upon him and a loaded whip in his hand, once a day opened the tall, narrow door and went within, we thought him brave as a god. Then the way the fierce beasts shrank cowering from him, the fashion in which they crouched on their bellies and heaved their shoulders up without taking their hind quarters off the ground, equally delighted and surprised us.

"Your father is almost as great a man as *my* father," said the Princess Helene, who, however, was rapidly forgetting her dignity. Indeed, already it had become little more than a fairy-tale to her. And that was perhaps as well.

One day, when I was about thirteen, or a little older, my father came out with a new short mantle in his hand, red like his own.

"Come hither, Hugo Gottfried!" he said, for he had learned the trick of the name from Helene.

I went to him tardy-foot, greatly wondering.

"Here, chick," he said, in his kindly fashion, "it is time you were beginning to learn your duties. Come with me today into the kennels of the blood-hounds."

But I hung back, shifting the new mantle uneasily on my shoulders, yet not daring to throw it off.

"I do not want to go, father," said I, edging away in the direction of the Playmate.

"What, lad!" he cried, slapping me on the shoulder; "they will not hurt thee with that cloak on. They know their masters better—as their fathers and mothers knew our fathers. Have we, the Gottfrieds, been the Hereditary Justicers of the Wolfmark for six hundred years to be afraid now of the blood-hounds that are kept to hunt the Duke's enemies and to feed on the Duke's carrion?"

"It is not that I am afraid of the dogs, father," I made answer to him. "I would quickly enough go among them, if only you would let me go without this scarlet cloak."

My father laughed heartily and loudly—that is, for him. A quick ear might have heard him quite three feet away.

"Silly one!" he exclaimed, "do you not know that even the Duke Casimir dares not set foot in the kennels—no, nor I myself, save in the garb they know and fear—as indeed do all men in this state."

Still I hung my head down and scraped the gravel with my foot.

"Haste thee," said my father, roughly. "Once it is permitted to a man to be afraid; to fear twice, and fear the same thing, is to be a coward. And no Gottfried ever yet was a coward. Let not my Hugo be the first."

Then I took courage and spoke to him.

"I do not wish to be executioner," I said; "I would rather ride a-soldiering far away, and be in the drive of battle and the front of danger. Let me be a soldier and a man-at-arms, my father. I am sure I could become a war-captain and a great man!"

Gottfried Gottfried stared blankly at me, and his blue-black hair rose in a crest—not with anger, of which he never showed any to me, but in sheer astonishment. He continued to rub it with his hand, as if in this manner he might possibly reach an explanation of the mystery.

"Not wish to be Hereditary Executioner? Why, are you not a Gottfried, the only son of a Gottfried, the only son of his father, who also was a Gottfried and Hereditary Red Axe of the Wolfmark? Why, lad, before there was a Duke at all in the Wolfsberg, before he and his folk came out of the land of the Poles to fight with the Ritterdom of the North, we, the Gottfrieds of Thorn, wore the sign of the Red Axe and dwelt apart from all the men of the Mark. For fourteen generations have we worn it!"

"But," said I, sadly, "the very children on the street hate me and spit on me as I pass; the maids will not so much as speak to me. They scyrry in-doors and slam the wicket in my face. Think you that is pleasant? And when as a lad of older years I set out to woo, whither shall I betake me? For what door is open to a Gottfried, to him who carries the sign of the Red Axe?"

"Ah, lad," said my father, patiently, "life comes and life goes. It is nigh on to forty years since even thus my father held out the curt mantle for me. And even so said I. Time eats up all things but the hearts of men. And they abide ever the same—yearning for that which they cannot have, but nevertheless accepting with a sharp relish the things which are decreed to them; even as do the Duke's carrion-eaters yonder, which, by-the-way, are waiting most impatiently for their meal while we thus stand arguing."

He was about to move away when his eye fell on Helene. At sight of her he seemed to remember my last words, about going a-wooing.

He considered a moment and then said: "You are young yet to think of courting, Hugo, but have no fear either for the love-making or the wedding. Sweet maids a many shall surely come hither. Why, there is one growing up yonder that will prove as fair as any. I tell you the Gottfrieds have married great ladies in their time—dames and dainty damsels. They have had princesses to be their sweethearts ere now. Come, then, lad—no more words, but follow me."

And for that time I went after him obediently enough, but all the same my heart was rebellious within me. And I determined that if I had to ran to the ends of the earth, I should never be Hereditary Executioner nor yet handle the broadaxe on the bared necks of my fellow-men.

We went in among the dogs—great, lank, cowering, tooth-slavering brutes. I followed my father till we came to the feeding-troughs. Then he bade me to stand where I was till he should set their meat in order. So he vanished behind, the barriers. Then, when he had prepared the beasts' horrid victual, though I saw not what, he opened the narrow gate, and the howling, clambering throng broke helter-skelter for the troughs, cracking and crunching the thigh-bones, tearing at the flesh, and growling at one another till the air rang with the ear-piercing din.

And outside the little Helene flung herself frantically at the split pines of the enclosure, crying, bitterly, "Take off that hateful mantle, Hugo Gottfried! I hate it—I hate it! Take it off!"

My father stood behind the dogs, whose arched and bristling backs I could just manage to see over the fence of wooden spars, and dealt the whip judicially among them—at once as a warning to encroachers and a punishment for greed.

Then all unharmed we went out, and as soon as my father had gone up to his garret-room in the tower, I tore the red cloak off and trampled it in the dirt of the yard. Then I went and hid it in a little blind window of the tower opposite the foot of the ladder which led to my father's room. For, because of my father's anger, I dared not destroy the badge of shame altogether, as both Helene and I wished to do.

Day by day the Little Playmate (for so I was now allowed to call her—the Princesshood being mostly forgotten) grew great and tall, her fair, almost lint-white hair darkening swiftly to coppery gold with the glint of ripe wheat upon it.

Old Hanne followed her about with eyes at once wistful and doubtful. Sometimes she shook her head sadly. And I wondered if ever the poor old stumbling crone, wizened like a two-year-old winter apple, had been as light and gay a thing as our dainty rose-leaf girl.

One day I was laboring at the art of learning to write, along with Friar Laurence—a scrawny, ill-favored monk, who, for good deeds or misdeeds, I know not which, was warded in a cell opening out of the lower or garden court of the Wolfsberg, when I heard Helene dance down the stairs to the kitchen of the Red Tower.

"Hannchen!" she cried, merrily, "come and teach me that trick of the broidering needle. I never can do it but I prick myself. Nevertheless, I can fashion the Red Axe almost as clearly as the pattern, and far finer to see."

Friar Laurence raised his great, softly solid face, blue about the jowls and padded beneath the eyes with craft.

"That little maid is over much with old Hanne," he said, as if he meditated to himself; "she will teach her other prickings than the needle-play. The witch-pricking at the images of wax was what brought her here. Aye, and had it not been for your father wanting a house-keeper, the Holy Office would have burned the hag, and sent her to hell, flaming like a torch of pine knots."

Now this was the first I had heard with exactness of the matter of old Hanne's having been a witch. And now that I knew it for certain I began to imagine all sorts of unholy things about the poor wretch, and grew greatly jealous of Helene being so often in the kitchen. Whereas before I had thought nothing at all about the matter, save that Hannchen was a dull, pleasant, muttering, shuffling-footed old woman, who could make rare good cream-cakes when you got her in the humor.

And that was not often.

CHAPTER VI

DUKE CASIMIR'S FAMILIAR

I mind it was some tale of years later that I got my first glimpse below the surface of things in the town of Thorn, and especially in the castle of the Wolfsberg.

Duke Casimir continued to move, as of yore, in cavalcade through his subject city. The burghers bowed as obsequiously as ever when they could not avoid meeting him. There were the old lordly perquisitions—thunderings at iron-studded doors, battering-rams set between posts, and the clouds of dust flying from the driven lintels, the screams of maids, the crying of women, a stray corpse or two flung on to the street, and then the procession as before, arms and legs, with a mercenary soldier between each pair, fore and aft. All this was repeated and repeated, till the dull monotony of tyranny began to wear through the long Teutonic patience to the under-quick of Wendish madness.

It chanced that one night I could not sleep. It was no matter of maids that kept me awake, though by this time I was sixteen or seventeen and greatly grown—running, it is true, mostly to knees and elbows, but nevertheless long of limb and stark of bone, needing only the muscle laid on in lumps to be as strong as any.

I had begun to steal out at nights too—not on any ill errand, but that I might have the company of those about my own age—'prentice lads and the wilder sons of burghers, who had no objection to my parentage, and thought it rather a fine thing to be hand-in-glove with the son of the Red

Axe of Thorn. And there we played single-stick, smite-jacket, skittles, bowls—aye, and drank deep of the city ale—the very thinnest brew that was ever passed by a bribed and muzzy ale-taster. All this was mightily pleasant to me. For so soon as they knew that I had determined to be a soldier, and not the Red Axe of the Wolfmark, they complimented me greatly on my spirit.

Well, as I lay awake and waited for the chance to slip down a rope from my bedroom window, whose foot should I hear on the turret stairs but that of my Lord Duke Casimir! My very heart quailed within me. For the fear of him sat heavy on every man and woman in the land. And as for the children—why, as far as the Baltic shore and the land of the last Ritters, mothers frightened their bairns with the Black Duke of the Wolfsberg and his Red Axe.

So now the Duke and the Red Axe were to be in conference—as indeed had happened nearly every day and night since I could remember. So that people called my father the Duke's Private Devil, his Familiar Spirit, his Evil Genius. But I knew other of it—and this night, of all nights in the year, I was to know better still.

It was a summer midnight—not like the one I told of when the story began, white with snow and glittering with the keen polish of frost. But a soft, still night, drowsy yet sleepless, with an itch of thunder tingling in the air—and, indeed, already the pulsing, uncertain glow of sheet-lightning coming and going at long intervals along the south.

I crouched and nestled in the hole in the wall where I had long ago hidden the hated red cloak, pulling my knees up uncomfortably to my chin. And great lumps of bone they were, knotted as if a smith had made them in the rough with a welding hammer and had forgotten to reduce them with the file afterwards. At that time I was thoroughly ashamed of my knees.

But no matter for them now. Duke Casimir passed in and shut the door.

"Gottfried," I heard him say, "I am a dead man!"

These words from the great Duke Casimir startled me, and though I knew well enough that Michael Texel, the Burgomeister's son, was waiting for me by the corner of the Jew's Port, I decided that, as I might never hear Duke Casimir declare his secretest soul again, I should even bide where I was; and that was in the crevice of the wall among the old clothes, which gave off such a faint, musty, sleepy smell I could scarcely keep awake.

But the Duke's next words effectually roused me.

"A dead man!" repeated Casimir. "I have not a friend in all the realm of the Mark besides yourself. And there is none of all that take my bounty or eat my bread that is sorry for me. See here," he said, querulously, "twice have I been stricken at today—once a tile fell from a roof and dinted the crown of my helmet, and the second time a young man struck at my breast with a dagger."

"Did he wound you, Duke Casimir?" asked my father, speaking for the first time, but in a strangely easy and equal voice, not with the distance and deference which he showed to his lord in public.

"Nay, Gottfried," replied Duke Casimir; "but he bruised my shirt of mail into my breast."

And I heard plainly enough the clinking of the rings of chain-armor as the Duke showed his hurt to my father. Presently I heard his voice again.

"And the Bishop has touched me in a new place," he said. "He declares that he will lay his interdict upon me and my people—ill enough to hold in hand as they are even now. When that is done they will rise in rebellion. My very men-at-arms and knights I cannot depend upon—only upon you and the Black Riders."

"In the matter of the Bishop's interdict, or in other matters, do you mean that you can trust my counsel, Duke Casimir?" asked my father.

"'Tis in the burial of the dead that the shoe will pinch first with these burghers of Thorn and among our soldiers at the Wolfsberg. For mass, indeed, they care not a dove's dropping—but that the corpse should be carried to a dog's grave, that they cannot away with. Red Axe, I tell you we shall have the State of the Mark about our ears in the slipping of a hound's leash—and as for me, I know not what I shall do."

"Listen, and I will counsel you, Duke Casimir! Care you not though the east wind brought Bishop Peters whirling over the Mark, as many as the January snowflakes that come to us from Muscovy. I, Gottfried Gottfried, tell you what to do. In every parish of the Mark there is a parson. Every clerk of them hath a Presbytery, in which he dwells with those that are abiding with him. Bid you the soldiers that are obedient to you to carry all the corpses of the dead to the Presbytery, and leave them there under guard. Then let us see whether or no the parsons will give them burial. What think you of the counsel, Duke Casimir?"

I could hear the Duke rise and pace across the floor to where my father sat on his bed. And by the silence I knew that the two men were shaking hands.

"Red Axe," said the Duke, much moved, "of a truth you are a great man—none like you in the Dukedom. These beard-wagging, chain-jingling gentry I have small notion of. And would you but accept it, I would give you tomorrow the collar of gold which befits the Chancellor of the Mark. None deserves to wear it so well as thou."

My father laughed a low scornful laugh.

"Because I bid you teach the parsons their own religion, am I to be made Chancellor of the Mark? A great gray wolf out of the forest were as suitable a Chancellor of the Mark as Gottfried Gottfried, the fourteenth hereditary Red Axe of Thorn!"

Then I heard him reach over his bed for something. I stole out of the hole in the wall and crouched down till my eyes rested at the great latchet hole through which the tang of leather to lift the bolt ordinarily goes. I could see my father sitting on his bed and the Red Axe lying across his knees. He took it in hand, dangling it like an infant. He caressed it as he spoke, and ran his thumb lovingly along the shining edge.

"Ah," he said, "my beauty, 'tis you and not your master they should make High Chancellor of this realm. 'Tis you that have held the power of life and death, and laid the spirit of rebellion any time these twenty years. And well indeed wouldst thou look with a red robe about thee" (here he reached for a cloak that swung from the rafters contiguous to his hand); "a noble presence wouldst thou be in a tun-bellied robe and a collar of shining gold! Bravely, great State's Chancellor of the Wolfmark, wouldst thou then lead the processions and preside at the diets of justice—as indeed thou dost mostly as it is."

And he made the Red Axe bow like a puppet in his hands as he swept the cloak of red out behind the handle.

I could see Duke Casimir now. He had drawn up a stool and sat opposite my father, with his elbows on his knees. One hand was stroking the side of his head, and his haughtiness had all fallen from him like a forgotten overmantle. He looked another man from the cruel, relentless Prince who had ridden so sternly at the head of his men-at-arms and looked so callously on at the death of men and the yet more bitter agony of women.

He stared at the floor, absorbed in his own gloomy thoughts, while my father regarded him with his eyes as though he had been a lad in his 'prenticing who needed encouragement to persevere.

"Duke," he said, steadily, "you have borne the rule many years, and I have stood behind you. Have I ever advised you wrong? Make peace with the young man, your nephew; he is now only the Count von Reuss, but one day he will be Duke Otho. And if he be rightly guided he may be a brave ruler yet. But if not, and he gather in his hand the various seditions and confused turbulences in the Dukedom, why, a worse thing may befall."

"You advise me," said the Duke, lifting his head and looking at his Justicer, "to recall my nephew and risk all that threatened us ere he fled to the Prince of Plassenburg—Karl, the Miller's Son."

Gottfried Gottfried continued to run his thumb to and fro along the edge of the Red Axe.

"Even so," he replied, without raising his head; "give him the command of the Black Riders of the Guard, who, as it is, adore him. Let him try his 'prentice hand on Bamberg and Reichenan. And if he offend, why, then it will be time to apply for further advice to this chancellor in the Red Robe, whose face so shines with wisdom."

The Duke rose.

"Well, on your head be it!" he said.

"Nay," said my father, "I but advise, it is for you to decide, my Lord. If Duke Casimir sees a better way of it, why, then the words of his servant are but as the tunes that the east wind whistles through the key-hole."

And at the mention of key-holes I imagined that I saw my father's eyes rest on the latchet crevice. So I bethought me that it was time for me to be retiring to bed. To my room, therefore, I went straightway, tiptoeing on the points of my hose. And with ears cocked I heard my father attend the Duke to the door, and on across the yard, lest any night-wandering traitor should take a fancy to make a hole in the back of Duke Casimir of the Wolfmark.

Presently came my father in again, and I heard his foot climb steadily up to my room. The door opened, and never was I in so deep a sleep. He turned down the coverlet to see that I was undressed—but that I had seen to. Whereat he departed fully satisfied.

Nevertheless this interview left me with a great feeling of insecurity. If the Duke Casimir were thus full of fears, doubts, misgivings, whence came the fierce and cruel courage with which he dominated his liege burghers and harassed the country round about for a hundred leagues? The cunning of a weak man? Say, rather, the contrivance of a strong servant to hide the frailty of a weak master.

Then first it was that I saw that my father Gottfried Gottfried was the true ruler of the Wolfmark, and that the man who had carried me on his shoulders and played with the little Helene was—at least, so long as Duke Casimir lived—the greatest man in all the Dukedom and first Councillor of State, whether the matter were one of peasant or Kaiser.

CHAPTER VII

I BECOME A TRAITOR

Much was I flattered, and very naturally so, when Michael Texel made so manifest a work about pleasing me and having me for his comrade. For though I was now nineteen, he was five years my senior, and his father, being both Burgomeister and Chief Brewer, was of the first consideration in the town of Thorn.

"Hugo," said Michael Texel, "there be many lads in the city that are well, and well enough, but none of them please me like you. It may be that your keeping so greatly to yourself has made you passing thoughtful for your age. And whereas these street-corner scraps of rascaldom care for nothing but the pleasing of pothouse Gretchens, we that are men think of the concerns of the State, and make us ready for the great things that shall one day come to pass in Thorn and the Wolfmark."

I nodded my head as if I knew all about it. But, indeed, in my heart, I too preferred the way of the other lads—as the favor of maids, and other lighter matters. But since one so great and distinguished as Michael Texel declared that such things were but useless gauds, unworthy of thought, I considered that I had better keep my tongue tight-reined as to my own desires.

I shall now tell the manner of my introduction to the famous society of the White Wolf.

From the very first time that ever I saw him, Michael Texel had much to say about a certain wondrous league of the young men of Thorn and the Wolfmark. He told me how that every man with a heart in him was enrolled among them: the sons of the rich and great, like himself; the sons of the folk of no account (like myself, doubtless); the soldiers of the Duke—nay, it was whispered very low in my ear, that even the young Count Otho von Reuss, the Duke's nephew and heir, had taken high rank in the society.

I asked Michael what were the declared objects of the association.

"See," he cried, grandly, with a wave of his hand, "this city of Thorn. It lies there under the Wolfsberg. With a few cannon like Paul Grete, the Margrave's treasure, Duke Casimir could lay our houses in ruins. Therefore, in the meantime, let us not break out against Duke Casimir. But one day there will come an end to the tyrant Duke. Tiles will not always break harmless on helmets, nor the point of steel always be turned aside by links of chain-armor. As I say, an hour will come for Casimir as for other malefactors. And then—why, there is the young Otho. And he has sworn the vows of the White Wolf to make of Thorn a free city with a Stadtholder—one with power and justice, chosen freely by the people, as in other Baltic cities. Is there a man of us that has not been plundered?—a maid that does not go in fear of her honor while Casimir reigns? Shall this thing be? Not surely forever. The White Wolf shall see to it. She has many children, and they are all dear to her. Let the Duke Casimir take his count with that!"

So, as was natural, I became after that more than ever eager to join this most notable league of the White Wolf.

One night I had sat late talking to the Little Playmate, who was now growing a great maid and a beautiful—none like her, so far as I could see, in all the city of Thorn—a circumstance which made me more ready to be of Michael Texel's opinion with regard to any flighty and irresponsible courting of the maids of the town. For had I not the fairest and the best of them all at home close by me? On this night of which I speak it was almost bedtime when I heard a knocking at the outer port, and went to open the wicket.

And lo! there was Michael Texel come all the way to the Red Tower for me, though it was by his own trysting that we had agreed to meet at the inn of the White Swan. Nevertheless there he was. So there was nothing for it but to bring him in. I presented him in form to the Little Playmate, who had quite forgotten her Princess-ship by this time in the sweetness of being our house-angel of the Red Tower.

I saw in a moment that Michael Texel was astonished at Helene's beauty, as indeed well he might be. But she, on her part, hardly so much as glanced at him, though he was a tall and well-grown youth enough, with nothing remarkable about him save pale hair of much the same color as his complexion, and a cut on one side of his upper lip which in certain lights gave him a sneering expression.

But to Helene he spoke very carefully and courteously, asking her whether she ever went to any of the Guild entertainments for which Thorn was famous. And upon her saying no—that my father did not think it fitting, Michael said, "I was sure of it; none could forget if once they had seen. For never in the history of Thorn has so fair a face graced Burgher dance or Guild festival, nor yet has a foot so light been shaken on the green in any of our summer outgoings."

Now this was well enough said in its way, but only what I myself had often thought. Not that the Playmate took any notice of his words or was in any degree elated, but kept her head bent demurely on her work all the time Michael Texel was with us.

Presently there entered to us, thus sitting, Gottfried Gottfried, who had come striding gloomily across the yard in his black suit from the Hall of Judgment, and at his entrance Michael instantly became awkward, nervous, and constrained.

"I must be going," he said; "the Burgomeister bade me be early within doors tonight."

"Is the noble Burgomeister lodging at the White Swan?" asked my father, with his usual simple directness, as he went hither and thither ordering his utensils without heeding the visitor.

"No," said Michael, startled out of his equanimity; "he bides in his own house by the Rath-house—the sign is that of the Three Golden Tuns."

The Red Axe nodded.

"I had forgotten," he said, indifferently, and stood by the great polished platter-frame over the sideboard, dropping oil on the screws of a certain cunning instrument which he was wont to use in the elucidation of the Greater Question.

I could see Michael turning yellow and green, but whether with anger or fear I could not tell. Helene, who loved not the tools of my father, had, upon his entrance, promptly gathered up her white cobwebs and lace, and had betaken herself to her own room.

"I must be bidding you a fortunate evening and wishing you an untroubled sleep," said Michael, with studious politeness, rising to his feet. Yet he did not immediately move away, but stood awkwardly fingering his hat, as if he wished to ask a question and dared not.

"It is indeed a fine place for a sound sleep," said my father, nodding his head grimly, "this same upper courtyard of the Wolfsberg. There are few that have once slept here, my noble young sir, who have ever again complained of wakefulness."

At this moment the hounds in the kennels raised their fierce clamor. And, without waiting for another word, Michael Texel took himself off down the stairs of the Red Tower. Nor did he regain his composure till I had opened the wicket and ushered him out upon the street.

Then, as the postern clicked and the familiar noises of the city fell on his ear—the slapping flat-footed lasses crying "Fried Fish," the sellers of "Hot Oyster Soup," the yelling venders of crout and salad—Michael gradually picked up his courage, and we proceeded down the High Street of Thorn to the retired hostel of the White Swan.

"Frederika," he cried, as he entered, "are the lads here yet?"

"Aye, sir, aye—a full muster," answered the old mild-faced hostess, who was busily employed knitting a stocking of pale blue in the porch, looking for all the world like the sainted mother of a family of saints.

Michael Texel walked straight through a passage and down a narrow alley, the beautiful apple-cheeked old woman following us with her eyes as we went.

Our feet rang suddenly on hollow pavement as we stooped to enter a low door in the side wall, almost concealed from observation by an overgrowth of ivy.

"Halt!" cried a voice from the dusk ahead of us, and instantly there was a naked sword at each of our breasts. We heard also the click of swords meeting behind us. I turned my head, and lo! there at my very shoulder I saw the gleam of crossed steel. My heart beat a little faster; but, after all, I had been brought up with sights and sounds more terrible than these, and, more than that, I had within the hour seen Michael Texel, the high-priest of these mysteries, turn all manner of rainbow colors at the howling of our blood-hounds and a simple question from my father. So I judged that these mighty terrifications could portend no great ill to one who was the son of the formidable Red Axe of the Wolfsberg.

Sometimes it is a mighty comfortable thing to have a father like mine.

I did not hear the question which was asked of my guide, but I heard the answer.

"First in charge," said Michael Texel, "and with him one of the Wolf's litter."

So we were allowed to proceed. But in the bare room which received us I was soon left alone, for, with another question as briefly asked and answered, the click of swords crossed and uncrossed before and behind him, and the screechy grind of bolts, Michael passed out of sight within. While as for me, I was left to twirl my thumbs, and wish that I had stayed at home to watch the nimble fingers of the Playmate busy at her sewing, and the rounded slenderness of her sweet body set against the light of evening, which would at that hour be shining through the windows of the Red Tower.

Nevertheless, it was no use repining or repenting. Here was I, Hugo Gottfried, the son of the Red Axe, at the inner port of a treasonable society. It was certainly a curious position; but even thus early I had begun to consider myself a sort of amateur of strange situations, and I admit that I found a certain stimulus in the thought that in an hour I might have ceased to be heir to the office of Hereditary Justicer of the ducal province of the Wolfmark.

Presently through the door there came one clothed in the long white garments of a Brother of Pity, the eye-holes dark and cavernous, and the eyes shining through the mask with a look as if the wearer were much more frightened than those who looked upon him.

"Child of the White Wolf," he said, in a shaking voice, "would you dare all and become one of the companions of the mysteries?"

But the accent of his voice struck me, the son of Gottfried Gottfried, the dweller in the enclosure of the Red Tower, as painfully hollow and pretentious. I had looked upon real terror, even plumbed some of the grimmer mysteries of existence, and I had no fears. On the contrary, my spirits rose, and I declared my readiness to follow this paltering, knock-kneed Brother of Pity.

We stopped and went through another narrow passage, in the midst of which we were stayed by thin bars, which were shot before and behind us, and by a cold point of iron laid lightly against my brow. In this constrained position my eyes were bandaged by unseen fingers.

The starveling Brother of the Wolf took me by the hand and led me on. Then in another moment came the sense of lights and wider spaces, the rustle of many people settling down to attention; and I knew that I was in the presence of the famous secret tribunal of the White Wolf, which had been set up in defiance of the authority of the Duke and against the laws of the Mark.

CHAPTER VIII

AT THE BAR OF THE WHITE WOLF

"Who waits at the bar with you, brother?" said a voice which, though disguised, carried with it a suggestion of Michael Texel.

The announcement was made by the officer who brought me in.

"'Tis one Hugo Gottfried, son of Gottfried Gottfried, hereditary executioner to the tyrant."

I could hear the thrill of interest which pervaded the assembly at the announcement. And for the first time I thought almost well of the honorable office to which I had been born.

"And what do you here, son of the Red Axe, in the place of the Sacred Fehme of the White Wolf?"

The question was the first addressed directly to me.

"I came," said I, as straightforwardly and simply as I could, "with Michael Texel, because he asked me to come. And also because I heard that there was good ale to be had for the drinking at the White Swan of Thorn, where we are now met."

A low moan of horror went about the assembly at the frivolity of my answer, which plainly was not what had been expected.

"Daring mocker!" cried a stern voice, "you speak as one unacquainted with the dread power of the White Wolf, which has within her grasp the keys of life and death—and has suckled great empires at her dugs. Beware, tempt not the All-powerful to exercise her right of axe and cord!"

"I do not tempt any," answered I, boldly enough—yet with no credit to myself, for I could have laughed aloud at all this hollow pretence, having been brought up within the range of that which was no mockery. "I am willing to become a loyal member of the Society of the White Wolf for the furtherance of any honest purpose. All things, I admit, are not well within the body politic. Let us, in the city of Thorn, strive after the same rights as are possessed by the Free Cities of the North. If that be your object, the son of the Red Axe is with you—with you to the death, if need be. But for God's sake let us take off these masks and set ourselves down to the tankard and the good brown bread with less mummery—a sham of which others have the reality."

"Peace, vain, ignorant fly!" cried the same speaker, one with a young voice, which he was trying, as I thought, to make grave and old; "terror must first strike your heart, or you cannot sit down with the Society of the White Wolf. You stand convicted of blasphemy against this our ancient and honorable institution—blasphemy which must be suddenly and terribly punished. Hugo Gottfried, I command you—make your head ready for the striker. Bare the neck and bow the knee!"

But I stood as erect as I could, though I felt hands laid upon my shoulders and the breathing of many close about me.

"Knights and gentlemen," said I, "I am not afraid to die, if need be. But ere you do your will upon me, I would fain tell you a tale and give you a warning. Here I am one among many. I am also of your opinion, if your opinion be against tyranny. But for God's sake seek it as wise men and not as posturing knaves. As for Michael Texel—"

"Name not the mortal names of men in this place of the White Wolf!" said the same grave voice.

At which I laughed a little.

"If you will tell me what to say instead in the language of the immortals, I will call my friend by that name. Till then Michael Texel, I say—"

I was pulled by force down upon my knees.

"Your pleasure, gentlemen," said I, as coolly as I might; "you may do with me as you will, but give me at least leave to speak. Your meetings here at the White Swan are known to the Red Axe, my father, and therefore to the Duke Casimir."

A low groan filled the wide hall. I could feel that my words touched them on the raw.

"Also this very night I saw one of your noblest members tremble with alarm—for the Society, not for himself, I warrant—when Gottfried Gottfried spake lightly of your meetings here as of a thing well known. I am not afraid of my life. In the sight of my father I went forth from the Red Tower in the company of Michael Texel. He knew of your place of meeting. And well I wot that if I am not within the precincts of the Red Tower by midnight, the officers of Duke Casimir and his Judgment Hall will come knocking at these doors of yours. I ask you, are you ready to open?"

"Rash mortal!" said the voice again to me, "you mistake the White Wolf if you think that she or her children are afraid of any tyrant or of his officers. You yourself shall die, as has been appointed. For none may speak lightly of the White Wolf and live to tell the tale!"

"So be it," I replied, calmly; "but first let me recount to you the story of Hans Pulitz. Not for the hiding of a belt of gold, as men say, was he condemned. But because he had plotted against the life of the Duke and of his minister of justice, the Red Axe. Would you know what happened? I will tell you briefly:

"Ten men, accounted strong, held Hans Pulitz. Ten men could scarce lead him through the court-yard to the chair on which sat Duke Casimir. I saw him judged. Was he not of the White Wolf? Did the White Wolf save him? Have her teeth ravened for those that condemned him? Or have you that are of that noble society kept close in your halls and played out your puppet shows, while poor Hans, who was faithful to you to the end, went—whither?"

A sough of angry whispering filled the room, rising presently into a roar of indignation.

"Traitor! Murderer! Spy!" they cried.

"Nay," said I, "'fore God, Hugo Gottfried was more sorry for the poor deceived slave than any here. For, in the presence of the Duke, I cried out against the horror. But being no more than a boy, I was stricken to silence by the hand of a man-at-arms. Then I saw Hans Pulitz cast loose. I saw him seized by one man—even by the Red Axe—raised high in the air, and flung over the barriers among the ravening and leaping blood-hounds. I heard the hideous noises that followed—the yells of a man fighting for his life in a place of fiends. I shut my ears with my hands, yet could I not shut out that clangor of hell. I shut my eyes, closer than you have shut them for me now. I fled, I knew not where, terror pursuing me. And yet I saw, and do now see, the Duke sitting with crossed hands as if at prayers, and the Red Axe standing motionless before the men-at-arms, pointing with one hand to the Duke's vengeance! Shall I tell you now why I am not afraid?"

After hearing these words it was small wonder that they cried yet more against me.

"Death to the traitor—bloody death—like that which he has rejoiced in!"

"Nay, my friends," said I, "it was because of the death of Hans Pulitz and that of others that I would strengthen the hands of liberty and make an end of tyranny. But not, an' it please you, with child's plays and the cast-off garmentry of tyrants. What can you do to me in the Inn of the Swan that can equal the end of poor Hans Pulitz—of whom they found neither bone nor hair, took up no fragment of skin or nail, save the golden chain only, tooth-scarred and beslavered, which he wore about his waist. And the belt you may see for yourselves any day if you give me your company within the Red Tower."

Now, as may well be understood, if the Society of the White Wolf was angry before, it was both angry and frightened now, which is a thing infinitely more dangerous.

"Let him die straightway! Let the taunting blasphemer die!" they cried. And again, for the third time, the hollow voice pronounced my doom.

"It is well," I shouted amid the din. "It is thrice well. But look ye to it. By the morrow's morn there shall not be one of you in your beds—aye, and those whose heads are rolled in the dust shall count yourselves the fortunate ones. For they at least will escape the fate of poor Hans Pulitz."

Now sorely do I wonder, at this distance of time, that they did not slay me in good earnest. But I have learned from that night in the Inn of the Swan that when defiance has to be made, it is ever best to deal in no half-measures. And, besides, coming from the Red Tower of the Wolfsberg, their precious Society of the White Wolf, with its mummery and flummery, filled me with a hot contempt.

"Kneel down!" cried the judge; "lay your head on the block! It has often been wet with the blood of traitors, never with that of a blacker traitor than Hugo Gottfried!"

So with that those about me thrust me forward and forced my head down. I was obliged to clasp the block with both my hands. As I did so I felt it well all over. Then I laughed aloud, with a laugh that must have appeared strange and mad to them.

For this their mock tribunal could not deceive one who had been brought up within the hum of judges of life and death, and with a father who as his daily business propounded the Greater and Lesser Questions. And their precious block, as smooth as sawn and polished timber, with never a notch from side to side, could not take in Hugo Gottfried, who had made a playmate and a printed book of the worn blocks of a hundred executions—to whom each separate chip made by the Red Axe had been a text for Gottfried Gottfried to expatiate upon concerning his own prowess and that of his fathers.

Nevertheless, it certainly gave me a strange turn when ice-cold steel was laid across my neck-bone. It burned like fire, turning my very marrow to water, and for the first time I wished myself well out of it. But only for a moment.

For there came a loud rattling of arms without, a thunderous and insistent knocking at the door, which disturbed the assembly.

"Open, in the name of the Duke!" cried, clamorously, many fierce voices without. I heard the rush and scuffle of a multitude of feet. The hands that had held me abruptly loosened their grip, and I was free. I raised my bound wrists to my brow and tried to push the bandage back. But it was firmly tied, and it was but dimly that I saw the hall of the White Wolf filled with the armed men of the Duke's body-guard, boisterously laughing, with their hands on their sides, or kicking over the mock throne covered with white cloth, the coils of rope, the axes of painted wood, and the other properties of this very faint-hearted Fehmgericht.

"But what have we here?" they cried, when they came upon me, bound and helpless, with the bandage only half pushed off my eyes.

"Heave him up on his pins, and let us look at him," quoth a burly guardsman. "I trust he is no one of any account. I want not to see another such job done on a poor scheming knave like that last, when the Duke Casimir settled accounts with Hans Pulitz!"

"Ha! ha!" laughed his companion; "a rare jest, i' faith; 'tis the son of our own Red Axe—a prisoner of the White Wolf and ready for the edge. We came not a moment too soon, youngster. What do you here?"

"Why," said I, "it chanced that I spoke slightingly of their precious nonsense of a White Wolf. But they dared not do me harm. They were all more frightened than a giggling maiden is of the dark, when no man is with her."

Then I saw my father at the end of the hall. He came towards me, clad in his black Tribunal costume.

"Well," he said, quaintly, like one that has a jest with himself which he will not tell, "have you had enough of marching hand-in-glove with treason? I wot this mummery of the White Wolf will serve you for some time."

I was proceeding to tell him all that had passed, but he patted me on the shoulder.

"I heard it all, lad, and you did well enough—save for your windiness about liberty and the Free Cities—which, as I see it, are by far the worst tyrannies. But, after all, you spoke as became a Gottfried, and one day, I doubt not, you shall worthily learn the secrets, bear the burden, and enlarge the honors of the fourteen Red Axes of the Wolfmark."

CHAPTER IX

A HERO CARRIES WATER IN THE SUN

With all which adventuring and bepraisement back and forth, as those who know nineteen will readily be assured, I went home no little elated. For had I not come without dishonor through a new and remarkable experience, and even defied the Mystery of the White Wolf, at perhaps more risk to myself than at the time I had imagined. For, as I found afterwards, there were those among the company at the Swan that night of sterner mould and more serious make than Michael Texel.

But, at all events, home to the Red Tower I strode, whistling, and in a very cocksure humor.

The little Helene was going about her house duties silently and distantly when I came down from my turret room on the forenoon of the morrow. She did not come forward to be kissed, as had been her wont every morning ever since I carried her, a little forlorn maid, up to mine own bed that chill winter's night.

"A good-morrow, Little Playmate!" I bade her, gayly. For my heart was singing a good tune, well pleased with itself and willing to be at amity with every one else—counting indeed, as is the wont of brisk hearts, a gloomy face little less than a personal insult.

But the maid did not answer, neither indeed did she seem to have heard me.

"I bade you fair good-morning, Helene," said I, again, stopping in my walk across to my breakfast platter.

But still she was silent, casting sand upon the tiled floor and sweeping it up with great vigor, all her fair body swaying and yielding to the grace, of movement at every stroke. Strange, it seemed she was now just about the age when I developed those nodosities of knee and elbow which troubled me so sore, but yet there was nothing of the kind about her, only delicate slimness and featly rounded grace.

I went over to her, and would have set my palm affectionately on her shoulder. But she escaped, just as a bird does when you try to put your hand upon it. It does not seem to fly off. It simply is not there when your hand reaches the place.

"Let be," she said, looking upon me haughtily. "By what right do you seek to touch me, sir?"

"Sweetheart," said I, following her, and much astonished, "because I have always done it and you never objected before."

"When I was a child, and when you loved me as a child, it was well. But now, when I am neither a child nor yet do you love me, I would have you cease to treat me as you have done."

"You are indeed no longer a child, but the fairest of sweet maids," I made answer. "I will do nothing you do not wish me to do. For, hearken to me, Helene, my heart is bound up in you, as indeed you know. But as to the second word of accusation—that I do not love you anymore—"

"You do not—you cannot!" she interrupted, "or you would not go out with Michael Texel all night to drinking-places, and worse, keeping your father and those that *do* love awake, hurting their hearts here" (she put her hand on her side), "and all for what—that you may drink and revel and run into danger with your true friends?"

"Sweetheart," I began—penitently.

The Little Playmate made a gesture of infinite impatience.

"Do not call me that," she said; "you have no right. I am not your sweetheart. You have no heart at all to love any one with, or you would not behave as you have done lately. You are naught but a silly, selfish boy, that cares for nothing but his own applause and thinks that he has nothing to do but to come home when his high mightiness is ready and find us all on our knees before him, saying: 'Put your foot, great sir, on our necks—so shall we be happy and honored.'"

Now this was so perilously near the truth that I was mightily incensed, and I felt that I did well to be angry.

"Girl," I said, grandly, "you do not know what you say. I have been abroad all night on the service of the State, and I have discovered a most dangerous conspiracy at the peril of my life!"

For I thought it was as well to put the best face on the matter; and, besides, I have never been able, all the days of me, to hide my light under a bushel, as the clerks prate about.

But I was not yet done with my adventuring of this eventful day. And in spite of my father setting me, like a misbehaving bairn, to the drudgery of the water-carrying, there was more in life for me that day than merely hauling upon a handle. For that is a thing which galls an aspiring youth worse than any other labor, being so terribly monotonous.

As for me, I did not take kindly to it at all—not even though I could see mine own image deep in the pails of water as they came up brimming and cool out of the fern-grown dripping darkness of the well. Aye, and though the image given back to me was (I say it only of that time) a likely enough picture of a lad with short, crisped locks that curled whenever they were wet, cheeks like apples, and skin that hath always been a trouble to me. For I thought it unmanly and like a girl's. And that same skin of mine is, perhaps, the reason why all my days I never could abide your buttermilk-and-roses girls, having a supply about me enough to serve a dozen, and therefore thinking but little of their stock-in-trade.

Now in the Wolfmark this is the common kind of beauty—not that beauty of any kind is over-common. For our maids—especially those of the country—look too much as if they had been made out of wooden pillows such as laborers use to lay their heads on of nights—one large bolster set on the top of two other little ones, and all three well wadded with ticking and feathers. But I hope no one will go back to the Wolfmark and tell the maids that Hugo Gottfried said this of them, or of a surety my left ear will tingle with the running of their tongues if there be any truth in the old saw.

It was three of the clock and the sun was very fierce on the dusty, unslaked yard of the Wolfsberg, glaring down upon us like the mouth of a wide smelter's oven. Fat Fritz, the porter, in his arm-chair of a cell, had well-nigh dissolved into lard and running out at his own door. The Playmate's window was open, and I caught the waft of a fan to and fro. I judged therefore that my lady knew well that I was working out there in the heat, and was glad of it—being a spiteful pretty minx.

Then I began to wonder who had given her that fan, for it was not like my father to do it, and she knew no other. "Ah!" I said to myself, as a thought struck me, "could it possibly be Michael Texel? He is rich, and Helene may have known him before. The cunning, dark-eyed little vagabond—to take my introduction yester-even as if she had never set eyes on the fellow before, while here it is as clear as daylight that he had all the time been giving her presents—fans and such like."

So I raved within me, half because I believed it, and half because she seemed so comfortable up there, with her feet on a stool and a cool jug of curds at her elbow, while I sweated and labored in the sun.

Very decidedly it must be Texel; devil fly up with him and scratch him among the gargoyles of the minster!

The fan wagged on. It looked distractingly cool within. But then my father—filial obedience was very distinctly a duty, and, also, Gottfried Gottfried, though kind, was a man not to be disobeyed—even at nineteen, and after defying the White Wolf.

It was, as I have said, about three by the sundial on the wall, the arch of which cast a shadow like jet on the scale, that my father came out through the narrow door from the Judgment Hall, opening it with his own key. For he had the right of entrance and outgoing of every door in the palace, not even excepting the bedchamber of Duke Casimir.

"Hugo," he said, "come hither, lad. I did not mean to keep you so long at work in the sun. You must have filled all the cisterns in the place by this time!"

I thanked him sincerely, but did not pursue the subject. For, indeed, I had not worked quite so hard as in his haste my father had supposed from my appearance.

"Go within," he said; "don quickly your saint's-day dress, and betake yourself down to the house of Master Gerard von Sturm, the city chamberlain, and tell him all that he asks of you—readily and truly."

"But, father," said I, "suppose he asks of me that which might condemn one who has trusted me, what am I to say?"

"Tut, boy," said my father, impatiently, "you mean young Michael Texel. Fear not for him. He was the first to inform. He was at Master von Sturm's by eight this morning, elbowing half a dozen others, all burning and shining lights of the famous Society of the White Wolf. You are the hero of the day down there, it seems."

"And lo! here I am flouted by a stripling girl, and set to carry water by the hour in the broiling sun!" I said within myself. I possessed, however, though without doubt a manifest hero, far too much of the unheroic quality of discretion to say this aloud to my father.

"I thank you, sir," I said, respectfully. "I will go at once and put on my finest coat and my shoes of silk."

My father smiled.

"You need not be particular as to the silk shoes. 'Tis to see Master von Sturm, not to court pretty Mistress Ysolinde, that I asked you to visit the lawyer's house by the Weiss Thor."

But I was not sorry to be able to proclaim my destination as loud as I dared without causing suspicion.

"Hanne," I cried down the turret stairs, "I pray you bring me the silken shoes with the ribbon bows of silk. I am going down to Master von Sturm's house; also my gold chain and bonnet of blue velvet with the golden feather in it which I won at the last arrow-shooting."

I saw the fluttering of the fan falter and stop. A light foot went pattering up the stairway and a door slammed in the tower.

Then I laughed, like the vain, silly boy I was.

"Mistress Helene," I said to myself, "you will find that poor Hugo, whom you flouted and despised, can yet pay his debts!"

So I put on the fine clothes which I wore on festal days and sallied forth. Now, though the lower orders still hated my father and all that came out of the Red Tower, or indeed, for the matter of that, out of the Wolfsberg, with hardly concealed malice—yet there were many in the city, specially among those of the upper classes, who began to think well of my determination to try another way of life than that to which I had been born. For I made no secret of the matter to Michael Texel and such of his comrades as joined us in our gatherings.

Indeed, now, when I come to think of it, it seems to me that my father was the only person of my acquaintance who did not suspect that I was resolved never to wear either the black robe of Inquisition or the crimson of Final Judgment.

Yet it wore round to within two years, and indeed rather less, of the time for my initiation into the mysteries of the Red Axe, and still I remained at home, an idle boy, playing at single-stick and fence with the men-at-arms, drinking beer in the evening with my bosom cronies, and in the well-grounded opinion of all honest people, likely enough to come to no good.

But I, Hugo Gottfried, had my eyes and my books open, and knew that I was but biding my time.

So it came about that I carried no taint of the dread associations of the Wolfsberg about me as I went down the bustling street to the Weiss Thor to call on that learned and well-reputed lawyer, Master Gerard von Sturm. So great was the fame of Master Gerard that he was often called in to settle the mercantile quarrels of the burghers among themselves, and was even chosen as arbiter between those of other towns. For, though accounted severe, he had universally the name of a just and wise man, who would not rob the litigants of all their valuables and then decide in favor of neither, as was too often the way with the "justice" of the great nobles.

As for Duke Casimir of the Wolfmark, no man or woman went near him on any plea whatsoever, save that of asking mercy or favor. And unless my father chanced to be at hand, mostly they asked in vain. For, as I now knew, he had to keep up the common bruit of himself throughout the country as a cruel, fearless, and implacable tyrant. Besides, his fears were so constant and so great, perhaps also so well-founded, that often he dared not be merciful.

CHAPTER X

THE LUBBER FIEND

At five of the clock I lifted the great wolf's-head knocker of shining brass which frowned above the door of Master Gerard von Sturm in the port of the Weiss Thor. Hardly had I let it fall again when a small wicket, apparently about two feet above my head, opened, and a huge round head with enormous ears at either side peeped out. So vast was the head and so small the aperture that one of the lateral wings of the chubby face caught on the sill, and the owner brought it away successfully with a jerk and a perfectly good-humored and audible "flip."

"Who are you, and what do you want?" said a wide-gashed mouth, which, with a squat, flattened-out nose and two merry little twinkling eyes, completed this wonderful apparition.

The words were in themselves somewhat rude. On paper I observe that they have an appearance almost truculent. But spoken as the thing framed in the window-sill said them, they were equal to a song of Brudershaft and an episcopal benediction rolled in one.

"I am Hugo Gottfried of the Red Tower, come to see Master Gerard," I replied. "Who may you be that asks so boldly?"

"I'll give you a stalk of rhubarb to suck if you can guess," was the unexpected answer.

As I had never in my life seen anything in the least like the prodigy, it was clearly impossible for me to earn the tart succulence of the summer vegetable on such easy terms.

"I should say," I replied, "if the guess savor not of insolence, that one might be forgiven for mistaking you for the Fool of the Family!"

The grin expanded till it wellnigh circumnavigated the vast head. It seemed first of all to make straight for the ears on either side. Then, quite suddenly, finding these obstacles insurmountable, it dodged underneath them, and the scared observer could almost imagine its two ends meeting with a click somewhere in the wilderness at the back of that unseen hemisphere of hairy thatch.

"Pinked in the white, first time—no trial shot!" cried the object in the doorway, cheerily. "I am the Fool of the Family. But not the only one!"

At this moment something happened behind—what, I could not make out for some time. The head abruptly disappeared. There was a noise as of floor-rugs being vigorously beaten, the door opened, and the most extraordinary figure was shot out into the street. The head which I had seen certainly came first, but so lengthy a body followed that it seemed a vain thing to expect legs in addition. Yet, finally, two appeared, each of which would have made a decent body of itself, and went whirling across the street till the whole monstrosity came violently into collision with the walls of the house opposite, which seemed to rock to its very foundations under the assault.

A decent serving-man, in a semi-doctorial livery of black cloth, with a large white collar laid far over his shoulders, and cuffs of the same upon his wrists, stood in the open doorway and smiled apologetically at the visitor. He was rather red in the face and panted with his exertions.

"I ask your pardon, young sir," he said. "That fool, Jan Lubber Fiend, will ever be at his tricks. 'Tis my young mistress that encourages him, more is the pity! For poor serving-men are held responsible for his knavish on-goings. Why, I had just set him cross-legged in the yard with a basket of pease to shell, seeing how he grows as much as a foot in the night—or near by. But so soon as my back is turned he will be forever answering the door and peeping out into the street to gather the mongrel boys about him. 'Tis a most foul Lubber Fiend to keep about an honest house, plaguing decent folks withal!"

By this time the great oaf had come back to the door of the house, and now stood alternately rubbing his elbow and rear, with an expression ludicrously penitent, at once puzzled and kindly.

"Ah, come in with you, will you?" said the man. "Certes, were it not for Mistress Ysolinde, I would set on the little imps of the street to nip you to pieces and eat you raw."

The angry serving-man held the door as wide as possible and stood aside, whereat the Lubber Fiend tucked his head so far down that it seemed to disappear into the cavity of his chest, and scurried along the passage bent almost double. As he passed the door he drew all the latter part of his body together, exactly like a dog that fears a kick in the by-going. The respectable man-servant stirred not a muscle, but the gesture told a tale of the discipline of the house by the White Gate at times when visitors were not being admitted by the main door, and when Mistress Ysolinde, favorer of the Fool Lubber Fiend, was not so closely at hand.

It was a grand house, too, the finest I had ever seen, with hangings of arras everywhere, many and parti-colored—red hunters who hunted, green foresters who shot, puff-cheeked boys blowing on hunting-horns; a house with mysterious vistas, glimpses into dim-lit rooms, wafts of perfume, lamps that were not extinguished even in the daytime, burning far within. All in mighty striking contrast to the bare stark strength of our Red Tower on the Wolfsberg with its walls fourteen feet thick.

As I followed the serving-man through the halls and stairways my feet fell without noise on carpets never woven in our bare-floored Germany, nor yet in England, where they still strew rushes, even (so they say) in the very dining-rooms of the great—surely a most barbarous and unwholesome country. Nevertheless, carpets of wondrous hue were here in the house of Master Gerard, scarlet and blue, and so thick of ply that the foot sank into them as if reluctant ever to rise again.

As I came to the landing place at the head of the stairway, one passed hastily before me and above me, with a sough and a rustle like the wind among tall poplar trees on the canal edges.

I looked up, and lo! a girl, not beautiful, but, as it were, rather strange and fascinating. She was lithe like a serpent and undulated in her walk. Her dress was sea-green silk of a rare loom, and clung closely about her. It had scales upon it of dull gold, which gave back a lustrous under-gleam of coppery red as she moved. She had a pale, eager face, lined with precision enough, but filled more with passion than womanly charm. Her eyes were emerald and beautiful, as the sea is when you look down upon it from a height and the white sand shines up through the clear depths.

Such was Ysolinde, daughter of Gerard von Sturm, favorer of Lubber Fiends and creator of this strange paradise through which she glided like a spangled Orient serpent.

As I made my way humbly enough across to Master Gerard's room his daughter did not speak to me, only followed me boldly, and yet, as it seemed to me, somewhat wistfully too, with her sea-green eyes. And as the door was closing upon me I saw her beckon the serving-man.

But I, on the inner side of the door, and with Master Gerard von Sturm before me, had enough to do to tell my tale and answer his questions without troubling my head about green-eyed girls.

Master Gerard was as remarkable looking to the full as his daughter, with the same luminously green eyes. But the orbs which in the maid shone as steadily clear as the depths of the sea, in the father glittered opalescent where he sat in the dusk, like the eyes of Grimalkin cornered by dogs in some gloomy angle of the Wolfsberg wall.

As soon as I had set eyes on him I knew that I had to do with a man—not with a walking show like my Lord Duke Casimir. It struck me that for good or evil Master Gerard could carry through his intent to the bitter end, and that in council he would smile when he saw my father change his black vesture of trial for the red of beheading.

The Doctor Gerard was little seen in the streets of Thorn. Many citizens had never so much as set eyes on him. Nevertheless his hand was in everything. Some said he was a Jew, chiefly because none knew rightly what he was or whence he had come. Thirty years had gone by since he had suddenly appeared one day in the noble old house by the Weiss Thor, from which Grätz the wizard and his wife had been burned out by the fury of the populace. Twenty years of artistic labor had made this place what it now was. And the little impish maid who used to break unexpectedly upon the workmen of Thorn from behind doors, or who clapped hands upon their shoulders in dusky recesses, scaring them out of their wits with suggestions of witch-masters long dead and damned, had grown into this maid of the sea-green eyes and silken draperies.

"A good-day to you, Hugo Gottfried!" said Master Gerard, quietly, looking at me keenly across the table. He wore a skull-cap on his closely cropped head. One or two betraying locks of gray appeared under it in front, but did not conceal a flat forehead, which ran back at such an angle that, with the luminous eyes beneath it, it gave him the look of a serpent rearing his yellow head a little back in act to strike. This was a look his daughter had also. But in her the gesture was tempered by the free-playing curves of a beautiful throat and the forward thrust of a rounded chin—advantages not possessed by the angular anatomy and bony jaw of the famous doctor of law.

Master Gerard, clad in a long robe of black velvet from head to heel, sat bending his fingers gracefully together and looking at me. His head was thrown back, I have said, and the lights of the colored windows striking on his gray hair and black skull-cap, caused him to look much more like some lean ascetic ecclesiastic and prince of the church than the chief lawyer of the ancient capital of the Wolfmark.

"You were present at this child's play yester-eve in the hostel of the White Swan?" he asked, boring into me with his uncomfortable, triangular eyes.

"Aye, truly," said I, "and much they made of me!"

For since my father said that I was accounted a hero in this house, I had determined not to hide away my deeds in my leathern scrip. I had had enough practice in playing at modesty in the Tower of the Red Axe.

Master Gerard shook his shoulders as though he would have made me believe that he laughed.

"You were over many for thorn, I hear great silly fellows—children playing with fire yet afraid to burn themselves. Why, since ten this morning I have had them all here—stout burgomeister's sons, slim scions of the Burghershaft, moist-eyed corporation children, each more anxious than another to prove that he had nothing to do with any treason. He had but called in at the White Swan for a draught of Frederika's famous stone ale, and so—well, he found himself somehow in the rear, and, all against his will, was dragged into the Lair of the White Wolf!"

He looked at me quietly, without speaking, for a while.

"And you, Master Hugo, did you go thither to distinguish yourself by breaking up their child's folly, or, like the others, to taste the stone ale?"

It was a question I had not expected. But it was best to be very plain with Master Gerard.

"I went," I replied, "along with Michael Texel, because he asked me. I knew not in the least what I was to see, but I was ready for anything."

"And you acquitted yourself on the whole extremely well," he nodded; "so at least they are all very ready to say, hoping, I doubt not, for your good offices with the Duke when it comes to their turn. You flouted them right manfully and defied their mystery, they told me."

At this moment I became conscious that a door opposite me was open and the curtain drawn a little way back. There, in the half-light, I saw Mistress Ysolinde listening. She leaned her head aside as though it had been heavy with its weight of locks of burned gold. She pillowed her cheek against the door-post, and let her dreamy sea-green eyes rest upon me. And the look that was in them gave me a sense of pleasure strange and acute, as well as a restless uneasiness and vague desire to escape out under the blue sky, and mingle with the throng of every-day men on the streets of the city.

CHAPTER XI

THE VISION IS THE CRYSTAL

Master Gerard, however, did not seem to be aware of her presence, for he continued his catechism steadily.

"You mocked at their terrors, did you not, and told them that you, who had seen the teeth of the Duke's hounds, had nothing to fear from the bare gums of the White Wolf?"

"I knew that they but played," I answered, "and that I had little to fear."

For with Ysolinde von Sturm watching me with her eyes I could not for very shame's sake make myself great.

"You told them more than that," the girl cried, suddenly flashing on me a look keen as the light on a sword when it comes home from the cutler. "You told them that you too desired a freer commonwealth!"

"I did," said I, flushing quickly, for I had thought to keep my thumb on that.

Nevertheless I was not going back on my spoken word, even in the presence of Duke Casimir's inquisitor. Besides which I judged that my father had influence enough to bring me out scathless.

"That is well and bravely said!" he replied, smiling with thin lips which in all their constant writhings showed no vestige of teeth within; "but the sentiment itself is somewhat strange in the son of the Red Axe and the future Executioner of Justice in the Wolfmark."

Then for the first time I permitted my eyes to rest on the lithe figure of the girl in the doorway. Methought she inclined her head a little forward to catch my answer as if it had been a matter of interest to her.

"I am indeed son of the Red Axe," said I, "but my own head would underlie it rather than that I should ever be Hereditary Justicer of the Mark."

A smile that was meant for me passed over the girl's face and momently sweetened her lips. She straightened her body and set a hand more easily to her waist. A certain kindness dwelt in her emerald eyes.

"Never be Duke's Justicer!" cried Master Gerard, looking up with his hand on a skull. "This is unheard of! Are not you the only son of Gottfried Gottfried, right hand of Duke Casimir, highest in favor with his Grace? And within two years, according to the law of the headsman, must you not also don the Red and the Black and stand at the Duke's left hand, as your father at his right, when he sits in judgment?"

I bowed my head for answer.

"Even so," said I; "but long before that time I shall be either in a far country waging the wars of another lord, or in a country yet farther— that to which the men of my race have directed so many untimeously."

"Have you at all thought of the land or the lord to whom you would transfer your allegiance?" said Gerard von Sturm, carelessly rapping with his fingers on the bare white of the skull before him.

"I have not," I replied as easily.

He looked down a moment, and drew his black robe thoughtfully over his knee as if turning the matter over in his mind. "What think you of Plassenburg and the service of Prince Karl?" he said at last.

"The place is too near and the man a usurper," I replied, brusquely.

"I am not so sure," Master Gerard mused, slowly, "that it might not be advantageous to bide near home. Duke Casimir is mortal, after all—long and prosperously may he live!" (Here he inclined his head piously, while naming his master.) "But who knows how long he may be spared to reign over a loving people. And after that, why, there may be more usurpers. For by the name 'usurper' the ignorant mostly mean men of the strong heart and sure brain, who can hold that which they have with one hand and reach out for more with the other."

While he spoke thus he looked at me with his green eyes half closed.

"But," said I, calmly enough, though my heart beat fast, "I am but a lad untried. I may never rise beyond a private soldier. I may be killed at the first assault of my virgin campaign."

Master Gerard looked up quickly. He beckoned to his daughter. For though by no faintest gesture had he betrayed his knowledge of her presence, he had yet clearly known it all the time.

"Ysolinde," he said, "bring hither thy crystal!"

The maid disappeared and presently returned with a ball in her hand of some substance which looked like misty glass.

"I have been looking in it already," she said, "ever since Hugo Gottfried came out of the Red Tower."

Her voice was soft and even, with the same sough in it as of the wind among poplar-trees which I had heard in the rustle of her silken dress as she came up the stair.

"And what," asked her father, "have you seen in the crystal, child of my heart?"

He looked up at me with some little shamefacedness, or so I imagined.

"I am a dry old man of the law," he went on, "dusty of heart as these black books up yonder—books not of magic but of fact, of crime and pain and penalty. But this my daughter Ysolinde, wise from a child, solaces herself with the white, innocent magic, such as helps man and brings him nearer that which is unseen."

The maid knelt by her father's knee, and held the crystal ball in the hollow of her hands against the sable of his velvet robe. She passed one hand swiftly twice or thrice over her brow, as though to clear away some cobwebs, gossamer thin, that had folded themselves across her vision. Then, in the same wistful, wind-soft voice, she began to speak. And as she spoke all that I had loved and known began to pass from before me. I forgot my father. I forgot the Red Tower. I forgot (God forgive me, yet help it I could not!) the little Princess Playmate and her sweetest eyes. I forgot all else save this lithe, serpentine maiden with the massive crown of burned and tawny gold upon her head.

"I see," she began, "a long street and many men struggling on it—the Wolf of the Wolfmark, the Eagle of Plassenburg are face to face. I see Red Karl the Prince. The young Wolf has the better of it. He bites his lip and drives hard. The Prince is down. He is wounded. He is like to die. The Wolf will drive all to destruction.

"But see—" she sighed, and paused the while as if that which she saw next touched her—"from the swelter in the rear comes a young soldier. He has lost his helmet. I see his head. It is a fair head with crisp curls. He has a sword in his hand and he lays well about him. He cuts a way to the Prince—he bestrides his body.

"Give way there, scullions, that I may see more!" she cried, impetuously, and waved her hand before her eyes, which were fixed expressionless on the crystal. "I see him again. Well done, young soldier! Valiantly laid on. It is great sword-play. Bravo! The Wolf is down. The Eagle of Plassenburg is up—I can see no more!"

And suddenly she dropped the ball, which would have rolled off her father's knee had he not caught it as it fell.

Ysolinde kept her head on Master Gerard's lap for a long minute, as if, after the vision of the crystal, she could not bear the common light nor speak of meaner things. Then, without once looking at me, she rose, gathered her skirts in her hand, and glided out of the doorway in which she had stood.

When she was quite gone her father reached a bony hand across to me.

"That is a great fate which she has read for you—never have I seen her so moved, nor yet her vision so clear and unmistakable. Surely the sooner you seek the service of the Prince of Plassenburg the better."

"But," said I, "how do I know that he will accept me? He may not wish to retain in his service the son of the Red Axe of the Wolf mark."

Master von Sturm smiled subtly at me.

"I cannot tell," he said, "why it is that I have an interest in you. But I desire to see you other than that which you are. I have, strange as it may seem in one of such humble degree here in the city of Thorn, whom all may consult without fee or reward, a certain influence and place in the councils of the reigning Prince of Plassenburg. If, therefore, you will take service with him, I can give you such an introduction as will guarantee you a place, not as man-at-arms, but as officer, so that your way may lie before you clear from the first. Also in this promotion you shall have a good sufficient reason to give those who may accuse you of changing your service."

I could not answer him for gladness. The hope seemed so unbelievable—the fortune too grateful to be true. I was overcome, and, as I guess, showed it in my face. For twice I essayed to speak and could not.

So that Master Gerard rose and glided over to me, patting me kindly enough on the shoulders and bidding me take courage, saying that he loved to see modesty in this untoward generation, in which there was little virtue and no gratitude at all.

So I grasped him by the hand and kissed his thin, bony fingers.

"Bide ye, bide ye," he said; "one day I may kiss yours an you be active. The wide spaces of Destiny lie before you, though I shall not live to see it. But you must bestir you, for I am an old man, and have not far to travel now to the place from which one leaps off into the dark."

He conducted me to the door of his chamber and gave me his hand again with the same inscrutable smile on his thin face, and his skull-cap pushed farther back than ever over the flat, ophidian brow.

"When you have all things ready," he said, "come to me for the letter of introduction, and also for that which may obtain you a worthy outfit for your journeying to Plassenburg. Or, if you are already Sir Proud-Heart, you can repay me one day, with usury if you will. I care not to stand on observances with you, nor desire that you should feel any obligation to a feeble old man."

"I am not proud," I said, "and my sense of obligation is already greater than ever I can hope to discharge."

"I thank you, my lad," he said. "Often have I wished for a son of the flesh like you as you passed the window with your companions—but go, go!"

And with his hand he pushed me out upon the stair-head and shut the door.

For a space I knew not where I stood. For what with the turmoil of my thoughts and the myriad of impressions, hopes, fears, visions, regrets to leave the Red Tower, the city of Thorn, the hope of seeing again that high-poised head of burned gold of the Lady Ysolinde, I paused stock-still, moidered and dazed, till a light hand touched me on the shoulder and the soft, even voice spoke in my ear.

"Master Hugo," said the Lady Ysolinde, bending kindly to me, "I am glad, very glad—aye, though you have made my head ache" (here she nodded blamefully and laid her hand upon her heart as if that ached too)—"it is the best of fortunes, and sure to come true. Because have I seen it at six o'clock of a Thursday in the time of full moon."

"Come hither," she said, beckoning me; "we shall try another way of it yet, in spite of the headache. It may be that there is more that concerns you for me to see in the ink-pool."

With this she took my hand and almost pulled me down the stairs by force. As we went I saw the wild head and staring eyeballs of Jan the Lubber Fiend peering at us. He was lying on the back staircase, prone on his stomach, apparently extending from top to bottom down the swirl of it, and with his chin poised on the topmost step. But as we came down the stair the head seemed to be wholly detached from any body. The red ears actually flapped with mirthful pleasure and anticipation at the sight of the Lady Ysolinde, and no man could see both the beginning and end of that smile.

"Lubber Jan," said she, "go and sit in the yard. The servants will be complaining of thee again, that they cannot come up the staircase, even as they did before."

"Then, if I do," mumbled the monster, "will you look out of window at least once in each hour, between every stroke of the clock. Else will Jan not stop in the yard, but come within to feast his eyes on thee."

"Yes, Jan," she said, smiling with a gentle complaisance which made me like her somewhat better than before, "I will look out at least once in the hour."

And turning a little she smiled again at me, still holding me by the hand. The Lubber Fiend pulled his forelock, and reaching downward his head, as if he had the power of stretching out his neck like an arm, he kissed the cold pavement where her foot had rested a moment before. Then he rather retracted himself, serpentwise, then betook him in Christian fashion down the stair, and we heard him move out amid a babel of servatorial recriminations into the outer yard.

"A poor innocent," said the Lady Ysolinde; "one that worships me, as you see. He is so great of stature and so uncouth that the children persecute him, and some day he may do one of them an injury. Years ago I rescued him from an evil pack of them and brought him hither. So that is the reason why he cleaves to me."

"An excellent reason, my lady," said I, "for any to cleave to you."

"Ah," she said, wistfully, "only fools think of Ysolinde in the city of Thorn. Some are afraid and pass by, and the rest are as the dogs that lick the garbage in the streets. Here I have no friends, save my father only, and here or elsewhere I have never had any that truly loved me."

"But you are young—you are fair," I answered. "Many must come seeking your favor." Thus did I begin lumpishly enough to comfort her. But at my first words she snatched her fingers away angrily, and then in a moment relented.

"You mean well," she said, giving her hand back to me again, "but it is not pity Ysolinde needs nor yet desires. But that is no matter. Come in hither and see what may abide for you in the depths of the black pool."

At the curtained doorway she turned and looked me in the eyes.

"If you were as other young men it would be easy for you to misjudge me. This is mine own work-chamber, and I bid you come into it, having seen you but an hour ago. Yet never a man save my father only hath set his foot in it before. Inquire carefully of your companions in the city of Thorn, and if any make pretension to acquaintance with the Lady Ysolinde of the White Gate strike him in the face and call him liar, for the sake of the favor I have shown you and the vision I saw concerning you in the crystal."

I stooped and kissed her hand, which was burning hot—a thin little hand, with long, supple fingers which bent in one's grasp.

"The man who would pretend to such a thing is dead even as he speaks," said I; and I meant it fully.

"I thank you—it is well," she answered, leading me in. "I only desired that you should not misjudge me."

"That could I never do if I would," I made her answer. "Here my every thought is reverence as in the oratory of a saint."

She smiled a strange smile.

"Mayhap that is rather more than I desire," she said. "Say rather in the maiden bower of a woman who knows well whom she may trust."

Again I kissed her hand for the correction. And, as I remembered afterwards, it was at that hour that the little Princess Playmate was used to look within my chamber to see that all was ready for me.

And, had I known it, even that night she stooped over and kissed the pillow where my head was to lie.

"Dear love!" she was used to say.

Alas that I heard it not then!

CHAPTER XII

EYES OF EMERALD

It was a strange little room into which the Lady Ysolinde brought me, full of quaint, changeful scents, and all ablaze with colors the like of which I had never seen. For not only were rugs and mats of outlandish Eastern design scattered over the floor, but there was vividly colored glass in the small, deeply set windows. Yet that which affected me most powerfully was a curious, clinging, evanescent odor, which came and went like a breeze through an open window. I liked it at first, but after a little it went to my head like a perfumed wine of Greece, such as the men of Venice sometimes send to our northern lands with their embassies of merchandise.

Altogether, it was a strange enough apartment for the daughter of a lawyer in the city of Thorn, within a mile of the bare feudal strengths of the Red Tower and the Wolfsberg.

All this while Ysolinde had kept my hand, a thing which at once thrilled and shamed me. For though I had never been what is called "in love" with the Little Playmate, nor till that day had spoken a word to her my father might not have heard, yet hitherto she had always been first and sole in my heart whenever I thought on the things which were to be.

The Lady Ysolinde having brought me to her chamber, bade me sit upon an oaken folding-stool beside a table on which lay weapons of curious design—crooked knives and poisoned arrows. Then she went to an ivory cupboard of the Orient (or, as they are called in Holy Writ, "an ivory palace"), and opening the beautifully fitting door, she took from it a small square bottle of red glass which she held between her and the light.

"It is well," she said, looking long and carefully at it; "it will flow."

And coming to the table and pouring some of a shining black liquid into the palm of her left hand, she sat down beside me on the stool and gazed steadily into the little pool of ink.

It was strange to me to sit thus motionless beside a beautiful woman (for such I then thought her)—so near that I could feel the warmth of her body strike like sunshine through the silken fineness of her sea-green gown. I glanced up at her eyes. They were fixed, and, as it seemed, glazed also. But the emerald in them, usually dark as the sea-depths, had opal lights in it, and her lips moved like those of a devotee kneeling in church.

Presently she began to speak.

"Hugo—Hugo Gottfried, son of the Red Axe," she said, in the same hushed voice as before, most like running water heard murmuring in a deep runnel underground, "you will live to be a man fortunate, well-beloved. You will know love—yes, more than one shall love you. But you will love one only. I see the woman on whom your fate depends, yet not clearly—it may be, because my desire is so great to see her face. But she is tall and moves like a queen. She goes clad in white like a bride and her arms are held out to you.

"But another shall love you, and between them two there is darkness and hate, from which come bursting clouds of fire, bringing forth lightnings and angers and deadly jealousies!

"Again I see you, great, honored, and sitting on a high seat. The woman whose face I cannot distinguish is beside you, clothed in a robe of purple. And, yes, she wears a crown on her head like the coronet of a queen."

Ysolinde withdrew her eyes gradually from the ink-pool, as if it were a pain to look yet a greater to look away. Then with a quick jerk she threw up her head, and tears were standing in her eyes ready to overflow. But the wetness made them beautiful, like a pebble of bright colors with the dew upon it and shone on by the sunshine of the morning.

"You hurt me," she murmured reproachfully, looking at me more like a child than ever I had seen her. She was very near to me.

"*I* make *you* suffer!" cried I, greatly astonished. "How can Hugo Gottfried have done this thing?"

For it seemed impossible that a poor lad, and one alien by his birth from the hearts of ordinary folk, should yet have the power to make a great lady suffer. For a great lady I knew Ysolinde to be even then, when her father seemed to be no more in the city of Thorn than Master Gerard, the fount and treasure-house of law and composer-general of quarrels.

But I might have known that he was no true lawyer to be so eager about that last. For upon the continuance and fostering of differences the law-men of all nations thrive and eat their bread with honey thereto.

As my father often said, "Better the stroke of the Red Axe than that of the scrivener's goose-quill. My solution is kindlier, sooner over, hurts less, and is all the same in the end!"

Ysolinde thought a little before she answered me.

"No man ever made me suffer thus before," she said, "though I have seen and known many men. I am older than you, Hugo, and have travelled in many countries, the lands from which these things came. But true love, the pain and the pleasure of it, have I never known."

She leaned her head on her hand and her elbow on the table, turning thus to look long and intently at me. I felt oafish and awkward, as Jan Lubber Fiend might have done before the King. Many things I might have wished to say and do with that slender figure and lissome waist so near me. But I knew not how to begin. Yet I think the desire came not so much from love or passion, but rather from a natural longing to explore those mysteries concerning which I had read so much after Friar Laurence had done me the service of teaching me French. But it was well that stupidity was my friend. For rebounding like a vain, upstart young monkey from my mood of self-depreciation, I must needs hold it for certain that all was within my grasp, and that the Lady Ysolinde expected as much of me, which thing would have wrought my downfall.

"Yon ride soon to Plassenburg, I hear," she said, after she had looked at me a long time steadily with the emerald eyes shining upon me. Then it was that I saw clearly that they were not the right emerald in hue so much as of the shade of the stone aqua-marine, which is one not so rare, but a better color when it comes to the matter of maiden's eyes.

"It is indeed true, my lady," I replied, disappointed at her words, and yet somehow infinitely relieved, "that I ride soon to Plassenburg by the favoring of your father, who has been gracious enough to promise me his interest with the Prince."

I saw her lip curl a little with scorn—the least tilt of a rose leaf to which the sun has been unkind.

She seemed about to speak, but presently thinking better of it, smiled instead.

"It is like my father," she said, after a little; "but since I also go thither, you shall be of my escort. A sufficient guard accompanies me all the way to the city, and I dare say the arrangement may serve your convenience as well as add to the pleasure and safety of my journeying."

"But how will your father do without your company, Lady Ysolinde?" I asked. For it seemed strange that father and daughter should thus part without reason in these disturbed times.

She laughed more heartily than I had heard her.

"My father has been used to missing me for months at a time, and, moreover, is well resigned also. But you do not say that you are rejoiced to be of a lady's escort in so long a travel."

"Indeed, I am much honored and glad to have so great a favor done to me. I am but a mannerless, landward youth, to have been bred in the outer courts of a palace. But that which I do not know you will teach me, and my faults I shall be eager to amend."

"Pshaw!—psutt!" said Ysolinde, making a little face, "be not so mock-modest. You do very well. But tell me if you have any sweetheart in the city to leave behind you."

Now this bold question at once reddened my face and heightened my confusion.

"Nay, lady," I stammered, conscious that I was blushing furiously, "I am over-young to have thought much of the things of love. I know no woman in the city save our old house-keeper Hanne, and the Little Playmate."

The Lady Ysolinde looked up quickly.

"Ah, the Little Playmate!" she said, in a low voice, curiously distinct from that which she used when she had interpreted her visions to me. "The Little Playmate! That sounds as though it might be interesting. Who is the Little Playmate?"

"She is a maid whose folks were slain long ago by the Duke in a foray, and the little one being left, my father begged her life. And she has been brought up with me in the Red Tower."

"How old is she now?" The Lady Ysolinde's next question leaped out like the flash of a dagger from its sheath.

"That," answered I, meditatively, "I know not exactly, because none could tell how old she was when she came to us."

"Tut," she said, impatiently tossing her head, "do not twist your answers to me—only wise men and courtiers have the skill to do that and hide it. As yet you are neither. Is she ten, or is she twenty, or is she mid-way betwixt the two?"

"I think she may be a matter of seventeen years of age."

"Is she pretty?" was the next question.

"No," said I, not knowing well what to say.

Her face cleared as she heard that, and then, in a little, her eyes being still bent steadily on me, reading my very heart, it clouded over again.

"You think her not merely pretty, then, but beautiful?" she asked.

I nodded.

"More beautiful than I?"

'Fore God I denied not my love, though I own I have many a time been less tempted, and yet have lied back and forth like a Frankfort Jew.

"Yes," said I, "I think so."

"You love her, then?" said the Lady Ysolinde, rising quickly to her feet; "and you told me that you loved none in this city."

"I love her, indeed," I said. "She is my little sister. As you mean love, I do not love her. But I love her notwithstanding. All my life I have never thought of doing anything else. And that she is beautiful, all who have eyes in their head may see."

This appeased her somewhat. I think it must have been looking for my fortune in the crystal and the ink-pool that made her so eager to know all that concerned me—which none had ever been so importunate to find out before.

"I must come and see this Little Playmate of yours," she said. "It is an ill-done thing that so fair a maid should be shut up in the tower of such a pagan castle—the Wolfsberg; it is indeed well named. Word has reached me today that the Princess of Plassenburg has need of a bower maiden. Now the Princess can make her choice from many noble families. But if the Little Playmate be as beautiful as you say, 'tis high time that she should not be left immured in the Red Tower of the Wolfsberg. True, the Duke, like a careful man, neither makes nor mells with womankind. 'Tis his only virtue. But any questing Ritterling or roaring free companion might bear her off."

"I think not," said I, smiling, "so long as the Red Axe of the Mark has a polished edge and Gottfried Gottfried can send it sheer through an ox's neck as he stands chewing the cud."

I hardly think that I ever boasted of my father's prowess before. And, indeed, I had some skill in the axe-play myself, but only in the way of sport.

"All one," said Ysolinde. "Your father, like great Caesar and Duke Casimir, is but mortal, and may stumble across the wooden stump some day himself and find his neck-bone in twain! None so wise that he can tell when the Silent Rider shall meet him in the wood, leading by the bridle the pale horse whose name is Death, and beckoning him to mount and ride."

The Lady Ysolinde paused a while, touching her lips thoughtfully with her fingers.

"Let your Playmate come," she said. "There is room, I warrant, for her and you both at Plassenburg. You shall keep each other company when you have the homesickness, and on the journey she can ride with us side by side."

Then going to the curtain she summoned the servitor who had first opened the door for me. He bowed before the girl with infinite respect. She bade him conduct me upon my way. I will not deny that I had hoped for a tenderer leave-taking. But all at once she seemed to have slipped back into the great lady again, and to be desirous of setting me in my own sphere and station ere I went, lest perchance I should presume overmuch upon her favors.

Yet not altogether so. For, relenting a little as I turned to leave her, she stood holding the curtain aside for me to pass, and, as it had been by accident, in dropping it her fingers rested a moment against my cheek. Then the heavy curtain of blue fell into its place, and I found myself following the eminently respectable domestic of Master Gerard down the stairs.

At the outer door, but before he opened it, the man put a sealed packet in my hand.

"From Doctor Gerard von Sturm," he said, bowing respectfully, yet with a certain sense of being a party in a favor conferred.

I thrust the letter into my inner pocket and went out into the street. The sun was still shining, yet somehow I felt that it must be another day, another world. The houses seemed hard and dry, the details of the architecture insufferably mean and insultingly familiar. I longed with all my heart to get away from Thorn into the new world which had opened to me—a world of perfumes and flowers and flower-like scents and Oriental marvels, of low voices, too, and the touching of soft hands upon cheeks.

In all the world of young men there was no greener or more simple Simon than I, Hugo Gottfried, as, playing a tune on the pipe of my own conceit, I marched up the High Street of Thorn to the entrance gate of the Wolfsberg.

The Little Playmate was standing at the door as I approached, sweet as a June rose. When she saw me she went into the sitting-room to show that she had not yet forgiven me. Though I think by this time, as was often the way with Helene, she had forgotten almost what was the original matter of my offending.

But I pretended to be careless and heart-free. And so—God forgive me!—I went whistling up the steps of the Red Tower to my room without so much as looking within the chamber where my Little Playmate had withdrawn herself.

Which thing I suffered grievously for or all was done. And an excellent dispensation of Providence it had been if I had lost my right hand, all for making that little heart sore, or so much as one tear drop from those deep gray eyes.

CHAPTER XIII

CHRISTIAN'S ELSA

It was about this time, and after we had made our quarrel up, that Helene began to call me "Great Brother." After all, there is manifest virtue in a name, and the Little Playmate seemed to find great comfort in thus addressing me.

And after that I had called her "Little Sister" once or twice she was greatly assured and treated me quite differently, having ascertained that between young men and women there is the utmost safety in such a relationship.

And as all ways were alike to me, I was willing enough. For indeed I loved her and none other, and so did all the days of my life. Though I know that my actions and conceits were not always conformable to the true love that was in my heart, neither wholly worthy of my dear maid.

But, then, what would you? Nineteen and the follies of one's youth! The mercy of God rather than any virtue in me kept these from being not only infinitely more numerous, but infinitely worse. Yet I had better confess them, such as they are, in this place. For it was some such nothings as those which follow that first brought Helene and me into one way of thinking, though by paths very devious indeed.

To begin with the earliest. There was a maid who dwelt in the Tower of the Wolfsberg opposite, called the Tower of the Captain of the Guard. And the maid's name was Elsa, or, as she was ordinarily called, "Christian's Elsa." She was a comely maid enough, and greatly taken notice of. And when I went to my window to con over my task for Friar Laurence, there at the opposite window would be—strange that it should always be so—Christian's Elsa. She was a little girl, short and plump, but with merry eyes and so bright a stain upon either cheek that it seemed as if she had been eating raspberry conserve, and had wiped her fingers upon the smiling plumpness there.

At any rate, as sure as ever I betook me to the window, there would be Christian's Elsa, busy with her needles.

And to tell truth I misliked it not greatly. Why, indeed, should I? For there is surely no harm in looking across twenty yards of space at a maid, and as little in the maid looking at you—that is, if neither of you come any nearer. Besides, it is much pleasanter to look at a pretty lass than at a vacant wall and twenty yards of uneven cobble-stones.

Now the girl was harmless enough—a red and white maid, plump as a partridge in the end of harvest. She was forever humming at songs, singing little choruses, and inventing of new melodies, all tunefully and prettily enough. And she would bring her dulcimer to the window and play them over, nodding her head to the instrument as she sang.

It was pleasant to watch her. For sometimes when the music refused to run aright, she would frown at the dulcimer, as if the discord had been entirely its fault and it was old enough to know better. Then sometimes she would look across abstractedly to the Red Tower, trying to recall a strain she had forgotten, with her finger all the while making the most bewitching dimple on her plump cheek. It was most sweet and innocent to see. And withal so entirely unconscious that any one could possibly be observing her.

I confess that I sat often and conned my book by the window, long after I knew my portion by heart, in order to watch her deft fingers upon the dulcimer sticks and the play of her dimples. But on my part also this was in all innocence and wholly thoughtless of guile.

Then would I be taken with a spasm of desire to play upon the recorders or the Bavarian single flute, and would pester my father to let me learn.

Now I never had any more ear for music than a deal board that has knot-holes in it. I had ears indeed. But the clatter of the mill-wheel and the lapper of water on the stones of the shore were ever better music to me than singing or playing upon instruments. Nevertheless, at this time, for some reason or other, I was in a great fret to learn.

And, curiously enough, my desire made the Little Playmate call me "Great Brother" more assiduously than ever. Though again I knew not why.

But Christian's Elsa she could not abide either sight or mention of. Which was passing strange in so sweet and charitable a maid as our Helene. Also the girl at the guard-house was a good daughter, besides being particular of her company, and in that garrison place untouched by any breath of scandal.

But no; Helene would have none of her.

"*Feech*!" she would say, making a little grimace of disgust which she had brought with her from her northern home; "that noisy, mewling cat, purring and stroking her face, in the window, I cannot abide her. I know not what some folks can see in her. There are surely more kinds of blindness than of those that wait about kirk doors with a board hung round their necks, saying, 'Good people, for the love of God, put a copper in this wooden platter.'"

"Why, Little Playmate, what ails thee at the maid? She is a good maid enough, and, I am sure, a pretty one."

So would I say to try her. Whereat the lass, being slender herself, and with a head that sat easily on her shoulders, would walk off like the haughty little Princess she was, and thrust her chin so far forward that even the pretty round of it bespoke a pointed scorn. And the poutlets would come and go on her red lips so quickly that I would come from the window, leaving my book and Christian's Elsa, and a thousand Elsas, just to watch them.

"So, Great Brother," Helene would say, "you think she is pretty, do you? 'Tis interesting, for sure. As for me, I see not anything pretty about her. Now, there is Katrin Texel, she is pretty, if you like. What say you to her?"

And this was because the minx knew well that I never could abide Katrin Texel, a girl all running to seed like a shot stalk of rhubarb, who would end up in the neighborhood of six foot in height, and just that "fine figure of a woman" which I never could abide.

"*Feech*!" I would say, copying her Wendish expression. "I would as soon set my feather bolster on end, paint it black and white, and make love to it as to Katrin Texel."

"You do worse every day of your life," retorted Helene, with pretty spite, tapping the floor with the point of one delicate foot.

"And, pray, what do I that is worse?" I said, knowing full well what.

The Little Playmate was silent a minute, only continuing to tap the flags with a kind of naughtiness that became her.

"Katrin Texel would not look at you, charming as you think yourself," she said, at last.

"Did she tell you so, Little Sister?" said I, drawing a bow at a great venture.

The arrow struck, and I was content.

"Well," she answered, somewhat breathlessly, "what if she did? Surely even your vanity can take nothing out of a girl saying that she cannot abide you."

But I answered nothing to this, only stroked the mustache which was beginning to thrive admirably on my upper lip.

"Of all the—" began Helene, looking at me fixedly. Then she stopped.

"Well," said I, pausing in the caressing of my chin, "what do I worse every day than make love to Katrin Texel?"

Her eyes fairly sparkled fire at me. They were "sweetest eyes" no more, but rarely worth looking into all the same.

"You go ogling and staring at that little she-cat in the window over there, that screeches and becks and pats herself, all for showing off! And you, Hugo Gottfried, like a great oaf, thinking all the time how innocent and sweet and—oh, I have no patience with you!—to neglect and think nothing of—of Katrin Texel, and—and then to go gazing and gaping after a thing like that!"

And I declare there were tears in the Little Playmate's eyes.

"Dear Little Sister, why are you so mindful about Katrin Texel?" said I. "Faith, my lass, wait till she comes again, and I will court her to your heart's content. There—there—I will be a very Valentine's true lover to your Katrin."

For all that she was not greatly cheered, but edged away, still strangely disconsolate when I came near and tried to pet her. Mysterious and hidden are the ways of women! For once, when I would have put my hand about her pretty slender waist, she promptly took me by the wrist, and holding it at arm's-length, she dropped it from her with a disgustful curl of her lip, as if it had been an intruding spider she had perforce to put forth out of her chamber into the garden.

Yet formerly, upon occasion when, as it might be, she was reading or looking out of the window, if I but came behind her and called her "Little Sister," I might even put my hand upon her shoulder, and so stand for five minutes at a time and she never seem to notice it.

CHAPTER XIV

SIR AMOROUS IS PLEASED WITH HIMSELF

For, as I say, women have curious ways, and there are a good many of them recorded in this book. And yet more I have observed which I cannot find room for in a chronicle of so many sad and bad and warlike happenings. But none of them all is more notable than this—that women, or at least (for it is no use saying "women," every one being different in temper, though like as pease in some things) many women, will permit that which it suits them to be oblivious of, when if you ask them for permission or make a favor of the matter, they will promptly flame sky-high with indignation. So my advice to the young man who honestly goes a-courting is to keep talking earnestly, to occupy his mistress's attention withal, and progress in her favors during the abstractions of high discourse.

Of course in this, as in all other similar enterprises, Sir Amorous must have a certain trading-stock of favor to start with. But if he have this much, 'tis not difficult to increase it by honest endeavor, and, as it were, the sweat of his brain. So at least I am told by those who have proved it. Nevertheless, for myself, I have used no such nice refinements, but rather taken with thankfulness such things as came in my way.

And now when I look back over my paper—lord! what a pother of writing about it and about! But my excuse is that many young lads and gay bachelors will read this tale, so I desire to import what of instruction I can into it. And not having the learning of the clerks, I must e'en put in what wisdom I have gotten for myself in my passage through the world. For I never could plough with another man's heifer—least of all with that of a college-bred Mess John. Not but what Mess John knoweth somewhat of the lear of love also among the well-favored dames of the city. Or else, by my faith, Mess John is sorely belied.

But where was I in my tale? And if this present errant discourse be forgiven, surely I will not transgress again, but drive my team straight to the furrow's end and then back again, like an honest ploughman that has his eye ever upon the guide-poles on the windy ridge.

Well, the Little Playmate lifted a toad from her waist—I mean my hand—and dropped it as far from her as her arm would reach.

And then after that she ran up-stairs, slammed the door of her own chamber, and came not down to our nooning, so that old Hanne had to call her three times.

And once, when I had occasion to cross the court-yard to the guard-house, I saw her standing pensively by the window. But so soon as she saw me she vanished within and was seen no more.

Yet, indeed and indeed, as all may see, there was no cause for all this fret. For I cared no more about Christian's Elsa than about Christian himself—less, indeed, for Christian was a good soldier and master-at-arms, and taught me how to handle the match-lock, the pistolet, and the other new weapons that had begun to come in from France. And often upon Saturdays and wet days he would let me spend long mornings in the armory with him, oiling and cleaning the ordnance. Which it certainly was a great pleasure to do.

And what if the little dumpling Elsa, with her red cheeks and her babyish eyes, did run in and out. Her father was ever with us, and even had I been willing there was no opportunity for more than a word or a touch of her fingers—well, save once, when her father went himself to seek the bottle of oil she had been sent to fetch, and was some time in finding it. But even that was a mere nothing, and might have happened to any one.

But when I came home again that night, you would have thought that the whole happening had been printed legibly on my face. The Little Playmate would not let me come within a hundred miles of her. And it was "Keep your distance, sirrah!" Not perhaps said in words, but expressed as clearly by the warlike angle of an arm, the contumelious hitch of a shoulder, or the scornful sweep of an adverse skirt.

And all about nothing! Mighty Hector! I never saw such things as women.

And yet in her good moments she would call me "Great Brother," and tell me that she thought only of my future welfare, desiring that I should not compromise myself in any entanglement with such as were not worthy of me. Oh, a most wise and prudent counsellor was the Playmate in these days.

And I used ever to say: "Helene, when I am truly in love I will e'en bring her here to you, and, by my faith, if you approve not—why, there is an end of the matter. Back she goes to her mother like a parcel of returned goods—aye, if she were the Kaiser's daughter herself!"

Whereat she pouted and was not ill-pleased.

"Ah, my man," she would reply, "after a girl hath said you nay a time or two, it will bring you down from these high notions, and be much for your soul's final good!"

But yet, when I could keep her in good-humor, it was exceedingly sweet to bide quietly in the house with the Little Playmate—far better than to gad about with Texels and meandering fools, which indeed I did oftentimes just because it made my little lass so full of moods and tenses—like one of Friar Laurence's irregular verbs in his cursed Humanities. For there is nothing so variously delightful as a woman when she is half in love and half out of it—more interesting (say some) though less delightful than when she is all and whole in love. Nevertheless, there are exceptions, and one woman at least I know more various, and more delicious also, since love's ocean hath gone over her head, than ever she was when, like a timid bather, she shivered on the brink or made little fearful plunges, as it were knee-deep, and so ran out again.

But I am not come to that in the story yet.

Well, on the afternoon of the next day, who should come to the house in the Red Tower but our Helene's gossip, for this week at least her bosom friend, Katrin Texel. She was even more impressive in manner than ever, and also a little pleasanter to behold. For her angles were clothing themselves into curves, and she was learning, perhaps from the Little Playmate, to leave off bouncing into a room like a cow at the trot, and to walk in sedately instead. By-and-by I knew she would come sailing down the street like a towered galleon from the isles of Ind. For all that, she looked not ill—an academic study for Juno, one might say. But to make love to—why, as Helene was wont to remark, *Feech!*

And the curious thing about Katrin Texel was that though her corporeal part might be a direct inheritance from her Burgomeister father and his substantial brewery, her spirit had been designed for an artful fairy of half her size, in order that it might go pirouetting into airy realms of the imagination. For she was gay enough and lightsome enough in her demeanor. She came in with a skip which would have been entrancing in some elfish mignonne who could dance light-foot on spring flowers without crushing them. But when this our solid Burgomagisterial Katrin tripped in, it nearly drove me wild with mirth. For it was as if some bland maternal cow out of the pasture had skipped with a hop and a circle of flying skirts into a ballroom or a butterfly of two hundred pounds' weight had taken to flitting from flower to flower.

And this Katrin talked in a quick, light voice, with ups and downs and skips and quivers in it, as spring-heeled as a chamois goat on the mountains of the south.

"Ah, Tiny-chen," she would cry, as she came undulating and cooing in to our Helene, "is it you, dearest? 'Tis as sweet to see you as for birds to kiss on bough! I have danced all day in the sunshine just to think that I should come to see you! And tell me why you have not been to visit me.

Ah, bad one—cruelest—as cruel as she is pretty" (appealing to me), "is she not? And there, our Michael, great oaf, sits at home desolated that he does not hear her foot on the stairs. The foolish fellow tells me that he listens for four little pit-a-pats every time that I come up from the courtyard, and is disappointed when there come back only my poor two."

And Katrin becked and nodded and set her head to the side—like to the divine Io-Cow playing at being little Jenny Wren.

And as for me, I kept my gravity—or, rather, how could I lose it, hearing such nonsense about that great stupid beer-vat, Michael Texel.

Michael Texel, indeed! I should admire to hear of Michael Texel so much as raising his eyes to the Little Playmate. Why, I would stave him on the open street like a puncheon of eight, and think nothing of the doing of it.

Michael Texel, indeed!

But I am forgetting. My business at this time was to make love to Katrin, so that I might banish the ill impression which Helene had formed concerning that pleasant, harmless little Christian's Elsa over there. I never heard anything so foolish in my life. But, then, what women will think and say passes the imagination of man.

Michael Texel indeed!

The thought of that young man of beef and beer recurred so persistently and forcibly to me that for a time I could scarce command myself to speak civilly to his sister. Though, of course, she was quite different, being a woman, and informed with such a quick and dainty spirit that at times it seemed as it had been imprisoned in her too massive frame and held "in subjection to the flesh," as the clerics say. God wot, I never knew I had so much religion and morality about me till I came to write. If I do not have a care this tale of mine will turn out almost as painful as a book of devotion which they set children to read on saints' days to keep them from being over-happy.

But I subdued my feelings and drew up somewhat nearer to Katrin.

"My Little Sister—" so I began, cunningly, as I thought—"my sister Helene is, indeed, fortunate to have so fair a friend, and one so devoted—"

"As my brother Michael, yes," she twittered, with her most ponderous, cage-bird manner; "yes, indeed, he *is* devoted to her."

"No," said I, hastily (confound the great hulking camel!), "I mean such a faithful friend as yourself. I, alas, have no friend. I am cut off from all society of my kind. Often and often have I felt the weight of loneliness press heavy upon me in this darksome tower."

I saw Helene rise, go to the window, and glance across with such a peculiar smile that I knew as well as if I had seen her that Christian's Elsa was at her window with her music, looking across for me between each bar. I cannot describe the smile which hovered on the face of the Little Playmate. But perhaps all the male beings who read my book may have seen something like it. All that I can say is, that the smile conveyed an almost superhuman understanding of men and their little ways, and, curiously enough, something of contempt too.

But I was not going to be discouraged by any smile, acid or sweet. Besides, I had something still to pay back.

Michael Texel, indeed!—faith, by St. Blaise, I will Texel him tightly an he comes sneaking to our gate!

So again I drew yet nearer to his sister. Katrin dimpled and showed her teeth, with a smile like the sun going about the world, till I had almost put my hand behind her shoulders to catch the ends of it when it got round. This illumination almost finished me, for it was not the kind of smile I had been accustomed to from—well, that was not the business I was on at present.

CHAPTER XV

THE LITTLE PLAYMATE SETTLES ACCOUNTS

But I admit that the smile discouraged me. Nevertheless I proceeded gallantly.

"Ah, Jungfrau Texel," said I, "you cannot know how your presence brightens our lives here in the Red Tower. Wherefore will you not come oftener to our grim abode?"

I thought that, on the whole, pretty well; but, looking up at Helene, I saw that her smile (so different from that of the Io-Cow Katrin) had become a whole volume of scathing satire. God wot, it is not easy to make love to a lass when your "Little Sister" is listening—especially to a woman-mountain set on watch-springs like Katrin Texel.

But, after all, Katrin was no ways averse to love-making of any kind, which, after all, is the main thing. And as for the Little Playmate, I did not mind her a bonnet-tag. She had brought it upon herself.

Michael Texel indeed!

So I went on. It was excellent sport—such a jest as may not be played every day. I would show Mistress Helene (so I said to myself) whether she would like it any better if I made love to Katrin than if I went over on an occasional wet day to clean pistolets and oil French musketoons in Christian's guard-house.

So I began to tell Katrin how that woman was the sacredest influence on the life of men, with other things as I could recollect them out of a book of chivalry which I had been reading, the fine sentiments of which it was a pity to waste. For our Helene would have stamped her foot and boxed my ears for coming nigh her with such nonsense (that is, at this time she would, doubtless—not, however, always). And as for the lass over the way—Christian's Elsa—she knew no more of letters than her father knew of the mathematics. Plain kissing was more in her way—as I have been told.

So I aired my book of chivalry to Katrin Texel.

"Fair maid," said I, "have you heard the refrain of the song that I love so well? It is like sweet music to me to hear it. I love sweet music. This is the latest catch:

"'My true love hath my heart and I have his.'

"How goes it, Helene?" I asked, turning to her as she stood smiling bitterly by the window. For I knew that it would annoy her to be referred to. "Goes it not something like this?"

And I hummed fairly enough:

"'My true love hath my heart and I have his.'" *** "And if it goes like that," said she, quickly, "it goeth like a tomcat mollrowing on the tiles in the middle of the night."

Now this being manifestly only spiteful, I took no notice of her work. "Helene does not love good music," said I; "'tis her only fault. But I trust that you, dear Katrin, have a greater taste for angelic song?"

"And I trust you love to scratch upon the twangling zither as cats sharpen their claws upon the bark of trees? You love such music, *dear* Katrin, do you not?" cried Helene over her shoulder from the window.

But Katrin, the divine cow, knew not what to make of us. I think she was of the opinion that Helene and I, with much study upon books, had suddenly gone mad.

"I do indeed love music," she said at last, uncertainly, "but, Master Hugo, not the kind of which my gossip, Helene, speaks. I love best of all a ballad of love, sung sweetly and with a melting expression, as from a lover by the wall to his mistress aloft in the balcony, like that of him of Italy, who sings:

"'O words that fall like summer dew on me.'

"How goes it?

"'O breath more sweet than is the growing—the growing—'"

She paused, and waved her hand as if to summon the words from the empty air.

"'*The growing garlic*,' if it be a lover of Italy," cried Helene, still more spitefully. "This is enough and to spare of chivalry, besides which Hugo hath his lessons to learn for Friar Laurence, or else he will repent it on the morrow. Come, sweetheart, let us be going. I will e'en convoy thee home."

So she spoke, making great ostentation of her own superiority and emancipation from learning, treating me as a lad that must learn his hornbook at school.

But I was even with her for all that.

"And so farewell, then, dear Mistress Katrin," said I. "The delicate pleasure of your presence shall be followed by the still more tender remembrance which, when you are gone, my heart shall continue to cherish of you."

That was indeed well-minded. A whole sentence out of my romance-book without a single slip. Katrin bowed, with the airy grace of the Grand Duke's monument out in the square. But the little Helene swept majestically off, muttering to herself, but so that I could hear her: "'O wondrous, most wondrous,' quoth our cat Mall, when she saw her Tom betwixt her and the moon."

The application of which wise saw is indeed to seek.

So the two maids went away, and I betook me to the window to see if I could catch a glimpse of Christian's Elsa.

But I only saw Katrin and Helene going gossiping down the street with their heads very close together.

At first I smiled, well pleased to think how excellently I had played my cards and how daintily I had worked in those gallant speeches out of the book of chivalry. But by-and-by it struck me that the Little Playmate was absent a most unconscionable time. Could it be—Michael Texel? No, that at least was plainly impossible.

I got up and walked about. Then for a change I paused by the window.

I had stood a good while thus moodily looking out at the casement, when I became aware of two that walked slowly up the street and halted together before the great iron-studded door which led to the Red Tower.

By the thirty thousand virgins—Helene and Michael Texel!

And then, indeed, what a coil was I in; how blackly deceitful I called her! How keenly I watched for any token of understanding and kindness more than ordinary that might chance to pass between them. But I could see none, for though the great soft lout of a ruddy beer-vat tried often to look under the brim of her hat, yet she kept her eyes down—only once, that I could observe, raising them, and that was more towards the Red Tower than in the direction of Michael Texel.

I think she wished to see whether I was watching. And when she had noted me it I wot well that she became much more animated, and laughed and spoke quickly, with color in her cheeks and a flash of defiance on her countenance, which were manifestly wasted on such a boastful, callow blubber-tun as Michael Texel.

Then it was: "Adieu to you, Master Texel!" "Farewell to you, fair maid!"

And Helene dipped a courtesy to him, dainty and sweet enough to conquer an angel, while the great jelly-bag shook himself almost to pieces in his eagerness to achieve a masterly bow. All this made me angry, not that I cared though Helene had coquetted with a dozen lads, an it had liked her. It was only the poverty of taste shown in being seen in the open High Street of Thorn along with such an oaf as Michael Texel. He had first been my friend, it is true, but then at that time I had not found him out.

By-and-by Helene came up the stairs, tripping light as a feather that the wind blows. Perhaps, though, she had turned in the doorway, where

I could not see her, to throw the lout a kiss—so I thought within me, jealously.

"You have convoyed your gossip Katrin home in safety, I trust," said I, sweetly, as she came in.

"Yes," said she; "but I fear she has left her heart behind her. So wondrously rapid a courtship never did I see!"

"Save on the street," answered I; "and with a pale, soft jack-pudding like Michael Texel! That was a sight, indeed."

At which Helene laughed a merry little laugh—well-pleased, too, the minx, as I could see.

"What are courtships on the street to you, Sir Hugo," she returned, "with your 'Twinkle-Twankle' singing-women over the way, and—Lord, how went it?

"'My true love hath my heart and I have his.'

"Ha! ha! Sir Gallant, what need you with more? Would you have as many loves as the Grand Turk, and invent new love-makings for each of them? Shall we maidens petition Duke Casimir to banish the other lads of the town and leave only Hugo Gottfried for all of us?"

And then she went on to other such silly talk that I think it not worth reporting.

Whereupon I was about to leave the room in a transport of just indignation, and that without speaking, when Helene called to me.

"Hugo!" she said, very softly, as she alone could speak, and that only when it liked her to make friends.

I turned me about with some dignity, but knowing in my heart that it was all over with me.

"Well, what may be your will, madam?" said I.

Helene came towards me with uplifted, petitionary eyes.

"You are not going to be angry with me, Hugo!" she said. And she lifted her eyes again upon me—irresistible, compelling, solvent of dignities, and able to break down all pride.

O all ye men who have never seen my Helene look up thus at you—but only common other eyes, go and hang yourselves on high trees for very envy. Well, as I say, Helene looked up at me. She kept on looking up at me.

And I—well, I hung a moment on my pride, and then—clasped her in my arms.

"Dear minx, thrice wicked one!" I exclaimed, "wherefore do you torment me—break my heart?"

"Because," said she, escaping as soon as she had gained her pretty, rascal way, "you think yourself so clever, Hugo, such an irresistible person, that you must be forever returning to this window and getting this book of chivalry by heart. Now you are going to be cross again. Oh, shame, and with your little sister—

"'That never did you any harm,
But killed the mice in your father's barn.'"

With such babyish words she talked the frowns off my face, or, when they would not go fast enough, hastened them by reaching up and smoothing them away with her finger.

"Now," she said, setting her head to the side, "what a nice sweet Great Brother! Let him sit down here on the great chair."

So I sat down, well pleased enough, not knowing what mischief the pranksome maid had now in her head, but judging that the matter might turn out well for me.

Then Helene stole round to the back of the chair, and, taking me by the ears, she gave first one and then the other of them a pull.

"That," she said, pulling the right, "is for listening to the little cat over the way that squalls on the tiles! And *that*" (giving the other a sound tug) "is for being a dandiprat when my gossip Katrin was here!"

She paused a moment as if to summon courage, and then she stooped quickly and kissed me on the neck.

"And *that* for Michael Texel!" she cried, and ran out of the room before I could get clear of the wide arms of the chair, and so run after and catch her.

She turned in the doorway and wafted me a kiss from her finger-tips, airily and a little mockingly.

"That for Hugo Gottfried!" she said, and was off to her own chamber with the *frou-frou* of a light skirt, the slam of a door, and the shooting of a bolt.

And after all this, it was heart's pity that ever anything should have come between us again, even for a moment.

Though, indeed, it was but for a moment.

CHAPTER XVI

TWO WOMEN—AND A MAN

It was the forenoon of a Sunday, a dull, sleepy time in all countries, and one difficult to get overpast. I was as usual busy with my accoutrement, recently bought with the loan of Master Gerard. The Little Playmate was just returned from the cathedral, and had indeed scarcely laid her finery aside, when there came a loud knocking at the outer gate of the Red Tower. Then one of the guard tramped stolidly from the wicket to the door of our dwelling.

"A lady waits you at the postern," said he, and so tramped his way unceremoniously back to his post.

I knew without any need of telling that it was the Lady Ysolinde. So I rose, and hastily setting my fingers through my hair, went to the gate. There, attended by the respectable servitor, was, as I had expected, the Lady Ysolinde.

"Good-morrow," she said very courteously to me, and I duly returned her greeting with a low obeisance of respect and welcome.

She wore a large garment, fashioned like a man's cloak, over her festal attire—which, with a hood for the head, wholly enveloped her figure and descended to her feet.

"I have come, as I promised, to see the Little Playmate." These were her first words as we paced together across the wide upper court under the wondering eyes of the men of the Duke's body-guard.

"Pray remember, Lady Ysolinde," said I, with much eagerness, "that I have as yet said nothing of the matter to Helene, and that my father only knows that I am to ride to Plassenburg in order to exercise myself in the practice of arms, before becoming his assistant here in the Red Tower and in the Hall of Judgment across the way."

My visitor nodded a little impatiently. She who knew so many things, of a surety might be trusted to understand so much without being told.

In the inner doorway Helene met us. And never had it been my fortune to see the meeting of two such women. The Little Playmate had in her hands the broidered handkerchiefs, the long Flemish gloves, and the little illuminated Book of the Hours which I had given her. She had been about to lay them away together, as is the fashion of women. And when she met the Lady Ysolinde I declare that she looked almost as tall. Helene was perhaps an inch or two less in stature than her visitor, but what she lacked in height she more than made up in the supple erectness of her carriage and the vivid and extraordinary alertness of all her movements.

"Lady Ysolinde," said I, as they met with the mutually level eyeshot of women who measure one another, "this is Helene—whom, for love and kindliness, we of the Wolfsberg call the 'Little Playmate.'"

The daughter of Master Gerard impetuously threw back the gray monk's hood which shrouded the masses of her tawny hair. She put out both hands to Helene, held her a moment at arm's-length to look into her eyes, even as she had done with me, but in a different way. Then, drawing her nearer, she leaned forward and kissed her on the brow and on both cheeks.

Now I am not ordinarily a close observer, and many things, specially things that pertain to the acts of women, pass by me unnoticed. But I saw in a moment that there was not, and never could be, more than the semblance of cordial amity between these two women.

I noted the Little Playmate instinctively quiver like a taken bird when she was thus embraced. It was, I think, the undying antipathy of Eve for Lilith, a hatred which is mostly on the side of Eve, the Mother-

Woman—its place being taken by sharper and more dangerous envy in the breast of Lilith-without-the wall.

There, face to face, stood the two women who were to make my life, ruling it between them, as it were, striking it out between the impact of their natures, as underneath the blows of two smiths upon the ringing anvil the iron, hissing hot, becomes a sword or a ploughshare.

It was impossible to avoid contrasting them.

Helene, of a bodily beauty infinitely more full of temptation, bloomful with radiant health, the blush of youth and conscious loveliness upon her lips and looking out under the crisp entanglement of her hair, all simple purity and straightness of soul in the fearless innocency of her eyes; the Lady Ysolinde, deeper taught in the mysteries of existence, more conscious of power, not so beautiful, but oftentimes giving the impression of beauty more strongly than her fairer rival, compact of swift delicate graces, half feline, half feminine (if these two be not the same). All these passed like clouds over the unquiet sea of her nature, reflecting the changing skies of circumstance, and were fitted to produce a fascination ever on the verge of repulsion even when it was strongest. Ysolinde was the more ready of speech, but her words were touched constantly with dainty malice and clawed with subtlest spite. She catspawed with men and things, often setting the hidden spur under the velvet foot deeply into the very cheek which she seemed to caress. Such as I read them then, and largely as even now I understand them, were the two women who moulded between them my life's history.

I suppose it is because I am of this Baltic North that I must need think things round and round, and prose of reasons and explanations—even when I write concerning beautiful maids—forever dreaming and dividing, instead of going straight, sword in hand, for their hearts, as is the way of the folk from the English land over-seas, or, more simply still, lying about their favors, which, I hear, is mostly the Frenchman's way.

But enough of intolerable theory.

Instinctively the Lady Ysolinde spoke to our maid of the Red Tower in a manner and tone very different from that which I had ever before heard her employ, at once more equal and more guarded.

"I was told by Master Hugo Gottfried here (whose acquaintance I made at my father's house on the day after his foolish boy's prank of the White Swan) that in the Red Tower of the Wolfsberg dwelt one of mine own age, like myself a maid solitary among men. So today I have come to solicit her acquaintance, and to ask her to be kind to me, who have ever been in this city and country as a stranger in a strange land."

It was prettily enough said, and our Helene, easily touched, and perhaps a little ashamed of her first stiffness, put out a hand which the other quickly and securely clasped. Then those two sat down together. Ysolinde von Sturm kept her eyes fixed on the Playmate, but our shy and slender Helene looked steadily past her out over the tumbled red roofs and peaked gables of the city of Thorn to the gray Wolfmark plains which lay spread beneath our windows like a picture in a book.

At intervals, as it came near the hour of their mid-day meal, the blood-hounds howled in the kennels, and by their tone I knew that my father had left the Hall of Judgment where he had been detained all the morning. Also I knew very well that the Lady Ysolinde wished me to find an errand elsewhere, in order that she might talk alone with her companion. But I saw also the appeal in the eyes of the Playmate, and I was resolved not to give her the chance.

"Are you never weary in this dull tower?" asked the lawyer's daughter, still holding the Playmate's hand.

"It is not dull," replied Helene. "I have my work. There are two men as shiftless and helpless as babes to attend to, and none to help me but old Hanne."

"Let men attend to themselves," cried Ysolinde; "that is ever my motto. They ought to be our servants, not we theirs."

It was said smilingly, yet there was bitterness under the words as well.

"But," said Helene, smiling back at her with a fresh directness all her own, "one of the men saved my life and brought me up as his own daughter, and the other is—is Hugo, here."

And as she spoke of my father and of me I saw the eyes of the Lady Ysolinde fixed upon her, as it had been to read her inner soul.

"And, by-the-way," she said, at last, after a long pause, "you have heard how this same Master Hugo proposes to himself to escape from the prison-house of this city, for a season to exercise himself in arms, and so in roving adventure fulfil that which is not granted to a maid, his 'wandering years.' He goes (so my father tells me) to the Court of the Prince of Plassenburg, with the promise of a company to command. And I am glad, for I shall ride thither under his escort. Indeed, and in truth, my home is far more there than here in Thorn. But I would fain have a companion of my own sex. So I have come to beg of you, Mistress Helene, that you will accompany me. The Princess, I know, has great need of a maid of honor near her person, and will gladly welcome a friend of mine for the post."

The Little Playmate looked up astonished, as well she might, at this direct assault, which was moreover spoken with a pretty shamefacedness and the air of asking almost too great a favor. And, indeed, if there was any patronage in the thing offered, it was at least carefully kept out of the manner of asking.

"Lady Ysolinde, I cannot accept your too overpowering favor," said Helene, after a pause, "but your kindness in thinking at all of me will always warm my heart."

At this critical moment came my father in, looking more than grave and severe, so that I judged at once that he had been talking to the Duke Casimir and had found his post of chief adviser both thankless and difficult. I knew it could be no matter of his office which worried him, for that day he wore his holiday attire of white Friesland cloth, and the broad bonnet in which I loved best to see him. There was no mark of his calling about him anywhere, save a little Red Axe sewed upon his left breast like a war veteran's decoration.

CHAPTER XVII

THE RED AXE IS LEFT ALONE

Gottfried Gottfried bowed to the guest of his house with the noble manner which comes to every serious-minded man who deals habitually in the high matters of life and death. I made his introductions to the Lady Ysolinde, and as readily and gracefully he returned his acknowledgments. For the rest I allowed Master Gerard's daughter to develop her own projects to him, which, indeed, she was no long time in doing.

As she proceeded I saw my father change color and become as to his face almost as white as the Friesland cloth in which he was dressed. Presently, however, as if struck with the sound of a well-known name, he looked up quickly.

"Plassenburg, said you, my lady?" he inquired.

The Lady Ysolinde nodded.

"Yes, to Plassenburg, where the Princess has great need of a maid of honor."

"Her Highness is often upon her travels, I hear it reported," said my father, "while the Prince keeps himself much at home."

"He esteems his armies more than all the marvels of strange countries," replied Ysolinde, "and thus he holds the land and folk in great quiet."

"And your father, Master Gerard, would have my son engage with this Prince Karl for a space. Well, I think it may be good for the lad. For I know well that the shadow of the Red Tower stalks after him through this city of Thorn, and there is no need that he should lie down under it too soon. But this of my little maid is a matter apart, and means a longer and a sorer parting."

"Fear not, my father," cried the Playmate, eagerly, "I would not leave you alone, even to be the Princess of Plassenburg herself."

My father took another strange look from one to the other of the two women, the import of which I understood not then.

"I know not," said he; "I think this thing also might be for the best. As I see it, there are strange times coming upon us in Thorn. And the town of Plassenburg under Karl the Prince is a defenced city, set in a strong province, content and united. It might be wisest that you also should go, little one."

"I cannot go," said Helene, "and leave you alone."

Gottfried Gottfried smiled a sad smile, wistfully pleasant.

"Already I am wellnigh an old man, and it is the nature of my profession that I should be alone. I work among the issues of life and death. Every man must be lonely when he dies, and I, who have lived most with dying men, am perforce already lonely while I live. It is well—a clearer air for the young bird! But yet it will be lonesome to miss you when I come in—the empty pot wanting the flower; the case without the jewel; silence above and below; your voice and Hugo's, that have changed the sombre Red Tower with your young folks' pleasantries, heard no more. Ah, God wot, I had thought—I had dreamed far other things."

He stopped and looked from one to the other of us, and I saw that Ysolinde of the White Gate read his thought. Whereat right suddenly the Little Playmate blushed, and as for me I kept watching the dull gold flash on the spangles of our guest's waist-belt, which was in form like a live serpent, with changeful scales and eyes of ruby red.

My father went over to where Helene sat. She rose to meet him and cast her arms about his neck. He laid his right hand on her head—that terrible hand that was yet not dreadful to us-who loved him.

"Little flower," he said, in his simple way, "God be good to you in the transplanting! It is not fair to your young life that my red stain should lie upon your lot. I have given you a quiet hermitage while you needed it. But now it is right that my house should again be left unto me desolate. It is already late summer with Gottfried Gottfried, and high time that the young brood should fly away."

He turned to me.

"With you, Hugo, it is a thing different; you were born to that to which you are born. And to that, as I read your horoscope, you must one day return. But in the mean time care well for the maid. I lend her to you. I give her into your hand. Cherish her as your chiefest treasure. Let her enemies be yours, and if harm come to her through your neglect, slay yourself ere you come again before me. For, by the Lord God of all Righteous Judgment, I will have no mercy!"

I saw the eyes of the Lady Ysolinde glitter like those of the snake in her belt as thus my father delivered Helene over to me.

But my father had yet more to say.

"And if any," he went on, in a deep, still voice, keeping his hand upon the downcast head of the Little Playmate—"if any, great or small, prince or pauper, harm so much as a hair of this fair head, by the great God who wields His Axe over the universe and sits in the highest Halls of Judgment, whose servant I am—I, Gottfried Gottfried, swear that he shall taste the vengeance of the Red Axe and drink to the dregs the cup of agony in his own blood!"

So saying, he kissed Helene and stalked out without turning his head or making any further obeisance or farewell.

We sat mazed and confounded after his departure.

The Lady Ysolinde it was who first recovered herself. She put out a kindly hand to Helene, who stood wet-eyed and drooping by the window, looking out upon the roofs of Thorn, though well I wot she saw nothing of spire, roof, or pinnacle.

"God do so to me and more also," she said, in a low, solemn voice, "if I too keep not this charge."

And I think for the moment she meant it. The trouble was that the Lady Ysolinde could not mean one thing for very long at a time. As, indeed, shall afterwards appear.

So it was arranged that within the week Helene and I should say our farewells to the Red Tower which had sheltered us so long, as well as to Gottfried Gottfried, who had ever been my kind father, and to the little Helene more than any father.

But in spite of all we wearied day by day to be gone. For, indeed, Gottfried Gottfried said right. The shadow of the Red Tower, the stain of the Red Axe, was over us both so long as we abode on the Wolfsberg. Yet what it cost us to depart—at least till we were out of the gates of the city—I cannot write down, for to both of us the first waygoing seemed bitter as death.

I remember it well. My father had been busy all the morning with his grim work on the day when we were to ride away. A gang of malefactors who had wasted a whole country-side with their cruelty had been brought in. And, as it was suspected that other more important villains were yet to be caught, there had been the repeated pain of the Extreme Question, and now there remained but the falling of the Red Axe to settle all accounts. So that when he came to bid us farewell he had but brief time to spare. And of necessity he wore the fearful crimson, which fitted his tall, spare figure like a glove.

"Fare thee well, little one!" he said, first to Helene. "Not thus, had the choice lain with me, would I have bidden thee farewell. But when it shall be that I meet you again I will surely wear the white of the festa day. I commit you to Him whose mistakes are better than our good deeds, whose judgments are kinder than our tenderest mercies."

So he kissed her, and reached a hand over her shoulder to me.

"Son Hugo," he said, "go in peace. You must return to succeed me. I see it like a picture—on the day when I lie dead you shall stand with the Red Axe in your hand waiting to do judgment. It is well. Keep this maid more sacred than your life—and, meantime, fare you well!"

So saying he left us abruptly.

Our horses were saddled in the court-yard, and as I rode last through the rarely opened gateway, I saw Duke Casimir looking out from his window upon the lower enclosure, as was his pleasure upon the days of execution. I heard the dull thud, which was the meeting of the Red Axe and the redder block as that which had been between fell apart. And for the last time I heard the blood-hounds leap and the pattering of their eager feet upon the barriers as they leaped up scenting the Duke's carrion.

Thus the latest I heard of the place of my nativity was fitting and dreadful. I was mortally glad to ride away into the clear air and the invigorating silence. But on my heart there still lay heavy the twice-repeated prediction of my father and of the Lady Ysolinde, that I should yet return and hold the Red Axe in his place.

But I resolved rather to die in the honest front of battle. Nevertheless, had I known the future, I would have seen that they and not I were right.

I was indeed fated to return and stand ready to execute doom, with the Red Axe in my hand and my father lying dead near by.

CHAPTER XVIII

THE PRIME OF THE MORNING

Now so strange a thing is woman that, so soon as we were started down the High Street of the city of Thorn, the Little Playmate dried her eyes, turned towards me in her saddle, and straightway began to take me to task as though I had been to blame.

"I have left," said she, "the only home I ever knew, and the only man that ever truly loved me, to accompany a young man that cares not for me, and a woman whom I have seen but once, to a far land and an unkindly folk."

"It is not fair," I said, "to say that I love you not. For, as God sees me, I have ever loved you—loved you best and loved you only, little Helenchen! And though you are angered with me now, I know not why—still till now you have never doubted it."

"I doubt it sorely enough now, I know," she said, bitterly; "yet, indeed, I care not whether you or any love me at all."

And this saying I was greatly sorry for. It seemed a sad wayfaring from our old Red Tower and out of my native city of Thorn.

"Helene, little one," said I, "believe me, I love none in the whole world but my father and you. Trust me, for I am to keep you safe with my life in the far land to which we go. Do not let us quarrel, littlest. There are only the two of us here that remember the old man my father and the little room to which you came as a babe, all in white."

So presently she was somewhat pacified, and reached me a hand from the back of her beast, on pretence of leaning over to avoid a swinging sign in one of the narrow streets near by the White Gate, where we were to meet the Lady Ysolinde.

"And yet more, Little Playmate," said I, keeping her hand when I had it; "do not begin by distrusting the noble lady with whom we are to travel. For she means well to us both, and in the strange country to which we go we may be wholly in her power."

"You are sure that you do not love that woman, then?" said Helene, without looking at me. For, indeed, in many things she was but a child, and ever spoke more freely than other maids—perhaps with being brought up in the Red Tower in the company of my father, who on all occasions spoke his mind just as it came to him.

"Nay," said I, "believe me, little love, I do not love her at all."

And now on horseback Helene looked all charming, and what with the exercise, the unknown adventure, and my reassurance, she had a glow of rose color in her cheeks. She had never before been so far away from the precincts of the Wolfsberg. I had even taught her to ride in the courtyard of a summer evening, on a horse borrowed from one of the Duke's squires.

We found the Lady Ysolinde waiting for us at her house, Master Gerard talking to her in the doorway, earnestly and apart. Both of them had a look of much solemnity, as though the matter of their discourse were some very weighty one.

Presently her father kissed her and she came down the steps. I leaped from my horse to help her to the saddle, but the respectable serving-man was before me. So that instead I went about and looked to the buckles and girths, which were all in order, and patted the arching neck of the beautiful milk-white palfrey whereon she rode. Then Master Gerard waved a hand and went within.

And as we fared forth out of the Weiss Thor into the keener air of the country, I thought what a charge I had—to squire two ladies so surpassingly fair, each in her own several graces, as our Helene and the Lady Ysolinde.

No sooner, however, were we past the outer barriers, at which the soldiers of the Duke Casimir kept guard, than a vast, ungainly wight started up from the road-side.

"Jan Lubber Fiend!" cried the Lady Ysolinde; "what do you here?"

The oaf grinned his awful, writhed smile and wriggled his great body after the manner of a puppy desirous of the milk-platter.

"Think you, my lady," said he, cunningly, "that your poor Jan would abide within the precincts of the city house with that funeral ape bidding me do this and do that, sit here and sit there, come in and go out at his pleasure? A thing of dough that I could twist into knots as easily as I can crack my joints."

And of this latter accomplishment he proceeded to give us certain examples which sounded like cannon-shots delivered at close quarters.

"Get home with you!" cried Ysolinde; "I cannot have thee following us. There are two men presently to meet us, to guard us to Plassenburg, and we do not need you, Jan Lubber Fiend. Get back and take care of my father."

"Oh, as for him," said the monster, sitting down squat upon the plain road in the dust, "he is a tough old cock, and will come to no harm. We can e'en leave him with a good cook, a prime cellar, and an easy mind. But this young man is not to trust to with so many pretty maids. Jan will come and look after him."

And with that he nodded his hay-stack of a head three times at me, and going to the hedge-root he laid hold of the top of a young poplar and turned him about, keeping the stem of it over his shoulder. Then he set himself to pull like a horse that starts a load, and presently, without apparently distressing himself in the least, he walked away with the young tree, roots and all.

Having shaken off the earth roughly, he pulled out a sheath-knife and trimmed the branches till he had made him a kind of club, with which he threatened me, saying, "If I catch that young man at any tricks, with this club will Jan Lubber Fiend break every bone in his skin, like the shells of so many broken eggs."

Then laughing a little, and seeing that nothing could be made of the fellow, the Lady Ysolinde rode on and we followed her. We thought that surely there would be no difficulty in shaking him off long ere we reached our lodging-place of the evening, and that he would find his way back to the city of Thorn.

But even though we set our horses to their speed, it seemed to make no difference to the unwieldy giant. He merely stretched his legs a little farther, and caused his great gaskined feet to pass each other as fast as if they had been shod with seven-league boots. So he not only kept up with us easily, but oftentimes made a détour through the fields and over the wild country on either side, as a questing dog does, ever returning to us with some quaint vagrant fancy or quip of childish simplicity.

But what pleased me better than the appearance of the Lubber Fiend was that ere we had gone quite two miles out of the city we found two well-armed and stanch-looking soldiers waiting for us at a kind of cross-road. They were armed with the curious powder-guns which were coming into fashion from France. These went off with a noble report, and killed sometimes at as much as fifteen or twenty paces when the aim was good. The fellows had swords also, and little polished shields on their left arms—altogether worthy and notable body-guards.

"These two are soldiers of the Guard from Plassenburg," said the Lady Ysolinde, "though now they are travelling as members of a Free Company desiring to enter upon new engagements. But they will make the way easier and pleasanter for us, as well as infinitely safer, being veterans well accustomed to the work of quartering and foraging."

As indeed we were to find ere the day ended.

So we rode on in the brilliant light, and the long, long day seemed all too brief to us who were young, and scarce delivered from the prison-house of Thorn. And to my shame I admit that my heart rose with every mile that I put between me and the Red Tower.

Indeed, I hardly had a thought to spend on my father. The hot quadrangle of the Wolfsberg, ever smelling of horses and the swelter of shed blood, the howling, fox-colored demons in the kennels, the black Duke Casimir—right gladly I forgot them all. Aye, I forgot even my father, and everything save that I was riding with two fair women through a world where all was love and spring, and where it was ever the prime of a young morning.

The Lady Ysolinde could not make enough of our Little Playmate. She laughed back at her over her shoulder when she let her horse out for a canter. She marvelled loudly at Helene's good riding, and at the unbound beauty of the crisp ringlets which clustered round her head like a boy's. And our Helene smiled, well pleased, and ceased to watch my eyes or to grow silent if I checked my horse too long by the side of the Lady Ysolinde.

Mostly we three rode abreast over the pleasant country. So long as we were crossing the plain of the Wolfmark we saw few tilled fields, and the farm-houses were fewer still. But wherever these were to be seen they were fortified and defended like castles, and had gates, great and high, with iron plates upon them and knobs like the points of spears beaten blunt.

The Lady Ysolinde, who had often ridden that way, told us that these were all in the Duke Casimir's country, and were mostly possessed by the kin of his chief captains—feudal tenants, who for the right of possession were compelled to furnish so many riders to the Duke's Companies.

"But wait," she said, "till you come to the dominions of the Prince of Plassenburg. You will find that he is indeed a ruler that can make the broom-bush keep the cow."

So we rode on, and passed pleasant and exciting things, more than I had ever seen in all my life before.

Once we saw half a dozen men driving cattle across our path, and it was curious to mark how readily they drew their swords and couched their lances at us, turning themselves about this way and that like a quintain till we were quite gone by, which made us laugh. For it seemed a strange thing that men so well armed should fear a company of no more than their own numbers, and two of them maids upon palfreys.

But Ysolinde said: "It is not, after all, so strange, for over yonder blue hills dwells Joan of the Swordhand, who can lead a foray as well as any man, and once worsted Duke Casimir himself when he beset her castle."

So the day went past swiftly, with good company and the converse of folk well liking one another. And ever I wondered how we were to spend the night, and what sort of cheer we should find at our inn.

CHAPTER XIX

WENDISH WIT

The gray plain of the Wolfmark, which we had been traversing ever since we descended out of the steep Weiss Thor of the city of Thorn, had now begun to break into ridges and mounded hills of stiff red clay. And I, who had often kept my watch on the highest pinnacle of the Red Tower, looked with astonishment back upon the city I had left behind. Seen from the plain, Thorn had an aspect almost imperial.

It rose above the colorless flat of gray suddenly, unexpectedly, almost insolently. The city, with its numberless gables, spires of churches, turreted gate-houses, occupied a ridge of gradually swelling ground which rose like a huge whale-back from the misty plain. Its walls were grim, high, and far-stretching. But as we travelled farther into the Wolfmark the city seemed to sink deeper into the plain and the dark castle of Duke Casimir to shoot ever higher into the skies. So that presently, as we looked back, we could only see the Wolfsberg itself, the abode of cruelty and wrong, standing black against the white sky of noon.

Its flanking towers stood up above the battlemented wall, their turrets climbing higher and higher towards heaven, till the topmost Red Tower—that in which my father's garrot was, and in which I had spent my entire life until this day—soared straight upward above them all, like a threatening index-finger pointing, not into the clear sky of a summer's noon, but into clouds and thick darkness.

I was glad when at last we lost sight of it. Then, indeed, I felt that I had left my old life behind me. And, in spite of the Lady Ysolinde's ink-pool prophecy and my love for my father (such as it was), I did not mean ever to trust myself within that baleful circle of gray and weary plain upon which the Red Tower looked down.

Seeing that the maids were inclined to talk the one with the other, or rather that the Lady Ysolinde spoke confidentially with Helene, and that Helene now answered her without embarrassment and with frank, equal glances, I dropped gradually behind and rode with the two stout men-at-arms. These I found to be honest lads enough, but of a strangely reserved and taciturn nature, each ever waiting for the other to answer—being, like most Wendish men, much averse to questioning and still more stiff as to replying.

"You are men of Plassenburg?" I said to the nearest, simply and innocently enough, for the purpose of improving the cordiality of our relations.

Whereupon he turned his head slowly about to his neighbor, as it were to consult him. The glance said as clearly as monk's script: "What shall we answer to this troublesome, inquisitive fellow?"

At first I thought that perhaps they spoke not the common dialect, and that as we were travelling towards regions roughly Wendish and but lately heathen, they might have some uncouth speech of their own. So, as is ever the custom with folk that are not accustomed to the speaking of foreign tongues, I repeated the question in mine own language in a louder tone, supposing that that would do as well.

"You are men of the country of Plassenburg?" cried I, as loud as I could bawl.

"We are not deaf—we have all our faculties, praise the saints!" said the more distant of the two, looking not at me but at his companion. He, on his part, nodded back at his comrade's reply, as if it had been delicately calculated at once to answer my question and at the same time not to commit them to any dangerous opinions.

I tried again.

"Your prince, I hear, is a true man, brave, and well-versed in war?"

The shorter and stouter man, who rode beside me, glanced once at my face, and slowly screwed round his head to his companion in a long, questioning gaze. Then as slowly he turned his head back again.

"Umph!" he said, judicially, with a movement of his head, which seemed a successful compromise between a nod and a shake, just as his remark might very well have resulted from an attempt to say "Yes" and "No" at the same time.

This was not encouraging to one who, like myself, was in high spirits and much inclined for conversation. But I was not to be so easily beaten off.

"The Prince of Plassenburg has a Princess," I said, "who is often upon her travels?"

It was an innocent remark, and, so far as I could see, not one in itself highly humorous. But it broke up the gravity of these red-haired northern bears as if it had been the latest gay sally of the court-fool.

"Ha! ha!" laughed the more distant, lanky man, rocking himself in his saddle till the pennon on his lance shook and the point dipped towards his horse's ear.

"Ho! ho!" chorused his companion, slapping his thigh jovially. "Jorian, did you hear that? 'The Prince of Plassenburg hath a Princess, and she is often upon her travels.' Ha! ha! ha! Ho! ho! ho!"

"He hath said it! Ho! ho! He hath said it! He is a wise fellow, after all, this beardless Jack-pudding of Thorn!" cried the other, tee-heeing with laughter till he nearly wept upon his own saddle-bow.

I began to get very angry. For we men of Thorn were not accustomed to be so flouted by any strangers, keeping mostly our own customs, and reining in the few strangers who ventured to visit Duke Casimir's dominions pretty tightly. Least of all could I brook insolence from these Wendish boors from the outskirts of half-pagan Borrussia.

"The Prince of Plassenburg hath churls among his retinue," said I, hotly, "if they be all like you two Jacks, that cannot answer a simple question without singing out like donkeys upon a common where there are no thistles to keep them quiet."

Sir Thicksides, the fat jolter-head nearest me set his thumb out to stick it into the side armor of Longlegs, his companion, who rode cheek by jowl with him.

"Oo-oo-ahoo!" cried he, crowing with mirth, as if I had said a yet more facetious thing. "'Tis a simple question—'Hath the Prince of Plassenburg a Princess, and is she not oft—ahoo!' Boris, prod me with thy lance-shaft hard, to keep me from doing myself an ill turn with this fellow's innocence."

"Hold up, Jorian!" answered the long man, promptly pounding him on the back with the butt of his spear. "Hold up, fat Jorian! Let not thy love of mirth do thee any injury. For thou art a good comrade, and fools were ever apt to divert thee too much. I have seen thee at this before—that time we went to Wilna, and the fellow in motley gave thee griping spasms with his tomfoolery."

Then was I mainly angry, as indeed I had sufficient occasion.

"You are but churls," I said, "and the next thing to knaves. And I will e'en inform the Prince when we arrive what like are the men whom he sets to escort ladies to his castle."

But though they were silenter after this, it was not from any alarm at my words, but simply because they had laughed themselves out of ply. For as I rode on in high dudgeon, half-way between the women and the men-at-arms, I could see them with the corner of an eye still nudging each other with their thumbs and throwing back their heads, and the breeze blew me scraps of their limited conversation.

"Ho! ho! Good, was it not? 'The Prince hath a Princess, and she—' Ho! ho! Good!"

The ridges of clay of which I have already spoken continued and increased in size as we went on. It was a dried-up, speckled, unwholesome-looking land. And people upon it there were none that we could see. The large fortified farms had ceased altogether. A certain frightful monotony reigned everywhere. Ravines, like cracks which the sun makes in mud, but a thousand times greater, began to split the hills perpendicularly to their very roots. The path wound perilously this way and that among them. And presently Jorian and Boris rode past me to take the lead, for Ysolinde and Helene were inclined to mistake the way as often as they came to the crossing and interweaving of the intricate paths.

And as these two jolly jackasses rode past at my right side I could see the thumb of long Boris curving towards the ribs of his companion, and the shoulders of both shaking as they chuckled.

"A rare simpleton's question, i' faith, yes. Ho! ho! Good!" they chorussed. "'The Prince hath a Princess'—the cock hath a hen, and she—Ha! ha! Good!"

At that moment I could with pleasure have slain Jorian and Boris for open-mouthed, unshaven, slab-sided Wendish pigs, as indeed they were.

Yet, had I done so, we had fared but ill without them. For had they been a thousand times jackasses and rotten pudding-heads (as they were), at least they knew the way and something of the unchristian people among whom we were going.

And so in a little while, as we wound our way along the face of these perilous rifts in the baked clay, with the mottled, inefficient river feeling its way gingerly at the bottom of the buff—colored ravine, what was my astonishment to see Jorian and Boris turn sharply at right angles and ride single file up one of the dry lateral cracks which opened, as it were, directly into the hill-side!

They did this without ever looking at the landmarks, like men who are anyways uncertain of their road. But, on the contrary, they wheeled confidently and rode jauntily on, and we three meekly followed, having by this time lost the Lubber Fiend, the devil doubtless knew where. For we must have followed Boris and Jorian unquestioningly had they led us into the bowels of the earth, as indeed, at first sight, they seemed to be doing.

CHAPTER XX

THE EARTH-DWELLERS OF NO MAN'S LAND

Then presently we came to a strange place, the like of which I have never seen, save here on the borders of the Mark and the northern Wendish lands. An amalgam of lime, or binding stuff of some sort, had glued the clay of the ravines together, and set it stiff and fast like dried plaster. So, as we went up the narrow, perilous path, our horses had to tread very warily lest, going too near the edge, they should chip off enough of the foothold to send themselves and their riders whirling neck-over-toes to the bottom.

All at once the Little Playmate, who was riding immediately before me, screamed out sharp and shrill, and I hastened up to her, thinking she had fallen upon a misfortune. I found her palfrey with ears pricked and distended nostril, gazing at a head in a red nightcap which was set out of a hole in the red clay.

"The country of gnomes! Of a surety, yes! And hitherto I had thought it had been but the nonsense of folk-tales!" said I to myself.

Which is what we shall say one day of more things than red-nightcapped heads.

But the Little Playmate uttered scream after scream, for the head continued coolly to stare at her, as if fixed alive over the gateway by the craft of some cave-dwelling imp of the Red Axe.

I noticed, however, that the head chewed a straw and spat, which I deemed a gnome would not do—though wherefore straws and spitting are not free to gnomes I do not know and could not have told. Yet, at all events, such was my belief. And a serviceable one enough it was, since it took the fear out of me and gave me back my speech. And when a man can speak he can fight. Contrariwise, it is when a woman will not fight that she can talk best, as one may see in any congress of two angry vixens. So long as they rail there is but threatening and safe recriminations, but when one waxes silent, then 'ware nails and teeth! And I am *not* in my dotage to use such illustrations—as not unnaturally sayeth the first to read my history.

"Good man," cried I, to Sir Red Cap in the wall, "I know not why you stick your ugly head out of the mud, but retract it, I pray you! For do you not see that it alarms the lady and affrights her beast?"

The man nodded intelligently, but went on coolly chewing his straw.

Then I went up to him, and, as civilly as I could, took him by the chin and thrust his head back into the hole. And as I did so I saw for the first time that the wall of the clay cliff, tough and gritty with its alloy of lime, had been cut and hewn into houses and huts having doors of wood of exactly the same color, and in some cases even windows with bars—very marvellous to see, and such as I have never witnessed elsewhere. Presently, at the trampling of the feet of so many horses, people began to throng to their doors, and children peered out at windows and cried to each other shrilly: "See the Christians!"

For so, being but lately pagans themselves, if not partly so to this day, these outlandish men of the border No Man's Land denominated us of the south.

Presently we came to an open space sloping away from the sheer cliff, where was a wall and a door greater than the others.

Jorian rode directly up to the gate, which was of the same dull brick-red as the rest of the curious town. He took the butt of his lance and thumped and banged lustily upon it. For a time there was no reply, but the number of heads thrust out at neighboring windows and the swarms of townsfolk on the pathways before and behind us enormously increased.

Jorian thundered again, kicking with his foot and swearing explosively in mingled Wendish and German. Then he took the point of his spear, and, setting it to a hole in the wall above his head, he hooked out an entire wooden window-frame, as one is taught to pull out a shrimp with a pin on the shore of the Baltic Sea.

Whereupon a sudden outcry arose within the house, and a head popped angrily out of the aperture so suddenly created. But as instantly it returned within. For Jorian tossed the lattice to the ground by the door and thrust his spear-head into the cravat of red which the man had about his throat, shouting to him all the while in the name of the Prince, of the Duke, of the Emperor, of the Archbishop, of all potentates, lay and secular, to come down and open the gates. The man in the red cravat was threatened with the strappado, with the water-torture, with the brodequins, and finally with the devil's cannon—which, according to our man-at-arms, was to be planted on the opposite bank of the ravine, and which would infallibly bring the whole of their wretched town tumbling down into the gulf like swallows' nests from under the eaves.

And this last threat seemed to have more weight than all the rest, probably because the Prince of Plassenburg had already done something of the kind to some other similar town, and the earth-burrowers of Erdborg had good reason to fear the thunder of his artillery.

At all events, the great door opened, and a man of the same brick-red as all the other inhabitants of the town appeared at the portal. He bowed profoundly, and Jorian addressed him in some outlandishly compounded speech, of which I could only understand certain oft-recurring words, as "lodging," "victualling," and "order of the Prince."

So, presently, after a long, and on the side of our escort a stormy, conference, we were permitted to enter. Our horses were secured at the great mangers, which extended all along one side; while, opposite to the horses, but similar to their accommodation in every respect, were stalls wherein various families seemed to be encamped for the night.

With all the air of a special favor conferred, we were informed that we must take up our quarters in the middle of the room and make the best of the hardened floor there. This information, conveyed with a polite wave of the hand and a shrug of the shoulders by our landlord, seemed not unnaturally to put Jorian and Boris into a furious passion, for they drew their swords, and with a unanimous sweep of the hand cleared the capes of their leathern jacks for fighting. So, not to be outdone, I drew my weapon also, and stood by to protect Helene and the Lady Ysolinde.

These two stood close together behind us, but continued to talk indifferently, chiefly of dress and jewels—which surprised me, both in the strange circumstances, and because I knew that Helene had seen no more of them than the valueless trinkets that had belonged to my mother, and which abode in a green-lined box in the Red Tower. Yet to speak of such things seems to come naturally to all women.

As if they had mutually arranged it "from all eternity," as the clerks say, Jorian and Boris took, without hesitation, each a door on the opposite wall, and, setting their shoulders to them, they pushed them open, and went within sword in hand, leaving me alone to protect the ladies and to provide for the safety of the horses.

Presently out from the doors by which our conductors had entered there came tumbling a crowd of men and women, some carrying straw bolsters and wisps of hay, others bearing cooking utensils, and all in various *dishabille*. Then ensued a great buzzing and stirring, much angry growling on the part of the disturbed men, and shrill calling of women for their errant children.

Our little Helene looked sufficiently pitiful and disturbed as these preparations were being made. But the Lady Ysolinde scarcely noticed them, taking apparently all the riot and delay as so much testimony to the important quality of such great ones of the earth as could afford to travel under the escort of two valiant men-at-arms.

Presently came Jorian and Boris out at a third door, having met somewhere in the back parts of the warren.

They came up to the Lady Ysolinde and bowed humbly.

"Will your ladyship deign to choose her chamber? They are all empty. Thereafter we shall see that proper furniture, such as the place affords, is provided for your Highness."

I could not but wonder at so much dignity expended upon the daughter of Master Gerard, the lawyer of Thorn. But Ysolinde took their reverence as a matter of course. She did not even speak, but only lifted her right hand with a little casual flirt of the fingers, which said, "Lead on!"

Then Jorian marshalled us within, Boris standing at the door to let us pass, and bringing his sword-blade with a little click of salute to the perpendicular as each of us passed. But I chanced to meet his eye as I went within, whereat the rogue deliberately winked, and I could plainly see his shoulders heave. I knew that he was still chewing the cud of his stale and ancient jest: "The Prince hath a Princess, and she—"

I could have disembowelled the villain. But, after all, he was certainly doing us some service, though in a most provocative and high-handed manner.

CHAPTER XXI

I STAND SENTRY

There are (say some) but two things worth the trouble of making in the world—war and love. So once upon a time I believed. But since—being laid up during the unkindly monotony of our Baltic spring by an ancient wound—I fell to the writing of this history, I would add to these two worthy adventures—the making of books. Which, till I tried my hand at the task myself, I would in no wise have allowed. But now, when the days are easterly of wind and the lashing water beats on the leaded lozenges of our window lattice, I am fain to stretch myself, take up a new pen, and be at it again all day.

But I must e'en think of them that are to read me, and of their pain if I overstretch my privilege. Besides, if I prove over-long in the wind they may not read me at all, which, I own it, would somewhat mar my purpose.

I was speaking, therefore, of being in the watch and ward of two women, each of whom (in my self-conceit I thus imagined it) certainly regarded me without dislike. God forgive me for thinking so much when they had never plainly told me! Nevertheless I took the thing for granted, as it were. And, as I said before, it has been my experience that, if it be done with a careful and delicate hand, more is gained with women by taking things for granted than by the smoothest tongue and longest Jacob-and-Rachael service. The man who succeeds with good women is the man who takes things for granted. Only he must know exactly what things, otherwise I am mortally sorry for him—he will have a rough road to travel. But to my tale.

Jorian ushered Ysolinde and Helene into the rooms from which he had so unceremoniously ousted the former tenants. How these chambers were lighted in the daytime I could not at first make out, but by going to the end of the long earth-hewn passage and leaning out of a window the mystery was made plain. The ravine took an abrupt turn at this point, so that we were in a house built round an angle, and so had the benefit of light from both sides.

"And where are our rooms to be?" I asked of the stout soldier when he returned.

Jorian pointed to the plain, hard earth of the passage.

"That is poor lodging for tired bones!" I said; "have they no other rooms to let anywhere in this hostelry?"

He laughed again; indeed, he seemed to be able to do little else whenever he spoke to me.

"Tired bones will lie the stiller!" said he, at last, sententiously. "There is some wheaten straw out there which you can bring in for a bolster, if you will. But I think it likely that we shall get no more sleep than the mouse in the cat's dining-room this night. These border rascals are apt to be restless in the dark hours, and their knives prick most consumedly sharp!"

With that he went out, leaving the doors into the passages all open, and presently I could hear him raging and rummaging athwart the house, ordering this one to find him "Graubunden fleisch," the next to get him some good bread, and not to attempt to palm off "cow-cake" upon honest soldiers on pain of getting his stomach cut open—together with other amenities which occur easily to a seasoned man-at-arms foraging in an unfriendly country.

Then, having returned successful from this quest, what was my admiration to see Jorian (whom I had so lately called, and I began to be sorry for it, a Wendish pig) strip his fine soldier's coat and hang it upon a peg by the door, roll up his sleeves, and set to at the cooking in the great open fireplace with swinging black crooks against the front wall, while Boris stood on guard with a long pistolet ready in the hollow of his arm, and his slow-match alight, by the doorway of the ladies' apartment.

I went and stood by the long man for company. And after a little he became much more friendly.

"Why do you stand with your match alight?" I asked of him after we had been a while silent.

"Why, to keep a border knife out of Jorian's back, of course, while he is turning the fry in the pan," said he, as simply as if he had said that 'twas a fine night without, or that the moon was full.

"I wish I could help," I sighed, a little wistfully, for I wished him to think well of me.

"What!" he exclaimed—"with the frying-pan? Well, there is the basting ladle!" he retorted, and laughed in his old manner.

I own that, being yet little more than a lad, the tears stood in my eyes to be so flouted and made nothing of.

"I will show you perhaps sooner than you think that I am neither a coward nor a babe!" I said, in high dudgeon.

And so went and stood by myself over against the farther door of the three, which led from the outer hall to the apartments in which I could hear the murmur of women's voices. And it was lucky that I did so. For even as I reached the door a sharp cry of terror came from within, and there at the inner portal I caught sight of a narrow, foxy, peering visage, and a lean, writhing figure, prone like a worm on its belly. The rascal had been crawling towards Helene's room, for what purpose I know not. Nor did I stop to inquire, for, being stung by the taunt of the man-at-arms, I was on Foxface in a moment, stamping upon him with my iron-shod feet, and then lifting him unceremoniously up by the slackness of his back covertures, I turned him over and over like a wheel, tumbling him out of the doorway into the outer hall with an astonishing clatter, shedding knives and daggers as he went.

It was certainly a pity for the fellow that Boris had taunted me so lately. But the abusing of him gave me great comfort. And as he whirled past the group at the fire, Jorian caught him handily in the round of his back with a convenient spit, also without asking any questions, whereat the fellow went out at the wide front door by which we had first entered, revolving in a cloud of dust. And where he went after that I have no idea. To the devil, for all I care!

But Boris, standing quietly by his own door, was evidently somewhat impressed by my good luck. For soon after this he came over to me. I thought he might be about to apologize for his rudeness. And so perhaps he did, but it was in his own way.

"Did you spoil your dagger on him?" he said, anxiously, for the first time speaking to me as a man speaks to his equal.

"No," said I, "but I stubbed my toe most confoundedly, jarring it upon the rascal's backbone as he went through the door."

"Ah!" he replied, thoughtfully, nodding his head, "that was more fitting for such as he. But you may get a chance at him with the dagger yet or the night be over."

And with that he went back to his door, blowing up his slow-match as he went.

Presently the supper was pronounced cooked, and, after washing his hands, Jorian resumed his coat, amid the universal attention of the motley crew in the great hall, and began to dish up the fragrant stew. Ho had been collecting for it all day upon the march, now knocking over a rabbit with a bolt from his gun, now picking some leaves of lettuce and watercress when he chanced upon a running stream or a neglected garden—of which last (thanks to Duke Casimir and his raiders) there were numbers along the route we had traversed.

Then, when he had made all ready, our sturdy cook dished the stew into a great wooden platter—rabbits, partridges, scraps of dried flesh, bits of bacon for flavoring, fresh eggs, vegetables in handfuls, all covered with a dainty-smelling sauce, deftly compounded of milk, gravy, and red wine.

Then Jorian and Boris, one taking the heap of wooden platters and the other the smoking bowl of stew, marched solemnly within. But before he went, Boris handed me his pistolet without a word, and the slow-match with it. Which, as I admit, made me feel monstrously unsafe. However, I took the engine across my arm and stood at attention as I had seen him do, with the match thrust through my waistband.

Then I felt as if I had suddenly grown at least a foot taller, and my joy was changed to ecstasy when the Lady Ysolinde, coming out quickly, I knew not at first for what purpose, found me thus standing sentinel and blowing importantly upon my slow-match.

"Hugo," she said, kindly, looking at me with the aqua-marine eyes that had the opal glints in them, "come thy ways in and sit with us."

I made her a salute with my piece and thanked her for her good thought.

"But," said I, "Lady Ysolinde, pray remember that this is a place of danger, and that it is more fitting that we who have the honor to be your guards should dine together without your chamber doors."

"Nay," she said, impetuously, "I insist. It is not right that you, who are to be an officer, should mess with the common soldiers."

"My lady," said I, "I thank you deeply. And it shall be so, I promise you, when we are in safety. But let me have my way here and now."

She smiled upon me—liking me, as I think, none the worse for my stiffness. And so went away, and I was right glad to see her go. For I would not have lost what I had gained in the good opinion of these two men-at-arms—no, not for twenty maidens' favors.

But in that respect also I changed as the years went on. For of all things a boy loves not to be flouted and babyfied when he thinks himself already grown up and the equal of his elders in love and war.

So in a little while came out Jorian and Boris, and, having carried in the bread and wine, we three sat down to the remains of the stew.

Indeed, I saw but little difference as to quantity from the time that Jorian had taken it in. For maids' appetites when they are anyways in love are precarious, but, after they are assured of their love's return, then the back hunger comes upon them and the larder is made to pay for all arrears.

Not that I mean to assert that either of these ladies was in love with me—far otherwise indeed. For this it would argue the conceit of a jack-a-dandy to imagine, much more to write such a thing. But, nevertheless, certain is it that this night they were both of small appetite.

CHAPTER XXII

HELENE HATES ME

However, when the provision came to the outer port, we three sat down about it, and then, by my troth, there was little to marvel at in the tardiness of our eating. For the rabbits seemed to come alive and positively leaped down our throats, the partridges almost flew at us out of the pot, the pigeons fairly rejoiced to be eaten. The broth and the gravy ebbed lower and lower in the pan and left all dry. But as soon as we had picked the bones roughly, for there was no time for fine work lest the others should get all the best, we threw the bones out to the hungry crew that watched us sitting round the stalls, their very jowls pendulous with envy.

So after a while we came to the end, and then I went to the entrance of the chamber where were bestowed the Little Playmate and the Lady Ysolinde. For I began to be anxious how Helene would be able to comport herself in the company of one so dainty and full of devices and convenances as the lady of the Weiss Thor.

But, by my faith, I need not have troubled about our little lass. For if there were any embarrassed, that one was certainly not Helene. And if any of us lacked reposefulness of manners, that one was certainly a staring jackanapes, who did not know which foot to stand upon, nor yet how to sit down on the oaken settle when a seat was offered him, nor, last of all, when nor how to take his departure when he had once sat down. And as to the identity of that jackass, there needs no further particularity.

Nevertheless, I talked pleasantly enough with both of them, and I might have been an acquaintance of the day for all the notice that the Little Playmate took of me, oven when the Lady Ysolinde told her, evidently not for the first time, of my standing sentry by the door and blowing upon the match at my girdle.

From without we heard presently the clapping of hands and loud deray of merrymaking, so I went to find out what it might be that was causing such an uproar.

There I found Jorian and Boris giving a kind of exhibition of their skill in military exercises. It might be, also, that they desired to teach a lesson for the benefit of the wild robber border folk and the yet more ruffianly kempers who foregathered in this strange inn of Erdberg on the borders of the Mark.

I summoned the maids that they might look on. For I wot the scene was a curious and pleasing one, and I could see that the eyes of the Lady Ysolinde glittered. But our little maid, being used to all these things from her youth, cared nothing for it, though the thing was indeed marvellous in itself.

When I went out our two men-at-arms had each of them in hand his straight Wendish Tolleknife, made heavy at the end of the Swedish blade, but light as to the handle, and hafted with cork from Spain.

Ten yards apart, shoulder to shoulder they stood, and, first of all, each of them poising the knife in the hollow of his hand with a peculiar dancing movement, set it writhing across the room at a marked circle on a board. The two knives sped simultaneously with a vicious whir, and stood quivering, with their blades touching each other, in the centre of the white. At the next trial, so exactly had they been aimed that the point of the one hit upon the haft of the other and stripped the cork almost to the blade. But Jorian, to whom the knife belonged, mended it with a piece of string, telling the company philosophically that it was no bad thing to have a string hanging loose to a Tolleknife, for when it went into any one the string would always hang down from the wound in order to pull it out by.

Then they got their knives again and played a more dangerous game. Jorian stood on guard with his knife, waving the blade slowly before him in the shape of a long-bodied letter S. Boris poised his weapon in the hollow of his hand, and sent it whirring straight at Jorian's heart. As it came buzzing like an angry bee, almost too quick for the eye to follow, Jorian flicked it deftly up into the air at exactly the right moment, and, without even taking his eye off it, he caught the knife by the handle as it fell. Thereafter he bowed and gave it back to the thrower ceremoniously. Then Boris guarded, and Jorian in his turn threw, with a like result, though, perhaps, a little less featly done on Boris's part.

All the while there was a clamant and manifold astonishment in the kitchen of the inn, together with prodigal and much-whispering wonder.

Then ensued other plays. Boris stood with his elbow crooked and his left hand on his hip, with his back also turned to Jorian. *Buzz!* went the knife! It flashed like level lightning under the arch of Jorian's armpit, and lo! it was caught in his right hand, which dropped upon it like a hawk upon a rabbit, as it sped through his elbow port.

Then came shooting with the cross-bow, and I regretted much that I had only learned the six-foot yew, and that there was not one in the company, nor indeed room to display it if there had been. For I longed to do something to show that I also was no milksop.

Now it chanced that there was in one corner a yearling calf that had been killed that day, and hung up with a bar between its thighs. I saw an axe leaning in the corner—an axe with a broad, cutting edge—and I bethought me that perhaps, after all, I knew something which even Jorian and Boris were ignorant of. So, mindful of my father's teaching, I took the axe, and, before any one was aware of my intent, I swept the long-handled axe round my head, and, getting the poise and distance for the slow drawing cut which does not stop for bone nor muscle, I divided the neck through at one blow so that the head dropped on the ground.

Then there was much applause and wonder. Men ran to lift the calf's head, and the owner of the axe came up to examine the edge of his weapon. I looked about. The eyes of the Lady Ysolinde were aflame with pleasure, but, on the other hand, the Little Playmate was crimson with shame. Tears stood in her beautiful eyes.

She marched straight up to meet me, and, clinching her hands, she said; "Oh, I hate you!"

And so went within to her chamber, and I saw her no more that night. Now I take all to witness what strange things are the mind and temper of even the best of women. And why Helene thus spoke to me I know not—nay, even to this day I can hazard no right guess. But as I have often said, God never made anything straight that He made beautiful, except only the line where the sea meets the sky.

And of all the pretty, crooked, tangled things that He has made, women are the prettiest, the crookedest—and the most distractingly tangled.

Which is perhaps why they are so everlastingly interesting, and why we blundering, ram-stam, homely favored men love them so.

But the best entertainment must at long and last come to an end. And the one in the inn of Erdberg lasted not so long as the telling of it—for the matter, being more comfortable than that which came after, I have, perhaps, not hurried so much as I might.

When at last both supper and entertainment were finished, and the earthenware platters huddled away into the hall without, there arose a mighty clamor, so that Jorian went to the door and cried out to the landlord to know what was the matter. The old brick-dusty knave came hulking forward, and, with greatly increased respect, he addressed the men-at-arms.

"What is your will, noble sirs?"

"I asked," said Jorian, "what was the reason of this so ill-favored noise. If your guests cannot be quiet, I will come among them with something that will settle the quarrels of certain of them in perpetuity."

So with sulky recurrent murmurs the fray finally settled itself, and for that time at least there was no more trouble. I went to the door of the Lady Ysolinde and the Little Playmate and cried in to them a courteous goodnight. For I had been sorry to have Helene's "I hate you!" for her last word. And the Lady Ysolinde came to the door in a light robe of silk and gave me her hand to kiss. But though I said: "A sweet sleep and a pleasant, Helene!" no voice replied. Which I took very ill, seeing that I had done naught amiss that I knew of.

Then Jorian, Boris, and I made us comfortable for the night, and, being instructed by Boris, I set my straw, with the foot of my bundle to the door, which opened inward upon us. Then, putting my sword by my side and my other weapons convenient to my hand, I laid me down and braced my feet firmly against the door, thus locking it safely.

Jorian and Boris did the same at the other entrances, and before the former went to sleep he arranged a tall candle that had been placed unlighted before a little shrine of the Virgin (for, in name at least, the folk were not wholly pagan) and lighted it, so that it shed a faint illumination down the long passage in which we were bestowed, and on the inner door of the ladies' apartment.

And though I was far from being in love, yet the thought of the wandering damsels, both so fair and so far from home, moved me deeply. And I was in act to waft a kiss towards the door when Jorian caught me.

"What now?" he said; "art at thy prayers, lad?"

"Aye, that am I," said I, "towards the shrine of the Saints' Rest."

Now this was irreverent, and mayhap afterwards we were all soundly punished for it. But at least it was on the level of their soldiers' wit—though I own, at the most, no great matter to cackle of.

"Ho! ho! Good!" chuckled Boris, under his breath. "One of them is doubtless a saint. But as to the other—well, let us ask the Prince. 'He hath a Princess, and she is oft upon her travels?' Ho! ho! ho!"

And the lout shook among his straw to such an extent that I bade him for God's dear sake to bide still, otherwise we might as lief lie in a barn among questing rattons.

"And the saints of your Saints' Rest defend us from lying among any worse!" said he, and betook him to sleep.

CHAPTER XXIII

HUGO OF THE BROADAXE

But as for me, sleep I could not. And indeed that is small wonder. For it was the first night I had ever slept out of the Red Tower in my life. I seemed to lack some necessary accompaniment to the act of going to sleep.

It was a long while before I could find out what it could be that was disturbing me. At last I discovered that it was the howling of the kennelled blood-hounds which I missed. For at night they even raged, and leaped on the barriers with their forefeet, hearing mayhap the moving to and fro of men come sleeplessly up from the streets of the city beneath.

But here, within a long day's march of Thorn, I had come at once into a new world. Slowly the night dragged on. The candle guttered. A draught of air blew fitfully through the corridor in which we lay. It carried the flame of the candle in the opposite direction. I wondered whence it could come, for the air had been still and thick before. Yet I was glad of the stir, for it cooled my temples, and I think that but for one thing I might have slept. And had I fallen on sleep then no one of us might have waked so easily. What I heard was no more than this—once or twice the flame of the candle gave a smart little "spit," as if a moth or a fat blue-bottle had forwandered into it and fallen spinning to the ground with burned wings. Yet there were no moths in the chambers, or we should have seen them circling about the lights at the time of supper. Nevertheless, ere long I heard again the quick, light "*plap!*" And presently I saw a pellet fall to the ground, rolling away from the wall almost to the edge of the straw on which I lay.

I reached out a hand for it, and in a trice had it in my fingers. It was soft, like mason's putty. "Plop!" came another. I was sure now. Some one was shooting at the flame of the candle with intent to leave us in the dark. Jorian and Boris snored loudly, sleeping like true men-at-arms. I need say no more.

I lay with my head in the shadow, but by moving little by little, with sleepy grunts of dissatisfaction, I brought my face far enough round to see through the straw the window at the far end of the passage, which, as I had discovered upon our first coming, opened out upon a ravine running at right angles to the street by which we had come.

Presently I could see the lattice move noiselessly, and a white face appeared with a boy's blow-gun of pierced bore-tree at its lips.

"Alas!" said I to myself, "that I had had these soldiers' skill of the knife throwing. I would have marked that gentleman." But I had not even a bow—only my sword and dagger. I resolved to begin to learn the practice of pistol and cross-bow on the morrow.

"Plap! Scat!" The aim was good this time. We were in darkness. I listened the barest fragment of a moment. Some one was stealthily entering at the window end.

"Rise, Jorian and Boris!" I cried. "An enemy!"

And leaping up I ran to relight the candle. By good luck the wick was a sound, honest, thick one, a good housewife's wick—not such as are made to sell and put in ordinary candles of offertory.

The wick was still red, and smoked as I put my hands behind it and blew. *"Twang! Twang! Zist! Zist!"* went the arrows and bolts thickly about me, bringing down the clay dust in handfuls thickly from the walls.

"Down on your stomachs—they are shooting crosswise along the passage!" cried Jorian, who had instantly awakened. I longed to follow the advice, for I felt something sharp catch the back of my undersuit of soft leather, in which, for comfort, I had laid me down to sleep. But I *must* get the candle alight. Hurrah! the flame flickered and caught at last. *"Twang! Twang!"* went the bows, harder at it than ever. Something hurtled hotly through my hair—the iron bolt of an arbalest, as I knew by the song of the steel bow in a man's hand at the end of the passage.

"Get into a doorway, man!" cried Boris, as the light revealed me.

And like a startled rabbit I ran for the nearest—that within which Helene and the Lady Ysolinde were lying asleep. The candle, as I have said, was set deep in a niche, which proved a great mercy for us. For our foes, who had thought to come on us by fraud, could not now shoot it out. Also, in relighting it, in my eagerness to save myself from the hissing arrows behind me, I had pushed it to the very back of the shrine. I had no weapon now but my dagger, for, in rising to relight the candle, I had carelessly and blamefully left my sword in the straw. And I felt very useless and foolish as I stood there to bide the assault with only a bit of guardless knife in my hand.

Suddenly, however, there came a diversion.

"Crash!" went a gun in my very ear. Flame, smoke—much of both—and the stifling smell of sulphur. Jorian had fired at the face of the popgun knave. That putty-white countenance had a crimson plash on it ere it vanished. Then came back to us a scream of dreadful agony and the sound of a heavy fall outside.

"End of act the first! The Wicked Angels—hum, hum—go to hell! All in the day's work!" cried Jorian, cheerily, recharging his pistolet and driving home the wadding as he spoke.

It may well be imagined that during our encounter with the assailants of the candle, whose transverse fire had so nearly finished me, the company out in the great kitchen had not been content to lie snoring on their backs. We could hear them creeping and whispering out there beyond the doors; but till after the shot from the soldier's pistolet they had not dared to show us any overt act of hostility.

Suddenly Jorian, once more facing the door, now that the passage was clear, perceived by the rustling of the straw that it began to open gradually. He waited till in another moment it would have been wide enough to let in a man.

"Back there, dog, or I fire!" he bellowed. And the door was promptly shut to.

After that there came another period of waiting very difficult to get over. I wished with all my heart for a cross-bow or any shooting weapon. Much did I reproach myself that I had not learned the art before, as I might easily have done from the men-at-arms about the Wolfsberg, who, for my father's sake (or Helene's), would gladly have taught me.

The women folk in the room behind my back were now up and dressed. Indeed, the Lady Ysolinde would have come out and watched with us, but I besought her to abide where she was. Presently, however, Helene put her head without, and seeing me stand by the door with my sword, she asked if I wanted anything. She appeared to have forgotten her unkind goodnight, and I was not the man to remind her of it.

"Only another weapon, Sweetheart, besides this prick-point small-sword!" said I, looking at the thing in my hand I doubt not a trifle scornfully.

Helene shut to the door, and for a space I heard no more. Presently, however, she opened it again, and thrust an axe with a long handle through to me. It was the very fellow of the weapon I had used on the pendent calf in the kitchen. I understood at once that it was her apology and her justification as well. For the Little Playmate was ever a straight lass. She ever did so much more than she promised, and ever said less than her heart meant. Which perhaps is less common than the other way about—especially among women.

"I found it on my incoming and hid it under the bed!" she said.

Then judge ye if I sheathed not my small-sword right swiftly, and made the broadaxe blade, to the skill of which I had been born, whistle through the air. For a mightily strange thing it is that, though I had ever a rooted horror at the thought of my father's office itself, and from my childhood never for a moment intended to exercise it, nevertheless I had always the most notable facility in cutting things. Never to this day have I a stick in hand, when I walk abroad among the ragweed waving yellow on the grassy pastures below the Wolfsberg, but I must need make wagers with myself to cut to an inch at the heads of the tallest and never miss. And this I can do the day by the length, and never grow weary. Then again, for pleasaunce, my father used to put me to the cutting of light wood with an axe, not always laying it upon a block or hag-clog, but sometimes setting the billet upright and making me cut the top off with a horizontal swing of the axe. And in this I became exceedingly expert. And how difficult it is no one knows till he has tried.

So it is small wonder that as soon as I gripped the noble broadaxe which Helene passed me I felt my own man again.

Then we were silent and listened—and ever again listened and held our breaths. Now I tell you when an enemy is whispering unseen without, rustling like rats in straw, and you wonder at what point they will break in next, thinking all the while of the woman you love (or do not yet love, but may) in the chamber behind—I tell you a castle is something less difficult to hold at such a time than just one's own breath.

Suddenly I heard a sound in the outer chamber which I knew the meaning of. It was the shifting of horses' feet as they turn in narrow space to leave their stalls. Our good friends were making free with our steeds. And, if we were not quick about it, we should soon see the last of them, and be compelled to traverse the rest of the road to Plassenburg upon our own proper feet.

"Jorian," cried I, "do you hear? They are slipping our horses out of the stalls! Shall you and I make a sortie against them, while Boris with that pistol of his keeps the passage from the wicks of the middle door?"

"Good!" answered Jorian. "Give the word when you are ready."

With axe in my right hand, the handle of the door in my left, I gave the signal.

"When I say 'Three!' Jorian!"

"Good!" said Jorian.

Clatter went the horses' hoofs as they were being led towards the door.

"One! Two! Three!" I counted, softly but clearly.

CHAPTER XXIV

THE SORTIE

The door was open, and the next I mind was my axe whirling about my head and Jorian rushing out of the other door a step ahead of me, with his broadsword in his hand. I cannot tell much about the fight. I never could all my days. And I wot well that those who can relate such long particulars of tales of fighting are the folk who stood at a distance and labored manfully at the looking on—not of them that were close in and felt the hot breaths and saw the death-gleam in fierce, desperate eyes, near to their own as the eyes of lovers when they embrace. Ah, Brothers of the Sword, these things cannot be told! Yet, of a surety, there is a heady delight in the fray itself. And so I found. For I struck and warded not, that being scarce necessary. Because an axe is an uncanny weapon to wield, but still harder to stand against when well used. And I drove the rabble before me—the men of them, I mean. I felt my terrible weapon stopped now and then—now softly, now suddenly, according to that which I struck against. And all the while the kitchen of the inn resounded with yells and threatenings, with oaths and cursings.

But Jorian and I drove them steadily back, though they came at us again and again, with spits, iron hooks, and all manner of curious weapons. Also from out of the corners we saw the gleaming, watchful eyes of a dark huddle of women and children. Presently the clamorous rabble turned tail suddenly and poured through the door out upon the pathway, quicker than water through a tide-race in the fulness of the ebb.

And lo! in a moment the room was sucked empty, save only for the huddled women in the corners, who cried and suckled their children to keep them still. And some of the wounded with the axe and the sword crawled to them to have their ghastly wounds bound. For an axe makes ugly work at the best of times, and still worse on the edges of such a pagan fight as we three had just fought.

So we went back victorious to our inner doors.

Then Jorian looked at me and nodded across at Boris.

"Good!" was all that he said. But the single word made me happier than many encomiums.

In spite of all, however, we were no nearer than before to getting away that I could see. For there was still all that long, desperate traverse of the defile before we could guide our horses to firm ground again. But while I was thinking bitterly of my first night's sleep (save the mark!) away from the Red Tower, I heard something I knew not the meaning of—the beginning of a new attack, as I judged.

It sounded like a scraping and a crumbling somewhere above.

"God help us now, Jorian!" I cried, in a sudden, quick panic; "they are coming upon us everyway. I can hear them stripping off the roof-tile overhead—if such rabbit-warrens as this have Christian roofs!"

Boris sat down calmly with his back against the earthen wall and trained his pistol upward, ready to shoot whatever should appear. Presently fragments of earth and hardened clay began to drop on the pounded floor of the corridor. I heard the soft hiss of the man-at-arms blowing up his match, and I waited for the crash and the little heap of flame from the touch.

Suddenly a foot, larger than that of mortal, plumped through our ceiling of brick-dust and a huge scatterment of earth tumbled down. A great bare leg, with attachment of tattered hose hanging here and there, followed.

Before the pistol could go off, Boris meanwhile waiting shrewdly for the appearance of a more vital part, a voice cried, "Stop!"

I looked about me, and there was the Lady Ysolinde come out of her chamber, with a dagger in her hand. She was looking upward at the hole in the ceiling.

"For God's sake, do not fire!" she cried; "tis only my poor Lubber Fiend. Shame on me, that I had quite forgotten him all this time!"

At which, without turning away the muzzle, Boris put it a little aside, and waited for the disturber of brick-dust ceilings to reveal himself. Which, when presently he did, a huge, grinning face appeared, pushing forward at first slowly and with difficulty, then, as soon as the ears had crossed the narrows of the pass, the whole head to the neck was glaring down and grinning to us.

"Lubber Jan," said Ysolinde, "what do you up there?"

The head only grinned and waggled pleasantly, as it had been through a horse-collar at Dantzig fair.

"Speak!" said she, and stamped her little foot; "I will shake thee with terrors else, monster!"

"Poor Jan came down from above. It is quite easy!" he said. "But not for horses. Oh no! but now I will go and bring the Burgomeister. Do you keep the castle while I go. He bides below the town in a great house of stone, and entertains our Prince Miller's Son's archers. I will bring all that are sober of them."

"God help us then!" quoth Jorian; "it is past eleven o' the clock, and as I know them man by man, there will not be so much as one left able to prop up another by this time!"

"Aha!" cried the head above; "you say that because you know the archers. But I say I shall bring full twenty of them—because I know the strength of the Burgomeister's ale. Hold the place for half an hour and twenty right sober men shall ye have."

And with that the Lubber Fiend disappeared in a final avalanche of brick-dust and clay clods.

He was gone, and half an hour was a long time to wait. Yet in such a case there was nothing for it but to stand it out. So I besought the maids to retire again to their inner chamber, into which, at least, neither bullets nor arrows could penetrate. This, after some little persuasion, they did.

We waited. I have since that night fought many easier battles, and bloody battles, too. Now and then a face would look in momentarily from the great outer door and vanish before any one could put a shot into it. Next, ere one was aware, an arrow would whistle with a *"Hiss!"* past one's breast-bone and stand quivering, head-covered in the clay. Vicious things they were, too, steel-pointed and shafted with iron for half their length.

But all waitings come to an end, even that of him who waits on a fair woman's arraying of herself. Erdberg evidently did not know of the little party down at the Burgomeister's below the pass of the ravine, or, knowing, did not care. For, just as our half-hour was crawling to an end, with a unanimous yell a crowd of wild men with weapons in their hands poured in through the great door and ran shouting at our position. At the same time the window at the end of the passage opened and a man leaped through. Him I sharply attended to with the axe, and stood waiting for the next. He also came, but not through the window. He ran at me, head first, through the door, and, being stricken down, completely blocked it up. Good service! And a usefully bulky man he was. But how he bled!—Saint Christopher! that is the worst of bulky men, they can do nothing featly—not even die!

One man won past me, indeed, darting under the stroke of my axe, but he was little advantaged thereby. For I fetched a blow at the back of his head with the handle which brought him to his knees. He stumbled and fell at the threshold of the maids' chamber. And, by my sooth, the Lady Ysolinde stooped and poignarded him as featly as though it had been a work of broidering with a bodkin. Too late, Helene wept and besought her to hold her hand. He was, she said, some one's son or lover. It was deucedly unpractical. But, 'twas my Little Playmate. And after all, I suppose, the crack he got from me in the way of business would have done the job neatly enough without my lady's dagger.

I tell you, the work was hot enough about those three doors during the next few moments. I never again want to see warmer on this side of Peter's gates—especially not since I got this wound in my thigh, with its trick of reopening at the most inconvenient seasons. But the broadaxe was a blessed thought of the little Helene's, and helped to keep the castle right valiantly.

Yet I can testify that I was glad with more than mere joy when I heard the "Trot, trot!" of the Prince's archers coming at the wolf's lope, all in each other's footsteps, along the narrow ledge of the village street.

"Hurrah, lads!" I shouted; "quick and help us!"

And then at the sound of them the turmoil emptied itself as quickly as it had come. The rabble of ill-doers melted through the wide outer door, where the archers received and attended to them there. Some precipitated themselves over the cliff. Others were straightway knocked down, stunned, and bound. Some died suddenly. And a few were saved to stretch the judicial ropes of the Bailiwick. For it was always thought a good thing by such as were in authority to have a good show on the "Thieves' Architrave," or general gallows of the vicinity, as a thing at once creditable to the zeal of the worthy dispensers of local justice, and pleasing to the Kaiser's officer if he chanced to come spying that way.

CHAPTER XXV

MINE HOST RUNS HIS LAST RACE

Hearty were the greetings when the soldiers found us all safe and sound. They shook us again and again by the hand. They clapped us on the back. They examined professionally the dead who lay strewn about.

"A good stroke! Well smitten!" they cried, as they turned them over, like spectators who applaud at a game they can all understand. Specially did they compliment me on my axe-work. Never had anything like it been seen in Plassenburg. The head of the yearling calf was duly exhibited, when the neatness of the blow and the exactness of the aim at the weakest jointing were prodigiously admired.

The good fellows, mellow with the Burgomeister's sinall-ale, were growing friendly beyond all telling, when, in the light of the offertory taper, now growing begutered and burning low, there appeared the Lady Ysolinde.

You never saw so quick a change in any men. The heartiest reveller forthwith became silent and slunk behind his neighbor. Knees shook beneath stalwart frames, and there seemed a very general tendency to get down upon marrow-bones.

The Lady Ysolinde stood before them, strangely different from the slim, willowy maiden I had seen her. She looked almost imperial in her demeanor.

"You shall be rewarded for your ready obedience," she said; "the Prince will not forget your service. Take away that offal!"

She pointed to the dead rascals on the floor.

And the men, muttering something that sounded to me like "Yes, your Highness !" hastened to obey.

"Did you say 'Yes, your Highness' ?" I asked one of them, who seemed, by his air of command, to be the superior among the archers.

"Aye," answered he, dryly, "it is a term usually applied to the Lady Ysolinde, Princess of Plassenburg."

I was never more smitten dazed and dumb in my life. Ysolinde, the daughter of Master Gerard, the maid who had read my fate in the ink-pool, whom I had "made suffer," according to her own telling—she the Princess of Plassenburg '.

Ah, I had it now. Here at last was the explanation of the threadbare and inexplicable jest of Jorian and Boris, "The Prince hath a Princess, and she is oft upon her travels !"

But, after all, what a Wendish barking about so small an egg. I have heard an emperor proclaimed with less cackle.

Ysolinde, Princess of Plassenburg—yes, that made a difference. And I had taken her hand—I, the son of the Red Axe—I, the Hereditary Justicer of the Wolfmark. Well, after all, she had sought me, not I her. And then, the little Helene—what would she make of it? I longed greatly to find an opportunity to tell her. It might teach her in what manner to cut her cloth.

The archers of the Prince camped with us the rest of the night in the place of the outcast crew. They behaved well (though their forbearance was perhaps as much owing to the near presence of the Princess as to any inherent virtue in the good men of the bow) to the women and children who remained huddled in the corners.

Then came the dawn, swift-foot from the east. A fair dawn it was, the sun rising, not through barred clouds, with the lightest at the horizon (which is the foul-weather dawn), but through streamers and bannerets that fluttered upward and fired to ever fleecier crimson and gold as he rose.

We rode among a subdued people, and ere we went the Princess called for the Burgomeister and bade him send to Plassenburg the landlord, so soon as he should be found, and also the heads of the half-dozen houses on either side of the inn.

Then, indeed, there was a turmoil and a wailing to speak about. Women folk crowded out of the huts and kissed the white feet of the palfrey that bore the Lady Ysolinde.

"Have mercy!" they wailed; "show kindness, great Princess! Here are our men, unwounded and unhurt, that have lain by our sides all the night. They are innocent of all intent of evil—of every dark deed. Ah, lady, send them not to your prisons. We shall never see them more, and they are all we have or our children. 'Tis they bring in the bread to this drear spot!"

"Produce me your husbands, then!" said the Lady Ysolinde.

Whereat the women ran and brought a number of frowsy and bleared men, all unwounded, save one that had a broken head.

Then Ysolinde called to the Burgomeister. "Come hither, chief of a thievish municipality, tell me if these be indeed these women's husbands."

The Burgomeister, a pallid, pouch-mouthed man, tremulous, and brick-dusty, like everything else in the village of Erdberg, came forward and peeringly examined the men.

"Every man to his woman!" he ordered, brusquely, and the women went and stood each by her own property—the men shamefaced and hand-dog, the women anxious and pale. Some of the last threw a, protecting arm about their husbands, which they for the most part appeared to resent. In every case the woman looked the more capable and intelligent, the men being apparently mere boors.

"They are all their true husbands, at least so far as one can know!" answered the Burgomeister, cautiously.

"Then," said the lady, "bid them catch the innkeeper and send him to Plassenburg, and these others can abide where they are. But if they find him not, they must all come instead of him."

The men started at her words, their faces brightening wonderfully, and they were out of the door before one could count ten. We mounted our horses, and under the very humble guidance of the Burgomeister, who led the Princess's palfrey, we were soon again upon the high tableland. Here we enjoyed to the full the breezes which swept with morning freshness across the scrubby undergrowths of oak and broom, and above all the sight of misty wisps of cloud scudding and whisking about the distant peaks-behind which lay the city of Plassenburg.

We had not properly won clear of the ravines when we heard a great shouting and turmoil behind us—so that I hastened to look to my weapons. For I saw the archers instinctively draw their quarrels and bolt-pouches off their backs, to be in readiness upon their left hips.

But it was only the rabble of men and women who had been threatened, the dwellers in those twelve houses next the inn, who came dragging our brick-faced knave of a host, with that hard-polished countenance of his slack and clammy—slate-gray in color too, all the red tan clean gone out of it.

"Mercy—mercy, great lady!" he cried; "I pray you, do execution on me here and now. Carry me not to the extreme tortures. Death clears all. And I own that for my crimes I well deserve to die. But save me from the strappado, from the torment of the rack. I am an old man and could not endure."

The Lady Ysolinde looked at him, and her emerald eyes held a steely glitter in their depths.

"I am neither judge nor"—I think she was going to say "executioner," but she remembered in time and for my sake was silent, which I thought was both gracious and charming of her. She resumed in a softer tone: "What sentence, then, would you desire, thus confessing your guilt?"

"That I might end myself over the cliff there!" said the innkeeper, pointing to the wall of rock along the edge of which we were riding.

"See, then, that he is well ended!" said the Princess, briefly, to Jorian.

"Good!" said Jorian, saluting.

And very coolly betook himself to the edge of the cliff, where he primed his piece anew, and blew up his match.

"Loose the man and stand back!" cried the Princess.

A moment the innkeeper stood nerving himself. A moment he hung on the thin edge of his resolve. The slack gray face worked convulsively, the white lips moved, the hands were gripped close to his sides as though to run a race. His whole body seemed suddenly to shrink and fall in upon itself.

"The torture! The terrible torture!" he shrieked aloud, and ran swiftly from the clutches of the men who had held him. Between the path and the verge of the cliff from which he was suffered to cast himself there stretched some thirty or forty yards of fine green turf. The old man ran as though at a village fair for some wager of slippery pig's tail, but all the time the face of him was like Death and Hell following after.

At the cliff's edge he leaped high into the air, and went headlong down, to our watching eyes as slowly as if he had sunk through water. None of us who were on the path saw more of him. But Jorian craned over, regarding the man's end calmly and even critically. And when he had satisfied himself that that which was done was properly done, as coolly as before he stowed away his match in his cover-fire, mounted his horse, and rode towards us.

He nodded to the Princess. "Good, my Lady!" quoth he, for all comment.

"I saved a charge that time!" said he to his companion.

"Good!" quoth Boris, in his turn.

We had now a safe and noble escort, and the way to Plassenburg was easy. The face of the country gradually changed. No more was it the gray, wistful plain of the Wolfmark, upon which our Red Tower looked down. No more did we ride through the marly, dusty, parched lands, in which were the ravines with their uncanny cavern villages, of which this Erdberg was the chief. But green, well-watered valleys and mountains wooded to the top lay all about us—a pleasant land, a fertile province, and, as the Princess had said, a land in which the strong hand of Karl the Prince had long made "the broom-bush keep the cow."

I had all along been possessed with great desire to meet the Prince of so noble and well-cared-for a land, and perhaps also to see what manner of man could be the husband of so extraordinary a Princess.

CHAPTER XXVI

PRINCE JEHU MILLER'S SON

Yet now, when she was in her own country, and as good as any queen thereof, I found the Lady Ysolinde in no wise different from, what she had been in the city of Thorn and in her father's house. She called me often to ride beside her, Helene being on my other side, while the Lubber Fiend, who had saved all our lives, gambolled about and came to her to be petted like a lapdog of some monstrous sort. He licked his lips and twisted his eyes upward at her in ludicrous ecstasy till only the whites were visible whenever the Princess laid her hand on his head. So that it was as much as the archers of the guard could do to hide their laughter in their beards. But hide it they did, having a wholesome awe of the emerald eyes of their mistress, or perhaps of the steely light which sometimes came into them.

It was growing twilight upon the third day (for there were no adventures worth dwelling upon after that among the cavern dwellings of Erdberg) when for the first time we saw the towers of Plassenburg crowning a hill, with its clear brown river winding slow beneath. We were yet a good many miles from it when down the dusty road towards us came a horseman, and fifty yards or so behind him another.

"The Prince—none rides like our Karl!" said Jorian, familiarly, under his breath, but proudly withal.

"He comes alone!" said I, wonderingly. For indeed Duke Casimir of the Wolfsberg never went ten lances' length from his castle without a small army at his tail.

"Even so!" replied Jorian; "it is ever his custom. The officer who follows behind him has his work cut out—and basted. Not for nothing is our Karl called Prince Jehu Miller's Son, for indeed he rides most furiously."

Before there was time for more words between us a tall, grim-faced, pleasant-eyed man of fifty rode up at a furious gallop. The first thing I noticed about him was that his hair was exactly the same color as his horse—an iron-gray, rusty a little, as if it had been rubbed with iron that has been years in the wet.

He took off his hat courteously to the Princess.

"I bid you welcome, my noble lady," said he, smiling; "the cages are ready for the new importations."

The Lady Ysolinde reached a hand for her husband to kiss, which he did with singular gentleness. But, so far as I could see, she neither looked at him even once nor yet so much as spoke a word to him. Presently he questioned her directly: "And who may this fair young damsel be, who has done me the honor to journey to my country?"

"She is Helene, called Helene Gottfried of Thorn, and has come with me to be one of my maids of honor," answered the Lady Ysolinde, looking straight before her into the gathering mist, which began to collect in white ponds and streaks here and there athwart the valley.

The Prince gave the Little Playmate a kindly ironic look out of his gray eyes, which, as I interpreted it, had for meaning, "Then, if that be so, God help thee, little one—'tis well thou knowest not what is before thee!"

"And this young man?" said the Prince, nodding across to me.

But I answered for myself.

"I am the son of the Hereditary Justicer of the Wolfmark," said I. "I had no stomach for such work. Therefore, as I was shortly to be made my father's assistant, I have brought letters of introduction to your Highness, in the hopes that you will permit me the exercise of arms in your army in another and more honorable fashion."

"I have promised him a regiment," said the Princess, speaking quickly.

"What—of leaden soldiers?" answered the Prince, looking at her mighty soberly.

"Your Highness is pleased to be brutal," answered the Lady Ysolinde, coldly. "It is your ordinary idea of humor!"

A kind of quaint humility sat on the face of the Prince.

"I but thought that your Highness could have nothing else in her mind—seeing that our rough Plassenburg regiments will only accept men of some years and experience to lead them. But the little soldiers of metal are not so queasy of stomach."

"May it please your Highness," said I, earnestly, "I will be content to begin with carrying a pike, so that I be permitted in any fashion to fight against your enemies."

Jorian and Boris came up and saluted at this point, like twin mechanisms. Then they stood silent and waiting.

The Prince nodded in token that they had permission to speak.

"With the sword the lad fights well," said Boris. "Is it not so, Jorian?"

"Good!" said Jorian.

"But with the broadaxe he slashes about him like an angel from heaven—not so, Boris?" said Jorian.

"Good!" said Boris.

"Can you ride?" said the Prince, turning abruptly from them.

"Aye, sire!" said I. For indeed I could, and had no shame to say it.

"That horse of his is blown; give him your fresh one!" said he to the officer who had accompanied him. "And do you show these good folk to their quarters."

Hardly was I mounted before the Prince set spurs to his beast, and, with no more than a casual wave of his hand to the Princess and her train, he was off.

"Ride!" he cried to me. And was presently almost out of sight, stretching his horse's gray belly to the earth, like a coursing dog after a hare.

Well was it for me that I had learned to ride in a hard school—that is, upon the unbroken colts which were brought in for the mounting of the Duke Casimir's soldiery. For the horse that I had been given took the bit between his teeth and pursued so fiercely after his stable companion that I could scarce restrain him from passing the Prince. But our way lay homeward, so that, though I was in no way able to guide nor yet control my charger, nevertheless presently the Prince and I were clattering through the town of Plassenburg like two fiends riding headlong to the pit.

Within the town the lamps were being lit in the booths, the folks busy marketing, and the watchmen already perambulating the city and crying the hours at the street corners.

But as the Prince and I drove furiously through, like pursuer and pursued, the busy streets cleared themselves in a twinkling; and we rode through lanes of faces yellow in the lamplight, or in the darker places like blurs of scrabbled whiteness. So I leaned forward and let the beast take his chance of uneven causeway and open sewer. I expected nothing less than a broken neck, and for at least half a mile, as we flew upward to the castle, I think that the certainty of naught worse than a broken arm would positively have pleasured me. At least, I would very willingly have compounded my chances for that.

Presently, without ever drawing rein, we flew beneath the dark outer port of the castle, clattered through a court paved with slippery blocks of stone, thundered over a noble drawbridge, plunged into a long and gloomy archway, and finally came out in a bright inner palace court with lamps lit all about it.

I was at the Prince's bridle ere he could dismount.

"You can ride, Captain Hugo Gottfried!" he said. "I think I will make you my orderly officer."

And so he went within, without a word more of praise or welcome.

There came past just at that moment an ancient councillor clad in a long robe of black velvet, with broad facings and rosettes of scarlet. He was carrying a roll of papers in his hand.

"What said the Prince to yon, young sir, if I may ask without offence?" said he, looking at me with a curiously sly, upward glance out of the corner of his eye, as if he suspected me of a fixed intention to tell him a lie in any case.

"If it be any satisfaction to you to know," answered I, rather piqued at his tone, "the Prince informed me that I could ride, and that he intended to make me his orderly officer. And he called me not 'young sir,' but Captain Hugo Gottfried."

"How long has he known you?" said the Chief Councillor of State. For so by his habit I knew him to be.

"Half an hour, or thereby," answered I.

"God help this kingdom!" cried the old man, tripping off, flirting his hand hopelessly in the air—"if he had known you only ten minutes you would have been either Prime-Minister or Commander-in-Chief of the army."

It was in this strange fashion that I entered the army of the Prince of Plassenburg, a service which I shall ever look back upon with gratitude, and count as having brought me all the honors and most of the pleasures of my life.

Half an hour or so afterwards the blowing of trumpets and the thunder of the new leathern cannon announced that the Princess and her train were entering the palace. The Prince came down to greet them on the threshold in a new and magnificent dress.

"The Prince's officer-in-waiting to attend upon his Highness!" cried a herald in fine raiment of blue and yellow.

I looked about for the man who was to be my superior in my new office—that is, if Prince Karl should prove to have spoken in earnest.

"The Prince's orderly to attend upon him!" again proclaimed the herald, more impatiently.'

I saw every eye turn upon me, and I began to feel a gentle heat come over me. Presently I was blushing furiously. For I was still in my riding-clothes, and even they had not been changed after the adventure of the Brick-dust Town. So that they were in no wise fitting to attend upon a mighty dignitary.

The Prince of Plassenburg looked round.

"Ha!" he said; "this is not well—I had forgotten. My orderly ought to have been duly arrayed by this time."

"Pardon, my Prince," said I, "but all the apparel I have is upon my sumpter horse, which comes in the train of the Princess."

My master looked right and left in his quickly imperious and yet humorous manner.

"Here, Count von Reuss," he said to a tall, handsome, heavily jowled young man, "I pray you strip off thy fine coat for an hour, and lend it to my new officer-in-waiting. The ladies will admire thee more than ever in thy fine flowered waistcoat, with silk sleeves and frilled purfles of lace!"

The young man, Von Reuss, looked as if he desired much to tell the Prince to go and be hanged. But there was something in the bearing of Karl of Plassenburg, usurper as they called him, the like of which for command I have never seen in the countenance and manner of any lawfully begotten prince in the world.

So, beckoning me into an antechamber, and swearing evilly under his breath all the time, the young man stripped off his fine coat, and offered it to me with one hand, without so much as looking at me. He gave it indeed churlishly, as one might give a dole to a loathsome beggar to be rid of his importunity.

"I thank you, sir," said I, "but more for your obedience to the Prince than for the fashion of your courtesy to me."

Yet for all that he answered me never a syllable, but turned his head and played with his mustache till his man-servant brought him another coat.

CHAPTER XXVII

ANOTHER MAN'S COAT

I followed the Prince without another word, and when he received the Princess I had the happiness of taking the Little Playmate by the hand and conducting her as gallantly as I could into the palace. And I was glad, for it helped to allay a kind of reproachful feeling in my heart, which would keep tugging and gnawing there whenever I was not thinking of anything else. I feared lest, in the throng and press of new experiences, I might a little have neglected or been in danger of forgetting the love of the many years and all the sweetness of our solitary companionship.

Nevertheless, I knew well that I loved those sweetest eyes of hers more than all the words of men and women and priests.

And even as I helped her to dismount, I went over and told her so.

It was just when I held her in my arms for a moment as she dismounted. She clung to me, and methought I heard a little sob.

"Do not ever be unkind, Hugo," she said. "I am very lonely. I wish, with all my heart, I were back again in the old Red Tower."

"Unkind—never while I live, little one," I whispered in her ear. "Cheer your heart, and tomorrow your sorrows will wear off, and you and I both shall find friendship in the strange land."

"I hate the Princess! And I shall never like her as long as I live!" she said, with that certain concentrated dislike which only good women feel towards those a degree less innocent, specially when the latter are well to look upon.

There was no time to reply immediately as I conducted her up the steps. For I had to keep my eyes open to observe how the Prince conducted himself, and in the easy ceremonial of Plassenburg it chanced that I happened upon nothing extravagant.

"But, Helene, you said a while ago that you hated *me*!" I said, after a little pause, smiling down at her.

"Did I?" she answered. "Surely nay!"

"Ah, but 'tis true as your eyes," I persisted. "Do you not remember when I had cut the calf's head off with the axe? You did not love the thought of the Red Tower so much then!"

"Oh, *that*!" she said, as if the discrepancy had been fully explained by the inflexion of her voice upon the word.

But she pressed my hand, so I cared not a jot for logic.

"You do not love her, you are sure?" she said, looking up at me when we came to the darker turn of the stairs, for the corkscrews were narrower in the ancient castle than in the new palace below.

"Not a bit!" said I, heartily, without any more pretence that I did not understand what she meant.

She pressed my hand again, momentarily slipping her own down off my arm to do it.

"It is not that I love you, Hugo, or that I want you to love me," she said, like one who explains that which is plain already, "except, of course, as your Little Playmate. But I could not bear that you should care about that—that woman."

It was evident that there were to be stirring times in the Castle of Plassenburg, and that I, Hugo Gottfried, was to have my share of them.

As soon as we had arrived at the banqueting-hall, the Prince beckoned me and presented me formally to the Lady Ysolinde.

"Your Highness, this is Captain Hugo Gottfried, my new officer-in-waiting."

The Princess bowed gravely and held out her hand. Her aqua-marine eyes were bent upon me, suffused with a certain quick and evident pleasure which became them well.

"Your Highness has chosen excellently. I can bear witness that the Captain Gottfried is a brave—a very brave man," she said.

And at that moment I was most grateful to her for the testimony. For behind us stood the young Von Reuss, pulling at his mustache and looking very superciliously over at me.

Then the Lady Ysolinde withdrew to her own apartments, and that day I got no more words with her nor yet with Helene.

The Prince also went to his room, and I remained where I was, deeming that for the present my duty was done.

The servant of the man whose coat I wore stood with another servitor close at hand—indeed, many of all ranks stood about.

"That is the fellow," I heard one say, tauntingly, meaning me to hear—"peacocking it there in my master's coat!"

His companion laughed contumeliously, at which the passion within me suddenly stirred. I gave one of them the palm of my hand, and as the other fell hastily back my foot took him.

"What ho, there! No quarrelling among the lackeys!" cried Von Reuss, insolently, from the other side of the room.

"Were you, by any chance, speaking to me?" said I, politely, looking over at him.

"Why, yes, fellow!" he said. "If you squabble with the waiting-men concerning cast-off clothes, you had better do it in the stables, where, as you say, your own wardrobe is kept."

"Sir," said I, "the coat I wear, I wear by the command of your Prince. It shall be immediately returned to you when the Prince permits me to go off duty. In the mean time, pray take notice that I am Captain Hugo Gottfried, officer-in-waiting to the Prince Karl of Plassenburg, and that my sword is wholly at your service."

"You are," retorted Von Reuss, "the son of my uncle Casimir's Hereditary Executioner, and one day you may be mine. Let that be sufficient honor for you."

"That I may be yours is the only part of my father's hereditary office I covet!" said I, pointedly.

And certainly I had him there, for immediately he turned on his heel and would have walked away.

But this I could not permit. So I strode sharply after him, and seizing him by his embroidered shoulder-strap, I wheeled him about.

"But, sir," said I, "you have insulted an officer of the Prince. Will you answer for that with your sword, or must I strike you on the face each time I meet you to quicken your sense of honor?"

Before he had time to answer the Prince came in.

"What, quarrelling already, young Spitfire!" he cried. "I made you my orderly—not my disorderly."

Von Reuss and I stood blankly enough, looking away from one another.

"What was the quarrel?" asked the Prince, when he had seated himself at table.

I looked to Von Reuss to explain. For indeed I was somewhat awed to think that thus early in my new career I had embroiled myself with the nephew of Duke Casimir, even though, like myself, he was in exile and dependent upon, the liberality of Prince Karl.

But, since he did not speak, I made bold to say: "Sire, the Count von Reuss taunted me with wearing a borrowed coat, and called me a servitor, because by birth I am the son of the Hereditary Executioner of the Wolfmark. So I told him I was an officer of your household, and that my sword was much at his service."

"So you are," cried the Prince—"so you are—a servitor! So is he—young fools both! And as for being son of the Hereditary Executioner, it is throughout all our German land an honorable office. Once I was assistant executioner myself, and wished with all my heart that I had been principal, and so pocketed the guilders. No more of this folly, Von Reuss. I am ashamed of you, and to a new-comer! Hear ye, sir, I will not have it! I will e'en resume my old trade and do a little justicing on my own account. Shake hands this instant, you young bantams!"

And the Prince sat back in his chair and looked grimly at us. I went a step forward. But Von Reuss held aloof.

"Provost Marshal!" cried the Prince, in a voice which made every one in the room jump and all the glasses ring on the table—"bring a guard!"

The Provost Marshal advanced, bowed, and was departing, when Von Reuss came forward and held his hand out, at first sulkily, but afterwards readily enough.

Then we shook hands solemnly and stiffly, of course loving each other not one whit better.

"Ah," said the Prince, "I thought you would! For if you had not, your uncle, Duke Casimir, might have been a Duke without either an heir to his Dukedom or a successor to his Hereditary Justicer."

"Now sit down, lads, sit down and agree!" he said, after a pause. "The ladies come not to table tonight. So now begin and tell me all the affair of the Earthhouses. I must ride and see the place. I declare I grow rotten and thewless in this dull Plassenburg, where they dare not stick so much as a knife in one another, all for fear of Karl Miller's Son! Since I cannot adventure forth on my own account, I am become a man that wearies for news. Tell me every part of the affair, concealing nothing. But if you can, relate even your own share in it as faithfully as becomes a modest youth."

So I told him at length all that hath already been told, giving as far as I could the credit to Jorian and Boris, as indeed was only their desert.

Whereupon the tale being finished, the Prince said: "Have the two archers up!"

And while the pursuivant had gone for them, the old Councillor leaned across the table and whispered: "Enter Field-Marshal Jorian and General Boris!"

But when the archers came in and stood like a pair of kitchen pokers, the Prince ordered them to tell the story.

Jorian turned his head to Boris, and Boris turned his head to Jorian. They both made a little impatient gesture, which said: "Tell it you!"

But neither appeared to be able to speak first.

"Wind them up with a cup of wine apiece!" cried the hearty Prince; "surely that will set one of them off."

Two great flagons of wine were handed to Jorian and Boris, and they drank as if one machine had been propelling their internal workings, throwing off the liquor with beautiful unanimity and then bringing their cups to the position of salute as if they had been musketoons at the new French drill. After which each of them, having finished, gave the little cough of content and appreciation, which among the archers means manners.

But nevertheless the Prince's information with regard to the affair of Erdberg was not increased.

"Go on!" he cried, impatiently, looking at Jorian and Boris sternly.

They were still silent.

"This officer, Captain Hugo Gottfried," said the Prince, looking at me, "tells me that the credit of the preservation of the Princess among the cave folk is due to you two brave men."

"He lies!" said Wendish Jorian, with a face like a blank wall.

"Good!" muttered Boris, approvingly.

"He did it himself!" said Boris, adding, after a pause—"with an axe!"

"Good!" quoth Jorian.

"He cut a calf's head off!" said Jorian, as a complete explanation of how the preserving of the Princess was effected.

Whereat all laughed, and the Prince more than any. For ever since he drank his first draught of wine, he had begun to mellow.

"Well, hearty fellows, what reward would you have for your great bravery?"

They turned their heads simultaneously inward without moving any other part of their bodies. They nodded to one another.

"Well," cried the Prince, "what reward do you desire?"

"Now for the Field-Marshal's wand!" said the Councillor near to me, under his breath.

"Twelve dozen Rhenish!" said Jorian.

The Prince looked at Boris.

"And you?" he said.

"Twelve dozen Rhenish!" said Boris, without moving a muscle.

"God Bacchus!" cried the Prince, "you will empty my cellars between you, and I shall not have a sober archer for a month. But you shall have it. Go!"

Jorian and Boris saluted with a wink to each other as they wheeled, which said, as plain as monk's script or plainer, "Good!"

CHAPTER XXVIII

THE PRINCE'S COMPACT

In spite of all drawbacks and difficulties (and I had my share of them) I loved Plassenburg. And especially I loved the Prince. The son, so they said, of a miller in the valley of the Almer, he had entered the guard of the last Prince of Plassenburg, much as I had now entered his own service. Prince Dietrich had taken a fancy to him, and advanced him so rapidly that, after the disastrous war with Duke Casimir of the Mark and the death of the last legitimate Prince, Karl, the miller's son, having set himself to reorganize the army, succeeded so well that it was not long before he found himself the source of all authority in Plassenburg.

Thereafter he gave to the decimated and heartless land adequate defences and complete safety against foreign foes, together with security for life and property, under equal laws, within its own borders. So, in time, no man saying him nay, Karl Miller's Son became the Prince of Plassenburg, and his seat was more secure upon his throne than that of any legitimate prince for a thousand miles all round about.

After the quarrel with Von Reuss, the Prince, for reasons of his own, favored me with a great deal of his society. He was often graciously pleased to talk concerning his early difficulties.

"When I was an understrapper," he was wont to say, "the land was overswarmed and eaten up by officialdom. I could not see the good meat wasted upon crawlers. 'Get to work,' said I, 'or ye shall neither eat nor crawl!'

"'We must eat—to beg we are not ashamed, to steal is the right of our noble Ritterdom,' the crawlers replied.

"'So,' said I, '*bitte*—as to that we shall see!'

"Then I made me a fine gallows, builded like that outside Paris, which I had seen once when on an embassy for Prince Dietrich. It was like a castle, with walls twelve feet thick, and on the beams of it room for a hundred or more to swing, each with his six feet of clearance, all comfortable, and no complaints.

"Then came the crawlers and asked me what this fine thing was for.

"'For the sacred Ritterdom of Plassenburg!' answered I, 'if it will not cease to burn houses and to ravish and carry off honest men's wives and daughters.'

"'But you must catch us!' quoth Crawlerdom. 'Walls fourteen feet thick!' said they.

"'Content,' cried I; 'there is the more fun in catching you. Only the end is the same—that is to say, my new, well-ventilated castle out there on the heath, fine girdles and neck-pieces and anklets of iron, and six feet of clearance for each of you to swing in.'

"So they went back to their castles, and robbed and ravished and rieved, even as did their fathers for a thousand years, thinking no evil. But I took my soldiers, whom in seven years' service I had taught to obey orders-two foot of clearance did well enough for the disobedient among them, not being either ritters or men of mark. And I, Karl the Miller's brat, as at that time they called me in contempt, borrowed cannon—great lumbering things—from my friend the Margrave George, down there to the south. A great work we had dragging them up to Plassenburg by rope and chain and laboring plough oxen. We shot them off before the fourteen-feet walls. Then arose various clouds of dust, shriekings, surrenderings, crying of 'Forgive us, great Prince, we never meant to do it,' followed, as I had said, by the six-feet clearances. But these in time I had to reduce to four—so great became the competition for places in my new Schloss Müllerssohn.

"But 'Once done, well done—done forever!' is my motto. So since that time the winds have mostly blown through my Schloss untainted, and the sons of Ritterdom, magnanimous captains and honest bailies of quiet bailiwicks, are my very good friends and faithful officers."

Prince Karl the Miller's Son was silent a moment.

"But I am still looking out for another man with a head-piece to come after me. I have no son, and if I had, the chances are ten to one that he would be either a milksop or a flittermouse painted blue. Milksops I hate, and send to the monkeries. I can endure flittermice painted blue, but they must wear petticoats—and pretty petticoats too. Have you observed those of the Princess?" said he, abruptly changing the subject.

"The Princess's flittermice?" I faltered, not well knowing what I said, for he had turned roughly and suddenly upon me.

"Aye, marry, you may say it! But I meant the Princess's wilicoats!"

"No," said I, as curtly as I could, for the subject had its obvious limitations.

"Ah, they are pretty ones," said Karl, "I assure you. She has at least an undeniable taste in lace and cambric. They say in other lands—not in this—though I would not hinder them if they did—that she wears the under-garments of men and rules the state. But I think not so. The Princess is a better Queen than wife, a better woman than either."

On this subject also I had nothing to say which I dared venture to the husband of the Lady Ysolinde.

"She read my horoscope," said I, weakly, searching for something in the corners of my brain to change the subject.

"How so?" said the Prince, quickly.

"First in a crystal and then in a pool of ink," I replied.

"It was a good horoscope and of a fortunate ending?"

"On the whole—yes!" said I; "though there was much in it that I could not understand."

"Like enow!" laughed the Prince; "I warrant she could not understand it herself! It is ever the way of the ink-pool folk."

Then ensued a silence between us.

Prince Karl remained long with his head resting on his hand. He looked critically at the twisted stem of his wineglass, twirling it between his thick fingers.

"The Princess loves you!" he said, at last, looking shrewdly at me from beneath his gray brows.

It was spoken half as a question and half as information.

"Loves me?" stammered I, the blood sucking back to my heart and leaving my head light and tingling.

The Prince nodded calmly.

"So they say!" said he.

"My Lord, it is a thing impossible!" cried I, earnestly. "I am but a poor lad—and she has been kind to me. But of love no word has been spoken. Besides—"

And I stopped.

"Out with it, man!" said the Prince, more like, as it seemed to me, a comrade inviting a confidence than a great Prince speaking to a newly made officer.

"Well, I—I love the Little Playmate."

It came out with a rush at last.

"Oh!" said he; "that is bad. I hope that is not a matter arranged, a thing serious. For if the Princess knows as much, the young woman will not have her troubles to seek in the Palace of Plassenburg."

I hung my head and said naught, save that Helene declared she loved me not, but that I thought she was mistaken.

"Ah, then," cried the Prince, like one exceedingly relieved, "it is but some boy and girl affair. That is better. She may change her mind, as you will certainly change yours—and that several times—among the ladies of the court. I was in hopes—"

And the Prince stopped in his turn, not from bashfulness, but rather like a man who desires more carefully to choose his words.

"I was in hopes," he went on, speaking slowly, "that if the Princess loved your boy's face and liked my conversation (which I may say without pride that I think she does) you and I together might have kept her at home. So over-much wandering is not good for the state. Also it gets her a name beyond all manner of ill-doing within-doors."

Once more I knew not well what to answer to this speech of the Prince's, so I remained discreetly silent.

"I have seen the Princess's flittermice about her before, often enough (I thank thee for the word, Sir Captain.), but this is the first time she has performed the ink-pool and crystal foolery with any man. There is no great harm in the Princess. In the things of love she is as inflammable as the ink, and as soft as the crystal. Fear not, Joseph, Potiphera may be depended upon not to proceed to extremities. But I was in some hopes that you and I could have arranged matters between us, being both men—aye, and honorable men."

I saw that Karl Miller's Son looked sad and troubled.

"Prince, you love the Princess!" said I, thrusting out my hand to him before I thought. He did not take it, but instead he thrust a flagon of wine into it, as if I had asked for that—yet the thing was not done by way of a rebuff. I saw that plainly.

"Pshaw! What does a grizzle-pate with love?" said he, gruffly. "Nevertheless, I was in hopes."

"Prince Karl," said I, "I give you word of honor, 'tis not as you say or they say. The Princess has indeed done me the honor to be friendly—"

"To hold your hand!" he murmured, softly, like a chorus.

"Well, to be friendly, and—"

"To caress your cheek?" put in the Prince, gently as before.

"Done me the honor to be friendly—"

"To play with your curls, lad?"

"The Princess—" I began, all in a tremor. For anything more awkward than this conversation I had never experienced. It bathed me in a drip of cold sweat.

"To kiss you, perhaps, at the waygoing?" he insinuated.

"No!" thundered I, at last. "Prince, you do your Princess great wrong."

He lifted his hand in a gentle, deprecating way, most unlike the rider who had ridden so fast and so hotly that night of our coming.

"You mistake me, sir," he said. "On the contrary, I have the greatest respect for the Princess Ysolinde. I would not wrong her for the world. But I know her track of old. You are a brave lad, and, after all, I fear there is something in that calf-love of yours—devil take it!"

I thought I could now dimly discern whither the Prince's plans were tending.

"Your Highness," said I, "I am a young man and of little experience. I cannot tell why you have chosen to speak so freely to me. But I am your servant, and, in all that hurts not the essence and matter of my love for the Little Playmate, I will do even as you say."

Prince Karl grasped my hand.

"Ah, well said!" he cried. "You are running your head into a peck of troubles, though. And you are likely to have some experience of womenkind shortly—a thing which does no brisk young fellow any harm, unless he lets them come between him and his career. Women are harmless enough, so that you keep them well down to leeward. I am Baltic-bred, and have ever held to this—that you may sail unscathed through fleets of farthingales, so being that you keep the wind well on your quarter, and see the fair-way clear before you."

I did not at the time understand half he said, but I knew we had made some sort of a bargain. And I thought, with an aching, unsatisfied heart, that though it might be well enough for an iron-gray and cynical old Prince, the thing would hardly commend itself to Helene, my Little

Playmate, to whom I had so recently spoken loving words, sweeter than ever before.

"Devil take all Princes and Princesses!" I said, as I thought, to myself. But I must have spoken aloud, for the Prince laughed.

"Do not waste good prayers needlessly," he said; "he will!"

And so, with a careless and humorsome wave of his hand to one side, he went down the staircase, and so out into the quadrangle of the Palace.

CHAPTER XXIX

LOVES ME—LOVES ME NOT

Now how this plan of my Lord Prince's worked in the Palace of Plassenburg I find it difficult to tell without writing myself down a "painted flittermouse," as the Prince expressed it. I was in high favor with my master; well liked also by most of the hard-driving, rough-riding young soldiers whom the miller's son had made out of the sons of dead and damned Ritterdom. I got my share of honor and good service, too, in going to different courts and bringing back all that Prince Karl needed. To exercise myself in the art of war, I hunted the border thieves and gave them short enough shrift. In a year I had made such an assault as that of the inn at Erdberg an impossibility all along the marches of our provinces.

The crusty old councillor, Leopold Dessauer, who had held office under the last Prince of the legitimate line, was ever ready to assist me with the kindest of deeds and the bitterest and saltest of words.

"What did I tell you about being Field-Marshal?" said he one day—"in Karl's kingdom the shorter the service, the higher the distinction. If you and the Prince live long enough, I shall see you carry a musketoon yet, and not one of the latest pattern, either. You will be promoted down, like a booby who has been raised by chance to the top of the class!"

"Well," said I, humbly, for I always reverenced age, "then I hope, High-Chancellor Dessauer, that I shall carry my musketoon as becomes a brave man!"

"I do not doubt it!" said he. "And that is the most hopeful thing I have seen about you yet. It is just possible, on the other hand, that you may yet rule and the Prince carry the piece."

"God forbid!" said I, heartily. For next to my own father, of all men I loved the Prince.

"The Princess hath a pretty hand," remarked Dessauer casually, as if he had said, "It will rain tomorrow!"

"I' faith, yes!" said I; "what have you been at to find out that?"

"Weak—weak!" he said, shaking his head. "I fear you will wreck on that rock. It is your blind peril!"

"My blind peril!" cried I. "What may that be, High Councillor?"

"Ah, lad," he said, smiling with that wise, all-patient smile which the aged affect when they mean to be impressive, yet know how useless is their wisdom, "it was never intended by the Almighty that any man should have eyes all round his head. That is why He fixed two in front, and made them look straight forward. That is also why He made us a little lower (generally a good deal lower) than the angels!"

I heard him as if I heard him not.

"You do me the honor to follow me?" he said, looking at me. He was, I think, conscious that my eyes wandered to the door, for indeed I was expecting the Little Playmate to come down every minute.

"Ah! yes, you follow indeed," he said, bitterly, "but it is the trip of feet, the flirt of farthingales down the turret steps. No matter! As I was saying, every man has his blind peril. He can see the thousand. He provides laboriously against them. He blocks every avenue of risk, he locks every dangerous door, and lo! there is the thousand-and-first right before him, yawning wide open, which he does not see—his Blind Peril!"

"And what, High-Councillor Dessauer, is my blind peril?"

"I will tell you, Hugo," he said; "not that you will believe or alter a hair. A man may do many things in this world, but one thing he cannot do. He cannot kiss the fingers of a Princess—dainty fingers, too, separating finger from finger—and kiss also the Princess's maid of honor on the mouth. The combination is certainly entertaining, but like the Friar's powder it is somewhat explosive."

"And how," asked I, "may you know all that ?"

The old man nodded his head sagely.

"Neither by ink-pool nor yet by scrying! All the same, I know. Moreover, your peril is not a blind peril only, but a blind man's peril. Ye must choose, and that quickly, little son—fingers or lips."

I heard the rustle of a skirt down the stair. It was the light, springing tread of the one I loved first and best, last and only.

"By the twelve gods, lips!" cried I, and made for the door.

And I heard the chuckling laughter of High-Chancellor Dessauer behind me as I followed Helene down the stairs. It sounded like the decanting of mellow wine, long hidden in darksome cellars, and now, in the flower of its age, bringing to the light the smiling of ancient vineyards and the shining of forgotten suns.

I found Helene arrived before me in the rose-garden. She did not turn round as I came, though she heard me well enough. Instead she walked on, plucking at a marguerite.

"Loves me—loves me *not*!" she said, bearing upon the last word with triumphant accent, as she continued to dismantle the poor flower.

And flashing round upon me with the solitary petal in her hand, she presented it with a low bow, in elfish mockery of the manner of the court exquisite.

"Ah, true flower!" she said, apostrophizing the bare stalk, "a flower cannot lie. It has not a glozing tongue. It cannot change back and forth. The sun shines. It turns towards the sun. The sun leaves the skies. It shuts itself up and waits his return. Ah,-true flower, dear flower, how unlike a man you are!"

"Helene," said I, "you have learned conceits from the catch-books. You quarrel by rote. Were I as eager to answer me, I might say: 'Ah, false flower, you grow out of the foulness underneath. You give your fragrance to all without discretion—a common lover, prodigal of favors, fit only to be torn to shreds by pretty, spiteful fingers, and to die at last with a lie in your mouth. Again I say—false flower!'"

"You can turn the corners, Sir Juggler, with the cup and ball of words," answered Helene. "So much they have already taught you in a court. But there is one thing that your fine-feathered tutors have not taught you—to make love to two women in one house and hide it from both of them. Hot and cold may not come too near each other. They will mix and make lukewarm of both."

A wise observation, and one that I wished I had made myself.

"May the devil take all princes and princesses!" I began, as I had done to the Prince himself.

Helene shook her head.

"Hugo," she said, "I was but a simpleton when I came hither, and knew nothing. Now I am wise, and I know!"

She touched her forehead with her finger, just where the curls were softest and prettiest.

"Oh, you have learned to be thrice more beautiful than ever you were!" I said, impetuously.

"So I am often told," answered she, calmly.

"Who dared tell you?" cried I, quick as fire, laying my hand on my sword.

"The false common flowers by the wayside tell me!" said Helene, pertly.

"Let them beware, or I will take their heads off for rank weeds!" I answered.

For at that time, in the Court of Plassenburg, we talked in figures and romance words. We had indeed become so familiar with the mode that we could use no other, even in times of earnestness. So that a man would go to be hanged or married with a quipsome conceit on his lips.

"I think, Sir Janus Double-tongue," she said, "that you would not be the worse of a little medicine of your own concocting."

And with that she swept her skirts daintily about and tripped down in to the pleasaunce of flowers, to make which the Prince Karl had brought a skilled gardener all the way from France.

I prowled about the higher terrace, moodily watching the sky and thinking on the morrow's weather. And by-and-by I saw one come forth from among the cropped Dutch hedges, and stride across to where Helene walked with something white in her hand. I could see her again picking a flower to pieces, and methought I could hear the words. My jealous fancy conjured up the ending, "Loves me not—loves me! Loves me not!"

She turned even as she had done to me. The newcomer was that sneering Court fop, the Count von Reuss, Duke Casimir's nephew—still in hiding from the wrath of his uncle. For at that time hardly any court in Germany was without one or two of these hangers-on, and a bad, reckless, ill-contriving breed they were at Plassenburg, as doubtless elsewhere.

Then grew my heart hard and bitter, and yet, in a moment afterwards, was again only wistful and sad.

"She had been safer," thought I, "in the old Red Tower than playing flower fancies with such a man!"

For I had seen the very devil look out of his eye—which indeed it did as often as he cast it on a fair woman. In especial, I longed to throttle him each time he turned to watch Helene as she went by. And here she was walking with him, and talking pleasantly too, in the rose garden of the palace.

"Ah, devil take all princes and princesses!" said I. This one, it is true, was only a count, and disinherited. But I felt that the thing was the Prince's doing, and that it was for the sake of the covenant he had made with me that I was compelled to put up with such a toad as Von Reuss crawling and besliming the fair garden of my love.

It was an evening without clouds—everything shining clear after rain, the scent of the flowers rising like incense so full and sweet that you could almost see it. The unnumbered birds were every one awake, responsive and emulous. The deep silence of midsummer was broken up. It was like another spring.

The Princess Ysolinde came out to take the air. She was wrapped in her gown of sea-green silk, with sparkles of dull copper upon it. The dress fitted her like a snake's skin, and glittered like it too as she swayed her lithe body in walking.

"Ha, Hugo," she said, "I thought I should find you here!"

I did not say that if another had been kinder she might have found me elsewhere and otherwise employed. I had at least the discretion to leave things as they were. For the time to speak plainly was not yet.

She took my arm, and we paced up and down.

"Princess—" I began.

"Ysolinde!" corrected she, softly.

It was an old and unsettled contention between us.

"Well then, Ysolinde, tomorrow must I ride to fight the men of mine own country of the Wolfmark. I like not the duty. But since it must be, for the sake of the brave Prince, it shall be well done."

"You do not say 'For your sake, Ysolinde'?" she answered, pensively.

"No," I said, bluntly, "'for the Prince's sake.'"

"You would do all things for the Prince's sake—nothing for mine!" said the Princess, withdrawing her hand.

"On the contrary, Lady Ysolinde," I made answer, "I do all things for your sake. Save for the sake of your good-will, I should now be elsewhere."

Which was true enough. I should have been in the garden pleasaunce beneath, and probably with my sword out, arguing the case with Von Reuss.

But she pressed my arm, for she understood that I had delayed a day from my duty for her sake. So touched at heart was Ysolinde that she slipped her hand down from my arm and took my hand instead, flirting a corner of her shawl cleverly over both, to hide the fact from the men-at-arms—as Helene could not have done to save her life. But every maid of honor who passed noted and knew, lifting eyebrows at once another, I doubt not, as soon as we passed, which thing made me feel like a fool and blush hotly. For I knew that ere they were couched that night every maid of them would tell Helene, and with pleasure in the telling too.

"Devil take—" I began and stopped.

"What did you say?" asked Ysolinde, almost tenderly.

"That if I come not back again from the Wolfmark it will be the better for all of us!" I made answer, which was indeed the sense if not the exact text of my remark.

"Nay," she said, shuddering, "not better for me that am companionless!"

"Why so?" said I, boldly. "You do not love me. Deep at the bottom of your heart you love your husband, Karl the Prince. You know there is no man like him. Me you do not love at all."

"You will not let me," she said, softly, almost like a shy country maiden.

"Ah, if I had, you would have slain me long ere this," said I, "for I read you like a child's horn-book that he plays battledore with. 'Have not—*love*! Have—*hate*.' There you are, all in brief, my Lady Ysolinde."

"It is false," laughed she; "but nevertheless I love greatly to hear you call me Ysolinde."

She netted her fingers in mine beneath the shawl. Well might the High Councillor say that she had a beautiful hand. Though, God wot, much he knew about it. For Ysolinde of Plassenburg could speak with her hand, love with it, be angry with it, hate with it—and kill with it.

"I am an experiment," said I; "one indeed that has lasted you a little longer than the others, my Lady Ysolinde, only because you have not come to the end of me so soon."

"Pshaw!" she said, pushing me from her, for we were at the turning of a path, "you love another. That is the amulet against infection that you carry. Yet sometimes I think that that other is only your hateful, plain-favored, vainly conceited self!"

I saw the Prince sit alone, according to his custom, in an arbor behind us at that very moment—and judge if I blushed or no. But the Princess saw him not, being eager upon her flouting of me.

"I tell you," she cried, scornfully and disdainfully, "there is nothing interesting about you but the blueness of your eyes, and that any monk can make upon parchment, aye, and deeper and bluer, with his lapis-lazuli. An experiment!—Why should I, Ysolinde of Plassenburg, experiment with you, the son of the Red Axe of the Wolfsberg?"

"Nay, that I know not," I answered; "but yet I am indeed no more than your arrow-butts, your target of practice, your whipping-boy, to be slung at and arrow-drilled and bullet-pitted at your pleasure!"

"I dare say," she said, bitterly; "and all the time you go scathless—no more heart-stricken than if summer flies lighted on thee. Away with such a man; he is the ghost of a man—a simulacrum—no true lover!"

"At your will, Princess. I shall indeed go away. I will tomorrow seek the spears. But, after all, you will not send me forth in anger?" I said, with a strong conviction that I knew the answer.

"And why not?" said she.

"Because," I replied, looking at her, "I am, after all, the one man who believes thoroughly in your heart's deep inward goodness. I believe in you even when you do not believe in yourself. I can affirm, for I know better than you know yourself. You cover the beauty of your heart from others. You flout and jeer. Above all, you experiment dangerously with words and actions. But, after all, I am necessary to you. You will not send me away in anger. For you need some one to believe in the soundness of your heart. And I, Hugo Gottfried, am that man!"

"Hence, flatterer!" cried the lady, smiling, but well pleased. "It is known to all that I am the Old Serpent—the deceiver—the ill fruit of the Knowledge of Evil. And now you say of Good also! And what is more and worse, you expect me to believe you. Wherein you also experiment! I pray you, do not so. That is to you the forbidden fruit. Goodnight. Go, now, and pray for a more truthful tongue!"

And with that she went in, the copper spangles glancing at her waist red as the light on ripe wheat, and all her tall figure lissome as the bending corn.

CHAPTER XXX

INSULT AND CHALLENGE

Now, because there is still so much to tell, and so little time and space to tell it in, I must go forward rapidly. In these dull times of grouting peace, when men become like penned pigs, waking up only at feeding-time, they have no knowledge of how swiftly life went when every day brought a new living friend or a new dead enemy, when love and hate awakened fresh and fresh with each morrow's sun—and when I was young.

Perhaps that last is the true reason. But when the Baltic norther snorts without, and mine ancient thigh-wound twinges down where my hand rests, naturally I have no better resource than to fall to the goose-quill. And lo! long ere I am done with the first page, and have the ink no more than half-way to the roots of my hair, I am again in the midst of the ringing hoofs of the foray. I hear the merry dinting of steel on steel; the sullen *chug-chug* of the wheels of Foul Peg, the Margrave's great cannon, which more than once he lent our Prince; the oaths of the men-at-arms shouldering her up, apostrophizing most indecently her fat haunches, and the next moment getting tossed aside like ninepins by her unexpected lurches. Ah, the times that were when I was young!

I see these gallants about our later courts—Lord help them, sons of mine own, too, some of them—year in and year out, crossing their legs and staring at the gilded points of their shoon. All are grown so tame—none now to ride a-questing in the Baltic forest for border brigands—indeed, there be no brigands to quest for.

But I forget. Time was when I looked love, and I too had shoon, aye, with golden tips to match the armor of honor which the Prince gave me after I had led my first regiment to victory—even as the Lady Ysolinde had said. And noble shoes of price they were.

And I could make love, too, when I had the chance. But, nevertheless, not more than one day in six—spending the rest in the new training of my men, the perfecting of their equipment, the choosing of their horses, and the providing for their stores.

God wot—it was a good time. I mind me the year when the Prince fell out with Duke Casimir, and we played over again the old tricks with him.

Never was I gladder of any quest than that to ride within sight of the Red Tower, and wave the blue and yellow of my master under the very ramparts of the Wolfsberg, and almost within hearing of the inhuman howling of its blood-hounds.

"Singe his beard!" said my master. And with a hundred riders I did it too. For though the burghers clattered to their gates, I rode to the very walls of the Wolfsberg, which for bravado I summoned to surrender. And the best of it was that no man knew me. For I had grown soldierlike and strong, and was most unlike the lad who had ridden away so meekly and almost in tears out of the gate of that very Wolfsberg.

Of my father, thank God, I saw nothing—though I doubt not he observed my troop. For doubtless he would be with his master—aged now, soured, and prone to cower about behind his guard, fearing the dagger or the poisoned bowl, seeing an enemy in every shadowy corner, and hearing the whistle of the assassin's bullet in every wind.

And, save when an honest burgher was slain by the Black Riders, the beasts of the kennels were fed on diet more ordinary than of old.

So we rode back with our prisoners, and as much plunder as we could screw out of old Burgomeister Texel and his citizens by threats of sacking the city—a deed which I was main sorry for afterwards, in the light of that which happened at a later day. But I knew not the future then, and it was as well. For the guilders paid nobly for the new-fashioned ordnance which stood us in such good stead that autumn, when we had sterner work in hand than singeing the gray beard of Duke Casimir.

Within Schloss Plassenburg things went on much as usual. Perhaps I was lax in my wooing—I cannot tell; I loved sincerely enough, of a certainty. Nor, after this, was I backward in telling Helene of it, and sometimes she would love me well enough, and then again she would not. So that I could not tell what she would be at.

Looking back upon everything now, I see clearly how that the rankling secret thorn was the accursed understanding with the Prince, that for his peace's sake I was to abide friendly with the Princess and let her try her fool experiments on me. Which she did, God wot, innocently enough— that is, for all the harm they did me. But, nevertheless, without knowing it, I kept the Little Playmate with a sore and aching heart for many and many a day.

But I made nothing of it—thinking, like a careless, ill-deserving soldier-lover, eager for success and dazzled with ambition, chiefly of my profession, of how to win battles and take fortresses against the surrounding princelings, our Karl's enemies, till one day I found Helene with her cheeks wet and her pretty lips bitten till the blood had come.

"What is't, little one? Tell me!" said I, going to her and putting my arm about her, as indeed I had some right to do, if no more than the right of having carried her up into the Red Tower in her white gown so long ago.

But she wrested herself determinedly out of my hold, saying: "Do not touch me, sir. 'Tis all your fault!"

"What is my fault, dear lass?" said I. "Tell me, and I will instantly amend it."

"Oh!" she cried, casting her hands out from her in bitter complaint, "there is nothing so meanly selfish as a man! He will say tender things— aye, and do them, too, when it liketh him. He can be, oh, so devoted and so full of his eternal affections. He is dying all for love! And then, soon as he passes out of the door he ties his sword-knot and points his mustache to his liking, and lo! there is no more of him. He goes and straightway forgets till it shall please his High Mightiness to call again. Oh! and we—we women, poor things, must stand about with our mouths open, like mossy carp in a pond, and struggle and push for such crumbs of comfort as he will deign to throw us from the full larder of his self-satisfaction!"

This was a most mighty speech for the Little Playmate, and took me entirely by surprise. For mostly she was still enough and quiet enough in her ways and speakings.

"'Tis true, sweetheart, that some men are like that," I replied, gently, "but not Hugo Gottfried, surely. When did you ever find me unkind, unthankful, unfaithful? When went I ever away and left you alone?"

"Oh, you did—you did," she cried, the tears starting from her lovely eyes, "or I should never have been insulted—treated lightly, spoken to as a staled thing of courts and camps!"

And Helene sank down beside the garden wall in an abandonment of sorrow—so that my heart grew hot and angry at the cause of her grief, to me then unknown.

I knelt down beside her and touched her lightly on one rounded, heaving shoulder.

"Dearest," said I, "I knew nothing of this. Tell me who has insulted you. As God is in His heaven, I will have my sword in his heart or nightfall, were it the Prince himself! Tell me, and by the Lord of the Innocents, I will make him eat cold steel and drink his own blood therewith!"

"Oh, it was my own fault—I know I should not have met him—let him speak to me in the garden. But you were so cold to me, Hugo. And then I thought—I thought that the Woman was taking you away from me. Also she sent me out to be—to be in his path!"

"In whose path, I bid you tell me, and what woman?"

Though the latter I knew well enough.

"The Princess," she answered, "and the Count von Reuss. Today he spoke to me of love, and spoke it hatefully, shamefully, when the Princess had bidden me go and carry her message to him. But it was with me that he desired to meet. And I—at first many days ago—I walked by his side and listened, for then he spoke courteously and like a gentleman. For you were on the high terrace, and I wished you to see. I thought—I hoped—"

And the little one broke off with tears.

"I know, I know!" cried I, contritely; "I am a blind, doting fool. In this Prince's court I thought no more of such dangers than when I had you safe and innocent, my Playmate of the Red Tower. But what did or said Von Reuss?"

"Truly he did naught, but only spoke—things for which I would have smitten him to death had I possessed a dagger. I bade him begone. And he swore he would execute his purpose yet in spite of every town's Executioner in the Empire."

"Ah, will he?" said I, a calm chill of hatred settling about my heart. "I, Hugo Gottfried, will execute him, if I have to send for my father's Red Axe to do it with—singed and scented monkey that he is."

"Nay," said Helene, "then I wish I had not told you. Perhaps he will not meddle with me again, and if you cross him he may slay thee. Remember, I have no friend here but you, Hugo!"

"Count von Reuss slay me! I could eat him up without salt or savory— a weak reed, a kerl without backbone save of buckram; why, I will shake him this day like a rat between my hands!"

So I spoke in my anger, hot with myself that I had let the Little Playmate suffer these things, and resolved that neither Prince nor Princess would stand between me and my love a moment longer.

But in all lands it takes more than Say-so to budge the stubborn wheels of circumstance.

CHAPTER XXXI

I FIND A SECOND

I meant to go directly to the Prince in his chamber and tell him that from this time forth Helene and I had resolved to battle out our lives together. But it chanced that I passed through the higher terrace on my way to the lower—a bosky place of woods, where the Prince loved to linger in of a summer afternoon, drowsing there to the singing of birds and the falling of waters. For our Karl had tastes quite beyond sour black Casimir, with his church-yard glooms and raw-bone terrors.

On the upper terrace I found Von Reuss, lolling against the parapet with other blue flittermice, his peers—he himself no flittermouse, indeed, but of the true Casimir vampire breed, horrid of tooth, nocturnal, desirous of lusts and blood.

At sight of him I went straight at mine enemy, as if I had been leading a charge.

"Sir," said I, "you are a base rascal. You have insulted the Lady Helene, maid of honor to the Princess, the adopted child of my father. Her wrongs are mine. You will do me the honor of crossing weapons with me!"

"I have not learned the art of the axe," said he, turning about, listlessly. "You expect too much, Sir Executioner!"

I wasted no more words upon him, for I had not sought him to barter insults, but to force him to meet me where I could have my anger out upon him, and avenge the tears in the eyes of my Little Playmate.

Von Reuss was drawing a glove of yellow dressed kid through his hand as he spoke. This I plucked from his fingers ere he was aware, and struck him soundly on either cheek with it before flinging it crumpled up in his face.

"Now will you fight, or must I strike you with my open hand?"

Then I saw the look of his uncle stand hell-clear in his eyes. But he was not frightened, this one, only darkly and unscrupulously vengeful.

"Foul toad's spawn, now I will have your blood!" he cried, tugging at his sword.

"We cannot fight here," said I, "within sight of the palace windows. But tonight at sundown, or tomorrow at dawn, I am at your service."

"Let it be tonight, on the common at the back of the Hirschgasse—one second, and the fighting only between principals."

Very readily I agreed to that, or anything, and then, with a wave of my hat, I went off, cudgelling my brain whom I should ask to be my second. Jorian, who was now an officer, I should have liked better than any other. But, being of the people myself, it was necessary that I should have some one of weight and standing to meet the nephew of the Duke of the Wolfmark and his friend.

Moodily pacing down the glade, which led from the second terrace and the pleasaunce, I almost overran the Prince himself. He was seated under a tree, a parchment of troubadours' songs lay by him, illuminated (to judge by the woeful pictures) by no decent monkish or clerkly hand. He had a bottle of Rhenish at hand, and looked the same hearty, hard-headed, ironic soldier he ever was, and yet, what is more strange, every inch of him a Prince.

"Whither away, young Sir Amorous," he cried, pretending great indignation at my absent-mindedness, "head among the clouds or intent as ever on the damosels? Conning madrigals for lovers' lutes, mayhap? And all the while taking no more heed of God's honest princes than if they existed only for trampling under your feet."

I asked his pardon—but indeed I had not come so nigh him as that.

"I am to fight in a private quarrel," said I, "and, truth to tell, I sorely want a second, and was pondering whom to ask."

The Prince sighed.

"Ah, lad," he said, "once I had wished no better than to stand up at your side myself. I was not a Prince then though; and again, these laws—these too strict laws of mine! But what is the matter of your duel, and with whom?"

"Well," said I, "I have slapped Count von Reuss's chafts with his own glove, in the midst of his friends, on the upper terrace."

'Tis possible I may be mistaken, I suppose, but I did think then, and still do think, that I saw evident tokens of pleasure on the face of the Prince.

"And the cause—"

I hesitated, blushing temple-high, I dare say, in spite of the growth of my mustaches.

"A woman, then!" cried the Prince. Then, more low, he added, "Not the—?"

He would have said the Princess, for he paused, in his turn, with a graver look on his face.

So I hastened with my explanation.

"He insulted the young Lady Helene, maid of honor to the Princess, who is to me as a sister, having been brought up with me in one house. Her honor is my honor, both by this tie, and because, as you know, we have long loved each other. Therefore will I fight Count von Reuss to the death, and a good cause enough."

The Prince whistled—an unprincely habit, but then all millers' lads whistle at their work. So Prince Karl whistled as he meditated.

"I see further into this matter than that—if indeed you love this maid. There be other things to be thought upon than vengeance upon Von Reuss! Does the Princess know of this?"

"Suspect she may," said I; "know she cannot. It was only half an hour ago that I knew myself."

"Ha," said he, musingly, with his beard in his hand, "it hath gone no further than that. Were it not, if possible, better to conceal the cause yet a while that our compact may go on? It were surely easy enough to invent an excuse for the quarrel."

"Prince," answered I, earnestly, "this bargain of ours hath gone on over long already, in that it hath brought a true maid's honor and happiness in question. And a maid also whom I am bound to love. I will ask you this, have I been a good soldier and servant to you or not?"

"Aye to that!" quoth the Prince, heartily.

"Have I ever asked fee or reward for aught I have tried to do?"

"Nay," he said; "but you have gotten some of both without asking."

"Will you grant me the first boon I have asked of you since you became Prince and Master to Hugo Gottfried?"

"I will grant it, if it be not to separate us as friend and friend," said my master at once.

It was like the noble Prince thus to speak of our relation. I took his hand in mine to kiss it, but this he would not permit.

"Shake hands like a man," he said, "or else kiss me upon the cheek. My hand is for young, blue-painted flittermice to kiss, for whose souls' good it is to put their lips to the hand that has shifted the meal-bags."

And with that Prince Karl embraced me heartily, and kissed me on both cheeks.

"Now for this request of yours!" said he, looking expectantly at me.

"It is this," I answered him directly: "Give me a district to govern, a tower to dwell in, and Helene to be my wife."

"Nay, but these are three things, and you stipulated but for one. Choose one!" he said.

"Then give me Helene to wife!" I cried, instantly.

"Spoken like a lover," said the good Prince. "You shall have her if I have the giving of her, which I beg leave to doubt. Something tells me that much water will run under the bridges ere that wedding comes to pass. But so far as it concerns me the thing is done. Yet remember, I have never been one wisely to marry, nor yet to give in marriage."

He smiled a dry, humorsome smile—the smile of a shrewd miller casting up his thirlage upon the mill door when he sees the fields of his parish ripe to the harvest.

"I wonder why, with her crystals and her ink-pools, the Princess hath not foreseen this. By the blue robe of Mary, there will be proceedings when she does know. I think I shall straightway go a-hunting in the mountains with my friend the Margrave!"

He considered a moment longer, and took a deep draught of Rhenish.

"Then the matter of a second," continued the Prince; "he is to fight, of course?"

"No," said I; "principals only."

"I wonder," said the Prince, meditatively, "if there be anything in that. It is not our Plassenburg custom between two young men, well surrounded with brisk lads. Three seconds, and three to meet them point to point, was more our ancient way."

"It was specially arranged at the request of the Count von Reuss," I told the Prince.

"If there is to be no fighting of seconds, what do you say to old Dessauer? He was a pretty blade in my time, and has all the etiquette and chivalry of the business at his finger-ends. Also he likes you."

"At any rate, he is ever railing upon me with that sharp tongue of his!" said I.

"But did you ever hear him rail upon any of these young men that lean on rails and roll their eyes under ladies' windows?" said the Prince. "Old Leopold Dessauer is even now no weakling. I warrant he could draw a good sword yet upon occasion. Anything more lovely than his riposte I never saw."

The Prince got upon his feet with the difficulty of a man naturally heavy of body, who takes all his exercise upon horseback.

"Page!" he cried. "My compliments to High State's Councillor Dessauer, and ask him to come to me here. You will find him, I think, in the library."

So to the palace sped the boy; and presently, walking stiffly, but with great dignity, came the old man down to us.

"How about the ancestors, the noble men my predecessors?" cried the Prince, when he saw him; "have you found aught to link the miller of Chemnitz with the Princes of Plassenburg?"

The Councillor smiled, and shook his head gravely.

"Nothing beyond that bit of metal which hangs by your side, Prince Karl," said Dessauer, pointing to his Highness's sword.

The Prince looked down at the strong, unadorned hilt thoughtfully and sighed.

"I would I had another to transmit this sword to, as well as the power to wield it, when I take my place as usurper in the histories of the Princes of Plassenburg."

"I trust your Highness may long be spared to us," replied Dessauer, gravely; "but, Prince Karl, in default of an heir to your body (of which there is yet no reason to despair), wherefore may not your Highness devise the realm back to the ancient line?"

"The line of Dietrich is extinct," said the Prince, booking up sharply.

"So says Duke Casimir, hoping to succeed to your shoes, when he could not to your helmet and your sword. But I have my suspicions and my beliefs. There is more in the parchments of yonder library than has yet seen the light."

Suddenly the Prince recollected me, standing patiently by.

"But we waste time, Dessauer; we can speak of ancestors and successors anon. I and Hugo Gottfried want you to take up your ancient role. Do you mind how you snicked Axelstein, and clipped Duke Casimir of his little finger at the back of the barn, when we were all lads at the Kaiser's first diet at Augsburg?"

Old Dessauer smiled, well pleased enough at the excellence of the Prince's memory.

"I have seen worse cuts," he said; "Casimir has never rightly liked me since. And had the Black Riders caught me, over to his dogs I should have gone without so much as a belt upon me. He would have kept them without food for a week on purpose to make a clean job of my poor scarecrow pickings."

"And now this young spark," said the Prince, "for the sake of a lady's eyes, desires to do your Augsburg deed over again with Duke Casimir's nephew. So we must give him a man with quarterings on his shield to go along with him."

"I am too old and stiff," said Dessauer, shaking his head mournfully, yet with obvious desire in the itching fingers of his sword-hand; "let him seek out one of the brisk young kerls that are drumming at the blade-play all the time down there in the square by the guard-rooms."

"Nay, it is to be principals only; there is to be no fighting of seconds. The Count has specially desired that there shall be none," said the Prince; "therefore, go with the lad, Dessauer."

"No fighting of seconds!" cried the Councillor, in astonishment, holding up his hands. And I think the old swordsman seemed a little disappointed. "Well, I will go and see the lad well through, and warrant that he gets fair-play among these wolves of the Mark."

"Faith, when it comes to that, he is as rough-pelted a wolf of the Mark as any of them!" laughed the Prince.

CHAPTER XXXII

THE WOLVES OF THE MARK

The Hirschgasse is a little inn across the river, well known to the wilder blades of Plassenburg. There they go to be outside the authority of the city magistrates, to make rendezvous with maids more complaisant than maidenly, to fight their duels, and generally to do those things without remark which otherwise bring them under the eye of the Miller's Son, as they one and all call (behind his back) the reigning Prince of Plassenburg.

It was on the stroke of seven, and as fine an evening as ever failed to touch the soul of sinful man with a sense of its beauty, that I set out to fight the nephew of Duke Casimir. I had indeed ridden far and fast, and withal kept my head since I left the Red Tower a poor homeless wanderer, otherwise I had scarce found myself going out with High Councillor Leopold von Dessauer as my second to fight my late master's heir, the proximate Duke of the Wolfmark.

What was my surprise to find the old man attired in the appropriate costume for such an occasion, a close-fitting suit of dark gray, of ancient cut indeed, and without the fashionable slashes and scallops, but both correct and practicable, either for the sword-play or the proper ordering of it in others.

Von Dessauer laughed a little dry laugh when I congratulated him on the youthfulness of his appearance. Indeed, he seemed little grateful for my felicitations. And if it had not been for the rheumatism which he had inherited from his father's campaigns on the tented field, and the weakness which came from his own in other fields, he would yet have proved as fit for the play of fence as any youngster of them all. So, at least, he averred. And tonight the wind was southerly, and his old hurts irked him not. Faith he was almost minded to try a ruffle with the cocks of the Mark on his own account.

"Mind you," he said, "guard low. The attack of the Mark ever comes from the right leg, half-way to the knee. But I forgot—what use is it to tell you, that are born of the Mark, and have learned sword-cunning in their schools?"

As we left the castle I looked about and secretly kissed a hand to that high window, where was the chamber of my Little Playmate, whose cause I was going out so gladly to champion.

Dessauer and I went quickly down through the lanes which led to the river edge where the ferry was, and more than once with the corner of my eye I seemed to see a man in a cloak and sword stealing after us. But as the sight of a man so attired going secretly in the direction of the Hirschgasse was no uncommon one, I did not pay any particular attention.

We crossed over in the large flat-boat which plied constantly between the banks before our fine new bridge was built. We found our enemies on the ground before us, and they seemed more than a little surprised when they perceived who my second was. For as we came up the bank I saw them go close and whisper together like men who hastily alter their plans at the last moment.

I presented my second in form.

"The High Councillor Leopold von Dessauer, Knight of the Empire!" said I, proudly enough.

Then the Count presented his, as the custom then was among us of the North:

"His Excellency Friedrich, Count of Cannstadt, Hereditary Cup-bearer of the Wolfmark."

Count Cannstadt was an impecunious old-young man, who, chiefly owing to accumulated gaming-debts and a disagreement with Duke Casimir concerning the payment of certain rents and duties, had sought the shelter of the Castle of Plassenburg—a refuge which the generous Prince Karl extended to all exiles who were not proven criminals.

The seconds bowed first to each other, and then to their opposing principals. In those days, duels were mostly fought with the combatants' own swords. And now Von Dessauer took my blade, and, going forward courteously, handed the hilt to Count Cannstadt, receiving that of Von Reuss in return. The seconds then compared the lengths, and found almost half an inch in favor of my opponent. Which being declared, and I offering no objection, the discrepancy was allowed and the swords returned us to fall to.

And this without further parley we did.

I was no ways afraid of my opponent. For though a pretty enough, tricky fighter, he had little practical experience. Also he had quite failed to strengthen himself by daily custom, and especially by practice at outrauce, with an enemy keen to run you through in front of you, and the necessity of keeping a wary eye on half a dozen other conflicts on either hand, as has constantly to be done in war.

The place where we fought was on a level green platform a little way above the roofs of the inn of the Hirschgasse, where many a similar conflict has been fought, and on which many a good fellow has lain, panting like a grassed trout, with the gasps growing slower and deadlier, while his opponent wiped his blade on the trampled herbage, and the seconds looked on with folded arms. There were many bushes and rocks about, and the place was very secluded to be so near a great city.

At first I did not trouble myself much, nor attempt to force the fighting. I was content to hold Von Reuss in play, and defend myself till the hunger edge of his attack was dulled. For I saw on his face a look of vicious confidence that surprised me, considering his inexperience, and he lunged with a venom and resolution which, to my mind, betokened a determination to kill at all hazards.

I knew, however, that presently he must overreach himself, so of set purpose I kept my blade short, and let him approach nearer. Immediately he began to press, thinking that he had me at his mercy. We had fought our way round to a spot on the upper side of the plateau, where for a moment Von Reuss had a momentary benefit from the nature of the ground. Here I felt that he gathered himself together, and, presently, as I had supposed he would, he centred his energy in a determined thrust at my left breast. This was well enough timed, for my guard had been short and a little high on purpose to lead him on, and now it took me all my time to turn his point aside. I saw the steel shoot past, grazing my left arm. Then with so long a recovery, and the loss of balance from lunging downhill, he was at my mercy.

As I did not wish to kill him I chose my spot almost at my leisure, and pinked him two inches below the spring of the neck and close to the collar-bone, which was running the thing as fine as I could allow myself.

What was my surprise to see my sword-blade arch itself as if it had stricken a stone wall, and to hear the unmistakable ring of steel meeting steel.

"Treachery!" cried Von Dessauer and I together; "you are villains both. He is wearing a shirt of mail!"

And the old man rushed forward with his sword bare in his hand and all a-tremble with indignation.

I heard the shrill "purl" of a silver call, and, turning me about, there was the gambler Cannstadt with a whistle at his lips. I dared not turn my head, for I had still to guard myself against the traitor Von Reuss's attack, but with the tail of my eye I could see two or three men rise from behind bushes and rocks, and come running as fast as they could towards us. Then I knew that Dessauer and I were doomed men unless something turned up that we wotted not of. For with an old man, and one so stiff as the High Councillor, for my only ally, it was impossible for me to hold my own against more than double our numbers.

Nevertheless, Von Dessauer attacked Cannstadt with surprising fury and determination, anger glittering in his eye, and resolution to punish treachery lending vigor to his thrust. I had not time to observe his method save unconsciously, for I had to change my position momentarily that I might take the points of the two men who came down the hill at speed, sword in hand.

But all this foul play among high-born folk gave me a kind of mortal sickness. To die in battle is one thing, but over against the very roofs of your home to find yourself brought to death's door by murderous treachery is quite another.

At this moment there came news of a diversion. From below was heard the crying of a stormy voice.

"Halt! I command you! Halt!"

And wheeling sufficiently to see, I observed through the twilight the figure of a stout man, who came leaping heavily up the hill towards us, waving a sword as he came. Well, thought I, the more there are of them the quicker it will be over, and the more credit for us in keeping up our end so long. Better die in a good fight than live with a bad conscience.

With which admirable reflection I sent my sword through Von Reuss's sword-arm, in the fleshy part, severing the muscle and causing him to drop his blade. I had him then at my mercy, and experienced a great desire to push my blade down his throat, for a treacherous cowardly hound as he had proved himself to me. But instead of this I had to turn towards the other two who came at the charge down the hill and were now close upon us.

I had just time to leap aside from the first and let him overrun himself when he shot almost upon the sword of the thick-set man, who came up the hill shouting to us to stop. The second man I engaged, and a stanch blade I found him, though fighting for as dirty a cause as ever man crossed swords in.

"Halt!" came the voice of command again—the voice I knew so well—"in the name of the State I bid you cease!"

It was the voice of Karl, Prince of Plassenburg.

"We must take the rough with the smooth now. We must kill them, every one, like stanch men of the Mark!" cried Von Reuss. "There is no safety for any of us else." And in a moment we were at it, the Prince furiously assaulting the second of the bravoes who came down the hill. More coolly than I had given him credit for, Von Reuss stuffed a silken kerchief into the hole in his shoulder, and repossessed himself of his weapon in his other hand.

It was the briskest kind of a bicker that ensued for a little while there on the bosky, broomy hill-side in the evening light. Ah, Dessauer was down at last and Cannstadt at his throat! I went about with a whirl, leaving my own man for the moment, and rushed upon the Count's false second. He turned to receive me, but not quite quick enough, for I got him two inches below where I had pinked his principal's ring-mail, and that made all the difference. Cannstadt did not immediately drop his sword. But his limbs weakened, and he fell forward without a sound.

Then as I looked about, there was the Prince manfully crossing swords with two, and the cowardly Von Reuss creeping up with his sword shortened in his left hand with intent to slay him from behind.

Whereat I gave a furious cry of anguish, that I should have been the means of bringing my noble master into such peril. The Prince Karl had at the same moment some intuition of the treacherous foe behind him, for he leaped aside with more agility than I had ever seen him display before on foot, and Von Reuss was too sorely wounded to follow.

Presently I was at my first bravo again, and the Prince being left with but one, Von Reuss took the opportunity to slip away over the hill.

The rest of the conflict was not long a-settling. There were loud voices from the stream beneath. The combat had been observed, and half a score of the Prince's guard were already swimming, wading, and leaping into small boats in their haste to be first to our assistance.

But we did not need their aid. I passed my blade through and through my assailant, almost at the same moment that the Prince spiked his man so directly in the throat, so that the red point stood out in the hollow of his neck behind.

Both went down simultaneously, and there was Von Reuss on horseback, just disappearing over the ridge. Prince Karl wiped his brow.

"What devil's traitors!" he cried. "Poor Dessauer, I wonder what he has gotten? Let us go to him."

We went across the plateau together, and knelt by the side of the old man. At first I could not find the wound, though there was blood enough upon his face and fencing-habit. But presently I discovered that his scalp had been cut from above the eye backwards to the crown of his head—a shallow, ploughing scratch, no more, though it had effectually stunned the old man.

Even as I held him in my arms, he came to and looked about him.

"Are they all dead?" he said, feeling about for his sword.

"You were nearly dead, dearest of friends," said my master. "But be content. You have done very well for so young a fighter. An you behave yourself, and keep from such brawling in the future, I declare I will give you a company!"

Dessauer smiled.

"All dead?" he asked, trying still to look about him.

"Your man is dead, or the next thing to it, two other rascals grievously wounded, and the scoundrel Von Reuss fled, as well he might. But my archers are already on his track."

Up the hill came Jorian and Boris leading the rout.

"Is the Prince safe?" cried Jorian.

"The Prince is safe," said Karl, answering for himself.

"Good!" chorussed Jorian, Boris, and all the archers together.

"Catch me that man on horseback there!" cried the Prince. "Take him or kill him, but if you can help it do not let him escape. He is the Count von Reuss, and a double traitor."

"Good!" cried the pair, and set off after him, all dripping as they were from their abrupt passage of the river.

CHAPTER XXXIII

THE FLIGHT OF THE LITTLE PLAYMATE

We carried Dessauer back to the boat with the utmost tenderness, the Prince walking by his side, and oft-times taking his hand. I followed behind them, more than a little sad to think that my troubles should have caused so good and true a man so dangerous a wound. For though in a young man the scalp-wound would have healed in a week, in a man of the High Councillor's age and delicacy of constitution it might have the most serious effects.

But Dessauer himself made light of it.

"I needed a leech to bleed me," he said. "I was coward enough to put off the kindly surgery, and here our young friend has provided me one without cost. His last operation, too, and so no fee to pay. I am a fortunate man."

We came to the gate of the Palace of Plassenburg.

My Lady Princess met us, pale and obviously anxious, with lips compressed and a strange cold glitter in her emerald eyes.

"So strange a thing has happened!" she began.

"No stranger than hath happened to us," cried the Prince.

"Why, what hath happened to you?" she demanded, quickly.

"Your fine Von Reuss has proved himself a traitor. He fought a duel with Hugo here all tricked in chain-armor, and when found out he whistled his rascals from the covert to slay us. But we bested him, and he is over the hill, with Jorian and Boris hot after his heel."

"And he hath not gone alone!" said the Princess, and her eyes were brilliant with excitement.

"Not gone alone?" said the Prince. "What do you know about this black work?"

"Because Helene, my maid of honor, hath fled to join him," she said, looking anxiously at us, like one who perils much upon a throw of the dice.

I laughed aloud. So certain was I of the utter impossibility of the thing, that I laughed a laugh of scorn. And I saw the sound of my voice jar the Lady Ysolinde like a blow on the face.

"You do not believe!" she said, standing straight before me.

"I do not believe—I know!" answered I, curtly enough.

"Nevertheless the thing is true," she said, with a curious, pleading expression, as if she had been charged with wrong-doing and were clearing herself, though none had accused her by word or look.

"It is most true," the Princess went on. "She fled from the palace an hour before sundown. She was seen mounting a horse belonging to Von Reuss at the Wolfmark gate, with two of his men in attendance upon her. She is known to have received a note by the hand of an unknown messenger an hour before."

I did not wait for the permission of the Princess, but tore up the women's staircase to Helene's room, where I found nothing out of place—not so much as a fold of lace. After a hurried look round I was about to leave the room when a crumpled scrap of paper, half hidden by a curtain, caught my eye.

I stooped and picked it up. It was written in an unknown and probably disguised hand—a hand cumbersome and unclerkly:

"Come to me. Meet me at the Red Tower. I need you."

There was no more; the signature was torn away, and if the letter were genuine it was more than enough. But no thought of its truth nor of the falseness of Helene so much as crossed my mind.

To tell the truth, it struck me from the first that the Lady Ysolinde might have placed the letter there herself. So I said nothing about it when I descended.

The Prince met me half-way up the stairs.

"Well?" he questioned, bending his thick brows upon me.

"She is gone, certainly," said I; "where or how I do not yet know. But with your permission I will pursue and find out."

"Or, I presume, without my permission?" said the Prince.

I nodded, for it was vain to pretend otherwise—foolish, too, with such a master.

"Go, then, and God be with you!" he said. "It is a fine thing to believe in love."

And in ten minutes I was riding towards the Wolfsberg.

As I went past the great four-square gibbet which had made an end of Ritterdom in Plassenburg, I noted that there was a gathering of the hooded folk—the carrion crows. And lo! there before me, already comfortably a-swing, were our late foes, the two bravoes, and in the middle the dead Cannstadt tucked up beside them, for all his five hundred years of ancestry—stamped traitor and coward by the Miller's Son, who minded none of these things, but understood a true man when he met him.

I pounded along my way, and for the first ten miles did well, but there my horse stumbled and broke a leg in a wretched mole-run widened by the winter rains. In mercy I had to kill the poor beast, and there I was left without other means of conveyance than my own feet.

It was a long night as I pushed onward through the mire. For presently it had come on to rain—a thick, dank rain, which wetted through all covering, yet fell soft as caressing on the skin.

I took shelter at last in a farm-house with honest folk, who right willingly sat up all night about the fire, snoring on chairs and hard settles that I might have their single sleeping-chamber, where, under strings of onions and odorous dried herbs, I rested well enough. For I was dead tired with the excitement and anxiety of the day—and at such times one often sleeps best.

On the morrow I got another horse, but the brute, heavy-footed from the plough, was so slow that, save for the look of the thing, I might just as well have been afoot.

Nevertheless I pushed towards the town of Thorn, hearing and seeing naught of my dear Playmate, though, as you may well imagine, I asked at every wayside place.

It was at the entering in of the strange country of the brick-dust that I met Jorian and Boris. They were riding excellent horses, unblown, and in good condition—the which, when I asked how they came by such noble steeds, they said that a man gave them to them.

"Jorian," said I, sharply, "where have you been?"

"To the city of Thorn," said he, more briskly than was his wont, so that I knew he had tidings to communicate.

"Saw you the Lady Helene?" I asked, eagerly, of them.

He shook his head, yet pleasantly.

"Nay," said he, "I saw her not. The Red Tower is not a healthy place for men of Plassenburg, nor yet the White Gate and the house of Master Gerard von Sturm. But Mistress Helene is in safety, so much Boris and I are assured of."

"Not with Von Reuss?" cried I, fear thrilling sudden in my voice that he had stolen her and now held her in captivity.

Boris held up his hand as a signal that I must not hurry his companion, who was clearly doing his best.

"She is with Gottfried Gottfried, the old man, your father, and is safe."

"Did she go to them of her own free will, or did my father send for her?" I went on, for much depended upon that question.

"Nay," answered Jorian, "that I know not. But certainly she is with him, and safe. The Count, too, is with his uncle, and they say also safe—under lock and key."

"Good!" quoth Boris.

"Let us all three go back to Plassenburg forthwith!" cried I.

"Good!" chorussed both of them together, unanimously slapping their thighs. "Choose one of our horses. He was a good man who gave us them. We wish we had known. We should have asked him for another when we were about it."

Nevertheless, I rode back to Plassenburg on the farmer's beast, sadly enough, yet somewhat contented. For Helene was with my father, and far safer, as I judged, than in the palace chambers of Plassenburg, and within striking distance of the Lady Ysolinde. And in that I judged not wrong, though the future seemed for a while to belie my confidence.

CHAPTER XXXIV

THE GOLDEN NECKLACE

The Chancellor Leopold von Dessauer, High Councillor of the Prince, with his head still bound up, was pacing the sparred gallery outside the private apartments of his master. It was in the heats of the late summer, before the ripening of the orchard fruits had had time to culminate, or the russet to come out slowly upon the apples, like a blush upon a woman's soft, dusky cheek.

The High Councillor was in a bad humor. For he had been kept waiting, and that by a man of no account. At last a forester in a uniform of dark green, with the Prince's bugle and sparrow-hawk in silver everywhere about him, made his appearance at the foot of the gallery, and stood waiting Dessauer's summons with his plumed hat of soft cloth in his hand.

"Hither, man!" cried the High Councillor, sharply. "What has kept you? Why were you not here half an hour ago? If this be the way you keep the Prince's forests, no wonder there are many deer taken by reiving rascals and the forest laws daily broken."

"High Mightiness," said the man, humbly, looking down, "it was my daughter—she would not give up the necklace. She hath had it for her own since she was a child, and she would not deliver it, though I threatened her with your well-born anger."

"And have you got it with you? Surely you and she have not dared to keep it!" began the Chancellor, with gathering fury on his eyebrow.

"Yea, truly, truly, an you will have patience, my Lord, I have it here,"- said the man, drawing a necklace of golden bars curiously arranged from his leathern wallet; and, kneeling on his knee, he presented it to the Chancellor.

"How did you prevail with the maid?" he asked, as soon as he had it in hand—"you used no constraint or force, I hope?"

"Nay, sir," said the man, "for my wife being dead and my daughter marriageable, she keeps house for me; and having a sweetheart betrothed a year ago she hath been laying aside plenishing gear and women's dainty gewgaws. So these I took one by one, beginning with a mirror of polished brass, and made as if I would dash them in pieces if she discovered not where the chain of gold was hid."

"And she revealed it?" said Dessauer.

"Aye," said the man, "but none so willingly, as you might suppose. I had Saint Peter's own trouble to get it from her. Indeed, I prayed to the Holy Apostle to aid me."

"What had Saint Peter to do with it?" said the Councillor, pausing and looking humorsomely at the man, like an ascetic sparrow with his head at one side.

"Because our Holy Saint Peter is the only saint who understands the trouble men have with the contrariness of women."

"Why so?" cried the Chancellor, rubbing his hand with a curious pleasure at the colloquy.

"Because he only among the Apostles was a married man and had experience of a mother-in-law."

"Art a wise forester. Where got you that wisdom?"

"Why," said the man, modestly, "partly by nature, partly because I also have been married, and so have graduated in the wars."

"It is the same thing," said the Chancellor, "according to your own telling."

"Aye, sir," quoth the man, "but yet the young fellows will take no warning. 'It is better to marry than to burn,' said the other Apostle. But methinks he knew nothing about it, being no better than a bachelor, or he would have amended it, 'It is better to burn than to marry *and* burn.'"

"Ha! art also a theologe, Sir Woodman?" cried Dessauer. "But enough; this touches on the Inquisition and the Holy Office. Let us despatch."

All this time the High Councillor had been gazing by fits and starts at the links of the necklace, turning it about and viewing it from every angle. It was composed of short bars of gold laid horizontally three and three together, and bound together with short chains of gold. And on each of the bars there was engraven a crest. Letters also were on the bars, cut in plain deep script.

"Now tell your tale and tell it briefly—that is, if brevity be in you, which I doubt," said Dessauer.

"As I said before," quoth the forester, "I was in the wars; I mean not only in the wars with womenkind, but also with mankind. And among other things I remember the night of the Duke Casimir's famous ride, when he took Plassenburg, because there was scarce a sober man within the walls."

"And his Highness the Prince Karl away on Baltic side with his men, else had Casimir never set foot within the city!" cried the High Chancellor.

"Ah, like enow," said the woodman, "I ken naught of that. But this I do know, Plassenburg was taken with much slaughter and grievous loss of goodly gear. They captivated many noble prisoners also, and, because I slept in the stables, they took me to help lead the horses. Yet I was not ill-treated, save that I had to keep pace with the horsemen upon my feet. But I saw the Prince—"

"Which Prince? Speak plainly," said the High Councillor, gruffly.

"Why, the Prince Dietrich Hohenfriedberg of Plassenburg," said the man. "He, as your well-born Wisdom remembers, was then the only

Prince in these parts—a good man, and born of the noblest, though not of the capacity of his present Highness the Prince Karl."

"Proceed somewhat faster. Yon move as slowly as one of your own forest oxen at the wood-hauling," cried the well-born Councillor in a testy tone.

"We were long in riding over to Thorn—two days and nights upon the way. It was a terrible time, and all the while those condemned beasts of the Wolfmark, Casimir's Black Riders, driving us with their spears like prick-goads, till our backs were all bleeding, gentle and simple alike. So at midnight of the third day we came to the city of Thorn, and up through the streets to the Wolfsberg. There was no gladness in the town, such as there would have been in our city had there been news of a victory, or even of some hundreds of the enemy's horses well driven. For then as now the town hated its Duke. And so they were all silent.

"Then in the darkness we came to the castle, and the word was: 'Dismount, and to the shambles!' Me and my like they meddled not with, but only the great ones. And it was then, as I told you, that I saw Prince Dietrich with the little maid in his arms. I had carried her part of the way for him, and faithfully delivered her up again, feeding her with the choicest meats I could obtain when she could eat. But she was tired, mostly, and would not look at food. So for this he gave me her necklace from about her pretty neck. But the rest of her noble golden gear, the belt and the clasps, were upon the maid when the headsman of Thorn delivered her to one that stood near by. So, being almost asleep with weariness and exhausted with terror, they carried her away, and I saw the maid no more.

"But the Prince Dietrich Hohenfriedberg was beheaded within the hour, and, as is their hellish custom, his body was thrown to the Duke's blood-hounds that were clamoring all the time behind their fence.

"God help us—such a disaster that night was for Plassenburg! Will the Prince never set about wiping away the disgrace?"

"Aye, that he will!" cried the High Chancellor, suddenly bursting into a fury, strangely unlike him. "He will wash it away in the blood of Duke Casimir and all his evil brood—the Wolves of the Mark truly are they named. And the Wolfsberg shall go up in flaming fire to heaven, so that the ashes of it shall be cast abroad to make the Mark yet grayer and more desolate—like the fell of the beasts that dwelt within it."

"Amen! Let it come quick, say I—that I may see it before I die!" cried the forester, bowing low before the Chancellor.

CHAPTER XXXV

THE DECENT SERVITOR

"This grows past all bearing," cried the Prince one morning, when he had summoned into his hall the Chancellor Dessauer and myself. For, though the Prince was still wont to command in person in any important action, and in the general policy of his realm took counsel with none, yet it had somehow come about that we, the old man and the young, had been constituted an informal council of two which was liable to be summoned at any moment, whenever the Prince was weary or troubled.

He struck one clinched hand into the palm of the other before he spoke again.

"Duke Casimir is either in his dotage, or his riders have gotten out of hand since Hugo and you drove the young wolf over to help the old. Both are likely enough, with a people praying for deliverance and yearning for their Duke's death. A bare board and an empty treasury may render a new course of plunder necessary abroad, in order to keep his Dukedom from toppling about his ears at home. After all, 'tis natural enough. But I had thought that he would have had enough of sense to let the borders of Plassenburg alone so long as its Prince lived."

"And what, my lord, has befallen?" asked the High Councillor.

"Why," cried the Prince, "the Black Riders of the Wolfmark are out again, and have left their ancient trail behind them in slain men and frantic women—and on our borders, too, among our kindly husbandmen, our honest, sunburnt peasants. Bitterly shall Casimir Ironteeth rue the day that he meddled with Karl Miller's Son."

"Your Highness," I said, "this is indeed madness. We have but to collect our forces, choose a time, and, lo! we are within the town of Thorn! Once there, we would be welcomed by man, woman, and child. We could then besiege the Wolfsberg, and in three days make an end."

"Aye, that is it," said the Prince, grimly; "you have hit it, Hugo. We *will* make an end."

"Also, my Prince," I went on, boldly, "so ye give me leave and approve of my design, I will go alone to the town of Thorn, and bring you back word of their power and dispositions. Save the Count von Reuss, there is none who could now recognize me within the city walls."

"What think ye, Dessauer?" said the Prince, looking over at the High Chancellor.

"I think well," said he, a little doubtfully; "but would it not be better that two should go than that one should adventure alone into the wolf's den?"

"Surely it were better to keep the matter between our three selves," the Prince made answer; "not even the Princess must know of our attempt. Keep a candle flame within the hollow of your palm, and though the wind blow the sparks will not fly far."

"I will go with the lad, Prince Karl," said the Chancellor, firmly. "In my youth I had some practice as a leech. I am acquainted with the art of healing. I could travel either as a doctor of healing, as a travelling philosopher seeking disputation with the scholars of each country, or, perhaps best of all, in mine own quality of a doctor of law. And in any case this young man might with all safety be my pupil or servant, whichever best liketh him."

"Servant, then," said I, "for the art of disputation I have hitherto chiefly undertaken with my fists and side-irons. And as to surgery, I am more practised in the giving of wounds than in the healing of them."

The Prince leaned his head upon his hand. He thought carefully over our proposal, taking up point after point, resolving difficulty after difficulty in his mind, as was his wont.

"How long would you be away?" he asked, looking up at us.

"Ten days, Prince," said I. "Give us but ten days and we will return."

"I will give you eight, and if ye are not home again on the eve of the last, as sure as I am Karl Miller's Son, the army of Plassenburg will be thundering on the walls of Thorn seeking for a wandering Chancellor and a lost Hugo Gottfried!"

And so it was arranged. We of the Prince's staff were indeed in great need of such a mission, for we had heard nothing from Thorn or the Wolfmark during many months; no tidings, at all events, that could be relied upon. For the cutting up of our frontiers by new raids, and the severance of all relations between us and the dwellers in the Wolfmark, through fear of reprisals, caused us to hear little news but such as was manifest lies.

As thus: Duke Casimir was collecting a great army, magnificent with cannon and munitions of war. He was shut up tight in the Wolfsberg, not daring to show his face to his own citizens. He would appear some fine day before the Palace of Plassenburg and slay every man of us. He was in a madman's cell, and Otho von Reuss was Duke of the Mark in his place.

These were only a few of the stories which were brought to regale us daily. And since there was no certainty anywhere, we were all in the dark concerning the military matters which it behooved us greatly to be acquainted with. Therefore I was honestly eager for my master's sake to undertake the perilous journey. But to tell the whole truth, the fact that I had not had a word from the Little Playmate, not so much as a line of script nor a verbal message since her disappearance, made me more eager to go than the high politics of a dozen provinces.

Since the duel, and the final declaring of my love for Helene, I had seen but little of the Princess. Indeed, I kept out of her way, so far at least as I could. And the Lady Ysolinde remained mostly in her own domains—to which, of late, I had been less and less invited. Nevertheless, when we met, she was more than kind to me—gentle, forbearing, pathetic almost in bearing and demeanor, like as a woman wronged, slighted, misconstrued.

Also there was sent to my quarters a new banner for my following, broidered and blazoned in yellow and blue, a saddle-cloth of silk for my horse, fine as a woman's robe, with a crowned Y faint and small in the corner, lettered in straw-colored gold. No man could help being touched by such kindly thought, which, after all, is more than mere liberality.

Yet I saw a sight upon her stairs one night which awoke me with a sudden start to the fact that we had one to reckon with in our journeying to the city of Thorn whom we had not as yet taken into consideration.

For it chanced that I was passing up to the Prince's apartments by the quicker way, through corridors and by stairs to which he had given me private access. And there, upon the steps leading to the Lady Ysolinde's rooms, I saw the decent servitor of Master Gerard stand waiting. He stared as hard at me as I did at him. But whereas his smooth, silent, secret face remained with me, and I knew him at a glance, it was, I judged, clean impossible that he could know the beardless stripling in the mustached leader of soldiers, walking well-accustomed and unafraid through palaces.

The man had a letter in his hand, and I saw him deliver it to a maid who came to the dividing curtain to take it.

So there was later news from the city of Thorn within the Palace of Plassenburg than we of the Prince's council of three possessed. Should I tell our Karl of this encounter? I thought it might be safer not. Because the Prince was the last man to attempt to obtain aught from his wife by compulsion, and any question, direct or indirect, might only put her upon her guard.

If I let him into the secret, the Prince would be most likely to stride straight into the Princess's rooms with the brusque words: "Gottfried has seen a letter come to you from your father—what were its contents?"

And that would not suit us at all.

So, rightly or wrongly, I kept the matter from my master, speaking of it only to Dessauer. And if aught befel from my reticence, it was at least I myself who bore the burden, and, in the final event, paid the penalty.

CHAPTER XXXVI

YSOLINDE'S FAREWELL

The next morning early, as I went about making my dispositions, and putting men of trust in positions fit for them—for the Prince has given me the command of all the soldiers within the city—the Lady Ysolinde came to me upon the terrace.

"Walk with me a while," she said, "in the lower garden. It is a quiet place, and I would speak with you."

It was a command that I dared not refuse to obey, yet my greatest enemy would not accuse me that I went lightly or willingly to such a tryst.

The Lady Ysolinde passed on daintily and proudly before me, and I followed, more like a condemned criminal lamping heavily to the scaffold than a lad of mettle accompanying a fair lady to a rendezvous of her own asking under the greenwood-tree.

But I need not have feared. The Princess's mood was mild, and I saw her in a humor in which I had never seen her before.

She moved before me over the grass, with her head a little turned up to the skies, as though appealing out of her innocence to the Beings who sat behind and sorted out the hearts of men and women.

At a great weeping-elm, under which was a seat, she turned. It formed a wide canopy of shade, grateful and cool. For the breezes stirred under the leaves, and the river moved beneath with a pleasant, meditative hush of sound.

"Hugo Gottfried, once you were my friend," she began; "what have I done that you should be my friend no more? Tell me plainly. I liked you when as a lad, the son of the Red Axe, you had come to my father's house about some boyish freak. I have not done ill by you since that day. And now that you are a leader of men and of rank and honor here in my husband's country of Plassenburg, I would be your well-wisher still. I am conscious of no reason for my having forfeited your liking. But that I would know for certain—and now."

As she threw back her head and let her clear emerald eyes rest upon me, I never saw woman born of woman look more innocent. Indeed, in these days of mistrust, it is innocence under suspicion which usually looks most guilty, knowing what is expected of it.

"Lady Ysolinde," I made answer, "you try me hard and sore. You put me by force in the wrong. You do me indeed great honor, as you have ever done all these years. In reverence and high respect I shall ever hold you for all that you have done—for your kindness to me and to Helene, the orphan girl who came from our father's roof with me. I know no reason why there should be any break in our friendship—nor shall there be, if you will pardon my folly and—"

"Tush!" she said, impetuously; "you speak things empty, vain, the rattling of knuckle-bones in a bladder—not live words at all. Think you I have never listened to true men? Do not I, Ysolinde of Plassenburg, know the sound of words that have the heart behind them? I have heard you speak such yourself. Do not insult me then with platitudes, nor try to divert me with the piping of children in the market-place. I will not dance to them, nor yet, like a foolish kitchen-wench, smile at the jingling of your trinketry."

"Your Highness—" I began again.

She waved her hand as if putting a light thing away.

"I was a woman to you before you knew that I was a Princess," she said; "you need not forget that I am a woman still, cursed with the plate-mail of rank added to the weariness and inaction of a woman's breaking heart."

I grew acutely conscious that I was not distinguishing myself in this interview. So I dashed again at the wall, and this time, for a moment at least, overbore interruption.

"Ysolinde, my dear lady," I said to her, "you are the Prince's and my good master's wife. And if I have stood aloof, it is that I wished that he should have the companionship which one day I desire to find for myself—and also that I might always have the right to look straight into my master's eyes."

"Now you talk like a silly prating priestling," she said. "You are both mighty careful of your honesty, your virtue, your companionship—your precious master and you. But you do not think what it is to starve a woman's heart, to bid her find her level among broiderers of bannerets and stitchers in tapestry. Ah! if the particular God who happened to be at the digging of us out of the happier pit of oblivion had only made me a man, I, at least, should neither have been a straitlaced Jackanapes nor yet a prating, callow-bearded wiseacre."

"And am I either?" said I, weakly enough.

"You are in danger of becoming both," she said, promptly. "Once I saw better things in you. I thought I had won me a friend, and that for once I might put my anchor down. My husband neglects me, so much cannot have escaped your eagle eye. He is twice my age, and he thinks more of you, more of Councillor Von Dessauer, more of his horse than of me, Ysolinde of Plassenburg. And I was made to be loved and to love. How much of either, think you, have I ever known? The true lot of a woman shut to me, the sweet love of man and woman wiled from me, even the communion of the spirit forbidden. I might as lief carry a wizened nut-kernel within my brain-pan as a thinking soul, for all that any one cares. I am a woman of another age stranded on the shores of a time made only for men. I am the woman priests talk against, or perhaps rather the witch-woman Lilith on the outside of Eden's wall. Or I may be the woman of a time yet to come, when she who is man's mate shall not be only a gay-decked bird to sit on his wrist, tethered with a leash and called back to her master with a silver lure."

These things I had never listened to before, nor, indeed, thought of. Nevertheless, though I could not answer her, I felt in my heart that she was wrong, and that a woman has always power over men, being stronger than all ideals, philosophies, kingdoms—aye, even our holy religion itself.

"After all," I said, piqued a little at her tone, as men are wont to be at that which they do not understand, "my Lady Ysolinde, wherefore should you not tell these things to the Prince, your husband, and not to me, that am neither your husband nor your lover?"

"And if you had been both?" she interjected, a little breathlessly.

"Then, my lady," I replied, stirred by her persistence, "you would have obeyed me and served me just as you say. Or else I should have broken your spirit as a man is broken on the wheel."

It was a prideful saying, and one informed with all ignorance and conceit. Yet the Lady Ysolinde gave a long sigh.

"Ah, that would have been sweet, too," she said. "You are the one man I should have delighted to call master, to have done your bidding. That had been a thing different indeed! But you love me not. You love a chit, a chitterling—a pretty thing that can but peep and mutter, whose heart's depths I have sounded with my finger-nail, and whose babyish vanity I have tickled with a straw."

This was enough and too much.

"Madam," said I, "the clear stars are not fouled by throwing filth at them, nor yet the Lady Helene—whom I do acknowledge that with all my heart I love—by the speaking of any ill words. You do but wrong yourself, most noble lady. For your heart tells you other things, both of the maid I love and of me that am her true servant, and, if I might, your true friend."

The Princess reached out her hand, looking, not with anger, but rather wistfully at me, like a mother at a son who goes to his death with blasphemy on his lips.

"Forgive me," she said, gently. "I would not at the last have you go forth thinking ill of me. Indeed, you think all too well, and make me do things that are better than mine intent, because I know that you expect them of me. I have done many ill and cruel things in my poor life, simply from idleness and the empty, unsatisfied heart. If you had loved me or taught me or driven me, I might have tried better things. Perhaps in the end, for great love's sake, I may yet do one worthy deed that shall blot out all the rest. Farewell!"

And without another spoken word she moved away, and left me in the green pleasaunces of the garden, with my heart riven this way and that, scarce knowing what I did or where I stood.

CHAPTER XXXVII

CAPTAIN KARL MILLER'S SON

Black, blank, chill, confining night shut us in as Leopold Dessauer and I rode out of Plassenburg. Our horses had been made ready for us at the little water-gate in the lower garden. Fain would I have taken also Jorian and Boris, but on this occasion the fewer the safer. For to enter Thorn was to go with lighted matches into a powder-magazine.

The rushes in the river rustled dry and cold along the brink. The leaves of the linden-trees chuckled overhead, rubbing their palms together spitefully. There was mockery of our foolhardy enterprise in the soft whispering sough of the water, as I heard it lapper beneath the ferry-boat that lay ready to cross to the other side. Old Hans, the Prince's ferryman, snored in his boat. Above in the women's chambers a light went to and fro. I judged that it was in the bower of the Lady Ysolinde. But not a string of my heart moved. For pity is so weak and love so strong that all my nature was now on the strain forward towards Helene and the Wolfsberg, like an eager hound that pulls at the unslipped leash.

"My love! my love!" I cried in my heart, "I am coming to you, I am going out to find you! Though I give my life for it, I shall at least see and touch you ere I die."

For during these last days my love had grown greatly upon me, being of that kind which gathers within a man, banks up, fills out his crevices, and he know it not. In the Wolfmark there are oft, in the heart of the limestone, caverns where the water sleeps deep and cool, while above, on the thin, rocky crust, the sun beats and the very lizards die for lack of moisture. It was only now that I had broken up the crust of my nature and found the caverns under, where love was abiding all undreamed of, deep, and eternal as the sea. It is a great thing and a beautiful to meet love for the first time face to face, not to nod to only as to an acquaintance, and to know how great and masterful he is; to say, "Love, I am yours. Do with me that which seemeth good to you. I was strong—now in your hands am I become weak. I was proud—now am I glad to be humble and kneel, waiting your word. You have made life and death the same thing to me, for the sake of the Beloved. I am ready to take either from your hands!"

But enough! We were riding out of the dark pleasaunces of the palace, the leaves were rustling and the sedges blowing. That was what began it, carrying away my thoughts.

Dessauer rode behind me, letting his horse follow mine, nose to tail. For, being used to the visitation of the city outposts, I knew the ground thoroughly.

At every hundred yards we were halted, and I answered. For I had posted the men myself, making sure that Plassenburg should not again be taken by surprise. On the other hand, I had determined that the spoiler should now be made despoiled, and that the foul den of the Wolf should be cleansed as by fire.

Then, like the breaking up of the Baltic ice in spring, the thought ran through me—my father and the maid of the Red Tower, what of them?

Why, at the very first (so I told myself), I should set a guard of the best troops in Plassenburg about the Red Tower, and carry them all—Helene, my father, and old Hanne—to a safe place till Prince Karl and I had made an end. With our stark veterans swarming in Thorn, that would easily be done. And so the plan abode to be altered, broidered, and recast in the imagination of my heart.

We were soon out on the darksome, unguarded road, and after that I steered chiefly by the lights of the palace behind me, Dessauer saying no word, but riding like a man-at-arms close behind me.

We had reached the crown of the green hill over whose slopes the path to the Wolf markwinds—the path by which, doubtless, Helene had travelled the night of the duel.

As I came to the summit, mounting the steepest part slowly, I was aware of a figure dark against the sky, no more apparent than a blacker patch of night where all was dark. It was in shape as of a horseman sitting his steed on the crest of the hill.

Instantly I drew my pistol, in which I had become expert.

"Your name and business?" cried I to the shape on the hill-side. For, indeed, none had any right to be abroad so near the city of Plassenburg, armed cap-a-pie, at that time of the night. And for a moment the thought flashed upon me that the tales we had heard might after all be true, and the armies of the Wolfmark nearer than we dreamed of.

"Hugo—Von Dessauer!" quoth right jovially to my ear a voice well known and ever dear to me, the voice of my master, the Prince Karl.

"The Prince!" cried I. "My lord, what do you here? This is stark madness—you, who should be within the walls of the palace, with the guards watching three deep about you. What would come to the State of Plassenburg if it wanted you?"

"Oh," said he, lightly, falling in beside us in the most natural fashion, "you and Von Dessauer in dual control would be a singular improvement on the present head of the State. You, Hugo, would keep the soldiers to their work, and Von Dessauer could look nobly after the treasury."

"But who would command us and be a gracious and beloved master to us?" said I. "My Prince, we must instantly return and put you in safety!"

"Indeed, that will you not. By God's truth, if I am not to come all the way to the city of Thorn with you, I will at least convoy you to the edges of the Mark. It is so dull, dragging out month by month at ease within the castle, and not nearly so much fun as it used to be when I was a poor captain of a free company under the old Prince. Young rattling blades like Dessauer and yourself make no allowance for the distractions of an aged and gouty Prince."

Within myself I felt some amusement stir. It was almost exactly what the Princess, his wife, had alleged as a reason for her wanderings. I could not help marvelling why these two had not long ere this found out their great affinity to each other. But now I see that this very likeness of nature was the first cause of their lack of agreement. Like may, indeed, draw to like, as the saw hath it. But in the things of love like and like agree not well together. Fair desires dark, stout and stark desire slender, slow desires quick, severe desires gay (though this often secretly). And so the world goes on, and in another generation, sprung from these desirings, once more dark desireth fair and fair dark.

There I am at it again. Oh, but I, Hugo Gottfried, am the wise man when I set out on my disquisitions. I could new-make all the saws of the world, set instances to them, and never breathe myself.

"Nay," said the Prince, "all is safe set within and without, thanks to my brave commander and wise Chancellor, and these other matters can e'en bide till I go back to them. Consider that I am but a captain of horse going a-wooing and needing to talk gayly for good comradeship by the road. Call me honest Captain Miller's Son."

So Captain Miller's Son rode with Herr Doctor Schmidt and his servant Johann. And a merry time the three of us had till we arrived at the borders of the Mark.

Now I have not time nor yet space (though a great deal of inclination) to tell of the wondrous pranks we played—of the broad-haunched countrywomen we rallied (or rather whom Captain Miller's Son rallied, and who, truth to tell, mostly gave as good as they got, or better, to that soldier's huge delight), the stout yeoman families into whose midst we went, and their opinion of the Prince. Of the last I have a good tale to tell. "A good man and a kindly," so the man said; "he has given us safe horse, fat cow, and a quiet life. But yet the old was good too. The true race to reign is ever the anointed Prince."

"But then, did not Dietrich, the anointed Prince, harry you? And worse, let others plunder you? And that is not the fashion of Prince Karl, usurper though he be!" said the Prince.

"Nay," the honest man would reply, "usurper is he not—a God-sent boon to Plassenburg rather. We love him, would fight for him, all my six sons and I. Would we not, chickens?"

And the six sons rolled out a thunderous "Aye, fight—marry, that we would!" as they sat, plaiting willow-baskets and mending bows about the fire.

"But, alas! he is cursed with a mad wife, and, after all said and done, he is not of the ancient stock," said the ancient man, shaking his head.

And the Prince answered him as quickly, tapping his brow significantly with his forefinger, "Are not all wives a little touched? Or are yon passing fortunate in your part of the country? Faith, we of the city will all come courting to the Tannenwald if you prove better off."

"We are even as our neighbors!" cried the yeoman, shrugging his shoulders. "Maul, my troth, what sayest thou? Here is a brisk lad that miscalls thy clan."

The goodwife came forward, smiling, comely, and large of well-padded bone.

"Which?" said she, laconically.

The farmer pointed to the Prince. The matron took a good look at him.

"Well," she said, "he is the one that should know most about us. He has been married once or twice, and hath gotten certain things burned into him. As for this one," she went on, indicating Dessauer, "he may be doctor of all the wisdoms, as ye say, but he has never compassed the mystery of a woman. And this limber young spark with the quick eyes, he is a bachelor also, but ardently desires to be otherwise. I wot he has a pretty lass waiting for him somewhere."

"How knew you that of me, goodwife?" I cried, greatly astonished.

"Why, by the way you looked up when my daughter came dancing in. You were in your lost brown-study, and then, seeing a pretty lass that most are glad to rest their eyes upon, you looked away disappointed or careless."

"And how knew you that I was of the ancient guild of the bachelors?" asked Dessauer.

"Why, by the way that you looked at the pot on the fire, and sniffed up the stew, and asked how long the dinner would be! The bachelor of years is ever uneasy about his meals, having little else to be uneasy about, and no wife, compact of all contrary whimsies, to teach him how to be patient."

"And how," cried the Prince, in his turn, "knew you that I had been wedded once?"

"Or twice," said the woman, smiling. "Man, ye cackle it like a hen on the rafters advertising her egg in the manger below. I knew it by the fashion ye had of hanging up your hat and eke scraping your feet—not after ye entered, like these other good, careless gentlemen, but with your knife, outside the door. I see it by your air of one that has been at once under authority and yet master of a house."

"Well done, good wife!" cried the Prince. "Were I indeed in authority I would make you either Prime-Minister or chief of my thief-catchers."

And so after that we went to bed.

CHAPTER XXXVIII

THE BLACK RIDERS

The next day we jogged along, and many were our advices and admonitions to the Prince to return. For we were now on the borders of his kingdom, and from indications which met us on the journeying we knew that the Black Riders were abroad. For in one place we came to a burned cottage and the tracks of driven cattle; in another upon a dead forest guard, with his green coat all splashed in splotches of dark crimson, a sight which made the Prince clinch his hands and swear. And this also kept him pretty silent for the rest of the day.

It was about evening of this second day, and we had come to the top of a little swell of hills, when suddenly beneath us we heard the crackling of timbers and saw the pale, almost invisible flames beginning to devour a thriving farm-house at our feet. There were swarms of men in dark armor about it, running here and there, clapping straw and brushwood to hay-ricks and byre doors.

"The Black Riders of Duke Casimir," I cried; "down among the bushes and let them not see us! We must go back. If they so much as suspected the Prince they would slay us every one."

But ere we had time to flee half a dozen of their scouts came near us, and, observing our horses and excellent accoutrement, they raised a cry. There was nothing for it but the spurs on the heels of our boots. So across the smooth, well-turfed country we had it, and in spite of our beasts' weariness we made good running. And while we fled I considered how best to serve the Prince.

"There is a monastery near by," said I, "and the head thereof is a good friend of ours. Let us, if possible, gain that shelter, and cast ourselves on the kindness of the good Abbot Tobias."

"Aye," said the Prince, urging his horse to speed, "but will we ever get there?"

Then I called myself all the stupid-heads in the world, because I had not refused to go a foot with the Prince on such a mad venture, and so put our future and that of the Princedom of Plassenburg in such peril.

But there at last were the gray walls and high towers of the Abbey of Wolgast. Our pursuers were not yet in sight, so we rode in at the gate and cast our bridles to a lay brother of the order, crying imperiously for instant audience of the Abbot.

As soon as my friend Tobias saw us he threw up his hands in a rapture of welcome. But I soon had him advertised of our great danger. Whereupon he went directly to the window of his chamber of reception and looked out on the court-yard.

"Ring the abbey bell for full service," he commanded; "throw open the outer gates and great doors, and lead these horses to the secret crypt beneath the mortuary chapel."

For the Abbot Tobias was a man of the readiest resource, and in other circumstances would have made a good soldier.

He hurried us off to the robing-rooms, and made us put on monastic and priestly garments over our several apparels. Never, Got wot, had I expected that I should be transformed into a rope-girt praying clerk. But so it was. I was given a square black cap and a brown robe, and sent to join the lay brethren. For my hair grew thick as a mat on top and there was no time to tonsure it.

Now, Dessauer being bald and quite practicable as to his topknot, they endued him with the full dress of a monk. But at that time I saw not what was done with the Prince. For my conductor, a laughing, frolicsome lad, came for me and carried me off all in good faith, telling me the while that he hoped we should lodge together. There were, he whispered, certain very fair and pleasant-spoken maids just over the wall, that which you could climb easily enough by the branches of the pear-tree that grew contiguous at the south corner.

As we hurried towards the chapel, the monks were streaming out of their cells in great consternation, grumbling like soldiers at an unexpected parade.

"What hath gotten into our old man?" said one. "Hath he overeaten at mid-day refection, and so is not able to sleep, that he cannot let honest men enjoy greater peace than himself?"

"What folly!" cried another; "as if we had not prayers enough, without cheating the Almighty by knocking him up at uncanonical hours!"

"And the choir summoned, and full choral service, no less! Not even a respectable saint's day—no true churchman indeed, but some heretic of a Greek fellow!" quoth a third.

Nevertheless, obediently enough they made their way as the bell clanged, and the throng filed into their places most reverently. It was a pleasant sight. I came into rank unobtrusively at the back, among the rustling and nudging lay brethren. In other circumstances it would have amused me to see the grave faces they turned towards the altar, and to hear all the while the confused scuffling as they trod on each other's toes, trying whose skin was the tenderest or whose sandal soles were the thickest. One or two even tried conclusions with me, but once only. For the first who adventured got a stamp from my riding-boot which caused him to squeal out like a stuck pig, and but for the waking thunder of the organ might have gotten him a month's penance in addition. So after that my toes were left severely alone among the lay brethren.

Then came the high procession, at which the monks and all stood up. In front there were the incense-bearers and acolytes, then officers whose names, not being convent-bred nor yet greatly given to church-craft, I did not know. Then after them came two men who walked together, at the sight of whom the' jaws of all the monks dropped, and they stood so infinitely astonished that no power was left in them. For, instead of one, two mitred abbots entered in full canonical attire—golden mitre and green, golden-headed staff, red embroidered robes lined with green. These two paced solemnly in abreast, and sat down upon twin thrones.

"The Abbot of St. Omer!" whispered one of the lay brothers, naming one of the most famous abbeys in Europe, and the word flew round like lightning. Whether he had been instructed or not what to say I do not know. But at all events I saw the tidings run round the circle of the choir, overleap the boundary stall, and even reach the officiating priests, who inclined an eager ear to catch it, and passed the word one to another in the intervals of the chanted sentences.

Then the news was drowned in the thunder of the anthem, and the organ dominating all. Everything was strange to me, but most strange the practice of the lay brothers, who chanted bravely indeed in tune, but who (for the words set in the chorals) substituted other sentiments of a kind not usually found in service-books.

"He looks a stout and be-e-e-fy o-o-old fel-low, this A-a-a-bot of St. Omer, don't you think? Glory, glo-o-ry. Takes his meals well, likes his qu-a-a-art of Rhenish or his Burgundy to swell his jolly paunch. A-a-a-men!"

Or, as it might be: "Are you coming—are you coming o-o-out tonight? There will be-ee, good compan-ee-ee. Dancing and deray—lots of pretty girls; no proud churls. Ten by the clock, when the doors all lock. As it was in the beginning, is now, ever shall be, world without end, A-a-a-men!"

These were, of course, only the lay brothers, and I hope the friars were better behaved. I decided, however, that for the sake of my respect for religion, I should ask Dessauer. Because I saw even the Abbot Tobias lean smilingly over to Abbot Prince Karl, and I marvelled what they spoke about. Not that I had long to wonder, for through the open door of the chapel there streamed a dismal host of invaders from the Wolfmark— black Hussars of Death, in dark armor, with white skeletons painted over them, all charnel-house ribs and bones in hideous and ridiculous array—which was one of Duke Casimir's devices to frighten children, and no doubt these scarecrows frightened many of these. Specially when these villanous companies were recruited from all the wild bandits of the Mark, and never punished for any atrocity, but, on the contrary, rather encouraged in evil-doing in order to spread the terror of their name.

Yet, when they came rushing in, even the cavaliers of death were daunted by the sight which met them. And as the solemn service proceeded, amid the thunder of the great organ pressing, throbbing against the roof and reverberating along the floor, hands stole to heads, helmets were lifted, and half-forgotten fear of Holy Church stirred in many a wicked and outcast heart. Some of the foremost, with their blades half-drawn, appeared to waver whether or no they should even yet stay the service with the bloody sword.

But as the monks calmly chanted, and the solemn responses were given, a stillness stole over the vociferous babble within the great open doors.

Higher and higher the voices of the choir mounted, breaking a way to heaven. Awe sat on every fierce face, and when the Abbot Tobias arose to pronounce the benediction, the other stood up beside him, and the Hussars of Death knelt awe-stricken before the two mitred dignitaries of the Church.

Without a murmur they arose and slunk away without so much as searching the abbey, and so departed on their errands, leaving us safe and unharmed.

Then, when the three of us were again united in the private rooms of the Abbot Tobias, that hearty ecclesiastic shook us all by the hand and said, "Good friends, we are well out of that. Nay, no thanks! My monks are not a bit the worse of a little additional exercise to keep them humble and lean. Nor is God the less well pleased that we have sought him in time of need—as Prince and Abbot, as well as soldier and peasant, require."

These being the only words of genuine piety I had heard within the walls of the monastery, I thought more of the Abbot Tobias from that moment that he was not ashamed to speak them in the presence of Prince and Councillor of State, as well as before a rough soldier like myself.

CHAPTER XXXIX

THE FLAG ON THE BED TOWER

It took us all our powers of persuasion with the Prince to induce him to depart homeward on the morrow, under escort of a dozen sturdy and well-armed lanzknechte attached to the monastery. But the thing was done at last.

"And remember," said our Karl, as he embraced us, "that if ye return not on the eighth day at eventide, the forces of Plassenburg will e'en be battering on the gates of Thorn by the hour of dusk. I am not going to have my farms burned, my peasants disembowelled and cast to the blood-hounds, my women ravished in their kindly home-steadings. God wot! the cup of Duke Casimir hath been brimming this many a day, and we will give him a deep and bitter draught to drink when we set it to his lips."

Thereupon we bade our dear and brave master a respectful adieu. Karl Miller's Son he might be, but for all that he was every inch a king—a right royal man, whom I would rather serve than the Kaiser himself.

And after he had gone from us a little way he turned again and waved his hand, crying: "On the eighth day report you without fail, friends of mine, unless ye wish me to come asking for you at the gates of Thorn, with some din and the spilling of much blood."

The worthy Abbot Tobias gave us a paper to the Bishop Peter, now restored to his bishopric of Thorn, and in some measure dwelling at peace with the Duke Casimir since that ruler's reconciliation with Holy

Church. In this paper it was set forth that the most learned Doctor of Law, Leonard Schmidt, with his servant Johann, were on their way to Ratisbon to dispute concerning the Practice of Law and Reason with another most learned Doctor of the Empire, and that, desiring to remain a day of two in Thorn, they were by the Abbot Tobias of Wolgast commended to Bishop Peter's kind hospitality.

For indeed the inns of Germany, and especially of the North, were not at that time such as wise and learned men could readily submit to—neither abide in, to be herded with dull, landward peasants and all the tankard-swilling gutter-knaves of the town.

Of the remainder of our journey I need not speak, seeing that more than once I have had to tell of that journey from Thorn to Plassenburg. It is sufficient that by evening the dark, frowning mass of the Wolfsberg lay imminent before us, each tower black against the sky. For even the new portions which Casimir had builded were of intention blackened with soot—mingled with the plaster and mortar, so that they should be of one piece of grim terror with the rest of the building.

"After all it is not strange," said I to the Councillor, for when there was no one in sight or very near us I rode with him instead of behind him, "that the man who shakes at every breeze among the aspens should take such pains to create the fiction and shadow of terror about him, when the substance and reality is dominant all the while in his own bosom."

Since we had come within the distressed and depopulated territory of the Wolfmark we had not spoken to any soul. Indeed, except a few poor, desolate peasant folk, burned black with the sun, scuttling from den to den at the sight of mounted men, we had not seen any living creatures. The cruelty which had marked the reign of the Black Duke seemed to have afflicted the very face of the country with a visible curse.

But the day of deliverance was at hand.

As we came nearer to Thorn, there before us was the Red Tower, at first dimly apparent, then prominent, then commanding, finally rising higher than all the buildings of the Wolfsberg. How many days had I not looked down from those windows! And my father was even now up there in his grim garret, his heart stirring calm and kindly within him, in spite of all the atmosphere of blood in which his life had moved, as untouched as though he had been a gardener working among the flowers of the parterre. Also the block was there, and against it the Red Axe was leaning.

Then I called to mind the prophecy of the Lady Ysolinde, that I should return to take up my father's dreadful trade. And I smiled thereat. For I thought that now I came in other circumstances—aye, even though riding in at the tail of the learned Doctor Schmidt with my shaven and chestnut-stained face, my flowing hair cropped to the roots, as in the manner of the servant tribe! Yet for all that was I not the virtual military commander of the Plassenburg and the right hand of the Prince, whose forces would soon be clamoring against the walls of Thorn and bringing down to destruction the hateful tyranny of the Black Duke Casimir?

"What is that?" said I, pointing to a standard of immense size which drooped from the Red Tower. It had been hanging limp and straight about the staff, and till now we had not observed it. But as we went toiling up to the Weiss Thor, and the last links of road lengthened themselves indefinitely out before us in their own familiar manner, suddenly a waft of hot wind from the sun-beaten plain of the Wolfmark blew out an immense black flag, which spread itself, fluttered feebly, and died down again flat against the pole.

"Nay," said the Doctor, "that I cannot tell. Surely you should know the customs of your own city better than I!"

For the heat had made the High Chancellor a little snappish, as well perhaps as the length of the way.

"Never in my time have I seen such a thing float above the Red Tower," I made answer. "Can it be a flag of pestilence?"

It seemed a likely thing enough. Cities were often made desolate in a few days by the plague—the people running to the hills, a weird devil's silence all about the gates. These might well betoken the presence of a foe to which the army of Plassenburg would seem as a friend.

As we rode under the Arch of the White Gate of Thorn we were summarily halted to be examined. We gave our names, and the Doctor showed his letters of authorization from a dozen learned universities. The Black Hussar who examined our credentials was of a taciturn disposition, and evidently no scholar, for he studied the parchments intently upsidedown, and appeared to have an idea that their genuineness was best investigated by smelling the seals.

"Where are you bound?" he asked.

"To the house of the learned and venerable Bishop of Thorn!" said the Doctor Schmidt.

So the Hussar, having finally approved of the quality of the scholastic wax, called a subordinate, and bade him guide us to the house of Bishop Peter.

In an instant we were in the familiar streets, narrow, sunken, and indescribably dirty, as they now appeared to me. For I had been accustomed to the wider, airier spaces, and to the bickering rivulets which ran down most of the steeper streets of Plassenburg, and which made it one of the cleanest towns in the world. So that the ancient and unreformed filth and wretchedness of Thorn appealed to my senses as they had never done before.

There were evidences too of the terror in which the inhabitants had long lived. The houses of the rich burghers were sadly dilapidated. No man thought it worth while to spend a pot of paint on a house which might be knocked about his ears that very night, if the Duke conceived there was money or gear to be found within the walls of it.

Here and there the same black banner appeared.

I asked the reason of it from our guide.

"Is it that the plague is in the city?"

"The plague has, indeed, been in the city—yes! But that is not the reason of the flag."

"And what then is the meaning of the black flag?" said I.

"Ye are strangers indeed!" answered the man. "Did you not know that the great Duke Casimir is dead, and that the black flag flies for him, and must fly on the Wolfsberg till his successor be crowned."

"And who is his successor?" said I.

"Who but young Otho, the worst of the Wolfs litter. But perhaps you are his friend?"

He turned with a keen look, like one who has been accustomed to deliver himself in company where he is sure of sympathy, and who suddenly has to consider his words in society the tone of which he is not sure of.

"Nay," said I, "we are travelling strangers and know nothing of your politics. But this Duke Otho, wherefore has he not been crowned?"

"Because," said the man, "the Duke Casimir, they say, hath been foully murdered, and that through the witchcraft of a woman. So by our laws, till the murderer is punished, the young Duke may not be crowned."

By this time we were at the entering in of the long, dull mass of building, which during most of my boyhood had stood unoccupied, owing to the quarrel between Bishop Peter and the Duke. Our guide led us unchallenged into the quadrangle, and then abruptly vanished without pausing to bid us good-day, or even deigning to accept the modest gratuity which my master, the learned Doctor, had in his front pouch ready for him.

As for me, I stood holding the horses and looking about for any of my own quality who might show me the way to the stables.

Presently a long, lean, lathy youth slouched out of one of the gloomy entries. He stood amazed at the sight of me. I went to him to ask where I might bestow the horses, now standing weary-footed, hanging their heads after the long journey and the toil of the final ascent from the plain.

"Will you fight, outlander?" were the first words of my lathy friend from the entry. He seemed to have been drawn up recently from a period of detention in some deep draw-well, and to have the mould of the stones still upon him.

"Why," said I, "of course I will fight, and that gladly, if you will find me a man to fight with!"

"I will fight you myself," he said, swelling himself. "For the end of this candle I will fight half a dozen such Baltic sausages as you be."

"Like enough," said I, "all in good time. But in the mean time show me the stables, that I may put up my master's horses."

"What know I about you or your master's horses?" cried my Lad of Lath; "and pray why should I show the way to Bishop Peter's good stables to every wastrel that comes sneaking in off the street and asks the freedom of our house. For aught I know you may have come to steal corn. Though, if that be so, Lord love you, you have come to the wrong place."

"Come, stable-master," said I, placably, "let me see a corner and a wisp of straw and I will ease the poor beasts. That will not harm the Bishop Peter, whom my master has gone to visit. He is a friend of his, a man learned in ecclesiastical affairs, who comes to hold disputations with the Bishop—"

"Disputations—what be those? Anything with money at the end of them? If so, he will be a welcome guest at this house. There is very little money at the tail of anything in this town."

I thought I would try the effect of a broad silver piece upon him, at the same time giving the lad the information that disputations were kinds of fights with the tongues of men instead of with their fists.

The silver sweetened his face like a charm. He seized me by the hand.

"My name," he cried, "is Peter of the Pigs. I am not stable-master, but feed the grouting piglings. And yet in a way I am indeed stable-master. For the Bishop hath had no horses since the Duke took them away to mount his cavalry for the raids into Plassenburg. So Peter of the Pigs looks after all about the yard, and precious little there is to look after—except one's own legs getting longer and leaner every day."

"And where is the Bishop this afternoon?" I said.

"Where should he be," cried Peter of the Pigs, "but at the trial of the witch-woman in the Hall of Justice? It must be a rare sight. They say she is to be put to the torture, and that they want a new executioner to do it."

"Why," said I, struck to the heart by his words, "what is the matter with the old one?"

"Oh," said the lad, "he is mortal sick abed. He happened an accident, or some one stuck a dagger into him—no great matter if he had stuck it through him, or cloven him to the chine with his own Red Axe!"

CHAPTER XL

THE TRIAL OF THE WITCH

At this point came my master back, looking exceedingly disconsolate. A starveling, furtive-eyed monk accompanied him.

"The Bishop," he said, "is gone forth of his house. He is in attendance at the trial of a woman for witchcraft, one whom some of the common city folk hold to be a saint. But the young Duke and others swear that she is a witch, and hath murdered the Duke Casimir. Haste thee with the horses, sirrah, and attend me to the Hall of Justice. I have sent a messenger forward with my credentials to the Bishop Peter."

So to the corner of the yard I went and rubbed down the horses with a wisp of straw which Peter of the Pigs brought me, and which smelled of his charges too. Then, with another piece of money in his hand, I sent him out to the nearest corn-chandler's to buy some corn for our beasts, the which I gave them, and stood by them till I saw them eat it too. For in such a poverty-stricken place, and with a gentleman of the capacity of Master Peter of the Pigs, one that is in any way fond of his horses cannot be too careful.

This done, I announced myself to my master as ready to accompany him.

Then, through the streets of Thorn, all strangely empty, we took our way. Women were leaning out of windows; every head turned castleward up the street.

They hardly deigned a glance at my master or at myself, but continued to gaze. And as each passenger came down the street from the direction of the Wolfsberg they cried questions at him, so that he ran the gantlet of a dropping fire of shrill queries.

"What are they doing to the sweet saint up yonder?"

"Hath she been put to the Question?"

"Who could be executioner in such a case? A man would be sent to hell-fire for daring to lay hand on her."

The popular sympathies ran clearly with the accused, which is not, as our old Hanne had reason to remember, the rule in trials for witchcraft.

Soon we were passing the gate of the Red Tower. It was barred and closed. The windows of my father's house looked barrenly down, like the eye-holes of skulls. I saw the window from which I used to gaze wistfully down upon the children, who would not play with me, but spat upon the tower when they saw me looking at their play and pipings upon the streets.

There above was the window of my father's garret, with the edge of the black flag blowing out above it.

The streetward door of the Judgment Hall was open, and a great crowd of people stood about, silent, anxious, respectful. Some of them talked in low tones, and whenever there was a word passed out of the door, within which men looked ten deep, it scattered all about like a wave which comes into a sea-cave by a narrow entrance, and then widens out till it breaks gently in the wide inner hall.

"She is not to be tortured; only the Hereditary Executioner may do that. They have threatened the old woman. She has confessed all!"

So ran the words about the crowd, and ever and anon, one would detach himself from the press, elbowing his way out, and then speed down the long street, crying the latest tidings of the trial.

It was manifestly impossible for us to obtain entrance by this door. So we looked about for another.

Then I minded me of the private passage which led from the inner court-yard which I knew so well. We skirted the crowd, with our attendant following, till we came to the side door, which led directly into the Hall of Judgment behind the judges' high seats.

It was the way by which many a time I had seen my father enter, either in his dress of black or in that of red. And I was always glad when I saw him put on the scarlet, because I knew that then the worst was over for some poor tortured soul.

But when my master proposed that the attendant of the Bishop should carry a letter into the hall to his master to inform him that we waited without, the man trembled in every limb, and the hair of his head shocked itself up in sheer terror.

"I cannot—I dare not," he cried; "it is the place of torture—of the engines—the strappado—the water-drop, the leg-crushers!"

And at this point the vision of what was contained within the fatal door became so appalling to him that he picked up his skirts and fled, looking over his shoulder all the while to make sure that the Red Axe was not after him full tilt.

So Dessauer and I were left standing. And if the matter had been less serious, it would have been comical to see us thus deserted upon mine own middenstead, as it were.

"Bishop Peter of Thorn seems a prelate somewhat difficult of approach," said the Chancellor. "I wonder if we shall ever lay any salt on his tail?"

"Let us risk it and go in," said I. "We are putting all our cards on the table, at any rate. And at least we can see all that is to be sees. If there is any risk of Von Reuss penetrating our disguises, it is as well to gulp and get it over at once, rather than suck gingerly at it till the fear of death chills our marrow."

"Go on, then," he said, somewhat crossly; "there is indeed naught to be gained by standing here as a butt for the eyes of evil-doers."

So I opened the door carefully, and with a trembling heart. The hum of a great assembly breathed turbidly upon us in a hushed chaos of sound. The warm, stifling atmosphere, heavy with a thousand respirations, the sound of a voice speaking loud and clear, the thunder of continuous heels on the paved floor, the voices of the ushers crying, "Silentium!" at intervals—these all came suddenly upon us as we shut out the air and sunshine and went into the Hall of Judgment.

We could not see the full assembly at first. We stood, as I had supposed, directly behind the judges' rostrum. Only the corners of the vast crowd which covered the floor and filled the galleries could be seen—a blur of white faces all bent towards one point. But at the corner, not far from us, a tall, spare, gray-headed ecclesiastic was speaking.

We stood still, in order that we might not interrupt by entering till he had finished.

What was our surprise when we heard his words.

"My Lord Duke," he was saying, "it is fortunate for the elucidation of this great mystery that I have this moment received word concerning a most learned and notable jurisconsult, a Doctor of the Law, wise in controversy and specially skilled in such cases, who has even now arrived in the city of Thorn, on his way to the Emperor at Ratisbon, before whom he is to dispute for the honor of truth and our holy religion.

"His name is the Learned, Venerable, and Reverend Doctor Schmidt, and I trust that we of the city and faculty of the Wolfmark shall have the honor of welcoming him as so distinguished a man deserves."

The pattern of the Bishop's speech is one that does not vary while the world lasts.

"Lord, they have made me a Doctor of Theology as well!" whispered the Chancellor to me. I gave him a little push.

"Now is your time," said I, "the hour and the Doctor!"

I lifted the skirt of his long black robe. He took hold of his marvellous beard, a triumph of the disguiser's art, and we stepped forward. I could hardly conceal a smile.

We had come in the very nick of time.

Then after this I have a vague remembrance of my master bowing this way and that. I seem to see the wise men of the law, the judges, the priests, and lictors rising and bowing in acknowledgment. I heard the hush of a thousand people all craning their necks to look round the heads of their neighbors, and the hum of whispered comment reach farther and farther back, till it lapped against the walls and ebbed out into the street from the great open door of the Hall of Judgment. It was a surprising sight, this great trial—the gloomy hall, black with age and deeds of darkness, lit by the rays of sunlight falling through windows of red glass, the faces of men flecked as with blood where the evening sunlight streamed luridly upon them.

In the midst there was a clear four-square space. A lictor, with a bundle of rods, stood at each corner. I looked, and there, alone in the centre, attired in white, the cynosure of eyes, I beheld—Helene.

CHAPTER XLI

THE GARRET OF THE RED TOWER

I felt my temples, my ears, my neck tingling with cold. I seemed to have fallen into a sea of ice. I think I would have fallen and fainted but that at that moment my master sat down beside the Bishop, and I was left free to retire into a darksome corner, where I staggered against a beam, slimy with black sweat, and hung over it with my hand clasping my brow, trying to think what had happened.

I do not know how long I remained in this position, nor yet when I came to myself. All was a dream to me, a nightmare of horrid whirlings and infinite oppressions. The faces of the folk that watched, the garmentry of the Bishop and his priests, the red robes of the young Duke and his assessors, spun round me in a hideous phantasmagoria.

At last I was conscious that a trumpet had blown. Whereupon all rose up. The secretaries stacked their papers unconcernedly with the feathers of their pens in their mouths. And then in the solemn silence which ensued the Duke and his judges filed out of the door, while the power of the Church, represented by Bishop Peter and his priests, went forth by another. Before I could realize the situation, Helene had vanished, as it seemed, down a trap-door in the floor.

My master accompanied Bishop Peter. As for me, I hardly knew what I did. I did not even stand up, till our conductor, he who had gone forward to announce us at the first, ran across to me, and, plucking me by the arm from the beam on which I leaned, whispered, hurriedly: "Art dead or drunk, man, that thou riskest thine ears and thy neck? Stand up while the Judges and the new Duke go by!"

So, dazed and numb, I hent me up, and lo! coming arm in arm towards me were Otho von Reuss and his newly appointed Chief Justice and assessor—who but mine old friend Michael Texel! The Duke bent a searching look on me as I bowed low before him, but he saw only the tan of my skin and the close bristle of my hair. And so all passed on.

"Ho, blackamoor, thy master waits thee! Run, if thou wouldst avoid the whipping-post!" cried another of the rout of servitors, with a small sniggering laugh.

So, putting out a hand to stay myself, I staggered weakly after my master. I found him at the door, in talk with the confessor of the Bishop.

"And so," he was saying, "this girl was reared in the executioner's house. And she went away to a far country in order to learn the secrets of necromancy, it is not known where. I would see this Duke's Justicer. Does he dwell near by? What! In that very tower? It is of good omen. Let us go in thither."

But the confessor excused himself, being in no wise desirous to visit the Red Axe, even in his time of sickness.

"I have business of the soul with Bishop Peter. I will speak with thee again at refection," he said, twitching his head up at the Red Tower with suspicious glances, as if he feared unseen ears might be listening, and that some of its fearful magic might even descend upon a man so notably holy as a Bishop's confessor.

Presently Dessauer and I were across the court-yard at the well-known door. I knocked, and listened, whereupon ensued silence. Again and yet again I made the quaint death's-head knocker thunder, and then, when the echoes ceased, there was once more a great silence in the tower.

I heard the blood-hounds of Duke Casimir howl. The indigo shadow of the pinnacled Hall of Justice stretched across and touched the Red Tower with an ominous finger.

"Let us go in," said I. And, pushing the unresisting door, I began to climb the stone stairs. Each smoothed hollow and chipped edge was familiar to me as my name. Indeed, much more so, for I was now passing under a false one. So I climbed, in a dazed way, up and up. There on my left was the sitting-room. It had been searched high and low, escritoires rudely tossed down, aumries rifled, household stuff, grain, white linen, empty bottles, all cast about and huddled together even as the searchers had left them.

Then above was the little room where Helene used to sleep. Here the wrack was indescribable—every hidingplace rifled, her pretty worked bedquilt lying across the doorway trampled and soiled, her dainty white clothing, some she had worn at Plassenburg, and even the tiny dresses of her childhood, all torn and confused together. And in the midst, what affected me more than everything else, a tiny puppet of wood my father had hewn her with his knife, and which she had dressed as a queen with red ribbons and crown of tinsel—ah, so long ago—and in such happy days.

"Father!" I called, loudly. "Father!"

But in this I forgot myself. There might have been enemies lurking anywhere in the house of pain and disaster.

My own room came next, and the way out upon the roof; but we tried not these. There remained only the garret of my father. I climbed up, with Dessauer behind me, and pushed the door open.

Then I stood in the entering-in, looking for the first time for years on the face of my father.

He lay on his conch, his head bound about with a napkin. The dark wisp of hair which rose like a cock's comb, sticking through the stained cloth which swathed his brow, was no longer blue-black, but of an iron-gray, splashed and brindled with pure white. His eyes were open, and shone, cavernous and solemn, above his fallen-in cheeks. It was like looking into the secrets of another world. That which he had so often caused other eyes to see, the Red Axe of Thorn was now to see for himself. The hand which lay—mere skin, muscle, and bone—on the counterpane had guided many to the door of the mysteries. Now at its own entrance it was to push the arras aside, for the Death-Justicer of the Mark was to go before the Judge of all the earth.

My father lay gazing at me with deep, mournful eyes. So sad they seemed that it was as if nothing in heaven or earth, neither joy nor sorrow, life nor death, could have power to change their expression of immeasurable sadness.

I entered, and my companion followed.

"You are alone? There is none with you here?" I said to my father, going to the bedside.

He started at the voice, and looked up even eagerly. But his eyes dulled and deadened again as he fell back.

"I did but dream!" he muttered, sadly.

"You have no one with you here, Gottfried Gottfried?" said I again, for in a matter of life and death it was as well to make sure even at risk of disturbing a dying man.

He set his hand to his brow as if trying to think.

"Who should be with me—except all these?" he answered, very solemnly. And swept his hand about the room as if he saw strange shapes standing in rows round the walls. "I wish," he went on, almost querulously, "whoever you may be, you would tell these people to keep their hands down. They point at me, and thrust their dripping heads forward, holding them like lanterns in their palms."

He turned away to the back of the bed, and then, as if he saw something there worse than all the rest, faced about again quickly, saying, with some pathetic intonation of his lost childhood, "There is no need for them to point so at me, is there? I did but my duty."

"Father!" said I, gently touching his cheek with my hand as I used to do.

"Ah, what is that?" he said, quickly. "Did some one call me father? Let me go! I tell you, sirs, let me go! She needs me. They are torturing her. I must go to her!"

"Father," I said again, putting him gently back, "it is I—your own son Hugo—come back to speak with you, to help if it may be—to die for the Little Playmate if need be."

"Hugo—Hugo!" he said. "Yes, yes—of course, I know—my little lad, my pretty boy!"

He pushed me back to look at me, eagerly, wistfully—and then thrust me sharply away.

"Bah!" he said; "you lie! What need to lie to a dying man? My Hugo had yellow hair and a skin like lilies. Yours is dark—"

"Father," said I, "I am here disguised. Help is coming, sure and strong, if we can only wait a little and delay the trial. But tell me all. Speak to me freely, if you love your daughter Helene—your daughter and my love."

He sat up now, and motioned me to come nearer. There was a dark, fierce, unworldly light in his eyes. I set a pillow to his back, and went and kneeled by the bed as I used to do at goodnight time when I said my Paternoster.

Then for the first time he knew me.

"Say your prayers, child!" he commanded, in his old voice.

So, though with the stress of wars and other things I had mostly forgotten, yet I said not only that, but the little Prayer of Childhood he had taught me. And then I kissed him as I used to do when I bade him goodnight.

"Yes," he said, softly, "it is true, after all. You are mine own only son. Hugo—I am glad you have come so far to see your father before he dies."

I told him how I had come, and brought Dessauer forward, introducing him as one great in the kingdom where I was, and to whom I was much beholden. He shook him by the hand with grave, intent courtesy, and again looked at me.

"Now, father," said I, "we have no long time to bide with you, lest the new Duke come upon us. We must hie us back to our lodging with the Bishop Peter, lest we be missed."

My father smiled.

"Ye will live but sparely there!" said he, with a flicker of his ancient smile.

"Tell us how you came to this," said I, "and, if you can, why Helene, our little Helene, stands so terribly accused."

My father paused a long time before he began to answer.

"It is not easy for me to tell you all," he said. "I know and I have the words, but, somehow, when I try to fit the words to the thing, they run asunder and will not mix, like water and oil. But see, Hugo, here is an elixir of rare value. Drop a drop or two on my tongue if ye see me wander. It will bring me back for a time."

CHAPTER XLII

PRINCESS PLAYMATE

Then began my father to tell the story slowly, with many a pause and interruption, now searching for words, now racked with pain, all of which I need not imitate, and shall leave out. But the substance of his tale was to this effect:

"After you had left us, the Dukedom went from bad to worse—no peace, no rest, no money. Duke Casimir took less and less of my advice, but, on the contrary, began again his old horrors—plundering, killing, living by terror and in terror. He threatened Torgau. He attacked Plassenburg. He stirred up hornets' nests everywhere. At home he made himself the common mark for every assassin.

"Then suddenly came his nephew back, and almost immediately he grew great in favor with him. Uncle and nephew drank together. They paraded the terraces arm in arm. I was never more sent for save to do my duty. Otho von Reuss rode abroad at the head of the Black Horsemen.

"But, at the same time, to my great joy, arrived the Little Playmate back to me. She was safer with me, she said. So that, having her, I needed naught else. She came with good news of you, making the journey not alone, for two men of the Princess's retinue brought her to the city gates."

"The Princess!" I cried; "aye, I thought so. I judged that it was the Princess who sent her back."

Dessauer motioned with his hand. He saw that it was dangerous to throw my father off the track. And, indeed, this was proven at once, for my unfortunate interruption set my father's mind to wandering, till finally I had to drop certain drops of the red liquid on his tongue. These, indeed, had a marvellous effect upon him. He sat up instantly, his eyes flashing the old light, and began to speak rapidly and to clear purport, even as he used to do in the old days when Duke Casimir would come striding across the yard at all hours of the night and day to consult his Justicer.

"What was I telling?" he went on. "Yes, I remember, of the homecoming of Helene under honorable escort. And she was beautiful—but all her race were beautiful, all the women of them, at any rate. But that is another matter.

"So things went well enough with us till, as she went across the yard one day to meet me at the door of the hall as I came out, who should see her but the Count Otho von Reuss. And she turned from him like a queen and took hold of my arm, clasping it strongly. Then he gazed fixedly at us both, and his look was the evil-doer's look. Oh, I know it. Who knows that look, if not I? And so we passed within. But my Helene was quivering and much afraid, nestling to me—aye, to me, old Gottfried Gottfried, like a frightened dove.

"After this she went not out into the court-yard or city any more, save with me by her side, and Otho von Reuss lingered about, watching like a wolf about the sheepfold. For, as I say, he was in high favor with Duke Casimir, and had already equal place with him on the bed of justice.

"Then there came a night, lightning peeping and blazing, alternate blue and ghastly white—God's face and the devil's time about staring in at the lattice. I lay alone in my chamber. But I was not asleep. As you know, I do not often sleep. But I lay awake and thought and thought. The lightning showed me faces I had not seen for thirty years, and forms I remembered, black against eternity. But all at once, in a certain after-clap of silence that followed the roaring thunder, I heard a voice call to me.

"'My father—my father' it cried.

"It was like a soul in danger calling on God.

"I rose and went, clad as I was in the red of mine office (for that day I had done the final grace more than once); even so, I ran down the stairs to the room of my little Helene.

"The lightning showed me my lamb crouched in the corner, her lips open, white, squared with horror, her arms extended, as though to push some monstrous thing away. A black shape, whose, I could not tell, I saw bending over her. Then came blackness of darkness again. And again my Helene's voice. Ah, God, I can hear it now, calling pitifully, like a woman hanging over hell and losing hold: 'Father—my father!'

"'I am here!' I cried, loudly, even as on the scaffold I cry the doom for which the malefactors die.

"And the room lit up with a flame, white as the face of God as He passed by on Mount Sinai, flash on continuous flash. And there before me, with a countenance like a demon's, stood Otho von Reuss."

I uttered a hoarse cry, but Dessauer again checked me. My father went on:

"Otho von Reuss it was—he saw me in my red apparel, and cried aloud with mighty fear. If God had given me mine axe in my hand—well, Duke or no Duke, he had cried no more. But even as he turned and fled from the room I seized him about the waist, and, opening the window with my other hand, I cast him forth. And as he went down backward, clutching at nothing, God looked again out of the skylights of heaven, and showed me the face of the devil, even as Michael saw it when he hurled him shrieking into the nether pit.

"Then I went back and took in my arms my one ewe lamb.

"Many days (so they brought me word) Otho lay at the point of death, and Duke Casimir came not near me nor yet sent for me. But by that very circumstance I knew Otho had not revealed how his accident had befallen. Yet he but bided his time. And as he grew well, Duke Casimir grew ill. He waxed more and more like an armored ghost, and one day he came here and sat on the bed as in old times.

"'I know my friends now,' he said, 'good Red Axe of mine, friend of many years. I have had mine eyes blinded, but this morning there has come a mighty clearness, and from this day forth you and I shall stand face to face and see eye to eye again, as in the days of old!'

"Then being athirst, he asked for something to drink. Which, when our sweet Helene had brought, he patted her cheek. 'A maid too good for a court—one among a thousand, a fair one!' he said; and passed away down the stairs, walking with his old steady tread.

"But even at the steps of the Hall of Justice he stumbled and fell. They carried him in, and there in the robing chamber he lay unconscious for a week, and then died without speech.

"When he was dead, and ere he had been embalmed, there arose a clamor, first among the followers of Otho von Reuss, and after that among those of the Wolfsberg who expected that they would be favored by the new Duke. It was first whispered, and then cried aloud, that the death of Duke Casimir had been compassed by witchcraft and potions.

"Cunningly and with subtlety was spread the report how my daughter and I had worked upon Duke Casimir. How he had gone to our house, drunken a draught, and then died ere he could come to his own chamber. But as for me, I went on my way and heeded them not. For just then the plague, which had stricken the Duke first, stalked athwart the city unchecked, and all through it this Helene of ours was as the angel of God, coming and going by night and day among the streets and lanes of the town. And the common folk almost worshipped her. And so do unto this day.

"Now perhaps I did not heed this babble as I ought to have done. But there came one night—how long ago I have forgotten—and with it a clamor in the court-yard. The Black Riders, the worst of them, fiends incarnate that Otho had of late gathered about him, thundered upon us without, and presently burst in the door.

"I met them with mine axe at the stair-head, and for the better part of an hour I kept them at a distance. And some died and some were dismembered. For at that business I am not a man to make mistakes. Then came Otho limping from his fall and shot me with a bolt from behind his men. And so over my body as I lay at the stair-head they took my love and left me here to die. And the new Duke will not kill me, for he desires that I shall see her agony ere my own life is taken. For that alone the fiend keeps me in life!

"And that," said my father, feebly, "is all."

But just as he seemed to ebb away a wild fear startled him.

"No," he cried, "there is yet something more. Hugo, Hugo, keep me here a little! Hold me that my mind may not wander away among the racking-wheels and the faces mopping and mowing. I have something yet to tell."

I held him up while Dessauer poured a drop or two of the potent liquid into his mouth. As before, it instantly revived him. The color came back to his cheeks.

"Quick, Hugo, lad!" he cried; "give me that black box which sits behind the block." I brought it, and from this he extracted a small key, which he gave me.

"Unlock the panel you see there in the wall," he said.

I looked, but could find none.

"The oaken knob!" he cried, sharply, as to a clumsy servitor.

I could only see a rough knob in the wood-work, a little worm-eaten, and in the centre one hole a little larger than the rest.

"Put in the key!" commanded my father, making as if he would come out of bed and hasten me himself.

I thrust in the key, indeed, but with no more faith than if I had been bidden to put it into a mouse-hole.

Nevertheless, it turned easy as thinking, and a little door swung open, cunningly fitted. Here were dresses, books, parchments huddled together.

"Bring all these to me," he said.

And I brought them carefully in my arms and laid them on the bed.

The eye of old Dessauer fell on something among them and was instantly fascinated. It was a woman's waist-belt of thick bars of gold laid three and three, with crests and letters all over it.

The Chancellor put his hand forward for it, and my father allowed him to take it, following him, however, with a questioning eye.

Then Dessauer put his hand into his bosom and drew out a chain of gold—the necklace of the woodman, in-deed—and laid the two side by side. He uttered a shrill cry as he did so.

"The belt of the lost Princess!" he cried; "the little Princess of Plassenburg!"

And, laying them one above the other, each group of six bars read thus:

```
o o o    H    o o o    H    o o o    H    o o o
         |             |             |
o o o    E    o o o    E    o o o    E    o o o      The Necklace
         |             |             |
o o o    L    o o o    L    o o o    L    o o o


o o o    E    o o o    E    o o o    E    o o o
         |             |             |
o o o    N    o o o    N    o o o    N    o o o      The Belt
         |             |             |
o o o    E    o o o    E    o o o    E    o o o
```

With delight on his face, like that of a mathematician when his calculations work out truly, Dessauer reached over his hand for the papers also, but my father stayed him.

"Who may you be that has a chain to match mine?" he asked, with his mighty hand on Dessauer's wrist.

"I am the State's Chancellor of Plassenburg, and it needed but this to show me our true Princess."

"Here, then," said my father, "is more and better."

And he handed him the papers.

"It meets! It meets!" cried Dessauer, enthusiastically, as he glanced them over. "It is complete. It would stand probation in the Dict of the Emperor."

"But yet all that will not prevent Helene Gottfried dying at the stake!" cried my father, sadly, and fell back unconscious on his bed.

* * * * *

We spent this heaviest of nights at the palace of Bishop Peter— Dessauer with the prelate—I, praise to the holy pyx, in the kitchen with the serving men and maids. Peter of the Pigs was there, but no more eager to fight. The lay brother who had gone with the letter, and the conductor who had run away from the dread door of the Hall of Justice, had returned, and had spread a favorable report of our courage.

Certainly the house of Peter the Bishop might be a poor one and scantily provendered, but there was little sign of it that night. For if the master went fasting and his guests lived on pulse (as they said in Thorn), certainly not so Bishop Peter's servants.

For there were pasties of larks, with sauce of butter and herbs, most excellent and toothsome. There were rabbits from the sand-hills, and pigeons from the towers of the minster. The clear chill Rhenish vied with the more generous wine of Burgundy and the red juice of Assmanhauser. For me, as was natural, I ate little. I spoke not at all. But I looked so dangerous with my swarthy face and desperate eye, I dare say, also I was so well armed, that the roysterers left me severely alone.

But I drank—Lord, what did I not drink that night! I poured down my gullet all and sundry that was given me. And to render these Bishop's thralls their dues, there was no lack and no inhospitality. But the strange thing of it was that, though I am a man more than ordinarily temperate, that night I poured the Rhenish into me like water down a cistern-pipe and felt it not. God forgive me, I wanted to make me drunken and forgetful, and lo! the dog's swill would not bite.

So I cursed their drink, and asked if they had no Lyons Water-of-Life, stark and mordant, or social Hollands, or indeed anything that was not mere compound of whey and dirty water. Whereat they wondered, and held me thereafter in great respect as a good companion and approven worthy drinker.

Then they brought me of the strong spirit of Dantzig, with curious little flakes of gold dancing in it. It was raw and strong, and at first I had good hopes of it. But I drank the Dautzig like spring-water, all there was of it, and though it had a taste singularly displeasing to me, it took no more effect than so much warm barley-brew for the palates of babes. Upon this I had great glory. For the card-players and the dicers actually left their games and gazed open-jawed to see me drink. And I sat there and expounded the Levitical law and the wheels of the Prophet Ezekiel, the law of succession to the empire, and also the apostolic succession— all with surprising clearness and cogency of reasoning. So that before I had finished they required of me whether it was I or my master who was sent for to dispute before His Sovereign mightiness the Emperor.

Then I told them that the things I knew (that is, which the Hollands had put into my head) were but the commonest chamber-sweepings of my master's learning, which I had picked up as I rode at his elbow. And this bred a mighty wondering what manner of man he might be who was so wise. And I think, if I had gone on, Dessauer and I might both have found ourselves in the Bishop's prison, on suspicion of being the devil and one of his ministrants.

But suddenly, as with a kind of recoil or back stroke, all that I had drunken must have come upon me. The clearness of vision went from me like a candle that is blown out. I know not what happened after, save that I found myself upon my truckle-bed, with my leathern money-pouch clasped in my hand with surprising tightness, as if I had been mortally afraid that some one would mistake my poor satchel for his own pocket.

So in time the morrow came, and by all rules I ought to have had a racking headache. For I saw many of those that had been with me the night before pale of countenance and eating handfuls of baker's salt. So I judged that their anxiety and the turmoil of their hearts had not burned their liquor up, as had been the case with me.

Now it is small wonder that all my soul cried out for oblivion till I should be able to do something for the Beloved—break her prison, hasten the troops from Plassenburg, or in some way save my love.

Hardly had I looked out of the main door that morning, desiring no more than to pass away the time till the trial should begin again, before I saw the Lubber Fiend, smirking and becking across the way. He had squatted himself down on the side of the street opposite, looking over at the Bishop's palace.

He pointed at me with his finger.

"Your complexion runs down," he said. "I know you. But go to the spring there by the stable, wash your face, and I shall know you better."

This was fair perdition and nothing less. For one may stay the tongue of a scoundrel with money, or the expectation of it, until opportunity arrive to stop it with steel or prison masonry. But who shall curb or halter the tongue of a fool?

Then, swift as one that sees his face in a glass, I bethought me of a plan.

"See," I said, "do you desire gold, Sir Lubber Fiend?"

He wagged his great head and shook his cabbage-leaf ears till they made currents in the heavy air, to signify that he loved the touch of the yellow metal.

"See then, Lubber," said I, "you shall have ten of these now, and ten more afterwards, if you will carry a letter to the Prince at Plassenburg, or meet him on the way."

"Not possible," said he, shaking his head sadly; "my little Missie has come to Thorn."

"But," said I, "little Missie would desire it; take letter to the Prince, good Jan, then Missie will be happy."

"Would she let poor Jan Lubberchen kiss her hand, think you?" he asked, looking up at me.

"Aye," said I; "kiss her cheek maybe!"

He danced excitedly from side to side.

"Jan will run—Jan will run all the way!" he cried.

So I pulled out a scrap of parchment and wrote a hasty message to the Prince, asking him, for the love of God and us, to set every soldier in Plassenburg on the march for Thorn, and to come on ahead himself with such a flying column as he could gather. No more I added, because I knew that my good master would need no more.

Then I went down with my messenger to the Weiss Thor, and with great fear and pulsation of the midriff I saw the idiot pass the house of Master Gerard. Then, at the outer gate, I gave him his ten golden coins, and watched him trot away briskly on the green winding road to Plassenburg.

"Mind," he called back to me, "Jan is to kiss her cheek if Jan takes letter to the Prince!"

And I promised it him without wincing. For by this time lying had no more effect upon me than dram-drinking.

CHAPTER XLIII

THE TRIAL FOR WITCHCRAFT

The Bed of Justice was set by eight of the morning. For they were ever early astir in the city of Thorn, though, like most early risers, they did little enough afterwards all day.

With a sadly beating heart, I accompanied Dessauer in the same guise as on the previous day. The crowd was even greater in and about the Hall of Judgment. And when the Duke had taken his seat and his tools set themselves down on either side, they brought in the Little Playmate.

She was dressed all in white, clean and spotless, in spite of prison usage. She glanced just once about her, right and left, high and low, as if seeking for a face she could not see, and from thenceforth she looked down on the ground.

The argument as to torture had been concluded on the day before, and it had been held inadmissible—not because of any kindly thought for the prisoner, but because, according to the laws of the Wolfmark, in the absence of the Hereditary Executioner, there was no one legally capable of inflicting it.

Then came the evidence.

The first witness against the Little Playmate was old Hanne. She was brought in by a cowled monk of dark and sinister appearance—in fact, as my heart leaped to observe, I saw that she was accompanied by Friar Laurence—he who had taught me my learning in the old days, and who even then had watched the Little Playmate with no friendly eyes.

As she passed the judges I saw the deadly fear mount to agony on the face of old Hanne. The look in her eyes of physical pain suffered and overpassed was the same which I had often seen in the wars after the surgeon has done his horrid work. That same look I saw now on the face of Hanne. So I knew that somewhere in the dark recesses under the Hall of Judgment the Extreme Question had been put to her, and to all appearance answered according to the liking of the persecutors, though they dared not torture so notable a public prisoner as Helene.

I saw a look of satisfied vindictiveness pass over the brutal features of Duke Otho. He changed his position and whispered to his colleagues.

It was Master Gerard von Sturm who rose to put the questions to the witness. And as he did so, I heard the steady sough of talk among the people rise mutteringly in a low growl of anger and contempt. The Duke's lictors struck right and left among the crowd, as men bent forward with fierce hate in their voices, lowing like oxen, as if to clear their lungs of a weight of contempt.

It was not thus in the old days, when there was no people's arbiter in all the Wolfmark so famous or so popular as Master Gerard of the Weiss Thor.

"What is the reason of that turmoil?" said I to my neighbor.

"This is the man who was her first accuser. Why, he dares not go outside his house without a guard of the Duke's riders," said the man, picking at his finger-nail with his teeth, as if it were a bone and he did not think much of its savoriness.

"You have already confessed," said the advocate to old Hanne, when they had propped up the poor wreck of skin and bone, "and you do now confess that this maid and yourself have ofttimes had converse with the Enemy of Souls?"

A spasm passed across the face of the witness, and a low sound proceeded from her mouth, which might have been an affirmative answer, but which sounded to me much more like a moan of pain.

"And you confess that she consulted you concerning the best means of killing the Duke Casimir—by means of a draught to be administered to him when he should, as was his custom, visit his Hereditary Justicer?"

"There was indeed a draught spoken of between us, noble sir," stammered the old woman, "but it was not for the Duke Casimir, nor yet for—for any evil purpose."

I saw the Friar Laurence incline his head a little forward and whisper in Hanne's ear from his place behind her.

At the words she clasped her hands and fell on the floor, grovelling: "I will say aught that you bid me, kind sir. I cannot bear it again. I cannot go back to that place. I am too old to be tormented. I will bear what testimony your excellencies desire."

"We wish only that you should tell the truth as you have already done of your own free will in your pre-examination," said Master Gerard, "the notes of which are before me. Was it not to kill the Duke Casimir that this draught was compounded?"

The old woman hesitated. Friar Laurence stooped again.

"Yes!" she cried; "God forgive me—yes!"

An evil look of triumph sat on the face of Otho von Reuss. I think he felt sure of his victim now.

"That is enough," said Master Gerard. "Take the old woman back to her cell."

"Oh no, great Lord!" she cried, "not there! You promised that if I said it I was to be let go free. Kill me, but do not send me back!"

The Duke moved his hand, and the old woman was led shrieking below.

Then came Friar Laurence, who testified that he had often seen old Hanne instructing the young woman who was now a prisoner in the art of drugs, in the preparation of images carven in dough—and it might be also in clay—things well known in the art of witchery.

Further, he had been with the Duke Casimir at the last, and the Duke had declared that he had partaken of a draught in the house of Gottfried Gottfried, and immediately thereafter had been taken ill.

There was not much else of matter in the Friar's evidence, but the most deep and vindictive malice against the prisoner was evident in every word and gesture.

Then Master Gerard rose to address the judges. His venerable appearance was enhanced by the sternly severe look on his face. He looked an accusing angel from the pit, swart of skin and with eyes of flame. He was tall and bent of figure, with the serpent-browed head set deep between hunched shoulders like those of a moulting vulture. He grasped his bundle of papers and rose to make his final speech.

The judges settled themselves to closer attention. The hush of listening folk broadened to the utmost limits of the great hall. At a whisper or a cough a hundred threatening faces were turned in the direction of the sound, so strained was the attention of the people and such the fear of the eloquence of this most famous pleader in all Germany. In these days when learning has reached so great a pitch, and is so general that in a largish city there may be as many as a thousand people who can read and write, of course there are many eloquent men. But in those days it was not so, and Grerard von Sturm was counted the one Golden Mouth of the Wolfmark.

And this in brief was the matter of his speech. The manner and the persuasive grace I cannot attempt to give:

"It has at all times been a received opinion of the wise that witchcraft is a thing truly practised—by which such women as the Witch of Endor in Holy Writ were able to call dead men out of their deep graves grown with grass; or, as in that famous case of Demarchaus, who, having by the advice of such a woman tasted the flesh of a sacrificed child, was immediately turned into a wolf.

"Further, the testimony of Scripture is clear: 'Thou shalt not suffer a witch to live'; and, again, as sayeth the Wise Man, 'Thou hast hated them, 0 God, because with enchantments they did horrible works.'

"Now, men may by conspicuous bravery guard their lives against assault by the sword of the enemy, against the spear of the invader that cometh over the wall, even against the knife of the assassin. But who shall be able to keep out witchcraft? It moveth in the motes of the midday sun. It comes stealing into the room on the pale beams of the moon. Witchcraft rides in the hurtling blast, and shrieks in the gust which shakes the roof and blows awry the candle in the hall.

"Enchantment can summon Azazeli, the Lord of Flesh and Blood, called in another place the Lord of the Desert, by whose spiriting of the elements even the pure water of the spring or the juice of the purple grape may become noxious as the brew of the serpent's poison-bag.

"Of such a sort was the ill-doing of this woman. For her own hellish purposes she desired and compassed the death of the most noble Duke Casimir. There may be those who try to discover a motive for such an act. But in this they do foolishly. For to those who have studied of this matter, as I have done, it is well known that enchanters and witches ever attack those who are the greatest, the noblest, and the most envied—not hoping for any good to result to themselves, but out of pure malice and envy, being prompted by the devil in order that the great and noble should be destroyed out of the land. Well was it spoken then, 'Ye shall not suffer a witch to live!'

"And if any plead hereafter of this evil-doer's youth, of her beauty, I call you to witness that the Evil One ever makes his best implement of the fairest metal. As the aged crone, her teacher and accomplice, hath confessed, this Helene was for long a plotter of dark deeds. By the trust of Duke Casimir in her maiden's innocence he was betrayed to death. That one so fair and evil should be turned loose on the world to begin anew her enchantments, and, like a pestilence, to creep into good men's houses, is a thing not to be thought of. Is she to go forth breathing death upon the faces of the young children, to sit squat, like hideous toad, sucking the blood of the new-born infant, or distilling poison-drops to put into the draughts of strong men which shall run like molten iron through their veins till they go mad?

"Hear me, judges, I bid you again remember the word: 'Ye shall not suffer a witch to live.' And in the name of the great unbroken law of the Wolfmark, which I hold in my hand, I conclude by claiming the pains of death to pass upon the witch-woman who by her deed sent forth untimely the spirit of the most noble Duke Casimir, Lord of the city of Thorn and Duke of the Wolfmark."

The pleader sat down, calmly as he had risen, and the judges conferred together as though they were on the point of delivering their verdict. There had been no sound of applause as Master Gerard had spoken—a hushed attention only, and then the muffled thunder of the great audience relaxing its attention and of men turning to whispered discussion among themselves.

"Prisoner," said Duke Otho, "have you any to speak for you? Or do you desire to make any answer to the things which have been urged against you?"

Then, thrilling me to my soul, arose the voice of Helene. Clear and sweet and girlish, without hurry or fear, yet with an innocence which might have touched the hardest heart, the maiden upon trial for her life said a simple word or two in her defence.

"I have no one to speak for me. I have nothing to say, save that which I have said so often, that before God, who knows all things, I am innocent of thought, word, or deed against any man, and most of all against Duke Casimir of the Wolfsberg."

And as she spoke the multitude was stirred, and voices broke out here and there:

"No witch!" "She is innocent!" "The guilty are among the judges!" "Saint Helena!" "If she die we will avenge her!"

And though the lictors struck furiously every way, they could not settle the tumult, and ever the mass of folk swayed more wildly to and fro. Nor do I know what might have happened at that moment but for a cry that arose in front of the throng.

"The Stranger! The Great Doctor! The Wise Man! Hear him! He is going to speak for her!"

CHAPTER XLIV

SENTENCE OF DEATH

And there, standing by the place of pleading, with his foot on the first step, I saw Dessauer, in his black doctorial gown, leaning reverently upon a long staff.

He made a courteous salutation to Duke Otho upon the high seat.

"I am a stranger, most noble Duke," he began, "and as such have no standing in this your High Court of Justice. But there is a certain courtesy extended to doctors of the law—the right of speech in great trials—in many of the lands to which I have adventured in the search of wisdom. I am encouraged by my friend, the most venerable prelate, Bishop Peter, to ask your forbearance while I say a word on behalf of the prisoner, in reply to that learned and most celebrated juriconsult, Master Gerard von Sturm, who, in support of his cause, has spoken things so apt and eloquent. This is my desire ere judgment be passed. For in a multitude of councils there is wisdom."

He was silent, and looked at the Duke and his tool, Michael Texel.

They conferred together in whispers, and at first seemed on the point of refusing. But the folk began to sway so dangerously, and the voice of their muttering sank till it became a growl, as of a caged wild beast which has broken all bars save the last, and which only waits an opportunity to put forth its strength in order to shiver that also.

"You are heartily welcome, most learned doctor," said Duke Otho, sullenly. "We would desire to hear you briefly concerning this matter."

"I shall assuredly be brief, my noble lord—most brief," said Dessauer. "I am a stranger, and must therefore speak by the great principles of equity which underlie all law and all evidence, rather than according to the statutes of the province over which you are the distinguished ruler.

"The crime of witchcraft is indeed a heinous one, if so be that it can be proven—not by the compelled confession of crazed and tortured crones, but by the clear light of reason. Now there is no evidence that I have heard against this young girl which might not be urged with equal justice against every cup-bearer in the Castle of the Wolfsberg.

"The Duke Casimir died indeed after having partaken of the wine. But so may a man at any time by the visitation of God, by the stroke which, from the void air, falleth suddenly upon the heart of man. No poison has been found on or about the girl. No evil has been alleged against her, save that which has been compelled (as all must have seen) by torture, and the fear of torture, from the palsied and reluctant lips of a frantic hag."

"Hear him! Great is the Stranger!" cried the folk in the hall. And the shouting of the guards commanding silence could scarce be heard for the roar of the populace. It was some time before the speech of Dessauer was again audible.

Ho was beginning to speak again, but Duke Otho, without rising, called out rudely and angrily:

"Speak to the reason of the judges and not to the passions of the mob!"

"I do indeed speak from the reason to the reason," said Dessauer, calmly; "for in this matter there is no true averment, even of witchcraft, but only of the administration of poison—which ought to be proven by the ordinary means of producing some portion of the drug, both in the possession of the criminal and from the body of the murdered man. This has not been done. There has been no evidence, save, as I have shown, such as may be easily compelled or suborned. If this maid be condemned, there is no one of you with a wife, a daughter, a sweetheart, who may not have her burned or beheaded on just as little evidence—if she have a single enemy in all the city seeking for the sake of malice or thwarted lust to compass her destruction.

"Moreover, it indeed matters little for the argument that this damsel is fair to the eye. Save in so far as she is more the object of desire, and that when the greed of the lustful eye is balked" (here he paused and looked fixedly between his knees), "disappointment oft in such a heart turns to deadly poison. And so that which was desired is the more bitterly hated, and revenge awakes to destroy.

"But if beauty matters little, character matters greatly. And what, by common consent, has been known in the city concerning this maid?

"I ask not you, Duke Otho, who have lived apart in your castle or in far lands, a stranger to the city like myself. But I ask the people among whom, during all these; past months of the plague, she has dwelt. Is she not known among them as Saint Helena?"

"Aye," cried the people, "Saint Helena, indeed—our savior when there was none to help! God save Saint Helena!"

Dessauer waved his hand for silence.

"Did she not go among you from house to house, carrying, not the poison-cup, but the healing draught? Was not her hand soft on the brow of the dying, comfortable about the neck of the bereaved? Day and night, whose fingers reverently wrapped up the poor dead bodies of your beloved? Who quieted your babes in her arms, fed thorn, nursed them, healed them, buried them—wore herself to a shadow for your sakes?"

"Saint Helena!" they cried; "Saint Helena, the angel of the Red Tower!"

"Aye," said Dessauer, in tones like thunder, "hear their voices! There are a thousand witnesses in this house untortured, unsuborned. I tell you, the guilt of innocent blood will lie on you, great Duke—on you counsellors of evil things, if you condemn this maid. Your throne, Duke Otho, shall totter and fall, and your life's sun shall set in a sea of blood!"

He sat down calm and fearless as the Duke raged to Michael Texel, as I think, desiring that the fearless pleader could be seized on the instant, and punished for his insolence. But as the folk shouted in the hall, and the thunder of cheering came in through the open windows from the great concourse without, Michael Texel calmed his master, urging upon him that the temper of the people was for the present too dangerous. And also, doubtless, that they could easily compass their ends by other means.

I saw Texel despatch a messenger to the lictors who stood on either side of Helene. The body-guard of the Duke stood closer about her as the Duke Otho himself stood up to read the sentence.

I saw that the form of it had been written out upon a paper. Doubtless, therefore, all had been prearranged, so that neither evidence nor eloquence could possibly have had any effect upon it.

"We, the Court of the Wolfmark, find the prisoner, Helene, called Gottfried, guilty of witchcraft, and especially of compassing and causing the death of our predecessor, the most noble Duke Casimir, and we do hereby adjudge that, on the morning of Sunday presently following, Helene Gottfried shall be executed upon the common scaffold by the axe of the executioner. Of our clemency is this sentence delivered, instead of the torture and the burning alive at the stake which it was within our power to command. This is done in consideration of the youth of the criminal, and as the first exercise of our ducal prerogative of high mercy."

With an angry roar the people closed in.

"Take her!" they cried; "rescue her out of their hands!"

And there was a fierce rush, in which the outer barriers were snapped like straw. But the lictors had pulled down the trap-door on the instant, and the people surged fiercely over the spot where a moment before Helene had stood. Before them were the levelled pikes and burning matches of the Duke's guard.

"Have at them!" was still the cry. "Kill the wolves! Tear them to pieces!"

But the mob was undisciplined, and the steady advance of the soldiers soon cleared the hall. Nevertheless the streets without continued angry and throbbing with incipient rebellion. Duke Otho could scarce win scathless across the court-yard to his own apartments. Tiles from the nearest roofs were cast upon the heads of his escort. The streets were impassable with angry men shaking their fists at every courier and soldier of the Duke. Women hung sobbing out of the windows, and all the city of Thorn lamented with uncomforted tears because of the cruel condemnation of their Saint of the plague, Helena, the maiden of the Red Tower.

CHAPTER XLV

THE MESSAGE FROM THE WHITE GATE

I rushed out into the street, distract and insensate with grief and madness. I found the city seething with sullen unrest—not yet openly hostile to the powers that abode in the Castle of the Wolfsberg—too long cowed and down-trodden for that, but angry with the anger which one day would of a certainty break out and be pitiless.

The Black Horsemen of the Duke pricked a way with their lances here and there through the people, driving them into the narrow lanes, in jets and spurts of fleeing humanity, only once more to reunite as soon as the Hussars of Death had passed. Pikemen cried "Make way!" and the regular guard of the city paraded in strong companies.

A soldier wantonly thrust me in the back with his spear, and I sprang towards him fiercely, glad to strike home at something. But as quickly a man of the crowd pulled me back.

"Be wise!" he said; "not for your own sake alone, but for the sake of all these women and children. The Black Riders seek only an excuse to sweep the city from end to end with the besom of fire and blood."

Then came my master out of the Hall of Judgment, his head hanging dejectedly down. As soon as he was observed the people crowded about, shaking him by the hand, thanking him for that which he had done for their maid, their holy Saint Helena of the plague.

"We will not suffer her to be put to death, not even if they of the Wolfsberg raze our city to the ground!"

"Make way there!" cried the Black Horsemen—"way, in the name of Duke Otho!"

"Who is Duke Otho?" cried a voice. "We do not know Duke Otho."

"He is not crowned yet! Why should he take so much upon him?" shouted another.

"We are free burgesses of Thorn, and no man's bond-slaves!" said a third. Such were the shouts that hurtled through the streets and were bandied fiercely from man to man, betraying in tone more than in word the intensity of the hatred which existed between the ducal towers of the Wolfsberg and the city which lay beneath them.

In my boyish days I had laughed at the assemblies of the Swan—the White Wolves and Free Companies. But, perhaps, those who had thus played at revolt were wiser than I. For of a surety these associations were yielding their fruits now in a harvest of hate against the gloomy pile that had so long dominated the town, choked its liberties, and shut it off from the new, free, thriving world of the northern seaboard commonwealths to which of right it belonged.

So soon as Dessauer and I were alone in my master's room at Bishop Peter's I tried to stammer some sort of thanks, but I could do no more than hold out a hand to him. The old man clasped it.

"It was wholly useless from the first," he said; "they had their purpose fixed and their course laid out, so that there was no turning of them. All was a mockery, so clear that even the ignorant men of the streets were not deceived. Accusation, evidence, pleadings, condemnation, sentence—all were ready before the maid was taken; aye, and, I think, before Duke Casimir was dead.

"Also there is no court in the Wolfmark higher than the mockery we have seen today. The arms of the soldiers of Plassenburg are our only court of appeal."

"It is two days before they can come," I answered. "I fear me all will be over before then."

"Be not so sure," said Dessauer. "There is at present no Justicer in the Mark capable of carrying out the sentence, so long as your father lies on his bed of mortal weakness."

"Duke Otho will not let that stand in his way—or I am the more deceived," said I, with a heavy heart.

At this moment there came an interruption. I heard a loud argument outside in the court-yard.

"Tell me what you want with the servant of the most learned Doctor!" cried a voice.

"That is his business, and mine—not yours, rusty son of a stable-sweeper!" was the answer.

I went out immediately, and there, facing each other in a position of mutual defiance, I saw Peter of the Pigs and the decent legal domestic of Master Gerard von Sturm.

"Get out of my wind, old Muck-to-the-Eyes!" said the servitor, offensively; "you poison the good, wholesome air that is needed for men's breath."

"Go back to your murderer of the saints," responded Peter of the Pigs, valiantly. "Your master and you will swing in effigy tonight in every street in Thorn. Some day before long you will both swing in the body—if a hair of this angel's head be harmed."

"I must see this learned Doctor's servant!" persisted the man of law, avoiding the personal question.

"Here he is," said I; "and now what would you with him?"

"I am sent to invite you to come to the Weiss Thor immediately, on business which deeply concerns you."

"That is not enough for me," said I. "Who sends for me?"

"Let me come in out of the hearing of this moon-faced idiot," said he, pointing contumeliously to Peter of the Pigs, "and I will tell you. I am not bidden to proclaim my business in the market sties and city cattlepens!"

"You do well, Parchment Knave," cried Peter; "for it is such black business that if you proclaimed a syllable of it there you would be torn to pieces of honest folk. Thank God there are still some such in the world!"

"Aye, many," quoth the servitor, "and we all know they are to be found in the dwellings of priestlings!"

I walked with the man to the gate, for I did not care to take him to where Dessauer was sitting. I feared that it might be some ill news from the Lubber Fiend, who, though I had seen him clear of the gate, might very well have returned and told my message to Master Gerard.

"Well," said I, brusquely, for I had no love for the Sir Rusty Respectable, "out with it—who sends you?"

"It is not my master," answered the man, "but one other."

"What other?" said I.

"The one," he said, cunningly, "with whom on a former occasion you rode out at the White Gate."

Then I saw that he knew me.

"The Princess—" I began.

"Hush," he said, touching my arm; "that is not a word to be whispered in the streets of Thorn—the Lady Ysolinde is at her father's house, and would see you—on a matter of life or death—so she bade me tell you."

"I will go with you," I said, instantly.

"Nay," he said, smirking secretly, "not now, but at nine of the clock, when the city ways shall be dark, you must come—you know the road. And then you two can confer together safely, and eke, an it please you, jocosely, when Master Gerard will be safe in his study, with the lamp lit."

I went back to Dessauer, who during my absence had kept his head in his hand, as if deeply absorbed in thought.

"The Princess is in Thorn!" said I, as a startling piece of news.

"Ah, the Princess!" he muttered, abstractedly; "truly she is the Princess, but yet that will not advantage her a whit."

I saw that he was thinking of our little Helene.

"Nay," I said, taking him by the arm to secure his attention, as indeed about this time I had often to do. "I mean the Lady Ysolinde, the wife of our good Prince."

"In Thorn?" said Dessauer. "Ah, I am little surprised. Twice when I was speaking today I saw a face I knew well look through a lattice in the wall at me. But being intent upon my words I did not think of it, nor indeed recognize it till it had disappeared. Now the picture comes back to me curiously clear. It was the face of the Princess Ysolinde."

"I am to see her at nine o'clock tonight in the house of the Weiss Thor."

"Do not go, I pray you!" he said; "it is certainly a trap."

"Go I must, and will," I replied; "for it may be to the good of our maiden. I will risk all for that!"

"I dare say," said he; "so should I, if I saw any advantage, such as indeed I hoped for today. But if I be not mistaken, our Princess is deep in this plot."

"And why?" said I. "Helene never harmed her."

"Helene is your betrothed wife, is she not?" he said. He asked as if he did not know.

"Surely!" said I.

"Well!" he replied, sententiously, and so went out.

CHAPTER XLVI

A WOMAN SCORNED

At nine I was at the door of the dark, silent house by the Weiss Thor. I sounded the knocker loudly, and with the end of the reverberations I heard a foot come through the long passages. The panel behind slid noiselessly in its grooves, and I was conscious that a pair of eyes looked out at me.

"You are the servant of the strange Doctor?" said the voice of the servitor, Sir Respectable.

"That I am, as by this time you may have seen!" answered I, for I was in no mood of mere politeness. I was venturing my life in the house of mine enemy, and, at least, it would be no harm if I put a bold face on the matter.

He opened the door, and again the same curious perfume was wafted down the passages—something that I had never felt either in the Wolfsberg nor yet even in the women's chambers of the Palace of Plassenburg.

At the door of the little room in which she had first received me so long ago, the Lady Ysolinde was waiting for me.

She did not shut the door till Sir Respectable had betaken him down again to his own place. Then quite frankly and undisguisedly she took my hand, like one who had come to the end of make-believe.

"I knew you today in your disguise," she said; "it is an excellent one, and might deceive all save a woman who loves. Ah, you start. It might deceive the woman you love, but not the woman that loves you. I am not the Princess tonight; I am Ysolinde, the Woman. I have no restraints, no conventions, no laws, no religions tonight—save the law of a woman's need and the religion of a woman's passion."

I stood before her, scarce knowing what to say.

"Sit down," she said; "it is a long story, and yet I will not weary you, Hugo—so much I promise you."

I made answer to her, still standing up.

"Tonight, my lady, after what you know, you will not be surprised that I can think of only one thing. You know that today—"

"I know," she said, cutting me short, as if she did not wish to listen to that which I might say next; "I know—I was present in the Judgment Hall."

"Then, being Master Gerard's daughter, you knew also the sentence before it was pronounced!" I said, bitterly, being certain as that I lived that the paper from which the Duke Otho read had been penned at this very house of the Weiss Thor in which I now sat.

Ysolinde reached a slender hand to me, as was often her wont instead of speech.

"Be patient tonight," she said; "I am trying hard to do that which is best—for myself first, as a woman must in a woman's affairs. But, as God sees me, for others also! You are a man, but I pray you think with fairness of the fight I, a lonely, unloved woman, have to fight."

"Will they carry out the terrible sentence?" said I, eagerly. For I judged that she must be in her father's counsels.

"Be patient," she said; "we will come to that presently."

Ysolinde sat silent a while, and when I would have spoken further she moved her hand a little impatiently aside, in sign that I was not to interrupt. Yet even this was not done in her old imperious manner, but rather sadly and with a certain wistful gentleness which went to my heart.

When she spoke again it was in the same even voice with which she had formerly told my fortune in that very room.

"That which I have to say to you is a thing strange—as it may seem unwomanly. But then, I did not ask God to make me a woman, and certainly he did not make me as other women. I have never had a true mate, never won the love which God owes to every man and woman He brings into the world.

"Then I mot you, not by any seeking of mine. Next, equally against my will, I loved you. Nay, do not start tonight. It is as well to put the matter plainly."

"You did not *love* me," said I; "you were but kind to me, the unworthy son of the Executioner of Thorn. Out of your good heart you did it."

I acknowledge that I spoke like a paltering knave, but in truth knew not what to say.

"I loved you—yes, and I love you!" she said, serenely, as though my words had been the twittering of a bird on the roof. "And I am not ashamed. There was indeed no reason for my folly—no beauty, no desirableness in you. But—I loved you. Pass! Let it be. We will begin from there. You loved, or thought you loved, a maid—your Little Playmate. Pshaw, you loved her not! Or not as I count love. I was proud, accustomed to command, and, besides, a Prince's wife. The last, doubtless, should have held me apart. Yet my Princessdom was but as straw bands cast into the fire to bind the flame. As for you, Hugo Gottfried, you were in love with your success, your future, and, most of all, with your confident, insolently dullard self."

She smiled bitterly, and, because the thing she spoke was partly true, I had still nothing to answer her.

"Hugo Gottfried," she said, "try to remember if, when we rode to Plassenburg in the pleasant weather of that old spring, you loved this girl whom now you love?"

"Aye," said I, "loved her then, even as I love her now."

"You lie," she answered, calmly, not like one in anger, but as one who makes a necessary correction, "you loved her not. You were ready to love me—glad, too, that I should love you. And since you knew not then of my rank, it was not done for the sake of any advancement in Plassenburg."

I felt again the great disadvantage I was under in speaking to the Lady Ysolinde. I never had a word to say but she could put three to it. My best speeches sounded empty, selfish, vain beside hers. And so was it ever. By deeds alone could I vanquish her, and perhaps by a certain dogged masculine persistence.

"Princess," I said to her, "you have asked me to meet you here. It is not of the past, nor yet of likings, imaginings, recriminations that I must speak. My love, my sister, my playmate, bound to me by a thousand ancient tendernesses, lies in prison in this city of Thorn, under sentence of a cruel death. Will you help me to release her? I think that with your father, and therefore with you, is the power to open her prison doors!"

"And what is there then for me?" cried the Lady Ysolinde, instantly, bending her head forward, her emerald eyes so great and clear that their shining seemed to cover all her face as a wave covers a rock at flood-tide.

"What for me?" she repeated, in the silence which followed.

"For you," said I, "the gladness to have saved an innocent life."

"Tush!" she cried, with a gesture of extravagant contempt. "You mistake; I am no good-deeds monger, to give my bread and butter to the next beggar-lass. I tell you I am the woman who came first out of the womb of Mother-earth. I will yield only that which is snatched from me. What is mine is more mine than another's, because I would suffer, dare, sin, defy a world of men and women in order to keep it, to possess it, to have it all alone to myself!"

"But," I answered, "who am I, that so great a lady should love me? What am I to you, Princess, more than another?"

"*That* I know not!" she answered, swiftly. "Only God knows that. Perhaps my curse, my punishment. My husband is a far better, truer, nobler man than you, Hugo. I know it; but what of that, when I love him not? Love goes not by the rungs in a ladder, stands not with the most noble on the highest step, is not bestowed, like the rewards in a child's school, to the most deserving. I love you, Hugo Gottfried, it is true. But I wish a thousand times that I did not. Nevertheless—I do! Therefore make your reckoning with that, and put aside puling shams and whimpering subterfuges."

This set me all on edge, and I asked a question.

"What, then, do you propose? Where, shall this comedy end?"

"End!" she said—"end! Aye, of course, men must ever look to an end. Women are content with a continuance. That you should love me and keep on loving me, that is all I want!"

"But," I began, "I love—"

"Ah, do not say it!" she cried, pitifully, clasping her hands with a certain swift appeal in her voice—"do not say it! For God's sake, for the sake of innocent blood, do not say that you love me not!"

She paused a moment, and grew more pensive as she looked stilly and solemnly at me.

"I will tell you the end that I see; only be patient and answer not before I have done. I have seen a vision—thrice have I seen it. Karl of Plassenburg, my husband, shall die. I have seen the Black Cloak thrice envelop him. It is the sign. No man hath ever escaped that omen—aye, and if I choose, it shall wrap him about speedily. More, I have seen you sit on the throne of Plassenburg and of the Mark, with a Princess by your side. It is *not* only my fancy. Even as in the old time I read your present fortune, so, for good or ill, this thing also is coming to you."

She never took her eyes from my face.

"Now listen well and be slow to speak. The Princedom and the power shall both fall to me when my husband dies. There are none other hands capable. So also is it arranged in his will. Here"—she broke off suddenly, as with a gesture of infinite surrender she thrust out her white hands towards me—"here is my kingdom and me. Take us both, for we are yours—yours—yours!"

I took her hands gently in mine and kissed them.

"Lady, Lady Ysolinde," I said, "you honor me, you overwhelm me, I know not what to say. But think! The Prince is well, full of health and the hope of years. This thought of yours is but a vision, a delusion—how can we speak of the thing that is not?"

"I wait your answer," she said, leaving her hands still in mine, but now, as it were, on sufferance. Then, indeed, I was torn between the love that I had in my heart for my dear and the need of pleasing the Lady Ysolinde—between the truth and my desire to save Helene. Almost it was in my heart to declare that I loved the Lady Ysolinde, and to promise that I should do all she asked. But though, when need hath been, I have lied back and forth in my time, and thought no shame, something stuck in my throat now; and I felt that if I denied my love, who lay prison-bound that night, I should never come within the mercy of God, but be forever alien and outcast from any commonwealth of honorable men.

"I cannot, Lady Ysolinde," I answered, at last. "The love of the maid hath so grown into my heart that I cannot root it out at a word. It is here, and it fills all my life!"

Again she interrupted me.

"See," she said, speaking quickly and eagerly, "they tell me this your Helene is an angel of mercy to the sick. If she is spared she will be content to give her life to works of good intent among the poor. This cannot be life and death to her as it is to me. Her love is not as the love of a woman like Ysolinde. It is not for any one man to possess in monopoly. Though you may deceive yourself and think that it will be fixed and centred on you. But she will never love you as I love you. See, I would knee to you, pray to you on my knees, make myself a suppliant—I, Ysolinde that am a princess! With you, Hugo, I have no pride, no shame. I would take your love by violence, as a strong man surpriseth and taketh the heart of a maid."

She was now all trembling and distract, her lips red, her eyes bright, her hands clasped and trembling as they were strained palm to palm.

"Lady Ysolinde, I would that this were not so," I began.

A new quick spasm passed over her face. I think it came across her that my heart was wavering. "God knows that I, Hugo Gottfried, am not worth all this!"

"Nay," she said, with a kind of joy in her voice and in her eyes, "that matters not. Ysolinde of Plassenburg is as a child that must have its toy or die. Worthiness has no more to do with love than creeds and dogmas. Love me—Hugo—love me even a little. Put me not away. I will be so true, so willing. I will run your errands, wait on you, stand behind you in battle, in council lead you to fame and great glory. For you, Hugo, I will watch the faces of others, detect your enemies, unite your well-wishers, mark the failing favor of your friends. What heart so strong, what eye so keen as mine—for the greater the love the sharper the eye to mark, prevent, countermine. And this maid, so cold and icy, so full of good works and the abounding fame of saintliness, let her live for the healing of the people, for the love of God and man both, and it liketh her. She shall be abbess of our greatest convent. She shall indeed be the Saint Helena of the North. Even now I will save her from death and give her refuge. I promise it. I have the power in my hands. Only do you, Hugo Gottfried, give me your love, your life, yourself!"

She was standing before me now, and had her arms about my neck. I felt them quiver upon my shoulders. Her eyes looked directly up into mine, and whether they were the eyes of an angel or of a tempting fiend I could not tell. Very lovely, at any rate, they were, and might have tempted even Saint Anthony to sin.

"Ysolinde," I said, at last, "it is small wonder that I am strongly moved; you have offered me great things tonight. I feel my heart very humble and unworthy. I deserve not your love. I am but a man, a soldier, dull and slow. Were it not for one man and one woman it should be as you say. But Karl of Plassenburg is my good master, my loyal friend. Helene is my true love. I beseech you put this thought from you, dear lady, and be once more my true Princess, I your liege subject—faithful, full of reverence and devotion till life shall end!"

As I spoke she drew herself away from me. My hand had unconsciously rested on her hair, for at first she had leaned her head towards me. When I had finished she took my hand by the wrist and gripped it as if she would choke a snake ere she dropped it at arm's-length. I knew that our interview was at an end.

"Go!" she commanded, pointing to the door. "One day you shall know how precious is the love you have so lightly cast aside. In a dark, dread hour, you, Hugo Gottfried, shall sue as a suppliant. And I shall deny you. There shall come a day when you shall abase yourself—even as you have seen Ysolinde the Princess abase herself to Hugo, the son of the Red Axe of the Wolf mark. Go, I tell you! Go—ere I slay you with my knife!"

And she flashed a keen double-edged blade from some recess of her silken serpentine dress.

"My lady, hear me," I pleaded. "Out of the depths of my heart I protest to you—"

"Bah!" she cried, with a sudden uprising of tigerish fierceness in her eyes, quick and chill as the glitter of her steel. "Go, I tell you, ere I be tempted to strike! *Your heart!* Why, man, there is nothing in your heart but empty words out of monks' copy-books and proverbs dry and rotten as last year's leaves. Ye have seen me abased. By the lords of hell, I will abase you, Executioner's son! Aye, and you yourself, Hugo Gottfried, shall work out in flowing blood and bitter tears the doom of the pale trembling girl for whom you have rejected and despised Ysolinde, Princess of Plassenburg!"

CHAPTER XLVII

THE RED AXE DIES STANDING UP

How I stumbled down the stairs and found myself outside the house in the Weiss Thor I do not know. Whether the servitor, Sir Respectable, showed me out or not has quite passed from me. I only remember that I came upon myself waiting outside the gate of Bishop Peter's palace ringing at a bell which sounded ghostly enough, tinkling like a cracked kettle behind the door.

The lattice clicked and a face peeped out.

"Get hence, night-raker!" cried a voice. "Wherefore do you come here so untimeously, profaning the holy quiet of our minster-close?"

"There was no very holy calm in the kitchen t'other night, Peter Swinehead!" said I, my wits coming mechanically back to me at the familiar sound.

"Ha, Sir Blackamoor, 'tis you; surely your chafts have grown strangely white, or else are my eyes serving me foully in the torchlight."

Instinctively I covered as much of my face as I could with my cloak's cape, for indeed I had washed it ere I went forth to see the Lady Ysolinde.

"'Tis that you have slipped too much of the Rhenish down thy gullet, old comrade," said I, slapping Peter on the back and getting before him so that he might remark nothing more.

At that, being well pleased with my calling him comrade, he lighted me cordially to my chamber, and there left me to the sleepless meditation of the night.

The next day was one of great quietness in the city of Thorn. An uneasy, sultry pause of silence brooded over the lower town. Men's heads showed a moment at door and window, looked furtively up and down the street, and then vanished again within. Plots were being hatched and plans laid in Thorn; yet, while there was the lowering silence in the city, up aloft the Wolfsberg hummed gayly like a hive. Once I went up that way to see if I could win any news of my father. But this day the door into the Red Tower stood closed, nor would any within open for all my knocking. So perforce I had to return unsatisfied. Several times I went to the Weiss Thor to spy the horizon round for the troops of Plassenburg. But only the gray plain of the Mark stretched itself out so far as the eye could penetrate—hardly a reeking chimney to be seen, or any token of the pleasant rustic life of man, such as in my youth I remembered to have looked down upon from the Red Tower. Beneath me the city of Thorn lay grimly quiescent, like a beast of prey which has eaten all its neighbors, and must now die of starvation because there are no more to devour.

The day passed on feet that crept like those of a tortoise, as the sullen minutes dragged by, leaden-clogged and tardy. But the evening came at last. And with it, knocking at the door of the Bishop's quadrangle and interrupting my long talk with Dessauer, lo! a messenger, hot-foot from the castle.

"To the learned Doctor and his servant, Gottfried Gottfried, being in death's utmost extremities, sends greeting, and desires greatly to have speech with them."

Thus ran my father's message in that testing hour where he had seen so many! Yet I was but little surprised. There was no wonder in the fact save the wonder that it should all seem so natural. Dessauer rose quickly.

"I will go with you," he said; "it will be safer. For at least I can keep the door while you speak with your father."

So, without further word, we followed the messenger up the long, narrow, wooden-gabled street, and heard the folk muttering gloomily in the darkness within, or talking softly in the dull russet glow of their hearth-fires. For there were but few lighted candles in Thorn that night. And I wondered how near or how far from us tho men of Plassenburg might be encamping, and thrilled to think that at any moment a spy might ride in to warn Duke Otho of the spy within his city, or the near approach of his foe.

But so far all was quiet at the Red Tower. The wicket-gate in the angle of the wall was open, and we passed in without difficulty. As I mounted the stairs I heard the key turn behind us. Obviously, therefore, we were expected. The gate of the Red Tower had been left open for our entrance; and so soon as the birds were in the snare, it was shut, and the silly goslings trapped.

Nevertheless we climbed up and up the dark stairs till we came to the door of my father's garret. I pushed it open without knocking, and entered.

"The most learned the Doctor Schmidt," I announced, lest there should be some stranger in the room. And indeed my precaution was necessary enough. For, from my father's bed-head, disengaging himself reluctantly, like a disturbed vulture napping up from the side of a dying steer, Friar Laurence rose out of the darkness, and, folding his robe about him, stalked to the door without a word or nod to either of us. I stood holding the edge of it till I had watched him well down the stairs. Then Dessauer relieved me at the stair-head as I went to approach my father.

I saw a change in him, very startling, indeed, to see. "In the uttermost extremity" he was, indeed, as he had written. A ghastly pallor overspread his face; his eyes were wild, his breathing came both quick and hard. The fire cast nickering lights over his face and on the outlines of his lank figure under the scarlet mantle which had been cast over him. One corner of it was cast aside, as if for air or coolness, and I could see a thing which gave me a cold chill in the marrow of my spine.

My father still wore the dress which he only donned when some poor soul was about to die and pay the forfeit.

At first Gottfried took no notice of me whatever, but lay looking at the ceiling, his lips muttering something steadily, though what the words were I could not hear.

"Father," I said at last, bending over him gently, "I have come to see you."

He turned to me, as if suddenly and regretfully summoned back from very far away. It was a movement I had seen in many dying men. He looked at me, a strange, luminous comprehension growing up gradually in his eyes.

"Hugo," he said, "you have come home at last! The Little Playmate has come home, too. We three will make a merry party in the old Red Tower. We have not been all together for so long. Lord Christ, but I have been a man much alone! Hugo, why did you leave me so long? Ah, well, I do not blame you, my son. You have been pushing your fortunes, doubtless, and you have—so they tell me—become a great man in Plassenburg. And the little maid is a lady of honor, and very fair to see. But now you two have come to the old garret, like birds homing to the nest."

"Yes, father," I said to him, "we have both come home to you, the Little Playmate and I. And now you will give us your blessing!"

"The Little Playmate—say rather the Little Princess," he cried, cheerfully, as, with the air of one who brings good tidings, he sat up in bed. Then he pointed to a chair on which a pillow had carelessly been flung. "Little Maid," he said, looking at the cushion as if it had been Helene, "I am glad you have come back to be wedded to my boy. That was like you. I ever wished it, indeed. But I never expected to see my children thus happy. Yet I always knew you and Hugo were made for each other. You are at your sewing, little maid. Well, 'tis natural. I mind me when my own love sat making dainties of just such delicate and wreathed whiteness."

He paused, and then, his countenance suddenly changing, he looked fearfully and fixedly at the chair.

"But, little maid, my own Helene," he cried, in a loud, gasping, alarmed tone, "what is this, best beloved? Why, you are sewing at a shroud? Surely such funeral-trappings become not bridals. A shroud—and there is blood upon it! Put it down—*put it down*, I pray you!"

The red flames on the fire crackled suddenly up about the back log and cast dancing shadows on his face.

"Lie down and rest, dear father," I said softly to him, "the Little Playmate is not here—I, Hugo, your son, am alone beside you."

"Hugo," he said, instantly appeased, and passing a lean arm about me, "my good son, my brave boy! You will be kind to the little Princess. She loves you. There is no man so beloved as you in all the city of Thorn. Many would have loved her besides Otho. Ah, but I threw him out of the window there. I threw a Grand Duke out of a window! Ha! ha! it was the bravest jest!"

He laughed a little at intervals, as at a tale that will bear infinite repetition. "I, Gottfried Gottfried, threw a proximate reigning Prince out of the window! How Casimir laughed! The thing pleased him well. And the little maid, do you remember her, Hugo? How she would teach me—me, the Red Axe of Thorn—how to dance that first night, and how totteringly she carried the Red Axe? The little one took heart that night. She will have a happy future, I know; so blessed, far away from this dark and damned place of the Wolfsberg. I am glad she is not here to see me die. That is a sight for men, not for fair young loving women."

"Hush, my father," I said, touching his dank brow; "you are not going to die. You will yet live to be strong and well, a man among men."

For one tells these things to dying men. And they smile and pass us by, amused at our childish ignorance, as you and I shall one day smile upon those others. And even thus did my father.

"Nay, Hugo, I am sped," he answered. "This night ends all. The door I have oped for so many is opening from within for me. God's mercy be on a sinful man! Ere the light of tomorrow's dawn the Duke's Justicer must face the Tribunal that has no assessor and no court of appeal."

He threw back the cloak which served him as a mantle, and crying, "Give me your hand, Hugo!" Gottfried Gottfried staggered to his feet.

"I will die standing up," he said, bending his brows and gazing about him uncertainly. He pointed to the walls of the garret. The fire was flickering low, but still making the place light enough to see easily. There beside the bed was the Red Axe, with its shining edge undimmed, leaning against the block. There across it was the crimson mask which was never more to bind his eyes as he did the office of final dread.

"Do you see them, son Hugo?" he cried, leaning heavily on my shoulder and pointing with his finger; "they are gibbering at me, mowing, processioning by, and pointing mockingly at me. Do you hear them laughing? That horrid one there with his head under his arm? Laughing as if there were no God! But I am not afraid. Mercy of Jesu! Hath God Himself no Justicer, that He should punish me because I have fulfilled my charge? I have all my life been merciful, ever giving the blow of mercy first, and the drop of stupefaction before the Extreme Question. Hence, fiends! Shapes inhuman, torment me not! For in my day I was merciful to you and never struck twice. I *will* die standing up. The devil shall not fright me—no, nor all his angels!

"God Himself shall not fright me! I appeal to His judgment throne! Get hence, false accusing spirits! I stand at Caesar's judgment-seat. Give me the axe, boy—I will cut down the evil, I will spare the good. Here is the Red Axe, my son. Take it! Strike with it strong and well. Strike, strike, and spare not!"

Totteringly he handed me the axe, and, clasping his hands, he stood looking up.

"God! God!" he cried in a great voice. "I see my Judge face to face; I am not afraid! But I will die standing up!"

And in this manner, even as I tell it, died Gottfried Gottfried, a strong man, standing up and not afraid. And these arms received him, as, being dead, he fell headlong.

CHAPTER XLVIII

HUGO GOTTFRIED, RED AXE OF THE WOLFMARK

Then cried Dessauer from the door to me as I stood thus holding my father in my arms:

"Haste you, lad; there are men coming across the yard with torches. They are gathering in groups about the door. Now they are on the stairs—many soldiers—and with weapons in their hands!"

And scarcely had he spoken when the sound of the tramping of men in haste came to us up the turret, and the door of the garret was thrust violently open. A turmoil of men-at-arms burst in on us. I stood still, holding Gottfried Gottfried, his head on my shoulder, though I knew that he was dead. But as one came forward with a paper in his hand I stooped and laid my father gently on his bed.

An officer of the Black Hussars, fantastically dressed in their churchyard array, with skull and cross-bones slashed in silver across his breast, accosted me.

"Hugo Gottfried, son of Gottfried Gottfried, in the name of the Duke Otho and the State of the Wolfmark, I arrest you! Also you, Leopold von Dessauer, Chancellor of the Princedom of Plassenburg. You are accused as spies and enemies of the commonweal. Yield yourselves therefore to me, without condition."

"I am indeed Hugo Gottfried," said I, "but you may see for yourselves the mission on which I have come hither. And for this hour, at least, you might have spared your brutal entry. Behold!"

I caught a torch from the nearest soldier, and let its light shine on the dead face of the fourteenth Hereditary Justicer of the Wolfmark.

The men started back. The terrible countenance of the dead affected them even more than the grim figure of the Red Axe as they had seen him stalking from the Hall of Justice to the block.

"Ah," said the officer, not wholly irreverently, "Gottfried Gottfried has gone now to the dark place to which he hath sent so many. But, after all, he is dead—and I heard a monkish clerk prate the other day, 'Let the dead bury their dead.' I have my orders, and the Duke Otho waits. Therefore I bid you follow me, Hugo Gottfried and Leopold von Dessauer."

So, leaving the body of my father lying on the bed in his garret, we were constrained to follow our captors down the stairs. Across the courtyard we were hurried, and through the Hall of Justice into the private apartments of the Duke.

Otho von Reuss, now Duke of the Wolfmark, was standing erect by the great chair in which, as my father had so often described him to me, Casimir had sat so many days with his head sunk on his breast. The new Duke stood up proudly, gazing at us with frowning brows and lowering, narrowed eyes. This was mighty fine, but I could not help thinking of the poor appearance he had made on the hill above the Hirschgasse as he slunk off when he saw an evil cause going desperately against him.

"So," he said, "gentlemen both, I have caught you spying in my land. You know what those have to expect who are caught in hostile territory in disguise."

I thought it was as well to take the high hand at once, especially since I saw that humility would avail us nothing at any rate.

"Before now I have seen Otho von Reuss in hostile territory, and a right cowed traitor he looked!" said I, boldly.

The Duke smiled upon me, like a man that has a complete retort on his tongue but who is content for the present to reserve it.

"My friend," he said, suavely, "I will reply to you presently. I have a word to speak to your betters."

He turned him about to Dessauer.

"And what, Lord High Chancellor of Plassenburg, think you of this masquerading? Dignified, is it not? And your wondrous speech in court that was to have done such great things. Will you be pleased to abide with us here in the Wolfsberg? Or must you forsake us to pleasure the Emperor, who, poor man, cannot sleep of nights in his bed at Ratisbon till the eloquent Doctor is come to cheer him with the full-flowing river of speech?"

"Duke Otho," said Dessauer, "my life is indeed in your hands. I hold it forfeit. A few years less or more are but little to Leopold von Dessauer now. But there is one who will most bloodily avenge us if a hair of our heads falls to the ground."

"Who?" said Otho, sneeringly. "Karl Miller's Son, I suppose. Ah, fool that you are, I hold your poor Karl in the palm of my hand!"

"It is like enough," said Dessauer, with a quick look, the look of a keen fencer when he sees an advantage. "I have often enough seen the palm of your hand approach Karl Miller's Son's treasury when I kept the moneys."

I saw the face of Otho twitch angrily. But he had evidently made up his mind to command his temper, sure of having that up his sleeve which would sufficiently answer all taunts.

"You mistake me," he said, with more subtlety than I had expected from the brute. "I had not meant to prove ungrateful. I am but newly come to my own here in the Wolfmark. I have learned from your host, Bishop Peter, how precious a thing forgiveness is. And now I am resolved to practise it. There is a time to love and a time to hate; a time to war and a time to be at peace. This is the last news I had from the holy clerk whose revenues I pay. So lay it to heart, as I have done."

"Glad am I," said Dessauer, courteously, as if he had been turning a phrase on the terrace at Plassenburg—"glad am I that in your hour you are to be mindful of old friends, for they are like old wine, which grows better and mellower with the years."

"It is indeed well," said Otho von Reuss, ironically. "I have known the Chancellor Dessauer many years, and he grows more honorable and more wise with each decade.

"But now 'tis with this young man that I would speak," he said, changing his tone. "He at least is mine own servant, and so I have other words for him. Hugo Gottfried, you remember that you insulted me, striking me on the face with a glove, because I offered certain civilities to a maid of honor to the Princess of Plassenburg. You wounded me in the arm. Your father, of whose death I have heard but now, cast me forth like a cur-dog from a chamber window. Between you ye have shamed me, and would shame me worse—for the sake of the murderess of mine uncle, Duke Casimir."

"Well do you know that the Lady Helene is innocent of that crime, or any other," said I; "she is purer than your eyes can look upon or your heart conceive. Yet, solely because she knows you for the foul thing you are, Helene lies condemned in your dungeons tonight. I ask you to grant me but one boon—that I may die with her!"

"Nay, my friend, gentlest squire of dames, defender of the oppressed, I have better things in store for you and your maid than that!"

He paused and looked a long while at me, as it seemed, chewing the cud of revenge upon that which he had to say to me.

At last he came a step nearer, that he might look into my eyes.

"Hugo Gottfried," he said, slowly, "son of Gottfried Gottfried, you are my servant now. I said that I would forgive you all for the sake of old times in exile together. And now you and I are both again in our own land. They that kept us out of our offices are dead, and we standing in their places. There is a maid down there in the Wolfsberg dungeons who tomorrow must meet her fate."

He paused a moment and laid his hand on my shoulder impressively.

"And you, Hugo Gottfried, Hereditary Justicer of the Dukedom, Red Axe of the Wolfmark, art the man who must carry out that doom!"

Again he paused—and the world seemed instantly to dissolve into whirling vapor at his words. I had never once thought of such a conclusion. Yet I was indubitably, by my father's death, Hereditary Executioner of the Wolfmark. Red Axe of Thorn I was, and by a terrible chance I had returned in time to be installed in mine office, even as the Lady Ysolinde had foretold.

But a strong thought swelled triumphant in my heart.

"Well," said I, looking the sneering tormentor in the face, "if so be that I am your Hereditary Justicer, it will be long ere a sentence so monstrous shall be carried out by me. I will not slay the innocent, nor pour out the blood of a virgin saint, for a million deaths. You can torture me with all your hellish engines, and you will find that a Gottfried has learned how to suffer, as well as, how to make others suffer, in fourteen generations. As God strengthens me, I will never carry out your sentence—do with me what you will."

"Nobly said, Justicer of the Mark!" said Otho. "I had thought of that! But in case you should refuse to do your lawful office, it may be well for you to remember that I have other instruments that mayhap will please you less."

He threw open a door suddenly, and we looked into an underground hall, where a dozen men were carousing—Duke Casimir's Hussars of Death, black-browed, evil-faced, slack-jowled villains every man of them, cruel and sensual. A blast of ribald oaths came sulphurously up, as if the mouth of hell had been opened.

"Listen!" said Otho, with his hand on my shoulder.

And a jest struck to our ears concerning the prisoner, the Little Playmate—a jest which sticks in my memory to this day. And even yet I hope to cleave the jester through the brain, meet him when I may.

The Duke shut the door, and turned to me again. His eyes narrowed to a thin line which glittered with hate and triumph.

"If you, Hugo Gottfried, Hereditary Executioner of the Mark, refuse to do your duty at the time appointed upon the prisoner condemned, I, Duke Otho, solemnly declare that I will cast your fair and tender lamb into that den of wolves down there to work their wills upon. Hark to them! They will have no misgivings—no qualms, no noble renunciations."

Then he turned to me airily and confidently.

"Well, my good Justicer, will you carry out the just and merciful sentence of the law, and baptize your Red Axe with the blood of her for whose sake you chose to insult and wound a Duke of the Mark?"

I turned away, sick at heart.

"Give me time. God's mercy—give me time!" I cried. "At least let me see Helene. I will give you my answer tonight. But, first of all, let me see my beloved."

"I am forgiving and most merciful," he said, smiling till his teeth showed. "Observe, I do not even cast you into prison to make sure of you. Go your ways" (he sat down and wrote rapidly); "here is a pass which will enable you to visit the prisoner. At midnight I shall expect you to tell me that tomorrow you will fulfil your office."

He handed me the paper and motioned us away.

"We are free to go?" said I, wonderingly.

"Surely," he replied, smiling. "Are you not both my friends, and can Otho von Reuss be forgetful of old times? Come and go at your pleasure. Be sure to be here to give me your answer at midnight tonight—or—"

He pointed with his hand to the door he had again opened, and with the fingers of his other hand beat time to the blasphemous chorus which came belching up from below.

CHAPTER XLIX

THE SERPENT'S STRIFE

Dazed and death-stricken by the horror of the choice which lay before me, I hastened down the street, hardly waiting for Dessauer, who toiled vainly after me. I knew not what to do nor where to turn. I could neither think nor speak. But it chanced that my steps brought me to the house of the Weiss Thor. Almost without any will of mine own I found myself raising the knocker of the house of Master Gerard von Sturm. Sir Respectable instantly appeared. I asked of him if the Lady Ysolinde would see me—giving my name plainly. For since Duke Otho knew me, there was no need of concealment any more.

The Lady Ysolinde would receive me.

I followed my conductor, but not this time to the room in which I had seen her on the occasion of my last visit.

It was in her father's chamber that I met the Princess. The room was as I had first seen it. Only there was no ascetic old man with keen, deep-set eyes and receding forehead to rear his head back from the table as though he would presently strike across it like a serpent from its coil.

For the moment the room was empty, but, ere I had time to look around, the curtains moved and the Lady Ysolinde appeared. Without entering, she set a hand on the door-post, and stood poised against the heavy curtain, waiting for me to speak.

Her face was pale, her thin nostrils dilated. Anger and scorn sat white and deadly on every feature.

"So," she said, intensely, as I did not speak, "you have come back already, most noble Hereditary Justicer of the Mark! Even as I told you—so it is. You come to ask mercy from the woman you despised, from the woman whose love you refused. You would beg her to spare her enemy. Ere you go I shall see you on your knees; ah, that will be sweet. I have been on my knees—can I believe it? Nay, I shall not forget it. I, Ysolinde of Plassenburg, have pled in vain to you—to you!"

And the accent of chill hatred and malice turned me to stone.

"My lady," said I, "well do you know that I would never ask aught for my own life, though the Red Axe itself were at my neck. But it is for the maid I love, for the little child I carried home out of the arms of the man condemned. I ask for her life, who never wronged you or any in all this world. You have heard that task which the Duke hath laid on me, because it is my misfortune to be my father's son—I must take away my love's sweet life, or, if I do not—" I could proceed no further for the horror which rose in my heart.

"I know it," she said, calmly; "my father hath told me all."

"Then," cried I, "if the power lie with you, as you hope for mercy to your own soul, be merciful! Save the maiden Helene from the death of shame, and me from becoming her murderer!"

"Ah," she answered, with delicatest meditative inflection, "this is indeed sweet. The mighty is fallen indeed. The proud one is suppliant now. The knee is bent that would not bend. Hearken, you and your puling babe, to the Princess Ysolinde! Were your lives in that glass, to save or to destroy—her life and your suffering—to make or to break, I would fling them to destruction, even as I cast this cup into the darkness!"

And as she spoke the wreathed beaker of Venice glass sped out of the window and crashed on the pavement without.

"Thus would I end your lives," she said, "for the shame that you two put upon me in the day of my weakness."

"Lady," I cried, eagerly, "you do yourself a wrong! Your heart is better than your word. Do this deed of mercy, I beseech you, if so be you can. And my life is yours forever!"

"Your life is mine, you say," cried she; "aye, and that means what? The wind that cries about the house. Your life is *mine*—it is a lie. Your life and love both are that chit's for whom you have despised—rejected—ME!"

And I grant that at that moment she looked noble enough in her anger as she stood discharging her words at me with hissing directness, like bolts shot twanging from the steel cross-bow.

"And, lest you should think that I have not the power to save you, I will tell you this—when you shall see the neck bared for the blade of the Red Axe, the fine tresses you love, that your eyes look upon with desire, all ruthlessly cut away by the shears of your assistants—ah, I know you will remember then that I, Ysolinde, whom you refused and slighted, had the power in her hand to deliver you both with a word, according to the immaculate laws of the Wolfmark. Aye, and more—power to raise you both to a pinnacle of bliss such as you can hardly conceive. In that hour, when you see me look down upon your anguish, you will know that I can speak the word. You will watch my lips till the axe falls, and under your hand the young life ebbs red. But the lips of Ysolinde will be silent!"

"Such knowledge is an easy boast, Lady Ysolinde!" I answered, thinking to taunt her, that she might reveal whether indeed she had the power she claimed.

"There," she said, pointing to the great collection of black-bound books and papers about the walls; "see, the secret is there—the secret for the lack of which you shall strike your beloved to the death to save her from the unnamable shame. I know it; my father has revealed it to me. I have seen the parchment in these hands. But—you shall never hear it, she never profit by it, and my vengeance shall be sweet—so sweet!"

And she laughed, with a strange crackling laugh that it was a pain to hear.

"God forgive you, Lady Ysolinde," said I, "if this be so. For if there be a God, you must burn in Great Hell for this deed you are about to do. Having had no mercy on the innocent, how shall you ask God to have mercy on you?"

"I will not ask Him!" she cried. "Instead of puling for mercy I will have had my revenge. And after that, come earth, heaven, or hell—I shall not care. All will then be the same to Ysolinde!"

I thought I would try her yet once more.

"The Little Playmate," I said, "the maid whom I have ever loved, though I am not worthy to touch her, is no chance child, no daughter of the Red Axe of Thorn. Leopold von Dessauer hath found and sent to Karl the Prince the full proofs that Helene is the daughter of the last and rightful Prince, and therefore in her own right Princess of Plassenburg."

"You lie, fool!" she cried—"you lie! You think to frighten me. And even if it were true—thrice, four times fool to tell me! For shall not I, the Princess of Plassenburg, the wife of the reigning Prince, stand for my own name and dignity. I would not help you now though a thousand fair heads, well-beloved, the desire of men, the envy of women, were to be rolled in the dust."

"Then farewell, Princess," I cried; "you are wronging to the death of deaths two that never did you wrong, who loved each other with the love of man and woman before ever you crossed their paths, and who since then have only sought your good. You wrong God also, and you lose your soul, divorcing it from the mercy of the Saviour of men. For be very sure that with that measure ye mete, it shall be measured to you again."

She did not answer, but stood with her hand still against the door-post, her head raised, and her lips curling scornfully, looking after me as I retired with a smiling and malicious pleasure.

So, without further speech, I went out from the presence of the Lady Ysolinde. And thus she had the first part of her revenge.

CHAPTER L

THE DUNGEON OF THE WOLFSBERG

And now I must see the Little Playmate. Judge ye whether or no my heart was torn in twain as I went up the long High Street of Thorn, back to the Wolfsberg, alone. For I had compelled Dessauer to return to Bishop Peter's, in order to avert popular suspicion, since our real names and errands were not yet known there.

And when I parted from him the old man was so worn out that I looked momently for him to drop on the rough causeway stones of the street.

Many pictures of my youth passed before me as I mounted towards the castle that night. I remembered the ride of the wild horsemen returning from the raid such long years agone, the old man who carried the babe, and the Red Axe himself, who now lay dead in the Tower—my father, Casimir's Justicer, clad now as then in crimson from head to heel.

Ere long I arrived at the Wolfsberg, and as I came near the Red Tower I saw that the gate was open. A little crowd of men with swords and partisans was issuing tumultuously from it. Then came six carrying a coffin. I stood aside to let them pass. And not till the last one brushed me did I ask what was their business abroad with a dead man at such a time of the night.

"'Tis one that had wrought much fear in his time," answered the soldier, for I had lighted on a sententious fellow—"one that made many swift ends, and now has come to one himself."

"You mean Gottfried Gottfried, the Duke's Justicer?" said I, speaking like one in a dream.

"Aye," he replied. "The Duke Otho is mightily afraid of the plague, and will not have a dead body over-night in his castle. Since they condemned the Saint Helena, God wot, the Duke is a fear-stricken man. He sleeps with half a dozen black riders at the back of his door, as though that made him any safer if a handful of minted gold were dealt out among the rascals. But when was a Prince ever wise?"

"My father's funeral," thought I. "Well, tonight it is, indeed, 'let the dead bury their dead'; Helene is yet alive!"

Surely I am not wanting in feeling, yet my heart was strangely chill and cold. Nevertheless, I turned and followed the procession a little way towards the walls. But even as I went, lo! the bell of the Wolfsberg slowly and brazenly clanged ten. I stopped. I had but two hours in which to visit the Little Playmate and tell her all.

"Goodbye, father," said I, standing with my hat off; "so you would wish me to do—you who met your God standing up—you who did an ill business greatly, because it was yours and you were born to it. Teach me, my father, to be worthy of you in this strait, to the like of which surely never was man brought before!"

The men-at-arms clattered roughly down the street, shifting their burden as if it had been so much kindling-wood, and quarrelling as to their turns. I heard their jests coming clear up the narrow street from far away.

I stood still as they approached a corner which they must turn.

I waved my hand to the coffin.

"Fare you well, true father; tonight and tomorrow may God help me also, like you, to meet my fate standing up!"

And the curve of the long street hid the ribald procession. My father was gone. I had made choice. The dead was burying his dead.

I went on towards the prison of the Wolfsberg; so it was nominated by a sort of grim superiority in that place which was all a prison—the castle which had lorded it so long over the red clustered roofs and stepped gables of Thorn, solely because it meant prisonment and death to the rebel or the refuser of the Duke's exactions.

Often had I seen the straggling procession of prisoners rise, head following head, up from that weary staircase, my father standing by, as they came up from the cells, counting his victims silently, like a shepherd who tells his flock as they pass through a gap in the sheepfold.

For me, alas! there was but one in that dread fold tonight. And she my one ewe lamb who ought to have lain in my bosom.

I clamored long at the gate ere I could make the drowsy jailer hear. As the minutes slipped away I grew more and more wild with fear and anger. At midnight I must face the Duke, and it was after ten—how long I knew not, but I feared every moment that I might hear the brazen clang as the hammer struck eleven.

For time seemed to make no impression on me at all that night.

At last the man came, shuffling, grumbling, and cursing, from his truckle-bed.

"What twice-condemned drunken roysterer may you be, that hath mistaken the prison of Duke Otho for a trull-house?

"An order from the Duke—to see a prisoner! Come tomorrow then, and, meanwhile, depart to Gehenna. Must a man be forever at the beck and call of every sleepless sot? 'Urgent'—is the Duke's mandate. Shove it through the lattice then, that a lantern may flash upon it."

I pushed under the door a broad piece of gold, which proved more to the purpose than much speech.

The door was opened and I showed my pass. That and the gold together worked wonders.

The jailer rattled his keys, donned a hood and woollen wrapper which he took down from a nail, and went coughing before me down the chill, draughty passages. I could hear the prisoners leaping from their couches within as the light of his cresset filtered beneath their doors. What hopes and fears stirred them! A summons, it might be, for some one in that dread warren to come up for a last look at the stars, a walk to the heading-place through the soft, velvet-dark night—then the block, the lightning flash of bright steel, a drench of something sweet and strong like wine upon the lips, and—silence, rest, oblivion.

But we passed the prison doors one by one, and the jailer of the Wolfsberg went coughing and rasping by to another part of the prison.

"'Tis an ill place for chills," he grumbled. "I have never been free of them since first I came to this place, no—nor my wife neither. She has been dead these ten years, praises to the pyx! Ah, would you?" (The torch threatened to go out, so he held it downward in his hand till the pitch melted and caught again, and meanwhile we stood blinded in the smoke and glare which the strong draught forced in our faces.)

At last came the door, a low, iron-spiked grating, like any other of the hundred we had passed.

"Key-metal is not often weared on this cell," the man chuckled. "Those stay not long above ground that bide here."

The door swung back on its creaking hinges. I slipped the fellow another gold piece.

"I must come in with you," he said; "you might do the wench an ill turn which would cheat the Duke of his show and me of my head tomorrow."

I slipped him another piece of gold, and then three together.

"Risk it, man," I said. "Have I not the Duke's own pass? I will do her no harm."

"Well," he said, "pray remember I am a man with five poor motherless children. My wife died of falling down a flight of steps ten years agone—praise the Lord for His mercies. For He is ever mindful of us, the sinful children of men."

The sound of his voice died away as the door closed. I turned, and was alone with the Beloved. The jailer had stuck the cresset in its niche behind the door, and its glow filled the little cell.

At first I could not see the Little Playmate—only a rough pallet bed and something white at the head of it. But as the cresset burned up more clearly, and my eyes became accustomed to the bleared and streaky light, I saw Helene, my love, kneeling at her bed's head.

I stood still and waited. Was she asleep? Was she—was she dead? I almost hoped that she might be. Then the Duke's vengeance would be balked indeed.

"Helene!" I said, softly, as one speaks to the dying—"Helene, dear, dear Helene!"

Slowly she looked up. Her face dawned on me as one day the face of the blessed angel will shine when he calls me out of purgatory.

"My love—my love!" she said, sweetly, like the first note of a hymn when the choir breathes the sweet music rather than sings it.

Ah, Lord of Innocence, that pure loving face, the purple deepness in the eyes, the flush on the cheek as on that of a little child asleep, the soft curled hair which crisped in the hollow of the neck—the throat itself—Eternal God, that I should be alive to think of the horror!

But time was passing swiftly. The minutes were slipping by like men running for their lives.

I raised Helene from her knees, and she nestled her head on my shoulder.

"You have come to me! I knew you would come. I saw you on the day—the day when they condemned me to die."

I broke into an angry, desperate, protesting cry, so that I heard my own voice ring strangely through that dumb, horrible place. And it was I who sobbed in her arms with my head on her shoulder.

"Hush, dear love," she said, clasping her arms caressingly about my head; "do not fear for me. God will keep your little one. God has told me that He will bring me bravely through. Hush thee, then; do not so, Hugo, great playmate! This I cannot bear. Help me to be good. It will not be long nor painful. Do not weep for your little girl! I think, somehow, it is for our love that I suffer, and that will make it sweet!"

But still I sobbed like a child. For how—how could I tell her?

Presently the power returned slowly to me, seeing her smiling so bravely up at me, and rising on tiptoe to kiss my wet face.

Then I told her all—in what words I hardly remember now.

"Love of mine," I said, "I have but an hour or less to speak with you—and ah! such terrible things, such inconceivable things, to say; a horror to reveal such as never lover had to tell his love before."

She drew one of my hands down and softly patted her breast with it.

"Fear not," she said; "tell it Helene. If it be true that love conquers all, your little lass can bear it!"

"I came," said I, "with purpose to see you, and by treachery (it skills not to ask whose) I was taken at my dead father's bedside."

"Our father dead?" she cried, going a step away to look at me, but coming back again immediately; "then there are but you and me in the world, Hugo!"

"Aye," said I, "but how can I tell you the rest? My father died like a man, and then they took me, still holding the dead in my arms. I was confronted with a fiend of hell in the likeness of Duke Otho."

As I mentioned the Duke's name I could feel her shudder on my neck.

"And—But I cannot tell you what he has bidden me do, under penalties too fearful to conceive or speak of."

She put her hands up, and gently, timidly, lovingly stroked my cheek.

"Dear love, tell me! Tell the Little Playmate!" she said, as simply and sweetly as if she had been coaxing me to whisper to her some lightest childish secret of our plays together in the old Red Tower.

I was silent for a space, and then, spurred by the thought of the swiftly passing time, the words were wrenched out of me.

"He says that I, even I, Hugo Gottfried, my father's son, being now hereditary Red Axe of the Wolfmark, must strike off the head of the one I love. And if I will not, then to the vilest of devils for vilest ends he will deliver her. Ah, God, and he would do it too! I saw the very flame of hell's fire in his eyes."

Then I that write saw a strange appearance on the face that looked up in mine. As on a dark April day, with a lowering sky, you have seen the wind suddenly stir high in the heavens, and the sun look through on the dripping green of the young trees and the gay bourgeoning of the flowers, so, looking on my love's face as she took in my words, there awakened a kind of springtime joy. Nay, wherefore need I say a kind of joy only. It was more. It was great, overleaping, sudden-springing gladness. Her eyes swam in lustrous beauty. She smiled up at me as I had never seen her smile before.

"Oh, I am glad, Hugo—so glad! I love you, Hugo! It will be hard for you, my love. And yet you will be brave and help me. I had far rather die at your hand than live to be the bride of the greatest man in all the world. Do that which will save me from, shame; do it gladly, Hugo. I fear it. I saw it in the eyes of that man Otho von Reuss. But *only* to die will be easy, with you near by. For I love you, Hugo. And I could just say a prayer, and then—well, and then—Do not cry, Hugo—why, then you would put me to sleep, even as of old you did in the Red Tower!

"Nay, nay, dear love! You must not do so. This is not like my Hugo. See, *I* do not cry. Do you remember when you took me up and laid me on your bed, and our father came and looked? You said I was your little wife. So I was, even though I denied it, and now I can trust you, my husband. I have never been aught else but your little wife, you see—not in my heart, not in my heart of hearts!

"I have been proud with you, Hugo—spoken unkind things. For love, you know, is like that. It hurts that which it would die for. But now you will know, once for all, that I love you. For death tests all. And you *will* help me. You will not cry then, Hugo—not then, when we walk, you and I, by the shores of the great sea. You will only send me a little voyage by myself, as you used to make me go to the well in the court-yard, to teach me not to be frightened!

"And then you will be with me when I go. You will watch me; soon, soon you will come after me. Yes, I am glad, Hugo—so glad. For—bend down your ear, Hugo—I will confess. Your little girl is such a coward. She is afraid of the dark. But it will not be dark—and it will not be long, and it will be sure. If my love stand by, I shall not fear. And, after all, it is but a little thing to do for my love, when I love him so."

What I said, or what I did, I know not. But when I came a little to myself, I found my head on my knees, and Helene soothing and petting me, as if I had been a child that had fallen down and hurt itself.

"I would have been a good wife to you, Hugo; I had thought it all out. At first I would have been such an ignorant little house-keeper, and you would have needed—oh, such great patience with me! But so willing, so ready, Hugo! And how I should have listened for your foot! Do you know, I used to know it as it came across the court-yard at Plassenburg. But I could not run and meet you then. I could only slip behind the window-lattice and throw you a kiss. But when I was indeed your wife, how I should have flown to meet you!"

I think I cried out here for very agony.

"Hush, Hugo!" she said. "Hush, lad, and listen. There are stairs up aloft—I saw them in a dream. I saw the angels and the redeemed ascending and descending as I prayed, even when you came in to call me back. I shall ask God to let me wait at the stair-head a little while for you—till it should be time for you to come, my dear, my dear. You would not be very long, and I could wait. I would listen for your feet upon the stair, dear love. And when at last you came, I should know your footfall; yes, I should know it ever so far away. You would not be thinking of me just then. And when you came to the top of the golden stairs, there—there, all so suddenly, would be your little lass, with her arms ready to welcome you!"

The door of the cell creaked open.

The jailer appeared. "It is time!" he said, curtly, and stood waiting. We stood up, and I looked in her eyes. She was smiling, dry-eyed, but I—the water was running down my face.

"You will be brave, Hugo, for my sake. Next to life with you—to die by your dear hand, knowing that you love me, is the best gift they could have given me. They thought to hurt, but instead they have made me so happy. Till we meet again, dear love—till we meet soon again!"

And she accompanied me to the door, and kissed me as I went out, standing smilingly on tiptoe to do it, even as of old she was wont to do in the Red Tower.

And the last thing I saw of her, as the door closed upon the darkness of the cell, was my love standing smiling up at me, her eyes filled with the splendors of the love that casteth out fear.

CHAPTER LI

THE NIGHT BEFORE THE MORN

Even as the dwarf on the ledge of the castle clocktower creaked his wires and clicked back his hammer to strike the midnight over the city, even as the first solemn toll of the hour reverberated over the Wolfsberg, I was at the door of the Duke's room waiting for admission.

The Chamberlain in attendance looked within, and seeing his master writing at a table, he was going out again without speech.

"Has Hugo Gottfried returned?" said the Duke, without looking up.

"Hugo Gottfried is here!" I replied, stepping unannounced into the room.

He looked up without smiling, a keen inquiring glance glittering from between eyelids so close together that only the faintest line of the pupil showed black under the lashes.

"Well?" he questioned.

"I will do the thing you have asked," answered I.

And said no more.

The Duke instantly became restless, and getting up, he began to pace about the floor like a caged beast.

"You have seen her?" he inquired, stopping in front of me, wide-nostrilled, like a dog that points the game.

"I *have* seen her," I replied, as simply.

"Well?" he queried again, with a keen, eager note of anxiety in his voice.

"I am ready to do that which you have asked."

He seemed to be on the point of saying something else. But, changing his mind, he touched a little silver bell.

The usher appeared.

"Show the Hereditary Justicer of the Mark to the Red Tower. Give him all that is necessary to eat and drink. Bid a man-at-arms attend him, and set a sufficient guard at the door!"

So I went out from the presence, and the Duke and the Duke's new Justicer bowed to each other gravely as I stood a moment on the threshold.

"Till we meet again, Red Axe of the Wolfmark!" said Duke Otho.

"Till we meet again!" said I, countering him like blade meeting blade.

In little more than ten minutes after I had entered them, I stood outside the Duke's apartments, and with my escort I strode across to the empty Red Tower, the home of so many memories. My head was reeling, and with the overpress of excitement I could not sleep. So, bribing the soldier, my companion—who had been charged by the Duke not to lose sight of me—to accompany me, I went up to my father's garret.

There I found all things as they had been when my father died.

I set the windows wide, cast the tumbled bedclothes out upon the dust-heap beneath, and bared the whole to the clean, large, wholesome breezes of the night. I saw the fateful Red Axe lean as usual against the block, and, taking it up, I found it keen as a razor. It was spotless, and the edge gave back the long low room and our one glimmering candle like a mirror. It must have been my father's last work in this world to polish it.

Then I went down to my own room and cast myself down upon the bed in which, on that night of the first home-coming of the Playmate, I had laid my little wife.

The soldier couched across the door, rolled in his cloak and some chance wrapping he found about the house.

God keep me from ever spending such a night again! I thought it would never come to an end. Out in the square in front of the Wolfsberg I could hear a knocking—dull, continuous, reverberant. At first I thought it must be within my own head. So I asked the soldier, after a little, if he heard it also. I had some faint idea that it might be Prince Karl of Plassenburg with his army thundering at the gates of Thorn.

"'Tis but the scaffold going up in the Grand Place without!" said the soldier, carelessly; "I heard that the Duke had bidden them work all night by torch-light."

I tried to sleep, but the knocking continued, aching across my brows till I thought I must go mad. After a while I rose and went to the window from which I had so often looked down wistfully upon the play of the city children.

Opposite me, in the middle of the open space, loomed a dark mass—a platform, it seemed, raised a dozen feet above the road—the black silhouette of a ladder set anglewise against it, and that was all. Lower, plainer, somehow deadlier than a gibbet with its flamboyant beam, which one never sees empty without imagining the malefactor aswing upon it; the heading-block did not frown, it grinned—yes, grinned like the eye-holes of a skeleton with a candle behind them, while the torches glinted through the interstices of the framework as it was being nailed together.

All night the dull *dunt-dunting* went on without. And I sat awake by the window and awaited the dawning.

The city seethed unslaked beneath. When first I looked from my chamber window the square was free to all who chose to enter it. But as the knocking went on the news spread through the town of Thorn.

"They are making the scaffold for our Saint Helena!" So the word ran.

And within an hour the courts and alleys of Thorn belched forth thousands of angry men. Pikes were carried like staves, the steel head hidden up the long white burgess sleeve. Working-men of the trades, 'prentices, and market porters drew their swords and came forth with the bare blades in their hands, leaving the scabbards at home to take care of themselves, as was their custom.

Wives cried from escalier windows to their men to come in by and lie decently down, to be ready for their work in the morning. And the men so addressed paid not the least heed, as the manner of men is. These things and many others I saw, scarce knowing what I saw.

And so, with the hum of gathering crowds, the hours passed slowly over. But the temper of the people in the square grew more and more difficult, and soon the guard had to be brought down from the castle. The great gates beneath me were open, and the Wolfsberg vomited the black men-at-arms to keep the Duke's peace.

But this brought only the quicker strife. Yells received them as soon as their steel partisans showed up in the square.

"Oppressors of the people, ye come to your reward!" cried many voices.

"We will give you your last breakfast—of cold, tempered steel!" cried another, from the bowels of the crowd.

"To the Wolfsberg—ho! Break in the doors! We will have our Saint Helena forth of their cursed prisons!"

It was no sooner said than done. Like a wave the people rushed in a black irregular mass at the front rank of the guard. The soldiers of the Duke were swept away like chaff; I could see one here and another there struggling in the vortices of the angry multitude.

"On to the Wolfsberg!" cried the crowd.

But when the first of them reached the castle gates, lo! they stood open, and there behind them stood file on file of matchlock men with their matches burning in their hands and their pieces trained upon their rests.

"Give them the fire!" cried a voice, that of Duke Otho, as the crowd halted a moment irresolute.

The bright red flame started out here and there from muzzle and touchhole, and then ran along the line in an irregular volley.

A terrible cry of fear went up from the folk. For though they had heard of the new ordnance, and even seen one or two, they had never realized the effect of a fusillade. And when a man on either side sank down with a hollow sound like a beast in shamble-thills, and the man in front fell over on his face without a sound, the multitude turned, broke into groups, fled, and disappeared in a moment like a whirl of snow which the wind canters down the street in a veering flurry.

Then the gates shut to, and the deep lines of matchlock men were hidden from view. After this the city thrilled and murmured worse than ever, humming like an angry hive. But the Wolfsberg kept its counsel. Not yet had deliverance arrived for the captives within its cells.

And the dread morning was coming fast.

At last, wearied out with crowding emotions, I went and cast me down on my bed, and, instantly falling asleep, I slept like a log till one touched me on the shoulder. Looking up, I saw the Duke Otho. He had come to make sure of his vengeance—the vengeance which I knew well was not his, but that of Ysolinde, Princess of Plassenburg.

CHAPTER LII

THE HEADSMAN'S RIGHT

"Rise, Justicer of the Wolfmark!" said Otho, smiling mockingly upon me like a fiend.

I started up and gazed about bewildered as the coming terrors of the morning broke upon me.

"'Tis scarcely an hour to sunrise," he continued, "and I warrant the noble Red Axe will desire to feel the edge of his tool and see that his assistants are in their places."

The Duke paused as he went out of the door, and looked at me.

"I can promise you a distinguished company at the first public performance of your honorable office," he said, with a polite gesture.

So soon as he was gone I rose to my feet. Across the broad, black oaken stool, whereon from boyhood it had been my habit to place my clothes neatly folded up, I found a suit of new red cloth, plain and rich, with an inscription upon a strip of vellum laid across the breast, bearing that these were a gift from the most Illustrious Duke Otho of the Wolfmark.

Since, after all, my fate was my fate, there was little use in straining at the gnat. So I set to and did upon me the garmentry of shame. They were made after the fashion of my father's, cap and hosen and shoon all of red, with a cloak of red to cover all.

Then I went to the Playmate's room, and before the niche where her little Prie-Dieu had stood, I kneeled me down and said such a prayer as at the moment I could compass. But little was needed. For I think God in heaven Himself was praying for us both that day.

When I went forth into the square, few there were who knew or remembered me, but all knew my attire. Then indeed it did my heart good to hear the great unanimous roar of execration which went up from the multitude as I came out. The soldiers had their work cut out to push a way for me to the scaffold.

"Butcher him—tear him to pieces—wolf's cub that he is—he that was her foster-brother to slay our Saint Helena!"

It made me proud to hear them. And as they rushed furiously against the escort, intent to kill me, we swayed from side to side.

"Down with the Red Axe!" they shouted. "Down with the bloody house of Gottfried and all that belong to it!"

And I felt inclined to cry "Amen!"

Then, when I had mounted the few steps which led to the platform on which stood the black headsman's block, I gazed about me in wonder, holding the Red Axe in my hand. And to my disordered vision I saw the crowd swell and whirl about me on earth and in the air, bubbling and tossing like a pot boiling furiously. Then I bethought me of the work I had to do, and prayed that I might be given strength to do it swiftly and featly, that the suffering of my love might not be long. Also I thought of the lecherous evil demons of the Black Riders, and thereat was somewhat comforted. At the worst I could give my love a better end than that.

Then appeared my Lord Duke Otho. An enclosure had been formed for him by the palace wall, covered with a red hanging, as though my sweetheart's death were a gala sight. And when he had come to the front and arranged his folk, lo! there by his side stood Ysolinde, Princess of Plassenburg, with her father, Master Gerard. They had a place close by the Duke, and Otho ofttimes bent over to confer graciously with his councillor. But Ysolinde looked neither to right nor left, nor yet spoke to any, keeping her eyes fixed, as it seemed, on the shining blade of the Red Axe in my hand.

Then, as these fine folk stood waiting and gloating among the festoons of their balcony, the devil or God (I know which, but I will not say, lest I be thought a blasphemer) put an intent into my heart. I walked to the edge of the scaffold, and I looked at the barrier of the enclosure. They were of the same height, and the distance between them little more than six feet.

I examined them again, and yet more intently. I saw the steely smile on Duke Otho's face. Already he was tasting the double sweetness of his revenge.

"Wait," I said, within my heart, as I also smiled a little, "only wait a little, Otho, Duke of the Wolfmark. Wait till this bright edge be sullied with my sweet love's blood. And then—then will I leap upon you, and the Red Axe shall crash deep into the brain that hatched and fostered this hellish intent. And by the gentle heart of her who is about to die, so also will I serve Gerard the lawyer, and Ysolinde, his daughter, for their treachery against the innocent. Then, amid the flash of steel and the heady whirl of battle, shall Hugo Gottfried be very content to die!" It would take more than one stroke to dull that which my father had sharpened. And I lifted up the Red Axe and felt the edge with my thumb. It was razor keen.

But the action was observed, and taken as a proof of callousness. And then what a yell of hate surged up around me! I could have taken those burghers of Thorn to my heart. And I thought if only our Karl would come. Alas! it was a full day too soon; for I felt sure that these burghers would proclaim him at the gates, and that the house of Otho and Casimir, the brood of the Wolf, would, like the shadow of the raven as it flits by in the sunshine, pass away. For by that time there would be no Otho. They would find him low enough, with an axe cleft in his head.

So soon as the sun's light tipped the eastern clouds with rose, the Black Hussars came riding forth. The guards and matchlock men lined the way from the castle gates. They blew up their matches to be ready. Suddenly in the midst of the armed throng there appeared a radiant figure coming down the steps of the castle from the Hall of Judgment.

At the sight the people threw themselves wildly in that direction. The dark lines of the guard reeled and wavered. There was the sharp click as the pikes engaged. The shouts of the captains of the matchlock men were heard. But the trained bands stood fast, and the rush was stayed. Then came our Helene down towards me, walking delicately, yet proudly erect as a young tree. She was clad all in white and wore her hair plaited high upon her head, so that the shape of her neck was clearly seen.

And I who stood there with the axe in my hand seemed to have a thousand years to think all these things, and even to mark the lace upon her dress. I saw her come nearer and nearer to me. Yet feeling was dead within me. I seemed to sleep and wake and sleep again. And when at last I awoke, there came a strange feeling to me. It was my wedding-day, and my bride was coming to me, lily pure, clad in whiteness.

Then at the foot of the scaffold there came one forth from the ranks, a captain of the Duke's guard, and with honor and respect offered Helene his arm.

She declined it with a proud smile, and all that were near could hear her clear voice say, "I thank you, sir, but I need no help. I am strong enough to walk thus far."

And she mounted the steps of the scaffold as though they had been those of the grand staircase at Plassenburg.

But when she saw me, standing in my habit of red from head to heel, she seemed a little taken aback. Quickly, however, she came forward and took me by the hand, looking up at me with the love-light making her eyes glorious.

"Hugo," she said, "I am glad you are here—glad that I am to die by no less loving hand. That will be sweeter than to live with any other. And, indeed, I deserve so much, for I have not known much joy in my life, save in the old days when I was your Little Playmate."

Then there came a stern voice from the enclosure:

"Executioner of the Mark, do your duty!"

It was the voice of Master Gerard.

And then I looked over and saw Gerard von Sturm standing a little in front, with his daughter's wrist held tightly in his hand as though he would drag her back. With that a loathing came over me, for I said within me, "Is the woman so anxious for the blood of the innocent whom she has hounded to death that she would intrude on the scaffold itself?"

Then I remembered the duty of the Justicers, ere the sentence was carried out, to recite the crimes of the condemned.

So I cried aloud, even as I had heard my father do.

"The crimes of Helene, Princess of Plassenburg, sole daughter of Dietrich, lately Prince thereof—guilty of no evil, save that she has been the savior of this people of Thorn and their deliverer in time of pestilence!"

The people hushed themselves with astonishment at my words. And then a cry went up.

"The Red Axe speaks true—she is innocent—innocent!"

But the voice of Gerard von Sturm came again, stern as that of the recording angel:

"Executioner of the Wolfmark, do your duty!"

Scarce knowing what I did, I went on with my formal accusation.

"Helene, Princess of Plassenburg, who is about to die, is also guilty of loving me, Hugo Gottfried, son of Gottfried Gottfried, and of none other crime. For this the Duke has decreed that she should die. It is her own will that she should die by my hand."

Helene came forward and put her hand in mine in token that I spoke truly, and there fell a great silence across the people. I saw the Lady Ysolinde straining at her father's hand, like a dog in a leash when the quarry rises.

Then my love kissed me once, just as though she had been saying goodnight in the Red Tower, simply and sweetly, like a child, and laid her head down on the block as on the white pillow of her own bed.

"God do so and more also to them on whose heads is the innocent blood of my love and my wife!"

The words burst from me rather than were uttered.

I raised the blade.

But ere the Red Axe could fall there arose a wild scream from the Duke's enclosure. Some one cried, "Let me go! He has said it! He has said it! I will not be silent any longer!" It was the Lady Ysolinde, who had broken away from her father's hand.

"The girl is his wife," she went on. "He has claimed her—according to the laws of the Wolfmark, that cannot be broken, he has called her his wife. It is the Executioner's right. One woman he can claim as his during his term of office—one only, and for his wife. Duke Otho, I call upon you to allow it! Chancellor Texel, I call upon you to read the law! I have it here in my hand. Head! Read! *I will save my soul! I will save my soul!*"

And ere any one could stop her, the Lady Ysolinde, sobbing and laughing both at once, had overleaped the light barrier, and was thrusting a parchment with a seal into the hands of the Chancellor Michael Texel.

"She is mad. Let the justice of the realm be done!" cried again the voice of Master Gerard.

And I think the Duke would have ordered it to be so. But there arose not only a roar from the people, but, what Otho minded far more, an ominous murmur among the nobles and gentlemen and from the ranks of men-at-arms.

"The law! The law! Read us the law!"

And even Otho dare not trifle with the will of the free companions of the Mark. For in all the realm they were now his only supporters. Helene had risen to her feet, and stood, pale of face but erect, resting, as was her wont, one hand on my shoulder.

Then Michael Texel read the scroll aloud.

"It is the immemorial privilege of the Hereditary Executioner of the Mark, being of the family of Gottfried, a privilege not to be abrogated or alienated, that during the term of office of each, he may claim—not as a boon, but as a right—the life of one man for a bond-servant, or the life of one woman for a wife. Thus, by order of the States' Council, to be the privilege of the Gottfrieds forever, it has been proclaimed!"

As Michael Texel went on, I saw the countenance of the Duke and the lawyer change. I knew that salvation had come to us like lightning from a clear sky, and I hastened to demand the right which was mine own.

So soon as he had finished I shouted with all my power:

"I CLAIM HELENE TO BE MY WIFE!"

Then went up such an acclaim from the people as never had been heard in the ancient city. Even the gentlemen within the enclosure threw their hats in the air. The soldiers put their helmets on the points of their spears, and the captains waved their colors as at a victory. The thunder of the cheering roused the very rooks and jackdaws from the towers of Thorn and the bastions of the Wolfsberg till they went drifting in a black cloud clamorously over the city.

Then Helene put her arms about my neck, and, upon the scaffold of death, before all the people, we plighted our troth.

"The Bishop—the Bishop Peter!" cried the people.

And, leaping upon an officer's horse, a messenger rode post-haste to the palace, the crowd making way for him. Duke Otho disappeared through a private door, for the thing was over-strong even for him. He knew his weakness too well to war with the immemorial privileges of the Wolfmark.

Rulers stronger than he had been broken in doing battle against ancient rights and amenities. Besides, the nobility were afraid of their own perquisites if one of so ancient a charter as that of the Hereditary Justicer were refused.

Then from the palace came the Bishop, with due and decorous attendance of crosier and solemn procession. And there, amid a turmoil of joy and the ringing of every bell in the city, we, that had gone out to be together in death, were joined in the bonds of youth and life.

But the Lady Ysolinde saw not—heard not. For they had carried her out white and still from the place where she had fallen fainting at the foot of the scaffold.

CHAPTER LIII

THE LUBBER FIEND'S RETURN

Al these things had overpast so quickly that when Helene and I found ourselves alone in the Red Tower it seemed to both of us that we dreamed.

We sat in a kind of buzzing hush, on the low window-seat of the old room, hand in hand. The shouts of the people came up to us from the square beneath. We heard the tramp of the soldiers, who cheered us as they passed to and fro. Being at last alone, we looked into each other's eyes, and we could not believe in our own happiness.

"My wife!" I said, but in another fashion than I had said it on the scaffold.

"My husband!" answered Helene, looking up at me.

But I think, for all that we realized of the truth, we might as well have called each other King and Queen of Sheba.

We had been conducted with honor to the Red Tower. For since it was in virtue of my hereditary office that I had obtained the great deliverance, I dared for the present seek no other dwelling-place. For Helene's sake, indeed, I should have felt safer elsewhere. Besides, desperate and full of baffled hatred as I knew Duke Otho to be, I did not believe that he would dare to molest us—for some time at least. The rage of the people, their unbounded jubilation at the deliverance of their Saint Helena from the jaws of death on the very scaffold, were too recent to be trifled with by a prince sitting so insecure in his ducal seat as Otho of the Wolfmark.

So here in the ancient Red Tower, I thought, we might at least be safe enough till my good fellows of Plassenburg, with the Prince at their head, should swarm hammering at the gates of Thorn.

To us, sitting thus hand in hand, there entered the Bishop Peter.

"Hail!" he said, blandly, and in his grandest manner, as we knelt for his benediction; "hail, bride and bridegroom! God has been good to you this day. Bishop Peter, the least of His servants, greets you very well. May you have long life and prosperity unfailing."

I thanked him for his gracious words.

"The folk of the city are full of joy," he said. "I think they would almost proclaim you Duke today."

"I desire no such perilous honor," I replied, smiling; "it were indeed an ill-omen to have a Duke habited all in red."

"It is your marriage-dress, Hugo," said Helene; "I will not have you speak against it."

Ever since the strain of the scaffold she had not once broke down—no, nor wept—but only desired to sit very close beside me, touching me sometimes, as if to make sure that I was real. Deliverance had been too great and sudden, and those things which had come so near to us both—Death and the Beyond—had left a salt and bitter spray on our lips.

"And what of the Lady Ysolinde?" I asked of the Bishop.

Now the Bishop Peter was a good man, but, like many of his brethren, a lover of great, swelling words.

"The Lady Ysolinde," he said, oratorically, "by the immediate assistance of the city guard, was placed in a litter and deported, all unconscious as she was, to her father's house in the Weiss Thor, where she still remains. But her most seasonable extract from the laws of the Wolfmark, which so opportunely saved the life of your fair wife, and led to this present happy consummation, I have here by me, even in my hand."

And with that the Bishop drew the rolled parchment from his pocket and handed it to me, with all the original seals depending from it. Now I have small gift for the deciphering of such ancient documents, being only skilled in the common script of the day, and not over-well in that. So that I had to depend upon the offices of Bishop Peter for the interpretation.

"I think," said the Bishop, after he had finished reading it over, "that this document had best remain in my own possession. It may be safer under the seal and protection of the Church—even as, to speak truth, you and your wife would also be. I am a plain man," the Bishop continued, after a pause, "but remember that there is ever a place of refuge at the palace—and one which even Duke Otho is not likely to violate, remembering the experiences of his predecessor, Duke Casimir, when he crossed his sword against the crosier of this unworthy servant of Holy Church."

"I thank you," said I. "I would that it were possible to avail myself of your all too generous offer. But it will be necessary to abide at least this one night in the Red Tower."

"Ah," he said, "why this night?"

"Great things may happen this night, my Lord Bishop!" said I, and glanced significantly in the direction of Plassenburg.

"Ah," said the Bishop again, "so then the power of Holy Church may not be the only restraint upon Duke Otho by tomorrow at this time!"

And, calling his attendants, the suave and far-seeing prelate made his way with gravity and reverend ceremony down the streets of Thorn towards his palace.

So, bit by bit, the long day passed away, and I thought it would never end. For Helene and I sat and waited for that which might happen, with beating and anxious hearts. Ofttimes I ran to the top of the Red Tower, and sometimes it seemed that I could see a moving cloud of dust, and sometimes a flurry of startled cattle afar on the horizon. But till dusk there came to our aching eyes no better evidence that the lads of Plassenburg were coming to our rescue and to the deliverance of the down-trodden city of Thorn.

The soldiers of the garrison were still encamped in the great square. There was also a constant swarming and mustering of men upon the ramparts of the Wolfsberg. Duke Otho had certainly enough men to make a creditable resistance. True, they were Free Companions, and without other loyalty than that which they owed to their paymaster.

And beneath this warlike show lay the city, rebellious and turbulent to the core, the merchants longing for unhampered rights of trade and security in the enjoyment of the fruits of their labors, the craftsmen claiming freedom to work in their guilds without a payment of labor-bond tithes to the Duke, and especially without the fear of being snatched away at any moment from their benches and looms to join in his forays and incursions.

Towards the gloaming I had come down from the roof of the tower, and was standing, gloomy, and little like a bridegroom, at the little window whence I had so often looked down upon the playing children of Thorn. Suddenly a great hand was reached up from the pavement, a folded paper was thrust in at the lattice, and I saw the face of the Lubber Fiend looking up at me from the street below.

"Come up hither, good Jan," I cried to him. "I will run and open the gate!"

But the Lubber Fiend only shook his head till his ears flapped like burdocks in the wind by the wood edges.

"Jan will come none within that gate to tell where he has been," he said. "Jan may be a fool, but he knows better than that."

"And where have you been?" I asked, eagerly.

Jan the Lubber Fiend stood on his tiptoes and whispered up to me with his elbows on the sill.

"You are sure the Duke is not behind you?"

"There is none here—except my wife," I said, smiling. And I liked speaking the word.

"I have seen the great Prince," said Jan, nodding backward, and smiling mysteriously, "and he is coming, but not by himself. There are such a peck of mad fellows out there. There will not be much to eat in Thorn when they all come in. Better make a good dinner today, that is my advice to you. And I was bid to tell you that when all was ready for their coming a fire is to be lighted on a high place, and then the Prince will come to the gates."

I longed much to hear more of his adventures, but neither love nor money would induce the thrice cautious Jan to set a foot within the precincts of the Red Tower.

"I will light a bonfire when it is dark at the White Gate," he said, as he retracted himself into the dusk. "I know what will make a rare blaze. And the Prince cannot come too soon."

So indeed I thought also, as I looked out and saw the swarms of Duke Otho's men in the court-yard and about the square, and reflected on our helplessness here in the Red Tower within the defenced precincts of the Wolfsberg.

CHAPTER LIV

THE CROWNING OF DUKE OTHO

But at long and last the most tardy-footed day comes to an end. And so, just as fast as on any common day, the sun at last dropped to the edge of the horizon and slowly sank, leaving a shallowing lake of orange color behind.

The red roofs of Thorn grew gray, with purple veins of shadow in the interstices where the streets ran, or rather burrowed. The nightly hum of the city began. For, under the cruel rule of the wolves of the castle, Thorn was ever busiest in the night. Indeed, the cheating of the guard had become a business well understood of all the citizens, who had a regular code of signals to warn each other of its approach.

Lights winked and kindled in the Wolfsberg over against me. I could see the long array of lighted windows where the Duke would presently be dining with Michael Texel, High Councillor Gerard von Sturm, and most of his other intimates. There, beneath, were the stables of the Black Riders, and before them men were constantly passing and repassing with buckets and soldier gear.

I wondered if the Duke had news of the approach of the enemy.

So soon as I judged it safe I went to the top of the Red Tower and unfolded the paper which Jan the Lubber Fiend had brought me. It was without name and address or signature, and read as follows:

"Tonight we shall be all in readiness. When the time is ripe let a fire be lighted upon some conspicuous tower or high place of the city. Then we will come."

Thereafter Helene, being lonely, climbed up and sat down beside me. I handed her the paper.

"Tonight will be a stormy one in Thorn and the Wolfsberg, little one," said I. "I fear you and I are not yet out of the wood."

The Little Playmate read the letter and gave it back to me. I tore it up, and let the wind carry away the pieces one by one, small, like dust, so that scarce one letter clave to another.

Her hand stole into mine.

"Ah," she sighed, "I am beginning to believe in it now! Tonight may be as dangerous as yesternight. But at least we are together, never to be separated. And to us two that means all."

It was a strange marriage night, this of ours—thus to sit on the roof of the Tower, under the iron beacon which had been placed there in my grandfather's time, and listen to the hum and murmur of the city, straining our eyes meanwhile through the darkness to catch the first spear-glint from the army of the Prince.

"If they do not come by midnight, or if Jan Lubber Fiend does not light his fire by the White Gate, we must e'en risk it and kindle this one here on the Red Tower."

So the night passed on till it was about eleven, or it might be a quarter of an hour later. Then all suddenly I saw a little crowd of men disengage themselves from that private entrance of the Hall of Judgment by which, on the day of the trial, Dessauer and I had entered. They made straight towards the Red Tower at a quick run.

"Dear love," said I to Helene, "see yonder! Be ready to light the beacon. I fear me much that our time has come to fight for life."

"Kiss me, then," she said, "and I will be ready for all that may be. At worst, we can die together, true husband and true wife."

Presently there came a thundering knock at the door of the Red Tower. I crouched on the stairs behind and listened intently. I could hear the breathing of several men.

"He is surely within," said a voice. "The tower has been watched every moment of the day."

Again came the loud knocking.

"Open—in the name of the Duke!" cried the voice. And the door was rattled fiercely against its fastenings.

But I knew well enough that it could hold against any force of unassisted men. For my father had ever taken a special pride in the bars and defences of the single low door which led into his much-threatened residence.

So I crouched in the dark of the stairs and listened with yet more quivering intentness. Presently I could hear shoulders set to the iron-studded surface, and a voice counted, softly, "One—two—three—and a heave!" But though I discerned the laboring of the men straining themselves with all their might, they might as well have pushed at the rough-harled wall of the Wolfsberg.

"It will not do," I heard one say at last. "We cannot hope to succeed thus. Bring the powder-bag and prepare the fuse."

So then I knew indeed that our time was at hand. I mounted the stairs three at a time till I came to the room where Helene was waiting for me in the dark.

"Fire the beacon on the Tower!" I bade her—"our enemies are upon us!"

"And after that may I come to you, Hugo?" she said.

"Nay, little one, it is better that you bide on the roof and see that the beacon burns. You will find plenty of tow and oil in the niche by the stair-head."

I could hear Helene give vent to a little sigh. But she obeyed instantly, and her light feet went pattering up the stairs.

Then I waited for the explosion, which seemed as if it would never come. I had my dagger in my belt, but of pure instinct my right hand seized the Red Axe. For I had more skill of that than any other weapon, and as I had cast it down when they brought us in from the scaffold that morning, it lay ready to my hand.

So I waited at the stair-head, and watched keenly the narrow passage up which the men must come one by one. I measured my distance with the axe-handle, and made a trial sweep or two, so that I might be sure of clearing the stones on either side. I could not see that there would be much difficulty in holding the place for a while, if only Prince Karl would haste him and come. For to me the game of breaking heads and slicing necks would be easy as cracking nuts on an anvil—at least, so long as they would come up singly.

Presently I heard the roar of burning fuel above me, and immediately after a cry from below. Through the narrow stairway lattice I could see the uncertain flicker of flames lighting up the street. Men ran backward across the open square, looking up as they ran. So by that I knew that Helene had done her work, and was now watching the burning beacon, as the flames flicked upward and clapped their fiery applausive palms.

But at the same moment, from the foot of the stairs, there came the loud report of the explosion beneath the door of the Red Tower, the rumble of stones, and then an eager rush of men to see what had been effected.

"Now for it!" I thought, as I gripped the Red Axe.

But it was not to be so soon. The iron bars, which my father had engineered so that they sank deep into the wall on either side, still held nobly, and I heard the loud voice crying again for a battering-ram. The soldiers of the attacking party went scurrying across the yard, and presently returned, carrying between them a young tree cleared of its branches, but with the rough bark still upon it.

Without, in the square, the turmoil increased, and the streets echoed with shouting. A wild hope came into my heart that Prince Karl had not awaited the summons of the beacon, and that his troops were already in the streets of Thorn. But even as the thought passed through my brain I knew that it was vain.

On the other hand, it was evident that in the town the general alarm had been given, for the trumpets blew from the ramparts of the Wolfsberg, and the call to arms resounded incessantly in the court-yard. I doubted not also that many a stout burgher was getting him under arms—and but few of them to fight for the Duke.

Suddenly the bars of the door jangled on the stones under the swinging blows of the battering-ram. I heard feet clatter on the stair. They came with a rush, but long ere they had arrived at the top the pace slackened. Only one man at a time could come up the stairway, and it is always a drag upon the enthusiasm of an assault when at least two cannot advance together. The light flickered and filtered in from the torches in the streets, and the reflected glow of the bonfire on the roof made the stair-head clear as a lucid twilight.

I waited, with the axe swinging loosely in one hand. A head bobbed up, clad in a steel cap. Bat as the unseen feet propelled it upward the Red Axe took little reck of the head. Betwixt the steel cap and the rim of steel of the body armor appeared a gray line of leather jerkin and a thinner white line of neck. The Red Axe swung. I bethought me that it was a bad light to cut off calves' heads in. But the Red Axe made no mistake. I had learned my trade. There was not even a groan—only a dull thud some way underneath, such as you may hear when the children of the quarter play football on the streets.

Then the foremost of the assailants were blocked by the fallen body, and the feet of the men behind were stayed as the strange round plaything rebounded among them.

"Back!" they cried, who were in front.

"Forward!" replied those who were hindmost and knew nothing.

"Come, men—on and finish it!" cried the voice which had commanded the powder-flask and the tree—the voice I now knew to be that of Duke Otho himself.

But the kick-ball argument of the Red Axe was mightily discouraging to those immediately concerned, and as I felt the muscles of my right arm and waited, I could hear Otho reasoning, threatening, coaxing, all in vain. Then his tones mounted steadily into hot anger. He reviled his followers for dogs, cowards, curs who had eaten his bread and now would not rid him of his enemies.

"A thousand rix-dollars to the man who kills Hugo Gottfried!" he shouted. "But, hear ye, save the girl alive!"

Yet not a man would attempt the first hazard of the stair.

"Knaves, traitors, curs!" he cried; "would that there were so much as a single true man among you—but there is not one worth spitting upon!"

"Cur yourself!" growled a man, somewhere in the dark—"you have most at stake in this. Try the stair yourself if you are so keen. We will follow fast enough!"

"God strike me dead if I do not!" shouted Otho; "if it were only to shame you cowards."

He paused to prepare his weapons.

"Follow me, men!" he shouted again; "all together!"

Again there was the clatter of iron-shod feet on the stone steps beneath me.

My grip on the Red Axe became like iron, but my joints were loose and swung easily as a flail swings on well-seasoned leathers.

"Welcome, Otho von Reuss!" I cried; "ye could not be crowned without the death of Helene my wife! Come up hither and I will crown thee once for all with the iron crown."

There, at last, was mine enemy at the turn of the stair, rushing furiously upon me, sword in hand.

"Traitor!" he cried, and his sword was almost at my breast, so fast he came.

"Murderer!" I shouted.

And almost ere I was aware the Red Axe flashed as it swept full circle with scarce a pause, but it took the head of a man with it on its way.

Otho von Reuss was crowned. Helene, the Little Playmate, was avenged.

CHAPTER LV

THE LADY YSOLINDE SAVES HER SOUL

The Duke's body sank down upon that of the soldier, still further blocking the passage. And as for his head, I know not where that went to. But the rush of his followers was utterly checked by the barrier of dead. With a wild cry, "The Duke is dead! Duke Otho is slain!" they rushed down and out of the Red Tower, eager at once to escape unharmed, and to carry to their companions in the Wolfsberg the startling news.

Nevertheless, I cleared my arm, wiped my axe, and again stood ready.

"Come!" I cried—"come all of you. You desire to kill me? Well, I am still waiting!"

But not a man answered. The stairway was clear, save of the headless dead. And then, sudden as summer thunder, through the dumb and empty silence, I heard clear and loud the clanging of the hammers of Prince Karl upon the gates of Thorn.

At that I felt that I must roar aloud in my fierce joy. I shouted angrily for more and more assailants to come up the stair, that I might kill them all. I yearned to be first at the gate, to see the men whom I had led break their way in to deliver the city. I, more than any other, had brought them there. I had trained them for that work. Best of all, across the stairway beneath me lay dead Otho, Duke of the Wolfmark, beheaded by the Red Axe of his own Justicer.

"Husband! Hugo! Are you wounded?" said a voice behind me, a voice which in a moment recalled me from my bloody imaginings and baresark fury of fighting.

"Helene!" I cried.

She approached, and would have thrown her arms about me. But I held out my hand to keep her off.

"Not now, child," I said; "touch me not. I am unwounded, but wet!"

And so I was, wet with that which had spouted from the neck of Otho von Reuss, as his trunk stood a moment headless in the stairway ere it fell prone—a hideous thing to see.

"Come, Helene," I said, "we must away. There is other work for your husband tonight. You I will place with the Bishop Peter. But my place is with the men of Plassenburg and with Karl, my noble Prince."

And I took her by the hand to lead her out.

"Not that way!" she cried, shrinking back.

For the bodies of the two slain men lay there. And the stairs ran red from step to step in red drips and lappering pools.

So I bethought me of what we should do, and ran forthwith for my father's cord, with which he was used to bind the malefactors upon the wheel.

"Come, Helene," said I, and straightway fastened the rope to the iron bar from which I had made so many descents to the pavement in the old days of the White Wolves.

I let myself down, and there in the angle of the tower wall, I waited to catch my wife. She delayed somewhat, and I could not think wherefore.

But at last she came, bringing the Red Axe in her hand.

"Go not weaponless!" she said, and I reached up and took from her hand that which had already served me so well. The Red Axe had done its work now, and she was grateful.

Then full lightly she descended to my side, and we went down the streets of Thorn, which were filled with hurrying burgesses, all with weapons in their hands, rushing to discover the cause of the clamor.

I took Helene hastily to the palace of the Bishop. And when I arrived there I saw Peter himself with his head out of a window.

"I come to claim your protection for my wife!" I cried.

He came down immediately with an attendant.

"Fear not," I said, "you will never be called in question for this kindly deed. The Duke Otho is slain, and the army of Prince Karl of Plassenburg is already at the gates."

"The Duke is dead!" he gasped. "Who slew him?"

"Who but the Hereditary Justicer of the Wolfmark should slay a traitor?" said I, smiling at his astonishment. And I held up the Red Axe, on which there was now no crystal-clear rim of shining steel. All was crimson from haft to edge—red as blood.

"Here, for an hour, Helene, little wife, I must leave you!" I said. But now she sobbed and clung to me as she had not done before, even in the dungeon.

"Stay with me," she said. "I need you, Hugo!"

I took her by the hand.

"Little one," I whispered, as tenderly as I could, "I would not be worthily your husband if I went not to meet those who are fighting to save us all this night. They have come from far to deliver us. I were false and recreant if I went not to their assistance."

"I know—I know," she said. "Go!"

And with that she gave a hand to the good Bishop and went quietly within, with no more than a smile over her shoulder, like a watery April sun-glint.

Then I betook me with all speed to the Weiss Thor, where I judged the chief struggle would take place. And as I came I heard the rattle of shot and the jarring thunder of the forehammers. The soldiers without shouted, and the men within more feebly replied.

I came in sight of the gate. There on my left hand was the house of Master Gerard von Sturm.

A fire was still flickering upon the tower of it.

Without I could hear the cheering and clamoring of the besiegers. But the gates remained obstinately shut. They were stronger than the Prince had anticipated.

As *I* stood, uncertain what to do, I saw a slim white figure, the figure of a woman, flash across the open space towards the gate. The men who defended the gate towers were all upon the top of the wall. Before any could stop her she had thrown herself upon the wheel by which the bars were unfastened, and with a few turns had drawn them as deftly as evil Duke Casimir had been wont to remove the teeth of the rich Hebrew folk when he wanted supplies.

The White Gate slowly opened upon creaking hinges. The faces of the soldiers of Plassenburg were seen without, the weapons gleamed in their hands as they came on shouting fiercely. The guards of the Duke rushed forward to close the gate. But the woman had clamped the wheel and stood holding the bar.

It was the Lady Ysolinde. She saw me as the soldiers of Duke Otho closed threateningly upon her. She waved her hand to me almost happily.

"*I have saved my soul, Hugo Gottfried!*" she cried. "*I have saved my soul!*"

At that moment a soldier of the Black Riders struck her fiercely with his lance. I saw the white bosom of her dress redden as he plucked his weapon to him again. I was in time to catch her in my arms as the soldiers of Plassenburg, with Prince Karl at their head, came through the White Gate like a spring-tide, carrying all before them.

The Prince stayed at his wife's side.

"Ysolinde!" cried the Prince, aghast, bending over her—not heeding, nor indeed, as I think, even seeing me.

"Karl!" she said, looking gently at him, "try and forgive me all the rest. But be glad that I opened the White Gate for yon. I, Ysolinde, your wife, did it for your sake."

I put her into her husband's arms. I saw at a glance that there was no hope. She could not live many moments with that lance-thrust through her breast.

She looked at him again.

"Karl—say 'Ysolinde, I love you!'" she whispered, almost shyly.

He looked down, and a rush of unwonted tears came to the eyes of the Prince of Plassenburg.

"Ysolinde, I love you!" he made answer, in a broken voice.

She smiled, and then looked over his shoulder up at me.

"Hugo Gottfried, have I not saved my soul?" she cried.

And so passed.

CHAPTER LVI

HELENA, PRINCESS OF PLASSENBURG

There was, however, deadly work yet before the men of Plassenburg. We found, indeed, that the townsfolk were with us almost to a man. Their guild train-bands gathered and mustered at their halls. The guards at the city gates fraternally turned their arms to the ground.

"The Prince will restore your ancient liberties!" I cried. And the people shouted. "Prince Karl of Plassenburg and our ancient liberties!"

Then we made our way up the street by different routes to the Wolfsberg. There was little fighting till we arrived under those vast and gloomy walls. The Black Riders had disappeared within. Those worst tools of grim tyranny had early withdrawn themselves, knowing that small mercy would be shown them by the people if once the Wolfsberg were taken. But the common soldiers of the fighting rank, sons and brothers of the women of Thorn, tore off the badge of the bloody Dukes and with loud shouts marched with us as comrades.

But when we came before the walls, and with sound of trumpet and loud shouts summoned the Wolfsberg to surrender, a discharge of musketry from the walls, and the determined faces of a multitude of defenders showed us conclusively that all was not yet over.

It was no use wasting men in attacking the great pile of buildings with the force at our disposal. We had men in plenty, but for breeching we needed the cannon left behind by these swift forces, which, marching day and night, had arrived in the very nick of time before the walls of Thorn.

Nevertheless, it was not the fate of the Wolfsberg to be taken by Lazy Peg and her compeers.

These ponderous pieces of ordnance were presently being dragged through the swamps and over the brick-dust barrens of the borderlands, and it might be three or four days before they could arrive to aid us. There was nothing, therefore, to do but to sit down and wait, drawing a cincture that not a mouse could creep through about the cliffs of the Wolfsberg.

But deep within the heart of the old Red Tower there was one stronger than Lazy Peg fighting for us.

"Fire! Fire!" cried the people in the streets. "The Wolfsberg is on fire!" And so, surely, it was. The flames burst out from the windows of the Red Tower and were rapidly carried by a dry fanning northerly wind along the wooden workshops and kennels to the main building, where the Hall of Judgment was soon blazing like a torch. The defenders seemed paralyzed by this misadventure. Some ran to the castle well. Some threw themselves desperately from the walls, others crowded to the gates, and through the bars besought our Prince's pledge that mercy would be shown them.

Then the crowd without were ill to deal with, for they cried aloud, "No mercy to the murderers! Show us our Saint Helena!"

Then it was that I leaped once more upon the scaffold, which had seen such a sight the day before, and cried, "Duke Otho is dead! I, Hugo Gottfried, slew him with this Red Axe. Prince Karl is come to save you, and to give you back your ancient liberties. Your Saint Helena is my wife, and is safe under the protection of Bishop Peter."

But though they cheered at my words they would not cease from crying, "Show us Saint Helena, and if she bid us we will have mercy on the wolves of the Wolfsberg!"

So it was necessary for Helene to be brought and to show herself to them, for the sake of the poor souls sore driven and in jeopardy 'twixt the fire and the knives.

"Have mercy on the poor folk!" she cried, when they had done shouting because of her safety. "At worst, they are but misguided, ignorant men!"

By this time the doors of the Wolfsberg were thrown open from within, and the men crowded out, casting down their arms in heaps on either side the gate. They were then marched, under charge of the soldiers of Plassenburg, to various strongholds which were pointed out by the Burgomeister and the chiefs of the guilds. The fortified halls of the trades were filled with them. By daybreak the whole of Thorn was in our hands, while the gray barrens of the Wolfmark were lit for leagues by the flaming Wolfsberg, which, on its craggy height, vomited fire and sparks into the blackness of night.

And the reek of this great burning hung for days after in the heavens. Thus was an end made to the iniquities of the house of the Black Duke Casimir and the Red Duke Otho. And the last Duke mixed his ashes with that of the fatal Tower. For on the morrow there remained only the blackened walls and glowing skeleton beams of all that mighty palace—which, indeed, has never been rebuilt. For the people of Thorn, under the mild and equitable rule which followed, erected a great memorial church upon the spot—as may be seen to this day, a landmark from far to witness if I have lied in the tale which has been told.

So the Prince Karl gave back to Thorn its liberties, as he had promised. But the regality of the Dukedom he kept for himself, and he took the Wolfmark and made it part of his dominions, till, as he had formerly undertaken, the broom-bush kept the cow throughout the length and breadth of Plassenburg and the Mark.

It was a noble home-coming when we returned to Plassenburg—victorious and famous; but also there was mourning deep and solemn for the Princess Ysolinde, who by her sacrifice had wrought such great things for the arms of Plassenburg, and had died in the moment of victory.

Then, when after the stately funeral of the dead Princess we returned back to the palace, it was the Prince's pleasure that Helene and myself should ride on either hand of him through the city.

And when we were announced in the court, and the councillors of state stood about, my wife was named by her true name, "Helena, Princess of Plassenburg!"

Whereat the courtiers opened their mouths and widened their eyes—thinking, perhaps, that that ancient wizard, Chancellor Leopold von Dessauer had suddenly gone mad.

But when the representatives of the cities of the Princedom, and the delegates from Thorn and the Mark, had been received with due honor, the Prince bade his Chancellor recount all he had learned from my father, and all that he had discovered in the archives of Plassenburg.

Then, when Dessauer had finished, Karl the Prince arose.

"I am," he said, "a plain, brusque man. And speech was never my stronghold. But this I say. When Karl the Miller's Son goes the way of King's son and beggar's son, it is his will that Helene, legitimate Princess of Plassenburg, shall reign over you. And also that her husband, Hugo, who, as you know, won her from dreadful death, shall stand by her right hand."

Then the nobles and great lords, fearing the Prince, and perhaps also envying a little the man who was the Prince's general of his armies, shouted amain:

"We swear to obey the Princess Helena!"

Whereat uprose the Little Playmate, very princess-like and full of sweet regal dignity.

"I thank you, noble Prince," she said. "I am glad that I can claim so honorable a name and lineage; but I had rather be no Princess, nor anything else than that which my husband hath made me—the wife of the captain-general of the armies of Karl, the only true and noble Prince of Plassenburg!"

Then the Prince rose and clasped her in his arms, kissing her fondly on both cheeks.

"Fear not," he said, "dear and loyal lady. If you live to be the Princess, your goodman shall be the Prince. Never shall the gray mare flaunt it first, in Plassenburg!"

And he gave us each a hand, and conducted us to a pair of seats which had been set level with his on the platform of the Council-chamber of the Princedom.

The Prince Karl lived many days after the winning of the Wolfmark and the ending of the ducal Wolves. But he gave less and less care to the regalities, leaving them even more completely to me, sitting mostly in the pleasaunce by the river-side, or in the far-regarding room which had been the Lady Ysolinde's.

Also he never looked again on the face of a woman—except as it might be to bid them good-day—save on that of my wife, Helene, who, as you who know her may guess, waxed but the sweeter and the fairer as the years went by.

And the blessing of children came to us, and in this thing the Prince Karl was even happier than we.

One day, however, it chanced that he was seated in full Council, and right noble he looked. I had just handed him a paper to sign. But he looked neither at me nor yet at the paper. His eyes were fixed on the locked doors of the privy bedchamber, through which only those of princely blood might come.

He stared so long at it that to recall him I put my hand on his sleeve and said, "Prince, the Council waits your pleasure!"

But he heard me not, his eyes being fixed on the door.

"Your pardon, my lords and knights," he said, at last, fighting a little stiffly with his utterance, "but it seemed that I saw the Princess, my wife, come through the door, clad in white, and beckon me with her hand. I must go to her, my lords; I think she waits for me. The Prince Hugo will take my place at the Council."

And the old man took a step from the high seat. But at the foot of the throne he stumbled and fell into my arms.

He said but one word after that, with his eyes still fixed on the bolted door.

"*Ysolinde!*"

And so the Prince Karl and his wife were united at last.

Since then we have lived long, the Little Playmate and I; but never have we been other than comrades and friends—lovers also, which is the best of all. And so (an the good God please) we shall abide till the end comes. And in the gloaming we two also shall see the beckoning finger from beyond the bolted door and turn our feet homeward, passing the bourne of the new life hand in hand—and undismayed.

THE END

CPSIA information can be obtained
at www.ICGtesting.com
Printed in the USA
LVHW020438050821
694513LV00004B/148